Julie Chan
Is Dead

Julie Chan Is Dead

A NOVEL

Liann Zhang

ATRIA BOOKS

New York   Amsterdam/Antwerp   London
Toronto   Sydney/Melbourne   New Delhi

ATRIA
BOOKS

An Imprint of Simon & Schuster, LLC
1230 Avenue of the Americas
New York, NY 10020

This book is a work of fiction. Any references to historical events, real people, or real places are used fictitiously. Other names, characters, places, and events are products of the author's imagination, and any resemblance to actual events or places or persons, living or dead, is entirely coincidental.

First Atria Books hardcover edition April 2025

Simon & Schuster strongly believes in freedom of expression and stands against censorship in all its forms. For more information, visit BooksBelong.com.

For information about special discounts for bulk purchases, please contact Simon & Schuster Special Sales at 1-866-506-1949 or business@simonandschuster.com.

The Simon & Schuster Speakers Bureau can bring authors to your live event. For more information or to book an event, contact the Simon & Schuster Speakers Bureau at 1-866-248-3049 or visit our website at www.simonspeakers.com.

Interior design by Davina Mock-Maniscalco

Manufactured in the United States of America

1   3   5   7   9   10   8   6   4   2

Library of Congress Cataloging-in-Publication Data
Names: Zhang, Liann, author.
Title: Julie Chan is dead : a novel / Liann Zhang.
Description: New York : Atria Books, 2025.
Identifiers: LCCN 2024050186 (print) | LCCN 2024050187 (ebook) | ISBN 9781668067895 (hardcover) | ISBN 9781668067901 (paperback) | ISBN 9781668067918 (ebook)
Subjects: LCGFT: Thrillers (Fiction). | Novels.
Classification: LCC PR9199.4.Z49 J85 2025 (print) | LCC PR9199.4.Z49 (ebook) | DDC 813/.6--dc23/eng/20241104
LC record available at https://lccn.loc.gov/2024050186
LC ebook record available at https://lccn.loc.gov/2024050187

ISBN 978-1-6680-6789-5
ISBN 978-1-6680-6791-8 (ebook)

To the early 2010 internet personalities who raised me.
But mostly to my mom, who actually raised me.

One thing needs to be made clear: I did not kill my twin sister.

1

A re you filming a video?"

"What?" I glance at the blond teen across the counter as I scan her box of supersized tampons. Three girls of similar font trail behind her in a cluster, their spidery eyes orbiting me with equal curiosity.

"A video," she clarifies, rather unhelpfully. "Is there a hidden camera somewhere?"

Her friends, thrilled at this proposition, examine the dusty ceiling beams, raking manicured hands over trashy tabloids as if a DSLR could hide between flimsy pages of celebrity scandals. One points toward the door. "I see it! There!" She smiles and waves.

I resist rolling my eyes. "That's a security camera. And please stop messing with the magazines. I don't know what you're going on about."

Only, I do.

I know exactly what they're talking about—*who*.

"You're Chloe Van Huusen, right?"

There it is.

Chloe Van Huusen.

"I'm a huge fan! Been watching since I was ten."

I flash a stiff smile, gritting my teeth. "I'm not Chloe. Would you like a plastic bag for ten cents?"

"Nah." She inserts her card into the reader. It's a Black AmEx. Of course.

This golden-haired teen with rich parents and no credit limit is exactly Chloe's demo.

"But, like, you are filming a video, right? I mean, why else would you be here? Let me guess! *Being a cashier for twenty-four hours challenge?*"

"Oh!" chimes another. "*Trying new jobs for a week challenge?*"

"Nope! Sorry!" I rip the receipt from the dispenser and shove it in the girl's hand. "Thank you *so* much for shopping at SuperFoods. Have a *super* day. Bye!"

She backs up, startled at my snippy tone, before scurrying away with her chittering pack, their hushed voices like buzzing mosquitos.

"That lady was kind of a bitch."

"It can't be her. Chloe is *so* nice."

"Oh my god."

"What?"

"Do you think it's her twin? From that video?"

A gasp. "Oh my god, *yes.*"

"What was her name? Janice?"

"Jordan?"

"Jade?"

"It's Julie!" I scream.

They jump and spin toward me, eyes wide. One of them lets out a squeak. The first girl drops her tampons. She picks up the box and they bolt out of the store as if I'm a rabid animal about to attack.

"You can't yell at the customers," Vera, the cashier in the aisle next to me, says. Her gold Employee of the Month badge catches the sunlight. "Everyone should feel *super* after leaving SuperFoods."

"Whatever."

Her jaw drops, eyes glinting with an opportunity to lecture me on the Ten Tenets of Super Employees at SuperFoods. Thankfully, a man walks up to her aisle, and she whips toward him. "Welcome to SuperFoods!" she chirps. "I hope you're having a super day!"

Stifling a yawn, I lean my hip against the counter when I notice my manager squinting at me through the grimy square window of his office door. Wary of his vigilance, I pull out a Kit Kat box and rearrange the red rectangles as a pretense of productivity while I zone out, thinking of the girls. Maybe I was too harsh. Being a young woman is already like existing in the seventh circle of hell. Not to mention one of them is on her period. Your internet idol's doppelgänger shouting at you is the last thing anyone wants.

But the last thing *I* want is any mention of my twin.

The mere whisper of her name short-circuits my brain and I tend to grow a little cross. Just a little. Like, the teeniest bit.

Although, if you knew my twin like I do, you'd applaud my reaction.

Here's the hard truth that Chloe Van Huusen fans fail to realize: she's far from the pretty little angel she pretends to be.

I only had to spend one afternoon with her to come to this conclusion.

We were twenty-one during our brief and highly publicized reunion, a whole seventeen years since some drunk driver crushed our parents under his pickup. The state had separated us before we learned to grieve, since the couple that fast-tracked Chloe's adoption only wanted one kid. I was sent to our aunt, a penny-pinching, foul-mouthed Cantonese woman who uses old Cheeto bags as folders for her tax returns, while my twin was adopted by an affluent white couple in New York City, legally rebranding herself a Van Huusen. She probably lived in a brownstone with *Sex and the City*–style steps, stomping into cliquey private schools with cashmere plaid skirts and pink feathery pens, while I shared a bunk bed with my cousin, who'd flick my bra strap for fun.

I knew of Chloe's high-profile life because people often looked at me with furrowed brows, a spark of recognition in their eyes. *Hey, you look like Chloe Van Huusen,* they'd say. My twin's luxurious lifestyle content had attracted over one million Instagram followers and six hundred thousand YouTube subscribers. While she was enjoying sponsored island retreats to the Bahamas and Bora Bora, wearing outfits from The Row and Loewe, I was scanning coupons behind a cash register. (Still am!) At night, I'd spend hours scrolling through her pages, passively absorbing our disparate lives through the screen. My thumb sometimes hovered over *Message* before swiping away.

Reaching out risked forming a connection. And forming a connection meant I'd have to acknowledge our differences, cementing the fact that

I—someone born from the same womb, formed from the same clump of cells—had failed everywhere she hadn't.

But then, out of nowhere, she popped into my life again.

I was working my usual morning shift, ringing up bananas (4011) and a bag of chia seeds for a platinum-haired lady with a shrieking baby clawing at her breast. Out of nowhere, a film crew ran up to my lane. One camera was pointed at me, the other pointed at the entrance.

Chloe sashayed through the sliding glass doors like the main character of a 2000s movie, her kitten heels *click, click, click*ing against vinyl, a ridiculous pink beret poised on her head, sun pooling on her back.

"Julie?" She gasped like she didn't know she'd find me here.

Seeing Chloe IRL was like looking in a fun-house mirror installed with Facetune. Her silky hair fell down her shoulders in loose waves, while mine resembled inked hay with split ends. Her skin was radiant from all her complimentary facials, while I looked like I hadn't slept for three days. And her hands looked soft, pliable, not a trace of labor in her sharp, shellacked nails, while I had chewed mine down to raw skin, tender hangnails clinging dryly for dear life.

"It's been so long!" Tears flooded her eyes as she wrapped her toned arms around me, cameras hovering. "I've missed you so much, Julie."

I was squished in Chloe's perfume-aisle-scented hug, immobile from shock. A million questions ripped through my mind—how she found me, why she was here—but they never left my gaping lips, since I was too over-stimulated by the crowd thronging around our sisterly reunion.

My answers came when I watched her video. Turns out, Chloe had hired a private investigator to locate me months ago. He had tailed me in a dark SUV, collecting footage of me obliviously staring down at my phone while walking to and from work, which was later edited over doleful royalty-free music like I was some endangered marsupial in a nature documentary. A week before her arrival, she had contacted my store manager for permission to film. Every employee on the clock that day knew she'd show up and they were delighted to play along in the production.

After our dramatic reunion, the manager dismissed me early (without pay!) so I could film the rest of my twin's video. In the parking lot, Chloe wrapped a blindfold tight around my eyes, stuffing me in the passenger seat of a car rigged with cameras for a "surprise." As we drove, my twin told an invisible audience the story of our childhood, narrating our parents' deaths and our separation, lacing her narrative with heartfelt details I didn't quite remember but that could've been true. Every now and then, she'd punctuate her sentence with a high-pitched "Right?" leaving a beat just long enough for me to nod, before continuing her exuberant song and dance down memory lane. After fifteen minutes, she let me out of the car, pushed a key into my fist, and released me from my blindness. Before I processed that we were on the other side of town, Chloe pointed to a house just down the block and shrieked: "It's your house now!"

"W-what?" When I watch the video back, I always cringe at my expression here. The ugly confusion next to my shiny twin. I looked like the *after crack* example of an antidrug campaign.

"With the cost of living these days, I figured you must be living paycheck to paycheck working at a grocery store. So, I decided to buy you a house!" She giggled as she took my clammy hand, traipsing through the newly renovated home.

I couldn't believe it. Both the fact that Chloe's fingers were intertwined with mine after so many years, and the fact that she had bought me a house.

A whole damn house.

On the dimly lit porch that reeked of fresh paint, we filmed a segment where she professed how much she had missed me. Her speech was breathless and cloying, so eloquent it must have been prepared. Yet, in the moment, once she whispered, "I've missed you so much, Ju-Ju," I unraveled entirely.

Ju-Ju sounds similar to "piggy" in Cantonese: 猪猪. I know, I know, that seems mean, bordering on fat-shaming. But it was affectionate—I swear. It meant I was cute and small, something to be coddled and adored, like McDull. As soon as that childhood nickname slipped through Chloe's glossy lips, she pried open the gates of my repressed emotions and released a flash flood of hot tears. I believed her lies with unbounded hope: she missed me, thought of me, loved me—she wanted me in her life again. I didn't realize how profoundly lonely I was, how much I had craved family and belonging, until she showed up. Until she called me a little pig again.

She was a messiah. A beautiful angel plucking me out of the gutter. *Creation of Adam* shit.

Then a crew member said, "That's a wrap." The cameras stopped rolling. Chloe stepped away from me. Her eyes flickered, brightness displaced by an eerie distance. "Bye, Julie." Then she was gone.

In her wake, she left me with a renovated home (featuring the landlord special: crumbling foundation, painted-over appliances, mushrooms sprouting from dank corners) and a YouTube video the next week: *"Finding My Long-Lost Twin and Buying Her a House #EMOTIONAL."* It hit ten million views in two days. People squealed about Chloe's generosity, how they'd cried watching the reunion, how lucky I was.

But she never called after the video—never gave me her phone number. Not even an Instagram follow.

I was demoted to a lurker, a measly data point within her growing subscriber count. Lost in her crowd of fans, I watched as she broke one million, then two, then three, then somehow skyrocketing to six million followers. As she opened a TikTok account. As she networked with celebrities at #NYFW. As she hard-launched a boyfriend, some ratty, tattooed white guy who looked one bad hair day away from starting a men's rights podcast. As she posted a breakup announcement shortly after.

When the occasional commenter asked: What happened to your twin? She'd reply: Julie isn't a public figure. We all need to respect her privacy. People believed her because she was the adored Chloe Van Huusen, who could do no wrong. Sometimes I wanted to reply, Hey! I'm here! She only used me for her video! And she's actually a huge fucking cunt!!!! But I could already imagine her rabid fans spamming me with hate messages, foaming at the mouth to defend their internet fave. She already bought you a house, what more could you want? You're just a knockoff, uglier version of her. No one cares about you! Desperate much?

Despite the explosive views (sitting pretty at twenty million!), people moved on from me quickly. I had my ten seconds of viral fame and after that, no one cared. I am a redundant replica floating in my twin's orbit, a footnote in her grand life, a fun fact in her fan Wiki—Did you know Chloe has a twin?

I accepted she'd never reach out after a year of silence, and I'd blocked her socials as a weak attempt to protect my sanity. But an online barricade can't be imposed onto reality.

My twin's soaring success meant more and more people mistook me for her. Now, I rarely go two weeks without a stinging reminder of her betrayal. Every time my twin is mentioned, I spiral, and at night, I sometimes hear her when the crumbling house shudders. *Ju-Ju,* the rooms groan. It's like her voice is trapped in an echo between walls, scraping at the dozen layers of white paint, desperate to crawl out.

————

"It's inappropriate to yell at customers," my manager says now. I have a feeling Vera snitched. Behind him is a photo of her, smiling with her dumb Employee of the Month certificate and a $50 coupon to SuperFoods. She bought forty-five cans of mushroom soup for our local charity. I hate her.

"Sorry."

"I'm also docking the gum you stole from your paycheck this week."

I was sure the gum rack was in a blind spot. Did Vera rat on me for this too?

He leans forward, his voice stern and low, breath pungent with the salami sandwich he had for lunch. "You've been a vital part of SuperFoods for a decade and that's why I'm being lenient. But this isn't the first nor the second offense. Don't let it happen again. Do you understand what I'm saying?"

I nod, staring at my dry cuticles.

He dismisses me.

I dread going home, knowing Chloe's voice will leak through the walls tonight. As a consolation, a packet of gummy bears finds itself in my bag.

I'm decapitating a white pineapple bear when I receive a call. Glancing at my screen, I almost choke on my candy.

The location under the number: *New York.*

I know only one person from New York.

Chloe.

2

"Hello?"

Heavy, disjointed breaths. Static.

"Hello?" I repeat. "Who is this?"

I can't make out the words clearly. It's like whoever is calling has a damp finger over the speaker, froth in their throat. I press my phone hard into my ear and squint as if that would help me hear better. "Hello?"

Then I hear her. My twin. Or at least I think I do. It's hard to make out. But it almost sounds like she's repeating *mistake, mistake, mistake.*

"Chloe? Is that you? What's a mistake?"

More coughing and moaning.

I turn my volume all the way up, put it on speaker. "Can you hear me? What's going on?"

"Ju-Ju . . . I'm sorry."

"What? Sorry for what? Chloe? Hello?"

The line goes dead.

I'm breathless. My tongue is dry and thick. A viscous layer of gummy bear coats my throat.

I dial her back. It rings and rings. *Hi, you've reached Chloe! Leave a voicemail or send me a text. Love you!* Instinctively, I hang up before the tone, my heart jogging. I'm not sure what to say. My thoughts aren't in order.

It's been three years since she spoke to me and now she suddenly calls?

Why? I didn't even know she had my number. I call her again. *Hi, you've reached Chloe! Leave—* I hang up.

Leaving a voicemail would be evidence that she still has power over me, that I care when I shouldn't. Chloe had heartlessly re-abandoned me after promising to reconnect, and I had stupidly believed her. I can't let myself be humiliated twice.

And what if, God forbid, it's a prank? *Tricking My Long-Lost Twin Sister into Thinking I'm Dying! #Hilarious.* It's not on-brand for her to do pranks. But she's diversified her content before—like buying me a house. Maybe she's trying something new. Aren't pranks having a resurgence these days?

I shove my phone in my pocket and continue home, chewing handfuls of gummy bears to stave off lingering doubts.

———

Chloe's whispers follow me everywhere. *Ju-Ju,* she says while I'm picking crusted lasagna sauce off the peeling kitchen counter. *Mistake,* she gurgles as I lie on the living room floor, staring at the dusty baseboards I'll never clean. *I'm sorry,* she whispers in the bathroom as I nurse a sugary stomachache.

She's with me as I shower, as I brush my teeth, as I blow-dry my hair.

No matter where I am, what I do, she won't leave me alone.

I don't sleep that night.

3

The next morning, I'm exhausted but I clock into my shift at SuperFoods and try going about my day.

"Would you like a bag?"

"How would you like to pay?"

"What a cute baby!" It's the ugliest baby I've ever seen.

I'm miserable, but the mindless work occupies my brain.

There's a lull in the afternoon. Michael Bublé's "Santa Claus Is Coming to Town" hums overhead. (The manager hasn't switched out the disc since December.) Vera regales me with a tale of her deworming her cat last night. She goes into excruciating detail. I think it might be her kink.

I lean against the register, nodding along to Vera's story like I'm so interested. *Yes, Vera, oh please! Tell me more about your pet's intestinal parasites!*

It is then, without warning, that Chloe crawls back, clinging to my shoulders so she can whisper into my ears, guttural and frothy.

Ju-Ju.

The more I try to ignore it, the louder it gets.

Mistake. Mistake. Mistake.

What if, by some small chance, something terrible happened and I was the only one she called?

"Julie?"

I jolt.

"You look a bit green in the cheeks, hon," Vera says. "Might be coming down with something."

I smooth my palm against my forehead. "Maybe a cold. I didn't sleep that well."

"That reminds me: Poochie Poo Senior caught a cold a few months ago. I know it's hard to believe since most people don't think about how animals can catch colds just like humans . . ." Vera drones on. I can't focus on her voice, attention drawn to my reflection in her lopsided glasses. Remnants of her greasy fingerprints blur my features, disturbing the details of my face until my twin is all I see. Her harsh voice lashes again, a bug burrowing through my eardrum. *Ju-Ju.* She's snagged onto me. I can't shake her away.

My shift drags on, Chloe in my thoughts.

I call her again on my lunch break.

No answer.

I can't focus. I even forget the PLU for bananas.

At home, I call her five more times.

On the sixth call, I finally swallow my pride and leave her a voicemail. "H-hey. It's Julie. Your twin—which, I'm sure you know. Um, I'm a bit worried about you. Can you call me back? I'll text you too." I cringe when I hang up, playing my voice back in my head.

I text her: hey, just checking if you're okay? I wait for the delivered status to change to read. It doesn't.

Concern gnaws at me as I pace around the kitchen.

Desperate for relief, I scroll through Instagram and read mean comments on Reels. An ad for a dress pops up in my feed. It's the style I'd rock in my mind: girly, with bows and ruffles, but would look frumpy IRL. I find myself on the shoddy site nonetheless. The dress is fifty-five dollars. I can tell it's going to be drop-shipped and will arrive on my doorstep in three months looking nothing like the images (if it arrives at all), but I still click on Purchase with 4 Installments, yearning for the temporary euphoria of impulse shopping. The confirmation pings in my email right as my bank notifies me of low funds. Regret spills into my chest. I click on the email, hoping to cancel the order. The link for customer support redirects to an empty web page.

Frustrated, I check my text to Chloe again. It hasn't been read.

Blistering anger suddenly ensnares me. I hate how I wasted money on a dress I didn't really want. I hate how Chloe took over my life with a single call, a few muttered words. I hate how I can't stop thinking about her, how much power my twin holds in my life. But what I hate the most is the knowledge that if she really gave me a chance, opened her arms, I would crawl on my knees and lick from her palm.

I type in her Instagram handle, click onto her page, and hover my thumb over unblock.

Since our reunion, I've tried my best to stay off Chloe's socials. Her pictures and videos are an addictive portal into a surreal, alternate dimension. As I watch her vlogs and scroll through her feed, our realities blend in my mind, until at some point, the liminal thresholds between what's Chloe's and mine become one. I start believing it's me waking up in her wide, king-sized bed, brushing my teeth by her Italian marble sink, applying my ten-step skincare routine in front of her backlit vanity, frying crackling eggs in her kitchen with the Turkish tile backsplash. It's so easy to lean into these delusions when you look the same. Sometimes, I let these imaginings marinate before bed, so when I dream, those visions carry on, lucid and real. But like anything good, it never lasts. The blare of my alarm inevitably expunges me from bliss, and when my eyes open to my cracking ceiling and painted-over light fixtures, the dissonance of our realities crashes harshly into my mind. Just like that, a simple unblock becomes a reminder of everything I don't have, everywhere I have failed.

This is my pattern. It's self-defeating and depressing, yet I can't stop myself. Chloe is my vice. I'm addicted to the way I grow hateful. Crave how it fills me with vitriol. Being angry and envious is better than being empty.

And this time, I need answers to satisfy my curiosity. There's a justification for what happens next.

I click unblock and refresh her page.

21

Chloe's most recent post is a sponsored selfie. She's on her white couch in a bathrobe and face mask, a bright smile on her glossy lips. Wine in hand. Caption: This is your sign to take a break from life. 🖤 🧘 Grab a glass of wine, a good face mask (my pick is the @KareKosmetics refreshing cucumber skin ampoule 24x hydration mask with hyaluronic acid), and tune in to your favorite new show. We all deserve a break. #selfcare #sponsored #Kare Partner.

I roll my eyes and scroll down to the date.

Posted two weeks ago.

Huh. Chloe normally uploads three times a week—minimum. I comb through her other socials. No uploads for the last two weeks. No announcement of a break either.

Judging from the hundreds of comments, her fans are just as uneasy as I am.

Are you okay?

Where did you go?

Did you die?

She was alive enough to call me yesterday.

Scrolling is like climbing down a ladder, each worried comment a rung lowering me until I'm chin-deep in a pool of her followers' concern. Overwhelmed, I throw my phone in my nightstand, shower, and try to go to bed early.

I can't fall asleep.

I'm pulled toward Chloe, unable to tamp down the unease. Something isn't right.

I call her five more times. Voicemail.

Maybe I should get someone to check up on her. Who? Her friends? I don't know any of them personally. I could call the police and ask for a safety check. But I don't know where she lives. In the past, if I had to contact her, it was always done through the real estate agent.

Then I remember the property deed. It had to have Chloe's address on it, since she's the legal owner of my house. Judging from the background of her videos, she hasn't moved in five years.

Where did I put it? The last time I looked at it was after my aunt tried to forge the deed into saying the property was in *her* name so she could illegally rent out the house as an Airbnb. (She only relented after I lied about Chloe having lawyers who would sue her broke.)

I search for hours before finding the papers in the drawer beneath the oven, smooshed between cookie sheets and instruction manuals. I wipe off the dust and breadcrumbs.

There it is on the first page, printed in shiny black ink: *New York.*

Her address is in my hands, yet I can't bring myself to dial 911, dread paralyzing my fingers. I'm reminded of the time the cops were called on me. A moment I never want to relive.

My aunt had opened a bank account for me when I was twelve and instructed me to start saving if I wanted a future. At the time, I saw it as a kind gesture. Throughout my teens I saved nearly every dime I earned working at SuperFoods. By eleventh grade, I had amassed over five thousand dollars. It wasn't a lot, but it was enough to move out, to dream.

But a week before my seventeenth birthday, my savings dropped to five hundred dollars. The bank informed me that since my account was started when I was underage, it was a custodial account, meaning my guardian had full control of the funds. When I confronted my aunt, she said: *Do you know how much it costs to raise you? To feed an extra mouth?*

At her words, a black hole formed in my chest, swallowing every ounce of motivation I had left. I became empty. For days after, I tried to identify what was wrong with me, wanting to rationalize my misfortune: dead parents, no family, an unreachable twin, a despicable aunt, isolation. It was mental self-flagellation. Recognizing problems is pointless when you have little motivation to fix them. And finding motivation is impossible when the mere idea of existing feels like a punishment.

Then, one night, a classmate had texted me, begging me to finish my section of a group project. I still don't know what came over me that evening. Why I replied with radical honesty. Maybe I was trying to justify my truancy; maybe I just wanted attention? But the message became lethal. She called the cops on me for a wellness check.

The check was anything but *well.* A cop car pulled up to my aunt's house with its sirens blasting, blue-red lights illuminating the night as the officers banged on the door like I was about to kill. The two cops—both men—were strapped for a shoot-out: bulletproof vests, batons, hands cupping their gun holsters. One had bloody ketchup smeared on his chin. The tang of greasy fast food settled thickly in my gut as I slumped into the living room sofa, enduring a barrage of close-ended questions about my safety and mental stability. Their stares made me feel worthless, a waste of air. The whole time, my aunt was smiling at the cops, offering them tea and pastries. Tricked by her grin, I thought she was finally sympathetic to me. But as soon as the cops left, she stomped over and slapped me in the face. *How dare you make a big fuss out of nothing!*

I was left with a chest full of embarrassment and shame, more helpless than ever. The mere idea of speaking to the cops became triggering. After all these years, I still can't bring myself to do it.

Maybe I'm making excuses for myself, but calling the police also seems premature. There's no point in making a fuss when I'm still not sure what happened to Chloe or if the cops are the right choice of intervention. (And let's be honest, they're rarely the right choice.)

I'm sitting on my dirty kitchen floor, biting my nails, staring at her New York address. I know if I keep ignoring Chloe, her voice will never leave me.

And if I'm being honest, I can't shake off one simple truth: I want to see her—*wanted* to before this. Viewing her through a screen was never enough.

I buy a bus ticket to New York for the following evening.

5

The next day, I fake coughing fits my whole shift. The manager tells me to take tomorrow off to recover. On my way out, I nab a sandwich from the deli in exchange for lost wages. When I get home, I pack a bag with a few essentials before heading out to the bus terminal.

I'm the last passenger to board, so I'm stuck with the spot next to the toilet.

The bus starts. My thighs rattle from the engines and my nose is congested from the exhaust fumes, which are muddled with the smell of piss and the remnants of someone's car sickness. My phone pings. A text from my manager:

7:45PM: We have you on tape stealing a sandwich.
7:46PM: I already warned you about this behavior. We need to have a talk once you come back. This is unacceptable.

I read the texts three times over, trying to conjure guilt. The bus pulls out of the station and chugs down the highway. After deleting my manager's messages, I log on to Reddit to doom-scroll. My eyes skim posts listlessly.

I'm distracted by thoughts of Chloe, a deluge of childhood memories inundating my mind.

I read an article that said our brains aren't capable of meaningful retention in early life. Most of our early memories are nothing more than fictionalized stories generated via stimuli we encounter in older age. A birthday candle there, a patch of grass here, a story muttered through Grandma's whistling dentures, and hey, presto! A manufactured memory, ready for you to relive as if it's real.

Logically, this checks out. Everything I remember is probably counterfeit. But the part of me who experiences the memories—who can close my eyes and play them like a reel, feel the textures of the room, smell the warm, salty air—*knows* they are real.

Memories of a mom and a dad. A family. A home.

Mom always wore dresses. Tight around the chest, loose past her hips. They'd drape near her thighs, and I'd grab at the soft cotton for her attention, smoothing my fingers along the tough embroidery adorning her hem. It was always some bird—black-capped chickadees, purple martins, hummingbirds—hand-stitched in shimmering threads. She always wore red lipstick, pink curlers caught in her hair. Her teeth were ragged, stained yellow from tea. Dad smelled of cigarettes and always wore polos, either white or sky blue, the collar pressed to perfection. He'd pair them with brown khakis and a leather belt. He never wore slippers inside, instead collecting dust and hairs on his stinky white socks, which Mom would yell at him about. Steamed rice and bone broth scented the house; something was always brewing on the stove, marinating on the sticky counters. Then there's Chloe, my twin, my older sister by seven minutes, the one who popped into the world first, paving the way so I could slip out in her great shadow. Armed with a charming grin, she'd hold my clammy hand and take me to places I'd never go alone.

A particular memory intrudes into my thoughts.

We were three years old and home alone—which might have been illegal. Dad was at work. Mom had run out to the store for oil and soy sauce. The trip never took more than ten minutes, and though we were toddlers, at three, we were more than independent. Perhaps because we had each other.

We found ourselves in the pantry, chubby hands fisting grains of rice. I was enamored by the sensory magic of the hard white pellets sliding through my little fingers. By the *crunch, crunch, crunch* when I squeezed my fist. The coarse powder left over on my tiny, oval nails. At some point, Chloe had walked out of the room without me noticing. Disappeared entirely.

By the time I heard Mom's keys jingling at the door, Chloe had been gone for who knows how long. I remember my mom's sharp panic, the plastic rollers in her hair clacking as she searched for Chloe, the groceries scattered on the floor. I followed her, searching, searching, searching, my fat, sweaty toes padding on smooth kitchen tile, around dusty corners, over stained carpets, as my eyes wandered for a me-shaped being. We scoured the laundry machine, the bedroom, under the tables, the closet, between couch cushions. Chloe was nowhere to be found.

Mom sobbed as she screamed at me. *Where did your sister go? You must know! Tell me now!* They say twins have a natural connection. Some telepathic bond. It wasn't true for me and Chloe. We looked identical, but we were always separate. Chloe was a toothy smile, a girl who always had dead leaves in her hair because she was too curious. Her mind and heart were otherwise pure mystery. I had no idea where Chloe was, where she went. Mom couldn't understand this or wouldn't believe me, even when my head shakes were paired with frustrated tears.

We found my twin eventually. She had escaped out the window and was naked but for her underwear, knee-deep in the garden bed, uprooting tomato plants. Mom sprang into the yard, her arms outstretched. *My baby, my baby,* she cried.

Watching Chloe and Mom from the back door, I remember feeling upset. I was the one who was crying, not Chloe. Chloe was happy, smiling in that bubbly-Chloe way, giggles rippling up her throat.

My baby, my baby.

Sometimes, it felt like Mom only ever had one baby.

Afterward, I holed up in the bathroom. I liked the warm, humid air, how it hugged me; the lack of windows that made me feel secure, shut out from the overstimulating world; the idyllic hum of the fan; the musk of mildew and bleach. I used to hide in the cabinet underneath the sink, smoosh myself between cleaning supplies and rolls of toilet paper, sweaty skin sticking onto cellophane. I sat there with my knobby knees tucked into my chest, wondering if Mom would go hysterical when she noticed me missing. She didn't. She never even looked.

It was Chloe who found me. She opened the cabinet doors, the warm bathroom light pooling in. When she smiled, it felt like she could see me, *really* see me, that at least my twin was the one person who cared. She shoved a plate of ripe mango wedges in my face, her nails crusted with soil. *Mama made this for me. Wanna share, Ju-Ju?* She didn't wait for me to say yes before moving the toilet paper rolls out of the cabinet. When there was enough space for two, she slipped in beside me and closed the doors. We ate mangoes together in the dark. Her chubby thigh touched mine. I felt safe.

This is the Chloe I want to remember. The Chloe I hope still exists behind the superficial social media persona. The Chloe I desperately wanted to be.

An announcement drones overhead: "Thirty minutes until arrival."

It's cloudy, past ten p.m. I wipe the condensation-covered windows, clearing the crawling frost, and peer into the freezing night. A line of bright city blinks up at the dark, starless sky.

I'll be in New York in thirty minutes. At her door in an hour.

Perhaps, as soon as I arrive, I'll see her digging around her garden, alive and well. Smiling brightly, not a care in the world.

6

Chloe lives in a Manhattan apartment that faces the Hudson River. She definitely does not have a garden.

A frigid breeze whips my face as I stare up at the towering building, at once awed and seized with vertigo. How can my twin, someone I shared a bed with, sudsed up in the bath with, have such a different life?

Her building requires fob access, which I don't have. I don't have a buzz code either. It's late and there's no one coming in and out. I wait awkwardly near the door in my baggy hoodie and jacket, backpack cutting into my shoulders. Each breath sends white clouds into the sky. I sniffle.

Something skitters in the distance, rummaging in the black trash bags and flattened cardboard boxes by the curb.

It pokes out its head. Beady black eyes. A rat. Holy shit, it's *giant*. A mutant the size of my forearm. It holds me in its gaze with a forlorn expression, its impossibly fat belly chafing the pavement. Judging by its size, this creature must eat better than I do, feasting on leftovers tossed out by rich New Yorkers while I feed on stolen grocery store sandwiches. As if the world wants to shame me further, my stomach rumbles, scaring the rat away.

I rub my forehead with my sleeve and groan with exhaustion. What am I doing? I can't believe I came all the way to New York only to wait outside Chloe's door and be jealous of a rat. She's probably fine. Maybe she had a brief panic attack, called me by accident, and I'm overthinking it. All the friends scattered on her socials would check up on her if something was awry. And her adoptive parents are caring in that picturesque, rich white people way: summer in the Hamptons, Christmas cards featuring matching red cashmere cardigans, calls every night to exchange *I-love-you*s. They'd make sure Chloe is safe.

Why did I even come?

THUMP! THUMP! THUMP!

I jump.

A harsh light blinds me. My heart pounds as I jerk my arms up to my eyes, shielding them from the rays. The light flickers off and I peek through my fingers.

A man stares at me, his creased eyes narrow and scrutinizing as he opens the door. He's wearing a crisp white button-down shirt and a burgundy tie. The polished bronze name tag clipped above his chest pocket reads: *Ramos, Security*. "Miss Van Huusen, what are you doing out in the cold? Come in."

He thinks I'm Chloe.

I don't know why this surprises me. We are twins, and after all, we're mistaken for each other all the time. "Thanks. I, uh . . . I forgot my fob." I fake a laugh.

He doesn't offer a chuckle of sympathy, the corner of his mustached lips twisting down in a gentle frown.

I pivot and head straight for the elevators. If he stares at me a second longer with those concerned dad eyes, I'm certain he'll realize I'm not Chloe.

Just before I press the button, he shouts, "Wait!"

I stop dead in my tracks, heart battering my rib cage.

"A few packages came for you. Would you like to sign for them?"

I blow a breath out, calm my nerves, and spin around. "Sure." My voice cracks but he doesn't comment on it. I walk over to the front desk as casually as possible.

He hands me two boxes. "More PR?"

"Um. Maybe." I sign for the packages with a scribble and hope he doesn't notice.

"Lately, my daughter keeps askin' me, *Daddy, Daddy, when is Chloe going to give me more stuff?* She loves you more than Santa!" He laughs, a deep belly laugh.

Has Chloe been giving product to his daughter? I guess it's on-brand for her. She did "give" me a house. I wonder if she made a video about this too. *Donating My PR to Less Fortunate Kids #Sustainable #Charity.* "I'll let you know as soon as I have more to give."

He places his hand on his chest. "You're an angel, Miss Van Huusen. An angel. I hope you're feeling better these days."

I smile tightly, take the packages, and make for the elevators before he can say more.

He follows in lockstep behind me, his heat on my back. Why won't he leave me alone? He reaches over and presses the elevator button with a smile.

Oh.

I muster a weird chuckle, unused to this type of service and attention. Should I tip him?

The elevator dings and he holds the door open for me.

"Thanks," I mumble.

He presses the number twenty-seven and waves. "Have a restful night, Miss Van Huusen."

"You too."

He disappears behind the closing doors.

The elevator is composed of gold mirrors and matching gold handrails. My sneakers sink into the plush red carpet. The LED display ticks through the ascending numbers. My ears pop and my pulse thrums, my stomach coiling tight.

7

I knock. Wait. Knock again.

No answer.

I press my ear against the tall wood door.

"Chloe?" Nothing.

I grab my phone from my back pocket to give her a call. A dark screen flashes with an empty battery graphic. "Fuck." Searching through my bag, I realize I forgot to bring a charger. *Just perfect.*

Tired and feeling like an idiot, I lean against the door and rest the heavy packages on the handle. The handle suddenly gives. The door swings open. I fall forward, landing hard on my hip. Sharp pain jars my body. Hissing, I clench my fists and crawl onto my feet. After a few curses, I manage to regain my composure and stare at the gaping entrance.

It's weird that she'd leave the door unlocked. Or maybe it isn't. Her building has security. People here are fancy and rich. She wouldn't be worried about someone breaking into her home—like I technically had.

I pick up the packages and stack them by the entryway table.

"Chloe?" My voice echoes through her apartment.

I recognize the white walls, the couch, the twinkling city skyline from her videos. Nonetheless, it's weird seeing her apartment in real life. It feels like stumbling onto a television set. I'm waiting for a camera to whip in front of my face, for someone to tell me everything is fake. *Gotcha!*

Her apartment is smaller than it looks on camera. Wooden floors, tall windows, and modern, soulless art. Pink carnations are stuffed into a vase shaped like a bust of some Roman hero. In a porcelain catch-all dish, her keys sit beside a ring embedded with two blue gemstones. I pick it up. It's weighty—must be real gold. I'm about to put it back when something stops me. Maybe it's the way the ring is cool against my clammy palms or the knowledge that this tiny object, which likely equals the value of my entire week's pay, was insignificant enough for Chloe to toss next to her dirty keys, but I can't quite leave it where I found it.

Clutching the ring tight in my fist, I shove my hand into my hoodie pocket, glancing down the hall of Chloe's apartment. Jealousy tugs at my chest, preventing me from stepping forward. I can't help but wonder: What if I was born first? What if I was adopted by the Van Huusens? What if I was famous online? What if I had all of this? This nice apartment with expensive rings lying innocently in a catch-all?

"I'm coming in." I make my way into her apartment and drop my backpack on the kitchen counter. "It's Julie, by the way, if you're here. I was worried after you called me." I turn on the lights as I pass by the switches. A fly whizzes by my ear.

There's something rancid in the air. A whiff of a Jo Malone candle from my right, but then something rotten. A bit like fruit. It's coming from the kitchen. She probably forgot to take out the trash.

My search makes me feel like a kid playing hide-and-seek. I look inside her bedroom. The bathroom. Her closet, which, oh my god, is a walk-in. It has a whole line of designer bags and shoes. A clear glass center table for accessories. Cartier bangles, Rolexes, sparkly rings and necklaces. There's even a sleek, fridge-like contraption that turns out to be a giant clothes steamer.

When I don't find Chloe, I circle back to the kitchen and living room. An open bottle of Elavil medication, 25mg, sits on her marble counter. It's half full. The packaging doesn't tell me what it's for; only printed with instructions—*take one tablet before bedtime*—and a warning to keep them out of reach of children. I figure it's some medication for anxiety, since every influencer seems to whine about being anxious these days. I screw on the top so the pills won't get dusty.

I continue my self-guided tour. At this point, I'm not even looking for her, I'm checking out her apartment like a prospective homebuyer. Evaluating the water pressure. Testing out the induction stovetop. Opening her fridge: a luxurious Miele double-door with a water fountain and ice dispenser. The contents are a bit surprising. Chinese take-out containers, a row of passion-fruit La Croix, and half-empty bottles of alcohol. There isn't a single piece of fresh fruit or salad. Not very clean-girl aesthetic of her.

Maybe I'm being a hater. She lives in New York and can run downstairs to a bodega if she needs anything. It's probably sustainable, or whatever, not to stock fresh produce in her fridge in case of spoilage.

After stealing a sip of chardonnay, the liquid burning my throat, I close the fridge and walk to examine the pantry shelf. The tips of my toes catch on something. My heart lurches as I flail toward the ground. At the last second, I catch myself on the window. Busy streets, cars the size of Lego pieces, wobble in my eyes. I upright myself with a relieved sigh.

I turn around to see what I tripped on.

And then I see her.

Chloe.

8

She's behind the kitchen island.

Her skin is blue and blotchy, sagging as if it doesn't sit quite right on her bones. A crusty line of spit and gunk trails from between her purple, cracked lips and down her cheek, splotching the dark wood floor. Red streaks her swollen face and neck like she'd been clawing, trying to peel off her skin with her chipped turquoise nails. Her hair is a mop, strands of black slashing across her face. Bloodshot eyes, glassy and empty.

I'm frozen. I don't feel anything. Not my heartbeat. Not the air. Time has stopped completely. I'm not sure if I'm even breathing. I want to look away, but I can't.

A fly buzzes by. Lands at the tip of her nose.

I'm snapped out of my daze. I fold over, limp. Hot sickness rushes up my intestines, my stomach, my throat—acrid, searing, wet. I bolt for the bathroom, puke into the toilet, empty everything, until all I spit up is foamy water and stomach acid. I don't even have the energy to flush. I fall backward, the bath mat soft against my head. Sweat slicks every crevice and limb. I tremble, hot and cold at the same time. Pins and needles prick my fingertips and toes. I can't control my breath. The room is flashing, blurring. Vision clips in and out, darkness in my periphery. I'm on solid ground but the earth seems to shift like waves, tossing me back and forth. At some point, I press myself against the hard ceramic bathtub, curled like a fetus in a womb.

I pray for the door to crack open, for Chloe—somehow alive—to appear, a plate of juicy mango wedges resting on her hand. I wish she would slink next to me, brush the sweaty hair out of my face, hold me, feed me, reassure me that this was all a big joke. That everything is fine.

But when the door stays shut, reality sloshes into me.

Chloe is dead.

I take a few sour, shaky breaths, crawl up to sit, and gather my thoughts.

Police. Yes. This time, I *must* call the police. There's no excuse anymore. I can't be scared. Chloe needs it.

With slippery fingers, I grab my phone, turn it on. No batteries. *Shit.*

Chloe must have a charger somewhere. I crawl toward the vanity, search around. Nothing. Of course not. Who keeps a charger in the bathroom?

The bedroom is my best bet. But that means exiting back into the kitchen. Seeing . . . her.

My mind spins, images of Chloe's dead body searing my retinas.

Okay. Stop thinking. Breathe. Breathe. *Breathe!*

When I'm stable enough, I grab the sink to help me stand. My hands are so sweaty I can't find purchase. Slowly, I use the wall, leaving damp fingerprints on the brocade wallpaper. I splash cold water onto my face.

When I look up, Chloe's bloodshot eyes stare back at me, her dry, cracked lips suspended in a silent shout, almost in warning.

I scream, jerking away from the sink.

But it's only my reflection. I didn't turn on the light, so my skin looked dark and blue. I almost laugh at how ridiculous it is, being afraid of my own face. The moment eases weight off my chest, the smallest distraction.

Okay. Focus.

I open the bathroom door and slide into the bedroom, keeping my eyes trained on the wall, my back to the kitchen. I find a charger on top of the nightstand, plug it in, and power on my phone.

Installing Automatic Updates. 0% . . . Estimated time: 1 hour and 15 minutes.

I blink. Blink again. "What the actual—" I claw at my hair. "Are you fucking kidding me?" I plant my face into her soft cotton pillow and scream. I scream and scream and scream until I have no voice left in me anymore.

I want to cry but I can't leave Chloe rotting there any longer. I have to contact the authorities *now*. If I can find her phone, I can use it to make an emergency call.

"Please, please, please," I mutter to myself, searching her bedroom, the living room, hoping her phone is anywhere but on her. No luck. Tears pool in my eyes as I glance at the kitchen.

With all my willpower, I step toward her. I breathe through my mouth, unwilling to inhale the scent of her decay, knowing it will make me sick again. My eyes are fixed to the smooth white ceiling, the fancy gold sconces, until I make it to where Chloe rests, hidden behind the kitchen island.

I squat next to her. "I'm so sorry." I pat around her body, her legs, searching her pockets, up her toned stomach. *There.* The hard plastic of a phone case. It's trapped under her. I try to poke it out, but her body is too heavy, the phone doesn't budge.

I have to move her.

"God, please. Let this be the last of it." I'm a cold, hard atheist, but I need anything I can get right now. "I'm so sorry, Chloe. Help will be on the way." I don't know why I'm talking to her like she can hear me.

With all my strength, I push her body off the phone. She rolls over, thumping onto her stomach. I grab the device and sprint into the bathroom. Forty percent battery. A flood of notifications populates the lock screen. I groan, swiping them away, trying to remember how to make an emergency call, when I notice the little lock at the top of the screen is already open.

My face unlocked Chloe's phone.

Maybe God *is* listening.

I swipe up, leaving a streak of sweat on the screen, and call 911.

The line responds immediately. "911, what's your emergency?"

"My sister . . . she . . . I think she's dead."

"Dead?"

"Yeah. No. I don't *think* she's dead. She's definitely dead. Like, for a day or two now. Maybe more. Fuck. I don't know." My heart is pounding up my throat. "Can you just *please* send someone to help?"

She asks for the address, and I give it to her.

"Do you know the cause of death, ma'am?"

"I-I don't know. I walked into the apartment and found her on the ground." My voice cracks. Sobs ripple from my chest.

"I hear you. I'm sending a team now. Are you able to get away from the body? Get some fresh air?"

"Y-yeah. Okay." I close my eyes as I hobble out of the bathroom, grasping at the walls to find my way. Once I'm outside the apartment, I sit on the plush hallway carpet, beside the door. "I'm outside."

"Emergency services should be with you soon. Hold on tight. Will you be okay if I let you go while you wait? Or do you want to stay on the phone with me?" What is she going to do? Sit over the line and coo at me until the police arrive? She probably has other emergencies to tend to.

I shake my head though she can't see. "I'm okay. You can go."

"All right. If we need anything, we will give you a call back on this number. Please be safe." The line goes dead.

9

I don't mean to snoop on her phone. Really.

It just happens. A natural reflex. I'm not proud to admit how much I use social media to cope. I struggle to exist without something flashing on the screen. Can't sit still without a video blasting to deaden my dark thoughts. Social media is the biggest thief of time but it's also an impossibly addictive form of escape.

As soon as that device leaves my ear, the phone app white and bright in my eyes, I swipe onto Chloe's home screen. The notifications haven't stopped. Every second, a banner pops up. Blah blah blah liked your Instagram post. Or New comments on your TikTok. Or Someone tagged you in a photo. How does Chloe handle this information overload? I'm already getting a headache from overstimulation. Then again, maybe it's because I'm too used to silence. Whenever I wake up, the only notification that greets me is my alarm.

Instinctively, I open TikTok first. Just to cope, to distract from the images of Chloe. After everything I've been through, I think I deserve it.

TikTok is my go-to, since the videos are curated through (likely invasive) algorithms. My personal feed is self-effacing story times or people injuring themselves in slapstick ways, quick bites of content that are guaranteed to make me laugh. But if Chloe's TikTok says anything about her, it's that she's boring. Her FYP consists of videos that replicate her lifestyle content. Occasionally, a TikTok pseudo-therapist pops up, lecturing me on ways to deal with guilt, depression, or some parent-child attachment complex. I groan. I'm looking for a cheap, distracting laugh, not to heal my inner child.

I swipe onto Instagram. The first thing I see is the little graphic that shows how many new followers, comments, and likes she's gained. Even though her last post was two weeks ago, her numbers still cap at one hundred for each value. It's chilling. All these people, all this attention, yet nobody knows she's dead.

Perhaps this is callous of me, but I can't help thinking: What happens to the sponsorship money now that she's out of commission? Does Chloe just not get paid? That's outrageous. Her last post got—I click on the analytics—more than three million impressions. Even if she's dead, the brand should still fork out that money. It's not like megacorporations don't have enough.

Out of pure curiosity, I visit her DMs. My eyes widen at the sheer number of blue checkmarks. From fellow influencers to singers to models to magazines to literal A-list celebs.

I click into her requested messages, which take a second to load due to volume.

Thousands—and I mean *thousands* of DMs—are from her followers clamoring for attention, parroting how much they love her, how much Chloe inspires them. A few hundred messages are from men asking if she'd like to see a picture of their penis and sending it anyway (preblurred by the app, thankfully). Some surprisingly detailed (and oddly creative) death threats. A number of smaller influencers trying to slide into her DMs. Hundreds of brands asking her to connect.

I can't resist going into her email. Her inbox has over two thousand unread, mostly spam. I navigate to the sidebar and find her second account for filtered correspondence. Only five unread. Everything else has been slotted into folders. She's neat.

The newest email is from Kare Kosmetics, dated three days ago. Title: Re: INVOICE for January.

It calls to me.

I click through.

Hi Chloe!

We loved your latest post and reel. Thank you for confirming the
analytics with us. As always, you impress us with your reach and
versatility. As per the contract, we have paid out your invoice at
the end of the month. Please see the attached file for reference.

We look forward to working with you next month. Can't wait to
see what you come up with!

Before I know it, I'm loading the pdf.

My eyes fly to the TOTAL. I clap my hand to my mouth.

I pinch the screen and zoom in. My eyes aren't tricking me. The number
is real.

For one Instagram Reel / TikTok cross-post and two static feed posts
over four weeks, Chloe received $45,000.

Forty. Five. Thousand. Dollars.

What. The. Actual. Flying. Fuck?

I barely make that much in a *year*, but she makes that with a few posts
of her in a shitty little face mask?

How can this be real?

My face scrunches with envy. I'm so disgusted by the unfairness of the
world that I want to hurt something.

Fuck her privacy. She's dead anyway. I scroll through her other emails
and open every file attached.

In the span of a few minutes, I've viewed about twenty invoices and
not a single payment is less than $10,000. Within a single month, Chloe
had raked in over $100,000 worth of sponsorship money. This doesn't even
include her YouTube channel, which must earn thousands per video.

No wonder she had bought me that house at the edge of town like it
was nothing. It *was* nothing. I looked up the property a while back. It was
listed on the market for $272,000. She could have bought the house with a
few months' worth of income. And who knows how much she earned from
the dozens of gratuitous ad rolls she implemented in that one hour-long
#EMOTIONAL video?

Actually . . . now I can find out. I log into her YouTube analytics, scroll three years back, and click on Earnings to Date. Fifty-seven thousand. Okay, not as much as I thought she'd get for twenty million views—wait. What the hell am I saying? She earned more than my salary with *one* measly video that exploited *my* vulnerabilities. And she didn't even give me a cut! How is that fair?

I remember there was a mid-video sponsorship for some app called Mansion-Scapes. (Through Mansion-Scapes, you can build your own home like Julie, design your own furniture, and have guests over by solving addictive puzzles! Jump-start your immersive gameplay with thirty free Mansion Coins by using code Chloe30. Thank you Mansion-Scapes for sponsoring this portion of the video.) I search her email for "Mansion-Scapes." There's an invoice dated three years back. The influencer coordinator gushed about the performance of the video. Of how over twenty thousand people downloaded Mansion-Scapes and redeemed her code.

The invoice totaled a staggering $125,000, with $75,000 in base pay and a casual $50,000 bonus for meeting an incentive number of downloads.

I'm so gobsmacked, I have to look away from the screen to process.

How can anyone make that much money with one video? It only gets worse as I read through the email thread from when Chloe had pitched the idea.

Evidenced in the attached analysis of YouTube's trending tab, philanthropic videos are attracting a favorable general audience, including those aged 8 to 20, who are most likely to download a game app. As this is a deviation from my typical content, I am confident that Julie's lower-middle-class life will be relatable to a wider viewership and would result in positive, empathetic engagement. I would love to see if it's within your budget to increase my compensation, especially reflecting the personal investments that would go into producing a video of this magnitude. Cheers, Chloe V.

And there it is. The truth.

I was nothing more than fodder for a video. An accessory for an ad. I meant absolutely nothing. I was a pawn.

It breaks me.

I cry, not for Chloe's death. I cry for *my* loss. Grief for that person I could have been.

I think back on my overwhelming gratitude when Chloe first found me, how misguided I was, when she only wanted to exploit me. How she used my childhood nickname, *Ju-Ju,* knowing how it must affect me. I wonder if she laughed internally as she said it, calling me a little pig and having me burst with appreciation. I grieve for how worried I was when she called. I wasted all that time and energy on her—time and energy I'll never get back. And for what? To find out she never cared? Not even for one second? That I was just some sad, lower-class example to be fed to her viewers? What type of fucked-up turn of events is this?

Pure hatred, hot and venomous, coils in my flesh, my muscles. I want to go into her apartment and tear into every piece of furniture. Cut into every designer bag, flush all her skincare down her ludicrous Toto toilet with its warm seat and bidet. She doesn't deserve any of it, not her material objects and wealth or my empathy and compassion. She is a vile, *vile* human being, selfish and narcissistic to the bone. I feel disgusted to be related to her— to have positive memories of her.

I sob and I shriek, loud and uncontrolled. Doors down the hall open. Neighbors' eyes fill with shock and concern. I don't care. I cry out from the depths of my chest, deep and guttural.

A hand grabs my shoulder. I jump.

It's Ramos. Behind him are a police officer and two paramedics with a stretcher.

A stretcher that will soon hold Chloe.

10

I'm hiccuping, eyes wet and swollen. I turn to the nosy neighbors in silk bathrobes. One person has his phone out, camera pointed at me.

"Are you okay?" Ramos tilts his head, brows furrowed.

"Y-yeah," I mumble, breathless.

"Is the deceased inside?" a paramedic asks.

I nod, biting my nails.

While the paramedics enter with a stretcher, the police officer pulls me aside. I'm thankful the cop is a woman. I'm more at ease. I tell her the truth, the parts that matter anyway: I walked into the apartment, saw my twin's body, made the call.

As she scribbles on her notepad, I catch her glancing at me. There's a spark in her eyes, a sharp, almost accusatory gaze. It makes me antsy. Does she think I have something to do with Chloe's death? Pulse humming with nerves, I clench and unclench my sweaty fists inside my hoodie pocket, feeling Chloe's ring.

"Do you know how she passed?" she asks.

I shrug. Watch her make notes. She glances at me again. I want to crawl out of my skin.

A paramedic joins us, flashing the bottle of Elavil. "Do you recognize these?"

I saw them on the counter, so I nod. But why is he asking? Does he think Chloe overdosed?

"Are they your pills?"

I'm so overwhelmed with the idea of Chloe overdosing that I nod without thinking. When I realize what he asked, I don't have the chance to correct myself because he moves on to the next question.

"Did your sister have a history with substance abuse?"

Chloe and substance abuse don't calibrate in my mind. She portrayed herself as a clean-cut girl, an advocate for ginger shots and celery juice, how-tos on healing your gut's microbiome. But social media is all about manufactured authenticity, a performative and controlled identity to appeal to the public.

I remember opening her fridge, seeing the bottles of alcohol. Could it be? Was she secretly an addict?

This realization kicks me in the gut. I thought she had a perfect life, but behind the screen, she and I were both fractured in different ways.

"I'm not sure," I say. "She hides things really well. Did she . . . you know . . . overdose or something?"

"I can't say for certain. It's difficult to OD on TCAs." He shakes the bottle of pills. "Unless she had a preexisting condition that would lead to a higher chance of seizures."

"Seizures?" The word shocks me so much it feels like a corset has suddenly bound my ribs.

"Her airways contained froth. That's uncommon for ODs on TCAs, unless she had a seizure."

I cross my arms and hold on to my trembling elbows. I'm reminded of her call to me, the gurgles, the choking.

"Do you know if your sister had epilepsy or any heart issues?"

"Maybe. I don't know."

Chloe's voice rips into my mind. *Mistake.* Did she accidentally take too many pills? Or had she intended to OD but was beginning to regret it? If so, why didn't she call 911? She had said *I'm sorry.* I'm sure I heard that. What was she apologizing for?

The paramedic, the cop, and Ramos are staring at me. Someone must have asked me a question, but I didn't hear it; I was tangled in thought.

I'm about to apologize when the paramedic says, "I see you're a bit rattled. We'll give you a second to breathe. Do you know where her ID is so we can make a report?"

"P-probably in the apartment."

"There was a backpack on the counter. Are her belongings there?"

She's talking about *my* backpack.

My identification.

The world is silent for a few beats, something stuck in my throat.

"Miss Van Huusen?" Ramos waves his hand in front of my eyes, his words ringing in my ears.

Miss Van Huusen.

A ridiculous idea slips into my mind.

So wrong yet so tempting, like stumbling across a bright red fire alarm, the insatiable urge to pull on the handle.

Everything slows as I glance into her apartment, the luxurious floors, pristine couches, expensive jewelry. Is it really fair for Chloe's life to go to waste? To become another tomb when so many would kill for her position? If I left tonight as Julie, I would have nothing. A rotting house. A dead-end job at SuperFoods. A drained bank account. No future. No friends. No family except for an aunt and cousin who never cared for me anyway. I wouldn't even have an asshole sister to be bitter about.

Chloe has everything. *Had* everything. Her life is all I've ever wanted and more. It's too precious to toss away, to zap into obscurity. I could do so much if I were her. So much more than she ever did. I could take what she had and better the world, give her assets to charity, start fundraisers, donate all my sponsorships to those in need—and not for some silly video.

I deserve it, don't I? Chloe had everything while I suffered with nothing. Isn't this karmic justice unfolding before me? Reparations for my hardships in the shape of a new, glittery influencer life? It's not like I asked for it. The world just placed the pieces in my palm, tempting me to puzzle them together. Who knows, this might be Chloe's final apology, her last gift for her dear twin: her life.

She'd want this for me. For family. Surely.

Surely.

"Miss Van Huusen?" Ramos says again.

It's his fault, really. It's Ramos's words that seal everything.

I can barely breathe as I answer, my heart blaring rapidly as I lie. "I-I think so, yeah. She always keeps her wallet in the front pocket."

The officer doesn't question it. She goes inside, returns with the wallet, and asks me to confirm if the ID is hers. "Julie Chan?"

I nod. Every crick in my neck bends and snaps.

She glances at the ID photo, then at me. Does she know I'm lying? I know that Chloe normally looks more put together, but compared to a corpse, I must look okay, right?

I bite my lip. It's not too late. I can take everything back. I can say I was confused, that I'm Julie and she's Chloe. I don't have to go down this path. I can stop before it all gets out of hand.

"And you . . ." the cop begins.

I should just tell the truth. Right now. Before she catches me in a lie.

"You're Chloe Van Huusen, right? Maybe I shouldn't be saying this, but uh . . ." She chuckles awkwardly. "I've been watching you since college."

I clench my teeth to stop my jaw from dropping. So that's why she kept glancing at me. It wasn't suspicion. She's a *fan*.

Her eyes gleam as if face-to-face with her idol at a meet and greet, as if there isn't a literal dead body on the other side of the wall. "I was curious why you kept your twin so private, but now I understand. If my sister was going through all of this, I wouldn't want her in the spotlight either."

"Oh . . ." is all I can mutter.

She closes her eyes and shakes her head. "Sorry. That was totally unprofessional. I don't know what got into me. I'm just . . . so sorry for your loss."

I don't know how to process this. What the fuck is happening?

"I know you're grieving, but I need to create a police report to make sure everything is in order. Can I ask you a few more questions?"

"S-sure." My heart is beating up my throat. Part of me screams to tell the truth. But how can I inform this cop that her internet idol is the one dead on the floor? How can I confess that I lied without incriminating myself? What if she grabs those metal handcuffs secured on her belt, arrests me, and drags me to jail for identity fraud?

But the cop is clearly sympathetic to me—er, Chloe. She's subconsciously primed to believe someone with my twin's face. Maybe, just maybe, I can work this to my advantage. Prevent this from all blowing up.

"It seems like your sister has been here for a while," she says. "Why didn't you call earlier? Were you not at home?"

I swallow. What would Chloe say? What would Chloe have been doing? "I-I was taking a break."

The cop nods. "Yes, I noticed."

Sweat beads down my back. "And I was, um, using that time to get away from the city. To be away from . . . all the stress. So, my sister was house-sitting for me." I can't bring myself to say *Julie* out loud. It feels too wrong.

"Did you go to your family home in the Hamptons?"

Holy shit. This cop is a big-time fan. She must have watched all of Chloe's summer vlogs. She's crafting my cover story without knowing it. I can lean into what she already believes. This is beyond luck. This is a miracle.

I nod.

She jots in her notebook. "Do you have a record of your travel, just in case we need to look into it?"

"Um . . ." Shit. Think. Think. *Think!* "I took a cab. Paid in cash. I didn't want my location to be accidentally leaked."

She sighs. "I hear you. You'd be surprised how often we respond to fans showing up at celebrity homes, or streamers being swatted. There are so many parasocial freaks out there. I'm sorry you have to go through all that trouble. Can anyone confirm that you were in the Hamptons?"

"N-no. I went there to lie low. To be by myself." The series of questions is making me nervous. The question bubbles up before I can stop it: "Am I under suspicion?"

"I'm only performing my due diligence. Most of these questions are routine." She meets my gaze. "Unless there's signs of foul play."

My eyes widen. "Foul play? Didn't she OD?"

"Since you weren't aware of a history of addiction or drug issues, we might have to get an autopsy to confirm."

Fuck. They can't get an autopsy. What if they find out she's actually Chloe? What happens to me then?

"I don't want to concern you, I'm not saying there's foul play," she continues. "We just want to make sure—"

"I lied!"

"Sorry?"

"I—" My throat catches. I'm so overwhelmed that I hiccup a sob. "I lied. She did have a history of addiction." What the hell am I saying? What am I doing? But I can't stop. I'm desperate to cover my tracks. I don't want to get in trouble. "I was used to protecting her and . . . I lied out of habit. I'm sorry." Tears stream down my cheeks, dripping off my chin in globs. I don't know if it's from the grief of losing my twin, fear of being caught, or guilt from sprinting down this path of lies. Perhaps it's everything. In this moment of panic, one lie has unlocked something inside me, released the floodgates. I'm caught in the currents, and I can't swim out.

"She's been having a lot of trouble recently. She was caught stealing at work and now she might get fired, she has no social support or family. And she once told me that back in high school, the police had to come to her house because she was suicidal."

The cop notes every word caught between breathless sobs. A history of misbehavior. A profile of deviancy. And it's all true. Maybe that's why they come out so easily. So quick and without thought. Maybe I've been wanting to confess my burdens and was simply waiting for someone to ask. To listen.

"I could tell she was hopeless and lost and really, *really* depressed, as if she was just going through the motions. I thought if I gave her a place to stay, she'd get better. But I wasn't thinking—I forgot about all my medication and now she's dead!" I let out another cry. "I feel so guilty. What do I do? I fucked up! I fucked everything up!" I *really* am fucking up. How can I keep lying like this? What is wrong with me?

My throat is tight. Breath struggles to enter my lungs. My fingertips are prickling. I see stars in my eyes.

"It's okay." The cop pats my back. "Breathe. You don't have to say any more. I understand."

I focus in on her face. When I stare at her misty eyes, wet with sympathy, I know I've gotten away with it. She's absorbed my words as truth, gobbled them up like grapes.

She believes me.

She believes that I'm Chloe.

The once cold and calming ring I've been squeezing in my fist is now hot from my sweaty palm. I slip it on my pointer finger. It slides into place without resistance, like it was meant for me all along.

"Do you have someone to stay with tonight to make sure you're okay?"

"I have family here." It comes out so naturally, I didn't even have to think. It's like Chloe's soul climbed into me, pulled on the tendons in my jaws, and sent words up my throat.

The paramedics come out with Chloe on a stretcher, her body covered by a blanket, face obscured. They carry her away. She disappears behind the elevator door. Just like that, she's gone.

The cop remains, letting me know in soft whispers that she just needs to copy the information off the ID. Date of birth, address, everything.

She's writing the end of Julie Chan's story.

And the start of mine.

11

I check into a hotel for the night.

I'm in a daze as I shower. Hot water sprays my bare skin, droplets draining down my thighs, steam pluming. The shampoo smells like peach and Bartlett pear. It marinates in my hair and skin, becoming nauseatingly sweet, like overripe fruit. Almost rotten. Like . . . Chloe's corpse. I snap my mouth shut, hold my breath, but the smell has already traveled through my nostrils and into my throat, sticking to my insides like tacky syrup. I gag and frantically rinse out the shampoo. In my frenzy, the foam drips down my forehead and traps itself between the thin skin of my eyelid and cornea, stinging, burning. I splash and rub my eyes. It lingers, persistent.

No matter how hard I try, I can't get rid of it. The burning and the smell. *Chloe's* smell.

Chloe. Chloe. Chloe.

I stumble out of the shower, soapsuds crackling in my hair, and wrap myself in a towel. I stand there, trembling like a sopping-wet dog, playing back every terrible decision from the last few hours.

My sister died, my twin, and yet . . .

I stole her life.

Replaced her.

Took everything.

The ring I put on earlier tonight suddenly feels too tight, too warm, a reminder of my wrongdoing, searing evidence of my cruelty. I wrench it off my finger and throw it. It skids against tile, clattering somewhere I can't see.

Why did I think I could get away with this? Lying to an incompetent cop with Chloe brain rot was one thing, but lying to the rest of the world? People who know about Chloe are bound to find out.

The Van Huusens.

What if they realize I'm not their daughter? What if they go to the police? Will I go to jail? Does the State of New York have the death penalty?

And Chloe. Even if she had tossed me aside, never truly cared about me, she was still my sister, my family. How could I do something so terrible? So stupid?

What the *fuck* is wrong with me?

Oh god. Oh god. Oh god.

I climb into the bed, wet hair squelching into the white sheets. Curling into a little ball, I sob, desperately alone and scared. I'm praying that this is all a nightmare. That I'll go to sleep, wake up, and everything will be fine. Chloe will be alive, and I will have done nothing wrong.

I don't know how long I cry until I pass out, exhausted from everything that's happened.

———

I'm awoken by the blaring sound of notifications. *Ding. Ding. Ding. Ding.* A phone call. My—Chloe's—phone vibrates off the end table, clunks on the floor.

I stare at the screen. Someone is trying to reach Chloe. I throw a pillow on top of my head, attempting to muffle the sound. As one call drops, another begins, unrelenting.

What if Chloe always picks up this person's phone calls? I must pick up. If I don't, they might realize something is wrong.

With a jolt, I straighten and grasp the device, squinting at the bright screen. It's 9:04 a.m. A thin ray of light streams in between the blackout curtains, casting a stripe of white across the wall.

I ignore all the messages from social media and read the texts. They're all from Fiona. She was cc'd in emails that Chloe sent out to brands. I think she might be a manager or an assistant.

I click on the text thread.

7:08AM: Hi Chloe! Hope Pilates is going well. I know you told me not to contact you unless it's necessary since you're taking a break. But this IS necessary.

So, Chloe had been taking a break. Also, what kind of psycho takes Pilates at seven in the morning?

7:09AM: A video of you is blowing up on that gossip subreddit, FauxMoi. You've already lost 10K followers on IG!!! But the good news: you're relevant enough to be on FauxMoi!!!!

I furrow my brow. What video?

7:35AM: Hello?
8:01AM: The video is gaining traction. It's been posted on TikTok and Instagram. I've tried to contact your neighbor to take it down. Call me back! This is urgent!!!

Neighbor? And then it dawns on me.

A guy had filmed me while I was having a breakdown in the hallway.

Chloe doesn't have Reddit on her phone, so I go into the App Store and download it. It uses my face for Face ID, which somehow still astounds me. As it downloads, I continue reading the text thread.

8:55AM: Stopped by your apartment and used the spare key when you didn't answer the door. It smells like shit in there by the way. (I already contacted a cleaner for you, ur welcome.) I called the Pilates studio and they said you no-showed? Are you okay? Call me.

They must be close if she has a spare. This isn't good. What if she finds out the truth?

9:00AM: This isn't funny, Chloe.

9:00AM: Call me.

9:00AM: Are you even alive?

9:04AM: I just spoke to the front desk guy. He said your twin died in your apartment? WTF. I thought you didn't talk to her because she was a loser. Why the hell was she at your house? Call me!!

9:04AM: IF this is true, let me know

9:04AM: We can use it.

9:05AM: Hello?

My pulse thrums as I finish reading the last message.

A laugh, of all things, escapes my throat. *Because she was a loser.* I'm not surprised. Fiona's text confirms that Chloe never cared about me. Not even a little.

I go on Reddit and log on to my own account. The video is on the front page of FauxMoi. Me, curled up against the beige walls of the hallway, the velvety carpet. Chloe Van Huusen Throws Tantrum in NYC.

I swallow, press play. The video starts off from afar, but slowly zooms in. I'm hysterical. Like I'm on drugs. I remember sobbing and screaming but I don't remember banging my fists against the floor, knocking my head into the wall, flailing around like a baby. The video is five minutes, but I pause at thirty-eight seconds, embarrassed. I look in the comments.

Chloe's a pretty big influencer. I used to watch her beauty tutorials in high school. What the hell happened to her?

In the replies: Entitlement is one hell of a drug.

Isn't her whole persona about positive mental health?

Are we even surprised? You're an idiot if you trust a single thing these influencers sell. There nothing more than society's parasites. Real-life snake oil salesmen.

They're*

My breaths are short and scattered as I read and expand every vile, vindictive thread. There's something addictive about it, seeing what people think of me, every cruel comment, every hateful sentence. I'm about to reply to one of the users, thumbs itching for vengeance, to clarify everything, when Fiona calls again.

12

I drop the phone with a yip.

Fiona's caller screen flashes in the dim hotel room.

Should I pick up?

I should, just to clarify the situation.

What if I pick up and she realizes I'm not Chloe?

But if I don't pick up, isn't that even more suspicious?

I lunge for the phone and answer before I can think myself into any more circles.

"H-hello?"

"What the hell?" Her high-pitched voice blasts into my eardrum. I flinch and turn down the volume. "What took you so long? I told you it's an emergency. We really need to make a statement. Is it really because your twin, like, died? If that's why, we should make a social post to clarify. I've drafted something in my notes for you." My phone dings, probably a text from her.

This is good. Fiona hasn't caught on yet.

"Hello? Earth to Chloe!"

"R-right. Yeah. Uh, I'll take a look at what you sent over."

There's a beat.

"So . . . did she die or not? Your twin."

My mouth dries, heart hammering. "She did."

Another person I lied to. Another nail in Julie's coffin. I've dived into the deep end and there's no way out. It's sink or swim.

She sighs. "I'm sorry, Chloe. That seriously sucks. Like, literally sucks so much. That's actually, like, legit so sad."

I have trouble telling whether she's actually sad or not.

"But honestly, like, RIP or whatever, I'm just kinda surprised. I thought you went no-contact after that video. What was she doing in your apartment?"

I gulp. "It's kind of a long story."

She doesn't say anything, waiting for said long story.

I make something up. Try to be convincing. "W-we weren't talking for a while. But, uh, y'know, Julie's always been a leech."

"Totally."

Okay. That hurt.

"She showed up unannounced," I continue. "I think . . . since it was our parents' death anniversary, she wanted my support." They died on a bright and hot summer morning. Not in the blustery winter. I'm hoping Fiona doesn't know this detail.

"You never told me it was your parents' death anniversary."

Ugh. "Yeah. I mean, y'know, I try to move on from it." Which is true. People say grief gets easier, but it never does. I'm haunted by what could have been if they were alive. Maybe I wouldn't be in this fucked-up situation, and maybe Chloe and I would be close, like real sisters. "If I keep thinking back on it, I'll never be able to heal. It's kind of like picking at old scars."

"Oh! Yes! That's a fantastic line!" The sound of her nails clicking on her screen. "I'm sending over a new statement draft." My phone dings. "I think you'll like it. It incorporates what you said earlier. Also, like, I know a grandma isn't the same as a twin or whatever, but I remember when my granny passed away, I was, like, legit, so, so, *so* sad, and the one thing that helped me was getting back to work. Like, grinding through the day." She laughs. All nasal. "Anyway. Can you give me a temperature check on the event for tomorrow?"

"Event?"

"For Bella Marie's brand launch? We had RSVP'd before you decided to take a break, so we're still on the list. I totally understand if you need time to grieve, but there's going to be, like, *so* many people there to network with. But of course, no pressure. Bella Marie will totally understand."

Bella Marie. There's no way it's *that* Bella Marie, right?

I put Fiona on speakerphone and search for her on Instagram. Her name, @bellamarie, pops up as soon as I type "B," since we're following each other.

Bella Marie Melniburg has thirty-two million followers on Instagram alone. I recognize her immediately. Her pale, almost transparent skin, lithe body, and blond, almost white hair. She has big blue eyes and plump lips, a perfect little nose, and the slightest tooth gap. The sight of her makes me gulp, sends a swirl into my stomach. Embarrassing memories I shoved into the dusty corners of my mind suddenly resurface. I had a small obsession with her back in middle school when she was *huge* on Tumblr. She occupied every "girl" niche from fashion to ED to travel. You couldn't scroll for more than ten seconds without her pale, stick-thin body popping up on your home feed. (I reblogged every picture.) At thirteen, Bella Marie was scouted at Wimbledon. By her late teens, she walked for Prada, Fendi, Dior, and had features in *Vogue*, *Allure*, and every teen girl's Pinterest board. But that's just the tip of the Bella Marie iceberg. She isn't just a model and an it-girl. She's basically royalty. Her father was a Russian oligarch, and her mother is a famous French aristocrat gymnast-turned-model-turned-film-star. Her mother succumbed to an addiction after her husband died and has been stuck in rehab since. Sometimes this detail seems made up, a perfectly shaped stain in Bella Marie's otherwise flawless life to make her seem more real. One thing is for certain: Bella Marie is rich. Old-money rich. Like she'd pay fifty dollars for a single banana without a blink, rich. She's always flying in private jets with a rotation of blond models or six-pack athlete boyfriends. One night in Paris, the next in Bali, a rosy little sunburn on the bridge of her perfect nose.

She has it all.

I wanted her, and I wanted to be her.

"Chl—I was invited to Bella Marie's event?"

"Uhhh. Yeah? All the Belladonnas are going."

Belladonnas? I want to ask more, but I fear it might arouse suspicion. "Right. My sister's death is scrambling my brain."

"Aw. Sad . . . But what's the vibes? Do you think you can make it? If not, I need to get in contact with Bella Marie's assistant to let her know."

I think about it. It's Bella Marie. Middle-school Julie would freak out. And okay, maybe grown-up Julie is freaking out a little too.

Attending an event right after my twin died is a terrible idea. It will be full of people who knew Chloe. People who could sniff me out as a fake. I'll be stepping into a tiger's den dressed as rare sirloin.

But . . . it's Bella Marie.

I think about how Chloe would act if I died.

She thought I was a loser. A leech.

She wouldn't care if I wasted away unless she could make a video out of it. She'd go.

"I'll be there," I say.

"Perf! I'll send over the invite again just in case you lost it. Oh, also, how did Julie die?"

"Drug overdose."

"Figures."

I hate the way she said it. *Figures.* I hang up before she can say anything else.

13

Fiona crafted an amazing statement.

Was she the one who penned Chloe's speech to me? I choose not to investigate this. I want to pretend a few words Chloe said were genuine.

After editing a few details (mainly the bit about my parents' death anniversary, I don't want anyone sleuthing around and calling me out on the lie), I post it as a screenshot from my Notes app.

The word is out now. Julie Chan is dead. Chloe Van Huusen is grieving. Everyone loves it.

Hello.

I'm here to address a video of me that has been going around. The video, which was filmed without my permission and taken out of context, featured me in front of my apartment, crying. I sincerely apologize to anyone who found the video disturbing. I want to make it clear: I am not on drugs. But I was having a mental breakdown.

I have always believed in transparency, even in matters most difficult. So, though it is with pained sadness, I will be honest about my circumstances. My twin, who you might have seen featured on my

YouTube channel, passed away last night. I discovered her body in my apartment, which led to a panic attack in the hallway.

The grief and pain of losing a loved one is an unparalleled experience. Losing a twin is even greater. Since birth, I have felt a connection to Julie. A connection that cannot be described in mere words. It is one of the soul. Of the spirit. And when she died, I felt a part of me die as well.

My grief was so overwhelming, it manifested in a breakdown outside my apartment. While I am disappointed that the video was filmed and posted without my consent, as a mental health advocate, I hope this might be a moment where I share the very real and ugly ways grief is expressed.

It is my personal philosophy that I will never be able to heal if I pick at old scars, so I will carry on with purpose and intention. I hope to live the life Julie would have wanted me to live if she were still with us.

Most importantly, check up on your loved ones and tell them you love them before it's too late.

Yours forever,
Chloe

124

I am flooded with love.

Within two hours, the apology doubles the engagement of Chloe's usual posts. People adore tragedy. The note was even covered in an article by some low-brow entertainment news site: Chloe Van Huusen's Honesty About Grief and Why We Love to See It.

Nearly every comment is in support of me. Praise for how honest and raw I am. They love me for my authenticity. Other influencers are clamoring into my DMs, asking how they can support me through this difficult time. Every like and positive comment injects me with a dose of pure ecstasy. I keep refreshing the post, watching the engagement creep. Eventually, I have to mute notifications since the sheer amount of activity is making my phone lag.

It's all going better than expected. No one suspects a thing.

After locating the ring I threw last night (inches away from falling down a drainpipe!) and slipping it back on my finger, I check out of the hotel and pay with Chloe's credit card. I take an Uber back to Chloe's apartment. (She has 4.9 stars.) I tip the driver 25 percent.

My heart thunders into my throat as I stand outside the apartment door. I can't bring myself to enter. The corpse is removed, and Fiona had sent a cleaner, yet the image of Chloe's bloated blue face twists in my thoughts. Her smell, rotten and sweet, spreads in my lungs.

I put down my things, stomp down the hallway, and knock on the door of the apartment next to mine. The guy answers, a plump pug in his arms. The creature struggles to breathe, snot bubbling from its flat snout, pink tongue dribbling saliva. Go figure. My neighbor is a sadist who films and posts other people's suffering, *and* an animal cruelty advocate.

When he sees my face, regret flashes in his eyes.

"Take the video down," I say.

His mouth parts. He swallows. "I'm sorry. I'll do it."

"Now. I want to see you delete it in front of me."

He puts the dog down. It patters like a miniature hippo into the apartment, stumpy tail trying to wag. He takes out his phone and deletes the video and post, clears his trash permanently. "I didn't know your sister died. I just thought you were having another one of your tantrums. It was getting on my nerves. The walls aren't that thick."

Chloe's been throwing regular tantrums? I googled her prescription this morning and learned it's often used to treat depression. Maybe her behavior is a side effect of her medication. Or maybe her tantrums are a symptom she's trying to treat. I'm starting to think Chloe was more messed up than anyone realized.

Regardless, the way he's trying to justify his behavior angers me. "It's fucked up to film someone's mental breakdown and post it on the internet for everyone to mock. How would you feel if someone killed your dog and filmed you hysterically crying?"

His face scrunches together like he's eaten something sour, and he steps away from me.

"Yeah," I spit. "I bet it would feel like shit." I close the gap, breathing hot into his face. "And if I ever catch you filming me again, you will be hearing from my lawyers." I don't know if Chloe has lawyers, but I get the reaction I wanted. He stumbles back, terrified. I grin at his horror before striding down the hall and into my apartment.

I press my back into the door as adrenaline ripples through my body. I'm on a high. Like I could run a marathon without breaking a sweat.

Is this how Chloe felt all the time? Or how my aunt felt when she belittled me? It's amazing. I don't know how I've ever lived without it.

15

The cleaner did an amazing job. The floor is scrubbed to a shine, not a trace of Chloe's remnants. They even lit a candle. Baies by Diptyque. It has a little golden carousel accessory on top that spins with the heat of the wick. Very fancy.

I take some time getting acquainted with my new living space. Find where Chloe stored her spices, her cutlery. I explore a cabinet I hadn't opened last night and discover a drawer full of prescriptions. Staring at the little containers makes me ill. How messed up must you be for a doctor to prescribe so many medications at once? At the same time, I'm a bit amazed. I wonder what insurance she has to afford all these meds. Maybe she paid out of pocket. She has the money. If I had all these little tablets, the support of doctors, the ability to pay for help, could I have lived with more purpose?

In the bathroom, makeup and skincare products are bursting out of the floor-to-ceiling cabinets. The products are separated into three sections. Unopened products at the bottom. Sponsored products, many of which are still sealed despite her claiming they saved her skin, in the middle. And products that are half empty, high-end stuff like Vintner's Daughter and La Prairie, within arm's reach.

I lie on her bed. The plush mattress snuggles my body; the sumptuous down pillows adjust to the shape of my neck.

I try on all her clothes. Some fit. Most don't. I'm a bit wider than she, with some extra belly and thigh fat. Makes sense, considering I'm mostly stationary while she's at Pilates by seven a.m. Luckily, our feet are the same size. I slip on every pair of Jimmy Choos and Manolo Blahniks. Every colorful sneaker and dead-stock dad shoe. I even try on her beat-up Birkenstocks. The topographical imprints of our soles are so identical it makes me a bit uncomfortable.

I'm slipping on a golden Rolex when someone knocks. I swear, if it's the damned neighbor again . . . With a sigh, I open the door and see a small Filipino woman standing in the hallway. At first, I just stare, wondering who she is, but then I catch sight of the IKEA-sized tote lugged over one shoulder and a garment bag on the other. I figure it's the cleaner Fiona hired returning with Chloe's dry cleaning. I'm afraid to say the first thing. I've never had help around the house before—if anything, *I* was the help. (I can't count the number of times I had to scrub my cousin's dried piss off the side of the toilet bowl because he refused to look away from his mobile games to aim.) Are hired cleaners supposed to stare at their employer with pure contempt stamped between their brows? Or maybe she's waiting for payment. A tip? Oh god, how much do cleaners cost?

"Christ," she utters. "You look like shit." Wow. Okay. "Well? Are you going to let me in or just stand there?"

Fiona. Her nasal voice is a dead giveaway. For some reason, I expected her to be a skinny white girl, not this small, Filipino woman with a liter of attitude. It makes sense why Fiona is absent from Chloe's content: she's not really "on-brand."

This reminds me, I need to go through every single person Chloe follows and familiarize myself with their faces. Read through DMs too.

"Sorry. Come in."

She barges inside. "Are you sick?"

"What?"

"You sound weird."

"Do I?" Shit. Voice and composure are how you pick out a fraud, at least according to my aunt. She could walk into a department store dressed like she's homeless, but if she carried the studied and condescending air of the elite, she could return a stolen La Mer container filled with Nivea without a receipt and come home with a crisp two grand in her pocket. (This worked five times before La Mer changed their refund policy.) As much as I hate to admit it, I might have to take a page from my aunt's book. Watch more of Chloe's videos, practice her sense of privilege, study her tone and her turns of phrase.

But for now, I'll lay into Fiona's preconceived beliefs. I clear my throat repeatedly. "I might be coming down with something."

"As long as you're not contagious. I *just* got over a case of mono."

"Thanks for sending a cleaner over, by the way."

"The apartment, like, literally smelled like a dead body. I would've killed myself if I had to breathe it in a second longer. Anyway, I picked up the dress for tomorrow. Do you want to do a quick fitting? I still have time to make last-minute adjustments if it's too big."

She unzips the garment bag and reveals a stunning emerald silk dress with a Van Gogh–style embroidery of a lily pond draping the skirt. If I could describe it in one word, it would be *expensive*. This looks like something a celebrity would wear on a red carpet.

I nod eagerly and take the dress to try on in the bedroom. I step into the garment from the neck. It goes past my hips with no resistance and the straps sit pretty on my shoulders. The jewel tones are perfect for my skin shade. But then I try to zip it up. The zipper moves an inch before it gets stuck. My stomach is way too big, and the silk has zero give.

Fiona knocks on the door. "How does it look? Can I come in?"

"No!"

"What? Why?"

"N-no. It's fine. It looks great. Like, literally perfect." I take off the dress, set it aside, and change back into my clothes before heading back out. I smile. "How much was this dress?" I might have to return it. There's no way I'll shove my bloat into that silk by tomorrow unless I pull off a miracle.

She looks at me like I'm stupid. Like the price is something I should know.

"Sister died. Brain's a mess." I try to laugh it off while pouring myself a glass of water.

Fiona sighs. "Custom from Slate Stan. Made from Japanese hand-spun cruelty-free mulberry silk, embroidered with angora-wool thread. Retail is sixteen K."

I almost choke on my water. One dress. Sixteen thousand? What on God's mighty green earth is wrong with this world?

"But we got it for free in exchange for a social post at Bella Marie's event."

"And, um, this is just purely hypothetical, what if I decide not to wear it tomorrow?"

She gapes.

"Like," I add, "if I feel like a different vibe?"

"This dress is custom-made for you. Slate can't resell it. So, you'd have to pay. But that's not the issue." She puts her hands on her hips and stares at me hard. "Don't you remember the lengths we went through to get him to accept your custom order? Literally months of lobbying! The optics would be foul if you go back on your word. Slate loves being an asshole and running his mouth about bad experiences with influencers. That's a part of his whole 'authentic' brand." She rolls her eyes and does air quotes for *authentic*. "Remember when Jasmine Davis got canceled after he flamed her on his socials? She lost half a mil in one week and only weird Amazon drop shippers sponsor her now. That's the whole reason every influencer wants to work with him. If he gives his seal of approval, it's a testament to our authenticity."

I didn't know a dress could be this serious. What the hell is wrong with these people? Men accused of sexual assault don't receive half this scrutiny.

"But my sister died. He'd understand, wouldn't he?"

"Maybe. *If* you don't plan on going to Bella Marie's event. But you are, so you *have* to wear his dress. And you can't renege on the event since I *just* confirmed your attendance with Bella Marie's assistant. And you *certainly* don't want to be on Bella Marie's bad side."

Why is this all so overly complicated? "I'll be there." I try not to show my panic. I can't let a *dress* be my demise when I barely had the chance to enjoy Chloe's life. "I was just asking . . . for curiosity's sake."

She nods slowly. "If you say so. Also, we have this meeting with—"

"Can you push everything back? Actually, you know what? Take the rest of the day off." I shove her toward the door. "Paid, of course. I just need some time to myself right now."

"But this is with Jessica Peters—"

I slam the door in her face and run into the bedroom, staring at the emerald silk garment.

My twin died and I stole her life, which might be a felony, yet somehow, my biggest concern right now is how to fit into a dress.

16

I have a mere four hours before Bella Marie's event.

The glam squad is scheduled to arrive in thirty minutes and I'm on the toilet fighting for my life. Have been for the past few hours.

Last night, I found Chloe's diet teas growing dusty in the pantry. She'd done a few paid posts for them in the past but stopped after people complained that she was promoting eating disorders.

I brewed six packs. Yes. Six.

I know, I know, a terrible decision. I'm probably stripping my intestines of good bacteria and weakening my colon. But I'm desperate, okay? How bad can it be? It's just laxatives.

Okay, fine.

It's pretty fucking bad.

I've been on the toilet so long, I think the Toto has made permanent indentations in my butt cheeks. I'm dehydrated and sweating from the intense abdominal cramps, and my asshole is on fire. I'm pretty sure I'm about to pop a hemorrhoid. Maybe two.

But it's all good. When I had a brief moment of reprieve, I weighed myself. Lost a staggering five pounds! It's probably all water weight that I'll gain back, but I can see the bloat in my stomach decreasing. And while I was waiting for the teas to take effect, I found several pairs of shapewear, size

XXXS. If I layer a few pieces, figure out how to stop breathing, and whisper a few prayers, I think I might be able to fit into the dress.

Someone knocks on the door.

Must be Fiona. I flush, wash my hands, spritz ylang-ylang spray all over, and wobble out of the bathroom. Each step makes me dizzy. I haven't consumed anything in the last twenty hours.

I open the door.

Fiona glances at me, a makeup artist and hairstylist behind her. She puckers her lips and nods. "You look skinnier. Good. I was worried because you looked horrible yesterday. Grief doesn't wear you well." She doesn't mince words.

I vaguely recognize the makeup artist and hairstylist from my cyber-stalking, but I hide in my bedroom and go on Instagram to remind myself of their names. The makeup artist is Fernanda. The hairstylist is Kim.

I return to the living room and try to remember how to have a conversation while they set up, stomach roiling. Butt in the makeup chair, I listen to Fiona's rundown of the event: who's going to be there, who I should take photos with, who I should avoid because they are close to getting canceled or are (allegedly) grooming underage fans. All the while, Fernanda is beating me with a beauty blender and Kim is pulling on my tangles. (I may have been fisting my hair in pain while I was on the toilet earlier.)

"Oh, and make sure you introduce yourself to Isla Harris."

"Isla Harris?"

Fiona shows me her iPad. @iloveisla, 312K followers. Her bio reads: "Digital Creator, single mom to two powerful Black girls 🖤 👧🏿. Romans 3:23." I scroll down her feed. A few reels of makeup videos. Some edgy magazine editorials. Candid pics of her family. She's censored her children's faces with emojis to protect their privacy.

"What's so special about her?"

"I was talking to some of the other assistants, and we all feel like she's going to be the newest Belladonna."

While on the toilet, I researched the Belladonnas. From what I could gather, Bella Marie has a habit of taking small-time influencers under her wing. Without fail, they explode in popularity after entering Bella Marie's orbit. These influencers are referred to as the Belladonnas because some haters find the group toxic, like the plant. (Pushing capitalism, overconsumption, vanity, unrealistic body types, selling out to major corporate brands, refusing to acknowledge their privilege, general tone deafness, etc.) The term is mostly used on catty gossip forums and hasn't caught on in the general social eco-space. I guess Fiona learned this label and started using it unironically.

Out of curiosity, I looked into when Chloe met Bella Marie.

Five years ago, Chloe had 300K on YouTube and 71K on Instagram. A year after becoming an alleged Belladonna, her following doubled. Since then, her socials have grown exponentially. Chloe had metamorphosed from a cringe YouTube try-hard to a certified A-list influencer.

"But why Isla?" I ask.

Fiona makes a *duh* expression. "Emmeline?"

I recognize Emmeline's name from my googling. @em94. Eleven million on Instagram and five million on TikTok. She's Bella Marie's cousin, equally blond and thin, but instead of piercing blue eyes, hers are brown. Earthly instead of heavenly. Her niche is travel and fashion. She has a podcast where she complains about her luxurious life, waxing philosophical about apparent "discoveries"—conclusions that regular folks had come to in their teens. I'd describe her niche as: *I'm rich and sad but also beautiful in that seemingly attainable way, so follow me, you peasants!* She runs a pet account for her dog, Madeline, a white Yorkie who looks like she'd bite your ankle for sport. The dog has two hundred thousand followers.

Recently, netizens uncovered years of racist tweets where she compared minorities to animals and complained about the influx of migrants. I wouldn't say any of them are *horrifically* racist—my bar is in hell—but they were very uncomfortable to read. She has since apologized in a tear-soaked video: *This was eight years ago. I was only in my teens. I have changed and am still growing. I surround myself with powerful people of color every day and live to uplift them. I am sincerely sorry for any hurt I have caused.* Her fans forgave her fast, probably because she's so damn pretty when she cries. She's young, commenters said. It was eight years ago! People change!

"You should be friendly with Isla," Fiona says, "seeing as you two will be the only people of color in the group."

I nod, which annoys Fernanda, who is trying to wing my eyeliner. I mouth a *sorry*.

While lurking the subreddit /r/chloevansnark I learned Chloe received some flak for only hanging out with white people. Chloe Van Huusen is a typical case of internalized racism, one commenter said. I don't think I've seen her around a single Asian person, even though she lives in the most diverse city on the planet! Not to mention, she only dates white men. She's begging for her body to be colonized. She probably wishes she were born a yt.

Only Chloe received these criticisms. No one complains when Bella Marie posts with her Scandinavian-featured friends. It's like they give Chloe a harder time because she's a minority and should be *one of us*. These commenters are clearly idiots. Even though she's biologically Asian, she grew up certifiably white. The Van Huusens look like the type of family who brag about distant ancestors being on the *Mayflower* as a show of their ancestral hardship while lounging in garden estates paid for by their generational wealth. Given her upbringing, it's no surprise Chloe ran around pale-faced crowds.

Still, I'm surprised Chloe's never pushed back at these people. Fiona is a POC; isn't that proof enough? And I'm sure she has other friends of color too. (I hope.)

I admit, it's unhealthy crawling around a Chloe snark subreddit. But it's impossible to resist. Every scroll and every mean post builds a tower of horrid fascination within me, each brick proving that I was right to take over Chloe's life.

The rabbit hole sucked me in and spat me out with the wildest conspiracies. Like how the Van Huusens only adopted Chloe because they said racist shit in a press conference for their green energy company. Something about how American-made solar panels are superior to the cheap products manufactured in the east. This slipup avalanched into Chinese investors pulling out of their projects. Considering how much capital China pours into renewable energy, they realized their fuckup fast. Regardless of their sociopolitical beliefs, anyone capitulates when enough dollar bills are ripped from their hands. As a result, they adopted a Chinese kid to prove they weren't actually racist. Wild, I know. It must be complete fiction, parasocial freaks making up degrading stories.

Then again, from what I've observed, it doesn't seem like Chloe had the best relationship with her adoptive parents. Their last text was in August, half a year ago, confirming attendance for dinner. And any messages before that were stilted and oddly formal. Since then, there's been a long stretch of no contact. They didn't reach out after my breakdown went viral either.

There was a press release stating the Van Huusens had retired a year ago. Maybe they're on vacation, lounging in Thailand with limited Wi-Fi.

Either way, it's better if their relationship is cold. If anyone were to find out I'm not Chloe, it would be the couple who raised her.

There's another thing I read and want to ask Fiona about.

Some believe that Bella Marie takes the Belladonnas on an annual trip in June. They go to some private island for a week, bankrolled by Miss Melniburg herself.

Except, here's the interesting part: while you'd expect these attention-hungry influencers to post every hour about the luxurious trip, the Belladonnas always keep it under wraps. Followers only caught on during the first year of Instagram Stories because influencers who'd live-post about their day went radio silent for a week. Upon deeper analysis, followers noticed that many of their static feed posts or videos were prescheduled. Then, a week after their silence, they returned to their selfies with a freshly bronzed glow, like they'd been relaxing on a beach, soaking up tropical sun.

Normally, I'd chalk this up to your typical internet conspiracy. But I noticed a week in June was blocked on Chloe's calendar for the last five years. Same this year.

"My brain is totally fried. Can you remind me about the trip in June?"

"The trip in June?"

I nod. "Where are we going this year? It's only a few months away."

She narrows her eyes. "Is this a test?"

"A test?"

Fiona frowns. "Last time I asked about the trip you ripped me a new one and told me to never bring it up again or you'd, like, literally kill me."

That's weird. I thought Fiona would know everything about Chloe's life. This only increases my curiosity.

"You passed!" I say, inhaling a breath of banana-scented setting powder, trying not to sound suspicious. "Congratulations."

Fiona rolls her eyes. "Julie seriously fucked you up."

17

I'm about to shit myself.

And it's not because of the diet tea. (Okay, maybe it's a little because of the diet tea.) It's because I'm nervous.

I'm in my Uber, staring at the event space that Bella Marie rented. It's a swanky hotel that has views of Central Park. I smell like hair spray mixed with Santal 33 and I can barely breathe due to the three shapewear sets strapping my core. But most importantly, I'll be surrounded by people Chloe knew.

Why did I even come here? This is such a mistake. I should have kept a low profile. Moved to Switzerland and rebranded to cottagecore so I don't have to interact with anyone IRL.

Why did I do this to myself? Am I insane?

Okay. Maybe I am. I did take my sister's identity after she died. That's dictionary-definition insane.

"Getting out, ma'am?" the Uber driver asks me.

I take a deep breath, wishing Fiona was here to walk me through this. "Yup." I open the door and step out, my pulse thrumming.

I take a few calming breaths before I head into the building. My Louboutins make me lumber around like Bigfoot incarnate. Paparazzi wait for the arrival of legitimate celebrities. (I swear I see an Armie Hammer look-alike. But wasn't he canceled for being a cannibal or something?) Some of the paps take photos of me and call my name—er, *Chloe*'s name—like I'm famous. I stand and pose for them awkwardly, unused to the pops of cameras and lights, before rushing into the building. The guard scans the invitation for the Belle by Bella Marie launch event and points me across a large hotel lobby, which is perfumed like an expensive Abercrombie, and into an elevator that is reserved for the event. A guy in a red bellhop suit waits in the corner, his sole job to press buttons. The door is about to close when someone yells, "Wait!"

The professional button-pusher obeys.

Out of breath, the woman utters a brief "Thank you" while straightening her black slip dress. She fingers her blond hair before stepping into the elevator. Her jaw drops, recognition flooding her hazel-green eyes.

"Oh my god! Chloe!" She squeals so loud it could break glass. Even the button-pusher cringes. She envelops me in a hug and kisses my cheeks like we're French, her air a plume of sugar and bergamot.

"You!" I squeal, trying to match her energy while scanning through my mental Rolodex of people Chloe follows. I watched every Instagram story to get a vague gist of who was in attendance via #getreadywithmes. But damn, there are too many blond-haired, hazel-eyed, lip-plumped white influencers in this world. Differentiating them is an Olympic sport.

The elevator door slides shut, and we head up.

She scans my outfit with a wide and adoring smile. "That embroidery! Don't tell me. Are you wearing Slate Stan?" I notice her snaggletooth, and it clicks. Amid the other influencers with razor-sharp veneers, her smile sticks out from the crowd.

@AngeliqueGray11. She has half a million followers on YouTube and TikTok and one million on Instagram. Her bio reads: "Author of #1 NYT bestseller Healing Through Dessert. Survivor with C-PTSD." I skimmed an article about her. She had abusive parents who starved her to the point of malnourishment. Now she's a pro baker making up for all the sweets she couldn't eat as a child. Pretty inspiring. Unsurprisingly, her internet niche is baking videos and recipes. Her feed also features clips of her famous hockey-player husband, Sommer. He's broad-shouldered with a chiseled jawline and has eyes that say he's gotten a concussion or two.

But most importantly, she is thought to be the most recent addition to the Belladonnas.

I laugh, glad I figured her out, and show off my dress, sucking in my stomach. "The one and only."

She puts a hand to her heart. "Obsessed. Like, *so* obsessed. You look gorgeous. Stunning. And your skin! It's that Korean in you, glass skin all day! Tell me your secrets."

I'm Chinese and only a few days ago, I used Dove bar soap for face wash and body lotion as serum. (Now I've switched to SkinCeuticals and La Mer.)

"It's all Kare Kosmetics." I laugh, glad she's not asking anything personal.

She laughs too. Hysterically. Like she also knows that no one who shills Kare Kosmetics uses it. "I am so obsessed with you." She gasps, clapping her palm to her mouth. "Oh no! I'm not being insensitive, am I? I heard about your twin. I'm so sorry about that. Remind me of her name again?"

"Julie."

It's so easy to say that now. The guilt isn't tangible anymore.

Julie Chan is dead. Julie Chan is dead. Julie Chan is dead.

See? Nothing.

In a way, Julie Chan *is* dead.

I'm not her anymore. Can never be her again. Julie Chan will never return.

"R.I.P. Julie," Angelique says. "She's in my thoughts and prayers."

I want to say, *You don't even know her.* Instead, I say, "Thanks."

The elevator door opens, and live music bounces into my ear. Bella Marie hired a whole symphony orchestra. There must be fifty people in tuxes jamming out to classical renditions of pop songs. I feel like I'm in *Bridgerton.* The event space is airy and wooden, decked out with an open bar and a million flower arrangements. In the center of the room are three long, rectangular tables holding golden candelabras, each with about thirty seats. A smaller table is at the head of the room with ten seats. Kind of like a wedding reception. There are little place cards in front of each dinner set, names written in elegant calligraphy. Thank god. I need those. I glance at the cards closest to me and discover that a handful of them are for reporters from major news and magazine outlets, their designation printed in small serif font under their name. From *Vogue* to *Vanity Fair*, *The New Yorker* to *Forbes*, the list goes on and on. And they aren't just fashion writers or small-time editors: the guests in attendance have titles like *Editor in Chief* and *President*. Bella Marie is better connected than I thought.

A server approaches us with a tray of golden champagne glasses and asks, "Would you like a welcome drink? It's freshly squeezed lemonade with imported water from Ville-d'Avray, Marie Antoinette's choice of water. We have alcoholic and virgin options."

This shit is so fancy I don't understand half the words coming out of the server's mouth. Either way, the last thing I need is a drink. It can push me toward itchy anxiousness, and my Asian glow will make me a human bull's-eye. "I'll pass."

The server tips her head. "Are you sure? We have a virgin option if you're alcohol-free."

I smile. "I'm sure. Thanks."

"But everyone else is having a glass. Bella Marie insists."

"No. I'm good."

Her eyes go buggy, almost frightened, before turning to Angelique.

"I'll take a virgin," she says.

"Are you sure you don't want one?" the server asks me after handing Angelique a glass. "It's very tasty. You won't regret it."

Christ. She's persistent. I grab one to get rid of her. I'm relieved when she moves on to the next guest.

Angelique turns to me with a glint in her eye. "Want to know a secret?" The way she says it, low and slow, makes my heart hammer with nerves. Did she notice I'm a fake? That I'm not really Chloe? She draws out the silence. The music swells in the background.

"I'm pregnant."

I don't know what I was expecting, but this isn't the worst.

I turn to her and gauge how I should feel. Being pregnant isn't always a good thing.

She's smiling . . . I think? It's a tight smile. Like she's trying to be happy, but something inside her is pulling her down. Or maybe I'm misreading it.

"Congratulations?"

"Thank you." She nods and looks away, her voice soft.

Okay. Maybe it isn't a good thing. Warm pity threads through my heart. I barely know this girl, yet I feel concerned for her. She seems sweet.

After putting down my drink, I follow Angelique through the swinging glass doors to the giant balcony that overlooks Central Park. Staff members, stationed between heat lamps and manicured evergreen bushes, eagerly offer to take our phones to help us capture photos. I studied some of Chloe's signature poses and I try to replicate them as best I can—a task more arduous than it sounds. Sucking in my core and smiling is a form of endurance exercise. I select the best of the photos and send to Fiona to Facetune. She replies: GORG!

Angelique brings me around and we mingle with a few other influencers. Thankfully, she opens conversations with *Oh my god! So-and-so!* and I don't have to play the name-guessing game. Everyone recognizes me as Chloe.

No one suspects a thing. Which is . . . surprising.

Don't get me wrong; I don't *want* to get caught. But a part of me feels sad for Chloe. None of these influencer "friends" truly know her. Their conversations are about brand deals, the algorithm, the show they are watching, or the newest social media scandal. Few ask questions about me—perhaps because they are so self-obsessed—and even when they do, they don't bat an eye when I make something up.

Eventually, two Belladonnas join Angelique and me. I recognize them instantly. The woman with sleek black hair is Kelly Hart. @harts4kelly. Four million on Instagram, twelve million on YouTube, thirteen million on TikTok. She's a social media veteran and one of the few creators I used to watch in middle school. She started filming videos when she was fourteen in her mom's basement and went viral at seventeen after teaching girls how to curl their hair with a straightener. (Thanks to her, I singed a section of my hair off.) Like most early creators, she fell off everyone's radar, including mine. Since then, she's shifted her content to reaction videos, aka saying *Damn, that's crazy* over and over and repeating what's said in the video, but louder. Essentially, she makes brain-dead content for overstimulated iPad kids. But this content has revived her career and tripled her following. Now, she's decked out in so much designer gear she might as well be a department store mannequin.

Then there's Lily Schmidt, a washed-up child-actress-turned-influencer. @lilyschmidt. Four million on Instagram, two million on YouTube, one million on TikTok. Two years ago, she made headlines after creating a series of videos about adopting a child with Down syndrome before returning him like a tampered bottle of Tylenol. She claimed, in a tearful video with melodramatic royalty-free music, that she wasn't well equipped to take care of a kid on the spectrum and that he was better off in whatever country she originally shipped him from. A year later, she adopted a young, neurotypical girl called Wendy from Thailand. Now she makes mommy content.

"Lately," Lily says, fingering her dirty-blond hair, "I'm just *so* tired all the time. Every day, I'm on the clock. Workout at five, meeting at seven, sponsored brunch at eleven, then I'm vlogging all day until six. Not to mention the emails."

"The emails!" Kelly groans.

"I barely have time to make dinner for Wendy. Thank god I have my two nannies."

Angelique blows a breath, shaking her head. "I feel for you."

"Sometimes I wish I were an office worker. They can clock out every day at five p.m. and live their lives. But influencers? Work, work, work. All the time, every second. People don't know how hard it is to be us."

"I know, right?" Kelly's satin red lips look like silicone Vienna sausages as she chews her spearmint gum. "It's like, try being an influencer for a day."

I arch my brow.

"So hard," replies Lily.

"One hundred percent," says Angelique.

They all glance at me. "Yeah," I say. "Totally."

"My brother is a consultant," Kelly continues, "and he gets four weeks' paid vacation. Guess what he actually gets to do? Vacation! If it were us, we'd have to be filming all the damn time, taking photos at the beach, reviewing restaurants. Ugh! It's so tiring! We never get a break. Speaking of breaks." Her spearmint-scented attention suddenly wafts my way. "I noticed you stopped posting. It's very unlike you, Chloe. I mean, your sister died and here you are, still grinding away. But how was your break?" The three women stare at me, blinking with curiosity.

I wish I hadn't put down my lemonade so I could sip and take time to think. "Uh, it was nice. I needed it."

"Nice . . ." Kelly narrows her eyes. "Good for you." There's something about her that rubs me the wrong way. Suspicion? I don't think that's it. Her words are sharp and bristly—almost angry. Did Chloe and Kelly have a fight no one knows about?

"I did this video where I was a service worker for a day," Lily says, changing the topic back to herself—thank god. "It was, like, low-key kinda easy."

"I saw that video!" Angelique exclaims. "The one where you work a shift at McDonald's?"

Lily nods. "The powers that be blessed me with that one. Six million views and counting. Surprising like-to-dislike ratio, though."

"There are so many haters out there," Kelly says.

"So many haters," Angelique echoes.

"Personally," Kelly continues, "I found the video very insightful."

"Very insightful," says Angelique.

Delete me from this conversation.

"I honestly don't know why service workers complain all the time." Lily's Cartier bangles clink and clack as she talks with her hands. "They have it so easy. Like, ring up a few orders, count some cash, put some stuff in a bag. It was brainless. Sometimes, I think about quitting it all and just working at Mc—"

The music stops and someone announces the dinner is starting. Perfect timing. If I spent another second in that conversation, I would have jammed my finger into someone's eye just to hear them scream.

As a group, we head into the main hall. I'm searching for my name amid all the place tags, when Angelique takes my hand and leads me confidently to the smaller table near the head of the room.

I'm about to tell her this is wrong, that I'm probably seated on one of the regular tables, when I see my name tag.

But that's not all.

I'm seated next to *the* Bella Marie. One seat off from the center.

Like where a best friend would sit.

My research didn't tell me Chloe and Bella Marie were particularly close. But this placement is evidence of their maid-of-honor-level friendship.

How is that possible?

I should have dived deeper, searched Chloe's room for diaries, scoured through gossip forums down to page one hundred twenty-eight. I'm so unprepared. Bella Marie will know something is wrong. Everyone is going to notice I'm a fraud. Why the fuck did I do this to myself? What is wrong with me?

Police sirens blare outside. Are they here for me? I'm reminded of that wellness check years ago. The hostility, that feeling of hopelessness. My aunt staring at me, her shrill voice berating me. Bile swims up my throat. Sweat breaks out across my back. I'm spiraling. I can't breathe.

I close my eyes and try to regain my composure. In the darkness, Chloe's face appears. Her limp body, purple lips, bloodshot eyes. But now there's wriggling maggots devouring her skin. Her teeth start chattering. *Click-click-click.* Suddenly, her pupils slide toward me. Dark and soulless. She parts her dry lips and whispers, *Hoax.* She lunges. Decaying arms reaching for me. Her fingers wrap hard around my upper arm.

I scream and yank away from her grasp.

But standing before me is not Chloe.

It's Bella Marie.

18

Bella Marie stares at me with her crystal-clear blue eyes. So bright that I see my shaking figure in them. I'm entranced. Chloe disappears into the dregs of my mind.

Bella Marie's features crease into the perfect concerned expression. "I didn't mean to scare you, darling."

Darling.

Her accent is vague, unrecognizable, like every European country is vying for a space in her beautiful mouth. I know that she's in her early thirties but she doesn't look a day over twenty. Her skin is youthful; her aura, holy. My throat swells with a stubborn feeling and I have a sudden instinct to look away, caught in a liminal space between fear and admiration.

She blinks and releases me from her hypnosis.

The room comes spinning back. Everyone is staring. Silent.

Right. I just screamed bloody murder after Bella Marie grabbed me.

I gulp. Turn toward the attendees. "I'm okay." I laugh it off, and people look away. The music comes alive again. I return my attention to Bella Marie, still avoiding her gaze. "S-sorry. My mind was somewhere else."

"No, no, don't apologize, darling. It's my fault for coming up from behind. I should have known better."

"Oh my gosh, no. Come at me from behind whenever!" I cringe. Words are spilling out of my mouth, unbridled. She probably thinks I'm a freak. I want to die.

My heart leaps when she laughs. Her breath, a plume of honey, fills the air. She leans close and we kiss our cheeks like Angelique and I did. My face warms where our skin touched. She guides me to my seat with a gentle hand on my back. "Sit down, sit down."

I smooth my sweaty palms against my tight dress. The seams are about to burst from my heavy breathing.

Bella Marie sits beside me, places a palm on my wrist to stop me from fidgeting. "You look splendid in emerald."

"I do?"

"Yes. But . . ." Her eyes drown in concern. "You look awfully nervous today. Are you okay?"

Oh, you know, it's just that I switched lives with my dead twin and now I'm in too deep with no way to climb out, and I'm sitting next to my middle-school icon who just said I look *splendid* and called me *darling*, and are those butterflies in my stomach or just remnants of the diet tea?

I give my usual excuse. "I think Julie's death is getting to me."

She clicks her tongue and tilts her head, a lock of white-blond hair trailing down her swanlike neck. "Poor thing." She rubs my back. "I'm so sorry for your loss. I can't even imagine your pain. My heart breaks for you."

And she's nice? God really created us unequal.

"Thank you," I say.

A head pokes out from behind her. She's blond and bears a striking resemblance to Bella Marie, except that her eyes are a dull brown. Right—the cousin, Emmeline. "I am so sorry to hear about Julie."

The Snow White–looking woman sitting beside her chimes in. "I sent you a message to see if you needed to connect for support. Did you not see it?"

"Same!" says another influencer, this one sporting a purple smoky eye.

"I sent one too," says Emmeline.

"Yes," Bella Marie says, "our group chat was mourning for you. But I don't think you saw the messages. We felt your absence greatly."

Group chat? Even with all my cyberstalking, I didn't see a group chat. And I read through a lot of DMs. "Sorry, I was just too overwhelmed."

"Aw," says Emmeline.

"So sad," says Snow White.

"So, so sad," says Smoky Eye.

"And a drug overdose, of all things." Bella Marie shakes her head with pity. "It's not an easy way to go."

I frown. "How do you know about that?" It isn't public information.

She answers without skipping a beat. "Lisa told me. You know how the assistants are, always trading secrets. It's like currency in their world." She tucks a loose strand of hair behind my ear, her fingers tickling my temple. I shiver. When was the last time someone touched me like that? "I hope you're coping all right. It must have been a huge shock. I don't want to make this all about myself, but I've been in your position. My mom struggles with alcohol, and I know how hard it can get. Our minds never fail to bring us to dark places."

I feel like a heroine in a romance movie, my heart swelling. "Thank you for saying that. I'm just trying to get life back on track. Everything is a bit crazy."

"Crazy times," says Emmeline.

"So, so crazy," echoes Snow White.

"Pure insanity," adds Smoky Eye.

"Mmm," Bella Marie hums. "Crazy indeed. Please let me know if there's any way I can support you."

Just then, Isla Harris walks up to our table with quick, rushed steps, her tight, pink-sequined dress limiting her range of motion. "Sorry I'm late," she whispers to Bella Marie, moving a tuft of curly hair from her brown eyes, which are outlined with electric-green pigment. "The kids were nagging me all afternoon and I couldn't get out the door in time."

Bella Marie tips her head with a soft smile, her eyes gliding down Isla's outfit for a beat too long. The shimmering pink dress is in stark contrast to the neutral or forest tones worn by other guests, like a Christmas ornament lost on a sandbank. Isla glances around the table nervously, and when our eyes meet, she smiles and nods in greeting.

I smile and nod back.

"I'm thankful you're here," Bella Marie says finally. "The dinner has yet to start. Have a seat."

Isla takes her seat at the far-left end, filling out the front table. In total, there are ten of us. Aside from Smoky Eye and Snow White, I'm struggling to identify the tall blonde with a healthy tan sitting next to Angelique. I predict a full night of cyberstalking ahead. Keeping track of everyone will be difficult.

Are we the Belladonnas? Bella Marie and her nine little disciples?

I notice Kelly staring at me intensely. When I catch her gaze, she smiles wide and blows her gum into a bubble. It pops, making me flinch. She grins happily at my reaction. Her tongue licks the remnants of sticky sugar. "This is the funniest thing. I almost complained to the host about the way we're arranged. Since *I* usually sit next to Bella Marie." She smiles tightly, envy glistening in her eyes. It's hard to believe she's the same girl who filmed wholesome videos teaching teens how to curl their hair. I still remember her neon-pink braces and the white sports bra peeking from under her turquoise top. She was soft-spoken, almost shy. Now she looks like she'd judge me for wearing a bikini. What happened to her?

Regardless, her passive-aggressive insinuations are clear. Bella Marie prefers me (Chloe, really) and she's envious. It doesn't put me down. You can only be jealous of someone above you. Her words dose me with a shot of confidence.

"Maybe it's time for a change."

"Change?" She laughs, throwing her chin high. "I know all about change. How do you think I lasted so long?" She leans in, breath all spearmint. "Don't get too confident. *You* should know exactly how replaceable we all are."

My stomach tenses at the word *replaceable*. It's probably a coincidence, but my mind rings with alarm. I shouldn't be making enemies so early in my new life. Envy is one thing, but suspicion is something I must avoid.

"I was just joking," I say, faking a chuckle.

"Oh! Me too. I thought you knew that." She tips her head to the side, eyes narrowing, lips curled slightly. "Has your sister's death made you soft?"

I bite my cheek. Was she being snarky . . . as a joke? I've heard there are people who roast each other out of affection. Maybe I've been interpreting her wrong the whole time. Are her mean comments a signifier of her sincerity? Some odd in-group friendship ritual?

"I think it's the grief," I begin to explain.

"I'm just surprised." She spits her gum into a napkin while holding my gaze, viscous saliva trailing from her tongue. "I mean"—she drops her voice to a whisper—"we're talking about Julie, of all people."

I swallow. "What do you mean?"

"You weren't close. We all told you to film more twin content—the internet loves twins. But you said you didn't want to risk people blending you two together. You thought she would ruin your brand. What did you say? That she was too pitiable? Made you uncomfortable? Something like that."

"Oh." Chloe's dislike of me was clear, but each word makes my heart sink deeper into my chest.

"It was fine, since we're all the family you need. That's what you said."

"I did?" My mind is blurry. I want this conversation to be over.

"You did. And it wasn't all that long ago when you still believed that."

The music stops, and I realize Bella Marie is standing. I'm grateful she broke up the conversation. She raises a crystal champagne flute and taps it with a knife. *Clink. Clink. Clink.* Everyone turns to her. I kid you not, the guests light up when they see her face. They clap and cheer like we've ended world famine. The noise is so loud and boisterous, so overwhelming, my bones rattle. I'm awed at their reaction. At how Bella Marie controls the room. She's magnetic, sparkling under the spotlight, her hair a cascade of golden perfection.

The crowd quiets.

"Welcome, everyone, and thank you for your attention." Even without a microphone, her voice rings clear through the hall. "I want to thank each and every one of you for attending the launch of Belle by Bella Marie. My team and I have put so much work into this brand, and I can't wait to unveil it through our immersive dinner experience. All I ask is that you put your phones away." Surprised moans in the audience. "I know it will be hard to resist taking photos, but sometimes we must disconnect to reconnect. We hope you'll be mindful and respect the artistry and labor that's gone into this event without distraction." She pauses, staring into the audience, a teacher controlling her class. People put their phones in their bags. Within seconds, no devices are in sight. "Now, without further delay, let our show begin!" She claps her hands twice with a winning smile.

The symphony comes alive with a familiar tune. I used to listen to angry classical music when I was feeling low. I think it's "Danse Macabre" by Camille Saint-Saëns. Admittedly, it feels . . . intense for the event.

A line of waiters file into the room as soft harp tones float through the air. There's a waiter for each guest. They stand behind us with a tray and metal cloches. Like a choreographed dance, the waiters bend forward as the solo violin cuts into the song, setting the trays on the table. My reflection in the cloche is stretched wide and ugly, features distorted. I'm reminded of Chloe, her bloated, sagging blue face. I'm rescued from the distasteful memory when a flute note signals a white glove to uncover the cloche, revealing . . . a thin slice of baguette with some caviar, gold flakes, and edible flowers on top.

Huh. A bit anti-climactic for the buildup. I expected something more substantial. But everyone loves it, judging from the applause. Maybe this is par for the course in fine dining. Once the waiters depart, a line of models strut around the tables with the rhythm of the violin. They're all dressed in beige, black, or gold. Flower accessories are nestled into their slicked hair like they had jumped into a spring swamp. Long and intricate earrings vine down their bodies, making it seem as if the plants are growing out of their ear canals.

I get it now. Immersive dinner. The models are literally dressed in the colors and flowers of the food. Once the models make one lap, they all pause where they are, evenly spaced around the room. Some climb onto the tables between the flower arrangements and candelabras to pose. They're still, like mannequins. We munch away at our baguettes. It's a little awkward, how close they are. Claustrophobic. I see the ribs of the woman in front of me. Her hollow cheeks and thinning hair. If it weren't for the lace gold collar, she'd look like a starved Victorian child in a little beige frock. I almost feel bad eating in front of them. It's a bit sadistic.

They leave once the waiters take away our plates.

The same choreographed dance occurs with each tasting course, the music changing every time. With the salads, it's "Valse Sentimentale" by Tchaikovsky, and the models stomp in green clothes with accessories that resemble the olive and fennel. When we're served a lime-infused duck with carrot puree, the symphony plays "Swan Lake," and models sashay in purple and orange with feather earrings. This goes on and on. I can't imagine how much planning and money went into this event. The guests eat it up. I'm enjoying myself too, as long as I ignore the odd choice in music and avert my gaze from the gaunt models, focusing on their clothes.

Then comes the main course: rare venison served with parsnips and beets. The orchestra plays "Lacrimosa" by Mozart. A choir belts out the baritone notes when the trombones begin. Their voices ripple across the high ceiling, vibrating the whole room. My heart pounds with the sheer power of the choir, the underlying sharp yet sorrowful strings.

I glance at the symphony, surprised. "Lacrimosa" is a song about grief. To illustrate the fear of impending death.

The music is incredibly off-putting, but no one else seems unnerved. Everyone is overjoyed, a grinning hive mind captivated by an exquisite yet haunting production.

Bella Marie is cutting into her venison peacefully, the movement of her wrist almost balletic as baby deer blood weeps onto her white dinner plate. She brings a small piece up to her pretty little mouth. *Chew, chew, chew. Swallow.* She sips her wine and notices me staring. Meeting my gaze, she smiles wide with her scarlet-stained lips, teeth bloody from the rare meat. Her cheerful expression doesn't reach her crystalline eyes, the blue so stark and icy that it reminds me of the undead.

"Something wrong with the venison?" There's a hollowness to her words.

I look away. Gulp. Heart beating up my throat. "N-no. It's great." I cut into the venison. Blood spurts onto my silverware. I place the meat on my tongue as a model pauses in front of me. She's not dressed in brown like the meat or white like the parsnips or purple for the beets. She's dressed in scarlet. Like the blood. Cheeks freckled with white spots like a doe. Her breaths are loud, heaving from clopping down the runway. I chew on my meat, metallic tang spurting into my throat, coating my tongue with gamey iron. I swallow. My stomach gurgles, sickness rising up in waves. The rough meat scratches my gullet as it goes down. Slithers through my esophagus in a clump as if it is alive. Clawing to get out.

19

’m alone, tucked away on the balcony garden after the dinner, huddling in a wool coat under a heat lamp that provides little refuge from the late-winter chill. The din of chatter and music pierces the cold air. I glance into the warm hall through the wide glass doors, observing the affluence from afar. I'm tempted to go back in, but I'm uncomfortable at the prospect of mingling further. The nauseating dinner made me feel distinctly out of place, unable to perceive the beauty of the experience that was apparent to everyone else.

I turn my gaze to the streets below. A line of cars gather like beads on a necklace, waiting for the traffic light. It blinks green and they move forward, only to stop at the red light a few yards ahead.

"It's Chloe, right?"

I jolt and turn to find Isla beside me.

"Sorry, I didn't mean to scare you." A woolly green cardigan is thrown over her shoulders. She hugs the opening tight to her chest, obscuring most of her pink dress.

"No, no. I was kind of zoning out."

"Deep in thought?"

"Sort of."

"I'm Isla." She extends a hand for me to shake. Her grip is firm.

"I know. Nice to meet you."

She leans against the railing with a sigh. "Did you enjoy dinner?"

I have the urge to be easygoing and say *Yes!* But the way she's looking at me, her brow slightly arched, lips curled like she's two seconds from telling an inside joke, makes me pause.

"Okay, don't tell anyone else this," I whisper with a sniffle. "Didn't the dinner feel a little—"

"Intense?" she finishes, also in a whisper, our breaths white between us.

"Exactly!" I say a bit too loudly. "Like the music was so . . . and the models?"

"It certainly was *immersive*." She retrieves a cigarette and lighter from her purse. It's the vintage type with a golden lid. "Is it okay if I smoke?"

"Go ahead."

She flicks her lighter open with a *schwing* and brings the blue flame to her cigarette. "At least the food was bomb. Is this how other Bella Marie events go? This is my first."

"They're . . . *something*." I hope this vague comment is enough to satisfy her curiosity.

"I was so nervous coming here. Especially since I was over an hour late. My youngest wouldn't stop crying until I watched like three episodes of *Bluey* with her. I didn't even get to taste those fancy drinks that everyone was raving about."

"Imagine shipping water across the world for lemonade. It's some rich white people shit."

She laughs and I try not to beam.

"You can call me Iz, by the way."

I'm glowing from the inside. Is this what it feels like for a cool kid to befriend you? A few days in Chloe's shoes and I'm already making friends. Fuck being yourself; being someone else is so much better.

"How did you get involved with Bella Marie?" I ask. "She doesn't really seem like your vibe."

Iz has a laid-back yet edgy aesthetic. Like she'd lounge on a fire escape and pass blunts to strangers. She's the polar opposite of Bella Marie's other peers, who leak the aura of legacy students at Ivies with trust funds as big as their egos.

Iz chuckles. "I see what you mean. Do you really want to know?"

I nod eagerly.

She takes a drag of her cigarette, the end glowing amber. White smoke curls into the dark sky, blossoms in my nose. "I was in a really abusive relationship."

Instantly, I regret asking. I've never been good at comforting people, probably because no one's ever comforted me. If I had a problem, my aunt would shut me out, leaving me to fester, or criticize me for giving her a headache. I redirect my attention at the park to avoid making eye contact.

"I don't even remember how he slowly isolated me from my friends and family—maybe it's a good thing I don't remember. But before I knew it, all I had was him and my babies. No job, no connections, no future aside from him." She flicks ash off her smoke and inhales again, long and deep. "But then I started an Instagram in secret and blocked all his accounts so he wouldn't find out. I would post on it whenever he was at work. When I got that first email for a sponsorship, it felt like a literal miracle. For a while, my socials were the only agency I had. The only place where I could use my voice. Where I could feel beautiful and seen. But then he found out and . . ." She shakes her head, cigarette ash scattering into the wind. "The police got involved. I finally decided to separate from him and file for sole custody of my daughters. I didn't feel safe staying in my hometown, so I fled across the country to New York."

I've developed a jaded view of social media influencers, viewing them as a toxic cesspool of self-aggrandizing narcissists who feed us images of their deceptively attainable wealth through LED screens connected to our palms. But her story softens me. It's easy to forget that genuine good can come from our interconnectedness. It's there for people who need it. If you're lucky, it can open up the world.

"It wasn't the smartest decision to move to the most expensive city in the world," Iz continues. "It only took a few months to realize how out of my depth I was. I could barely afford rent, despite taking every brand deal that came my way. I had to get a second job writing articles for an indie magazine. A month in, I published an article about my story and boom, Bella Marie follows me on Instagram. We start messaging, bumping into each other at events, and next thing I know, I'm invited to this launch. I couldn't pass this opportunity up, especially considering how well connected she and her whole family are. Industry leaders float around her as if she owns them. Just by show-ing up tonight, I was able to get my name in with a few brand coordinators and major fashion houses who wouldn't have looked my way otherwise. You have to associate with people like them to move up in our world."

She puts emphasis on the word *them* and the corners of my mouth curve upward. I wonder if she knows about Emmeline's tweets.

She turns to me. "But what about you? How did you two meet? You two must be pretty tight since you sat next to her at dinner."

It didn't feel that way. Throughout the whole dinner, Bella Marie barely spoke to me. Then again, there wasn't much conversation to be had. Mouths were preoccupied by chewing, ears deafened by the dour orchestra.

I clear my throat. "Yeah, I guess we're close. I can't remember how we met. It's a blur. I think it's been over five years and so much has changed since then." I hope she believes me.

"I know how you feel. This past year has been like . . ." She blows a rasp-berry, hand waving to signify *crazy*, when an alarm goes off on her phone. "Shit. I gotta run and relieve the babysitter." She stubs out her cigarette and walks it to the nearest trash can.

"I'm gonna head out too," I say. "I think I'm about to explode out of this dress."

She laughs. "I'll see you around." It sounds like a promise.

Alone, I hobble back to the main hall, where guests are sipping cocktails and mingling, while models are on little pedestals dotted throughout, lights bleaching them to porcelain. I can tell where Bella Marie is by the swarm of people surrounding her. She's like a queen bee wafting pheromones to attract helpers. There's no way I'll get to her in under thirty minutes, so I don't even try.

Before I go, I find Angelique. She's the only one I care to say bye to.

I tap her on the shoulder and she turns around with her snaggletoothed smile. "Leaving already?"

"I'm exhausted."

She pouts like she'll miss me. "I'll see you around."

As I'm about to leave, I remember the odd gap in Chloe's calendar. "Hey, are you going on the trip?"

Her mouth parts, something clouding her eyes. She cocks her head. "What trip?"

I frown. "You know. The trip in June?"

The people around us turn to listen.

Angelique laughs tightly. "Silly goose. I think you've had too many drinks. I have no idea what you're talking about."

Huh. She is the newest Belladonna—is it possible she's never been on the annual trip? "Never mind."

"Okay. Toodles!" She returns to her conversation with an air of urgency, and I walk away, somewhat uneasy.

I'm calling for the elevator, when someone shouts, "Chloe!"

"Hey!" I say, avoiding the blonde's name. It's one of the three Belladonnas who isn't instantly recognizable.

Meeting so many new people is overwhelming. It's like scrolling through an Instagram comment section and trying to commit every user to memory.

She catches up to me with three long strides. She's at least a foot taller than me, built like a gazelle or an athlete with her long limbs and sleek blond hair.

"Can't wait to see you tomorrow morning."

"Tomorrow?"

"Yeah, I saw you on my class list. Nabbed yourself a front-row seat, like always." She winks.

"Totally! I'll be there." I have no idea where *there* is.

"I'm so glad to see you in high spirits, especially after your sister passed." She puts a hand on my shoulder and squeezes tight. Like, *really* tight. Her grip strength is insane. "Just remember to reach out if you ever need help. We all know what it's like to be in your place."

The elevator dings. The door opens.

"I won't hold you hostage any longer. Keep strong and oh—I sent some positive affirmations that I thought would help you. Check your DMs. See you tomorrow!" With that, she waves and gallops across the event space to Bella Marie's side, joining the dozens already congregated near the queen.

Inside the elevator, I peek at Chloe's calendar. There's only one event in the morning: SoulCycle at seven a.m., aka my personal idea of hell.

20

Ripping off the Slate Stan dress feels like unclasping a million bras from my body. I can finally breathe!

After my shower, I plop into bed, and immediately pick up my phone.

I upload the photos Fiona edited to my Instagram. I thought she'd touch up my makeup, but she slimmed my body three sizes and gave me a nose job. Rude. But whatever. I tag Slate Stan and paste the description Fiona made for me. The second it uploads, likes pour in. Though I've experienced a similar brigade of dopamine hits with Julie's death post, it's even better when the likes are about my appearance. I spend some time interacting with commenters and delete spammy messages about cryptocurrency.

Iz comments on my post: U inspire me. 🖤

Grinning, I DM her right away.

It was so nice meeting you at the event tonight!

I sit in the chat room for a while, but she hasn't seen the message, so I move on to my next task: a deep dive into the women I didn't recognize at Bella Marie's table.

Social media makes stalking easy.

Snow White is Ana Klein. @analuvsu. Four million on Instagram, eight million on TikTok. She's hot. That's it. That's her content. She's just fucking hot. Giant tits, soulful eyes, plump lips, nice ass. She posts off-rhythm dance videos on TikTok and gets millions of views because her boobs bounce. I can understand the appeal. Sometimes she writes poetry. Here's her magnum opus:

> When I'm with you
> my emotions
> emote
> like emojis.

It takes keen talent to write something less profound than the back of a shampoo bottle.

Smoky Eye is Maya Smith. @mayasmakeup. Five million followers on Instagram, twenty-eight million on TikTok. She's one of those new-age influencers who exclusively posts short-form content. Her feed is cluttered with makeup tutorials where she slathers half a bottle of foundation onto her face as a base. She's teasing a makeup line, One Drop, where only one drop of foundation is needed. Pretty genius, all things considered. Recently, she denied plastic surgery allegations on a podcast by claiming her nose naturally shrank due to Accutane.

Sophia Chambers is the blond woman who spoke to me before I left. @sophchambers. Three million on Instagram, five million on TikTok, one million on YouTube. She was a Team USA volleyball athlete until she broke her arm in a freak accident a week before the 2016 Summer Olympics. Now she's a full-time fitness influencer moonlighting as a SoulCycle instructor for fun. Her ventures include a fitness app and a clothing collab with a popular sports bra company. Most of her posts are things like, It's a great day to have a great day. Or Remember to be happy! Or When you are feeling sad, think positive thoughts. Her followers eat it up. I think depression is scared of her.

In addition to Angelique, Emmeline, Lily, Kelly, Iz, Bella Marie, and me, these three women make up what I presume to be the Belladonnas.

This assumption is confirmed when I discover Chloe had muted and archived all their DMs. But she didn't just mute them on Instagram—she muted them across all social platforms and iMessage. I find the Instagram group chat nicknamed Hot Girls Only and read the latest messages.

Maya: I can suggest an amazing therapist, she's done heaven's work for my grief.
Angelique: We're always here for you.
Sophia: Think of all the positive memories you have of Julie.
Lily: You're in my thoughts.
Emmeline: I'm sorry for your loss.
Kelly: We are family.

Ana even penned me a poem:

> Death.
> Everyone will face it
> At some point in
> Time.
> Hope you feel better.

Well. It's the thought that counts.

The most recent message is from Bella Marie herself: We've all experienced significant loss. You know where to find us when you are ready. Xoxo.

My lips spread into a smile and my chest warms. Older messages are mostly the girls sending support to one another, asking for advice in negotiations for brand deals, pooling connections for potential partnerships, questions about which photos to place on the cover of carousels, etc.

I don't understand why Chloe muted them when they've only been supportive. So what if they seem a little superficial at times? They're influencers, what can you expect? They live busy lives, have photos to post, brand deals to negotiate, companies to build. Yet they still took the time out of their crowded schedules to send supportive messages. If I had friends like them while I was Julie—a social safety net, a community, people who cared and followed up with me— everything could have been different.

I take the chat out of my archives and unmute every Belladonna. By the time I've replied to each of them in earnest, I'm drained, but my heart is abuzz. I'm enamored with this new world I've claimed for myself. All these new, genuine connections.

I glance at the time. Two fifteen a.m. I want to stay up and absorb this moment for longer, but I'm crushed with fatigue. Five hours of pretending to be Chloe is not easy. Thankfully, it went off without a hitch. I think I'm getting the hang of this.

After dimming the lights and turning my phone to do not disturb, I sink into the memory foam and try to rest.

But without the bright LED screen shining in my eye, the constant ping of notifications, the silent darkness becomes a confrontation, and every sense that I dulled with my distracted scrolling suddenly sharpens. A swollen unease burgeons in my stomach as Chloe's fragrant apricot shampoo infiltrates my nose like she's in bed next to me. I shift, trying to find comfort.

Something sharp pricks my thigh. I flinch, turn on the light, and examine my leg. A long, black hair has pierced my skin like a splinter. It looks like mine yet I'm sure of it.

It's Chloe's.

Only her hair would try to skewer me in my sleep. Heart racing, I pull it out and rush to the bathroom, flushing the hair down the toilet like it's a bug that could come back and bite me, watching, breathless, until I'm sure it's been swallowed by the swirling water.

Stripping the bed, I toss everything into a giant black trash bag. I consider using the other set of sheets I spotted in the linen closet, but I'm uneasy. What if there are little remnants of Chloe in there too? Instead, I lay a towel on the bare mattress and rest on top of it. I'm scrunching my eyes hard, willing sleep to arrive so I can escape the disquiet thumping in my brain, when my phone rings.

Didn't I silence it? I grab the device and squint at the screen. Nothing pops up.

The phone is still ringing.

I smack it like a broken remote. The screen shows nothing.

Then I realize it.

The sound is coming from somewhere else.

It's not Chloe's phone that's ringing.

It's *my* phone.

21

I lurch out of bed and search for my phone, which I had tossed into the nightstand drawer, hands trembling as I rummage through Chloe's sex toys. Eventually, my fingers grasp hard metal. I pull it to my face right as the call drops.

Notifications pop up on my lock screen: Missed Call from: (13) DANGER! DO NOT PICK UP. (6) Voicemail.

Fuck.

Fuck, fuck, fuck, fuck, *fuck*.

My phone rings again and I yelp, throwing the device away. It has what feels like ten seconds of airtime before it slams into the wall, leaving a dent, and clatters on the floor.

The ringing. It won't stop. I push my palms against my ears, trying to drown out the sound. How could I forget?

My aunt.

I've been so carried away living as Chloe that I've ignored my previous life as Julie. My aunt was my emergency contact. The authorities must have called her after they took Chloe's body.

But if she knows Julie is dead, why is she calling Julie's phone like she's alive?

Maybe she's trying to reach Chloe.

That makes sense. Julie was discovered in Chloe's apartment, so Auntie could be calling to get the phone back. She probably wants to factory reset the device and sell it secondhand like the penny-pincher she is. I wouldn't put anything past her. She's as unscrupulous as a person could be. I still remember when I found my fourth-grade classmate's wallet at a park. It had a grand total of $11.24 in quarters and pennies, yet she still pocketed the money before asking me to return the wallet. Of course, I was accused of stealing the money, and when I tried to tell the truth, the teacher called my aunt and she put the blame on me without remorse. I was a fourth grader. Nine years old. For a month afterward, she refused to pack a lunch or give me two dollars for the lunch program since I tried to snitch on her. I had to live off the occasional sympathetic teacher and the snacks I stole from the corner store.

The call drops. Silence.

Deep breaths.

Everything is okay. There's no way she knows.

My sweat-soaked pajamas stick onto my skin as my heart plows through my chest. I reach for the phone like it's a venomous spider.

"Calm down," I tell myself. "Listen to the voicemail. It will be fine."

Finding the courage to pluck my phone from the ground, I swipe my damp thumb on the lock screen and go to voicemail.

Five seconds of static silence. The sound of someone washing dishes in the background. Maybe she called by accident. Like a butt dial?

But then she speaks.

"*Wai!* A'Patrick, come here." Her Cantonese is gruff and short. "What the hell is this? Why is there no noise from the phone?"

"You're supposed to leave a voicemail, Ma."

I groan. The last thing I want to hear is Patrick's voice. When I was living with them, he spent every second glued to his gaming computer in our shared bedroom, screeching when he head-shotted someone in *Call of Duty*, or screaming racist and homophobic obscenities every time he died. His voice triggers me. He's a PMS migraine incarnate.

"Voicemail?" my aunt asks.

"Just talk if you want to leave a message. It will record you and send it to her."

"How do you know if Julie will listen to it?"

My heart drops. It's visceral. A rock plummeting from my chest down to my stomach. I break out in a shivering cold sweat.

How do you know if Julie will listen to it?

Julie.

She knows.

She knows I'm alive.

"Well," Patrick says, "you don't, Ma."

"Hah?"

"And I doubt she will. She was posting at some party. She won't be checking her phone."

My ears ring. They know about Bella Marie's event. About me pretending to be Chloe. How? How did they piece it together?

She clicks her tongue. "Useless. Get out of my face! I'll call her again." The voicemail ends.

Another voicemail starts. In this one, she only mumbles a few Cantonese swear words before it cuts. Ever eloquent.

There are a few more of these, each voicemail getting shorter because she learns to hang up before the beep until it's just missed calls.

I drop the phone and cradle my head in my hands, rocking back and forth. A maelstrom rips through my mind. Should I call her back? Lie? Double down on the fact that I'm Chloe?

But what if she has proof? How is she so confident that I'm Julie?

If they decide to report me, it's over. What if they get a last-minute autopsy on Chloe's body and discover she's not me? Is that even possible? Can they tell identical twins apart? Either way, I know she'd only reach out to me for nefarious reasons.

I want to believe I'm overreacting. Family would never do something so terrible, right? Especially Asian families. There are stereotypes about us, how we always support each other, send money back to the homeland, how we have this sacred bond of ancestry and blood.

But who am I kidding? That shit doesn't exist anymore. One feud between sisters and a whole generation is at war, the effects trickling into their children.

I don't know the exact details, but it didn't take the most inquisitive mind to understand my aunt's hatred for my mom. My beautiful mom. The darling of the family. She married a handsome man and had beautiful twin girls. My aunt, short and stout, married an alcoholic who abandoned her when Patrick was two. She never felt it beneath her to insult my dead mom in front of me. If anything, she might have felt more joy knowing her sister's daughter was forced to absorb her jealous words.

When I was seven, I asked her why she adopted me and not Chloe. She answered simply: "There was no choice. Chloe was already adopted. Trust me, I would have taken you both out of the kindness of my heart. Someone needs to straighten out the sins your mother birthed into you." This was said while she searched the mail for my monthly adoption subsidy like a rabid, frothing dog.

The phone rings again. I flinch and turn the device on silent.

My heart pounds. I know I have to talk to them before this all gets out of hand, but I can't bring myself to answer. Not when I'm so fatigued and panicked. If I pick up, I'll only say the wrong thing, fall into their trap.

I need to rest, take a breather. Yes. Tomorrow morning, when I'm calm and collected, I'll give my aunt a call.

Everything will be okay.

I head to the living room and throw the phone onto the couch. Searching through Chloe's prescriptions, I find a bottle of Ambien. I take a pill, chew it to a fine powder, and swallow it with a gulp of tap water.

Back in the bedroom, everything is silent. Still. Safe.

Stripping off my sweat-soaked clothes, I slide naked onto the towel I laid out and pull the duvet up to my chin. My eyes are closed for a long time, but sleep doesn't come.

I stare at the dim ceiling. Squiggles and lines appear in the darkness. Something isn't right. I blink and the squiggles suddenly turn into worms and centipedes, their bodies forming weird shapes. Molding, stretching, bloating. My pulse buzzes with horror as I try to look away.

But I can't.

I can't move. Can't control my body. "Lacrimosa" plays as the ceiling twists and morphs into a face. Chloe's face. Her round eyes, black hair, small lips. She's discolored, almost blue-gray. No, not her. *Go away.* I whimper, shutting my eyes hard, but the vision of her naked gray limbs invades my consciousness, seeps through my eyelids. Chloe looms over me, purple veins snaking down her neck like claw marks. Her skin is peeling, flaking off. Her black hair drapes over me like a cocoon. I yearn to escape but I am frozen. Tied to the bed. We are encased together in a void made of her hair; nothing else exists except the two of us and darkness. Then, a noise. A heartbeat. We're in the womb again. It's warm and wet. She is mere centimeters away, holding me captive in her unblinking gaze. My twin. Her irises have turned gray and glassy, rotted away from the inside out like a dead fish. I try to say *I'm sorry* as if an apology would stop the haunting, *I'm sorry for taking your life,* but my lips don't move; it's like they're sewn together. Then she opens her mouth. Wide. Dislocates her jaw like she wants to swallow me whole. But instead, something falls out of the black hole that is her throat. A grain of rice. No. It squirms. A maggot. Then another. And another. And another. Until a waterfall of maggots is expelled from her gullet, burying me. The tiny, writhing bugs crawl into my nostrils, slither underneath my eyelids, burrow in my ear canals, chew the thin lining of my eardrums. They munch and bite and eat me alive until I'm drowning, until I suffocate, until I can't breathe I can't breathe I can't breathe I can't—

22

I jerk awake, quivering, covered in sweat. The duvet is wet and cold. My mouth is dry and full of phlegm. Tears dribble down my cheeks and land on my damp chest.

Chloe flashes before my eyes again. I flinch into my headboard like she's here, ready to tie me down. But there's just darkness, a sliver of orange light escaping through the blinds.

It's 5:41 a.m. I fell asleep. It was all a nightmare. Pure fiction.

It's early but I can't think of going back to sleep. I get out of bed, shower with freezing-cold water. I pat in my skincare, brush my teeth. I avoid looking in the mirror, scared I'll see Chloe's face in the reflection. "Lacrimosa" hums in my head. I can't stand it. I tell the Alexa in the living room to play happy music. Pharrell booms through the speakers. That shitty song from *Minions*.

I make myself a coffee. Three espresso shots, no creamer. I never want to sleep again.

Then I remember the Ambien. I google for side effects: nightmares, night terrors, hallucinations, among many other dreadful symptoms. Stomping to my bedroom, I flush the rest of the pills down the toilet. I'd rather be an insomniac than ever experience that again.

I sit down with my coffee and stare at the stark gray New York skyline. The sun stretches its golden rays through the foggy clouds, ripening the sky

·to a burnt yellow. I'm unable to relax, Chloe clawing through my mind in horrific fragments.

I need to get her out of my head. But how?

I am reminded of Sophia. She said she sent me some positive affirmations. Normally, I'd find affirmations to be bullshit woo-woo, but I'm at my wits' end. I open her messages and read the quotes:

I am thankful for what I still have.

I am patient with myself and my sorrow.

I will take care of myself as I heal.

I am thankful to be safe and healthy.

I close my eyes and repeat the positive thoughts in my head, throwing in one of my own.

I am thankful for what I still have.

I am patient with myself and my sorrow.

I will take care of myself as I heal.

I am thankful to be safe and healthy.

I am not being haunted.

I repeat them a hundred times until I start to believe them. Until I feel like I'm on solid ground.

I open my eyes.

A bird flaps by my window to say hello. I take a cool breath and blow out warm air. My mug emanates heat into my palms. I sip coffee until I feel at peace. Until the memory of Chloe fades into the recesses of my mind.

I am safe.

I am good.

Everything is okay.

Huh. Maybe positive affirmations aren't all bullshit.

When I get up to put my cup away, I see *my* phone on the floor and avoid it. I'm not ready to deal with my aunt.

Thankfully, I have a perfect distraction: SoulCycle. For the first time in my life, I am excited about exercise—anything to take my mind off last night. I change into a teal sports bra and legging set from GymFish, take a picture in front of the mirror (I suck in for dear life), and tag the brand on my stories with my discount code. Within minutes, email notifications roll in about people using my affiliate link. Three dollars, four dollars, sixteen dollars in commissions. After reading through a few replies complimenting my body for a boost of serotonin, I take some preworkout powder I found in the pantry that turns water into liquid Skittles and makes my skin itch in a good way. I debate on riding the train or walking like a true New Yorker, but go for an Uber instead. The whole six-minute ride, I'm blasting music through my headphones, drowning out my thoughts. I feel like Kendall Roy at the start of *Succession*. On top of the world.

23

I make it to SoulCycle with ten minutes to spare. The girl at the front desk recognizes me and signs me in without asking. She hands me a pair of cycling shoes and tells me to enjoy my class. The dimly lit walls of the studio are decorated with inspirational messages telling me I'm a warrior legend and to believe in myself. I strap into the bike Chloe had booked, which happens to be in the front row. Glancing over my shoulder, I realize everyone will be able to see me. I've never taken a spin class before. What if I make a fool of myself?

"Chloe!" It's Lily Schmidt, the Belladonna who exchanged the boy with Down syndrome for the neurotypical Thai girl.

"Lily!" It feels good to know her name. We do the weird cheek-kiss thing before she straps in next to me.

"It was so nice to see you last night. Hope you're not too hungover."

"Oh, I didn't drink."

She arches her brow. "Seriously?"

I remember all the alcohol in Chloe's fridge. Maybe the Belladonnas knew about the tendencies Chloe hid from her clean-girl feed. "I'm thinking of going sober for a bit," I say, hoping to clear any confusion. "After Julie's death, I don't want to fall into bad habits."

She places both hands over her heart. "That's admirable. It takes a lot of courage."

I smile from her words even though she reacted to a lie.

"Good morning, everyone! Are you ready to sweat?" Sophia gallops into the room and everyone quiets their conversations. She's dressed in a matching neon-green gym set, the dim lights accentuating her cut abs and rippling thigh muscles. She hops on her bike and starts the class. Neon lights flash like we're at a rave. The music is a medley of upbeat #girlboss songs that reverberate straight into my chest. Beyoncé, Katy Perry, Christina Aguilera, the like.

Indoor cycling is harder than I thought it would be. I'm out of breath within the first five minutes, but then Sophia yells, "We're closing out on our warm-up, beautiful people. Get ready for our first climb!"

My heart monitor says I'm clocking in at 175 beats per minute, and this is only the *warm-up*?

I'm winded as we start our climb, pushing our resistance up several levels, legs aching. Lily glances at my bike display, clearly making sure she's going a bit faster and harder than me. When we start something called a Tabata, I think I'm about to pass out. Not enough air can enter my lungs. I'm heaving. Bile swims up my stomach, heart hurling against my chest, wanting to break my ribs. I slow down even though everyone else is pedaling for their lives, pushing their legs with the beat of the music. I start wondering if cardio classes are the elite's answer to self-harm.

As I reach to turn down my resistance, Sophia's eyes lock on mine.

"I want to see everyone push their limits this morning. Your body can do more than you think! It's by powering through these difficulties, breaking through our physical fatigue, that we can build resiliency and excellence!" She's staring at me so hard my classmates turn in my direction. A rush of pure embarrassment kicks my chest. The dose of group shame forces my hands off the resistance knob and I begin pedaling again even though I can't feel my legs.

"Show your mind who's boss!" Sophia shouts. "On the count of three, I want you all to scream '*I can do it!*' One. Two. Three!"

Shouts course through the room. "I can do it!"

"I-I can do it!" I join in, breathless.

Sophia points a finger in the air, drenched in glistening sweat. "Now push! Push! *Push!*"

I push, even though my muscles are screaming to stop.

By the end of the class, I'm clipping in and out of death. I have become sweat. My pores, Niagara Falls. There's a puddle on the hardwood floor below me. I see the strobing afterlife; it smells like sweat and sounds like pop music. It is hell.

Lily pats me on the back, her hand sliding off my slick skin. She has a gloating expression, like she just whooped me in a competition. Which she did. "Good ride."

I nod because I have zero breath in my lungs.

"But I guess a few weeks off the bike can really do a number on us."

"Huh?" I mumble, almost vomiting.

Her gaze lands on my stomach. An inch of my belly fat has rolled over the top seam of my leggings. I sit straighter, suddenly hyperaware of my own body, the circumference of my waist, the lack of definition in my abs, the flab in my arms. Can she tell that something is off? That I'm a different person? I can edit my body in photos, but I can't alter reality.

I desperately change the subject. "Hey, about that trip in June—"

Her Apple Watch lights up. "Gotta drop Wendy off at school. See you next week!" She waves to Sophia and jogs out of the class. How does she have so much energy? Either way, I'm glad she didn't say anything more. Her abrupt exit saved me from having to spin more lies.

I'm fumbling with the pedals, trying to unclip myself, when Sophia helps me out. She's glowing. An oiled Greek goddess that crushed a triathlon, ready to be immortalized in marble.

"You okay? I noticed you weren't keeping up like you usually do." I cringe and try to take some calming breaths while simultaneously sucking in my stomach. Thankfully, she's not staring at my body like Lily.

While trying to dig up an excuse, I push back my sweaty ponytail. It whips droplets of sweat across the floor. "I guess there's stuff on my mind." My aunt trying to reach me even though she should think I'm dead, my sister dying, identity theft . . . lies upon lies upon lies. "Julie" is all I say.

"Ah. I should have figured." She shakes her head sympathetically. "I still remember the grief from when I broke my arm right before the Olympics. One wrong step during a yacht party and . . ." She blows a long breath. "I holed myself up in my room for months, depressed. I'm glad you're getting to this step of recovery faster than I did. Today's sweat and pain is good for you. Exercise is the best way to deliver dopamine to our brains."

Though my situation isn't quite the same, I get what she's saying. During those brief moments of strenuous exercise, I didn't think about my issues one bit—mostly because the stinging lactic acid in my muscles overwhelmed any possibility of thought. But hey, nothing about Chloe or my aunt for a solid forty minutes. That's something, right?

"Thanks for your encouragement." I smile. "And the affirmations."

"The affirmations are all thanks to Bella Marie." She tips her head to the ceiling with a soft smile. "When I first got to know her after my accident, she gave me a jar full of them, handwritten, and asked me to read one every day until the jar was empty. She had written a whole year's worth of affirmations for me. It was"—she sighs and shakes her head—"*so* special. If it wasn't for Bella Marie, I wouldn't be where I am today."

I wonder if Bella Marie did similar acts of kindness for Chloe, if she'll ever do one for me.

"I have to head out to a brand event," she says. "But if you ever need to take your mind off things, come in for another class. We're always here."

I think I'm starting to understand why Chloe works out every day.

I'm sticky and exhausted but I feel good inside. Like I've accomplished something, even though I technically traveled nowhere. I'm revitalized as I walk out of the studio, the dusty New York air whipping in my face: a pleasant mix of trash, car exhaust, and coffee. I take a photo in front of the SoulCycle logo looking sweaty, body steaming into the winter morning, and post it to my stories. Always time for some @SoulCycle. Shout-out to my favorite instructor @sophchambers, you rock! 🖤 Remember, unleash your inner warrior. #strong #beautiful

As I walk—yes, walk—back to my apartment, I watch the reactions flood in. A follower replies: you are such an inspiration. you help me get through my day. I send them a heart and reply: You have so much strength within! Don't discount yourself! They flood me with more love.

I understand why Chloe invested so much time and energy into her following now. It bolsters me, empowers me. I didn't know how good it could feel to have a community of supportive fans at my fingertips. How much I've desired it. One tap and the world floods me with love. I feel like a god.

Iz replies to my story: Looking good girl.

Angelique also replies: You are so beautiful. We should cycle together sometime!

In fact, all of the Belladonnas reply, complimenting my body, my work ethic. I grin, elated that I finally have a group of friends who support me. By the time I'm back at my apartment, I know I can conquer anything. I pick up my phone from the floor to dial my aunt back.

I can do anything I put my mind to. I am a boss. A warrior legend.

24

SoulCycle lied. I am not a warrior legend. I am a fraud. A fraud who wishes she could go back in time and never pick up the damned phone.

"Do you think I'm stupid?" my aunt shouts in Cantonese. "You could barely swallow your Tylenol when you got a fever. You had to grind it up and sprinkle it into your water because you're scared of tablets getting caught in your throat. A pill overdose is the last way you'd go."

"I-I don't know what you're talking about," I stammer in Cantonese. "This is Chloe."

"Do you think some girl raised by gweilo speaks fluent Cantonese? Mandarin maybe, but Cantonese? You're not fooling anyone."

Oh god. Why didn't I think before speaking? I pace back and forth, my damp sports bra digging into my shoulders. "W-what do you want, Auntie?"

"Transfer your house ownership to me and pay me ten thousand dollars."

That's it? "Okay—"

"For every month you mooched off me. And pay for your sister's funeral expenses too. I'm not spending a single dime on a girl I didn't know."

I plug the numbers into the calculator app. Ten thousand times twelve times the thirteen years I lived with them. A staggering $1,560,000. "Are you crazy? That's over a million dollars!"

"Do you know how much it cost to raise you all those years? To feed an extra mouth?"

It's the same lame excuse she used when she stole my savings. "Was all the money you took from my bank account not enough? Were the government checks not enough?" I'm exhausted. I wish I could hide away and be done with this. How long will she follow me, chasing after me like a feral dog?

"How dare you talk back to me!" Her voice blares into my ear. "Fine! I'll go to the police! Tell them about how you killed your sister and stole her life!"

"K-killed?" I stop dead in my tracks. "Are you insane? I didn't kill anyone!"

"And you just happened to be in New York when she died?"

"She called me! It was all a coincidence. When I arrived, Chloe was already dead."

"Will the police believe you? You took her identity without remorse. You've already proven yourself to be a liar and a criminal."

I'm shaking, heart hammering. "You can't prove anything. Our genes are one hundred percent the same. There's no way anyone can tell Chloe and me apart." At least I hope so. I really need to google it.

She bursts out laughing. "I don't need genetic testing. I have all the evidence in my hands."

My mouth dries. "What do you mean?"

"We've been recording you the whole time," Patrick says. "You admitted to switching lives on tape."

"Wha—" My mouth stays parted but no words escape except for a gurgle. I hang up in a panic, throw my phone onto my couch, and scurry into the bathroom to hyperventilate.

Oh god, oh god, oh god. Why the hell did I go to SoulCycle and convince myself that I'm a warrior legend? I'm nothing more than a sheep. And now they have a recording of me admitting to my crime. How much jail time is that?

But I'm innocent—at least in terms of murder.

Breathe.

I rinse out my mouth and splash cold water on my face.

Okay. Think.

Would she really risk getting the police involved? Extortion is illegal. If she decides to submit the recording, she could also get in trouble. Would she risk that? But even if she doesn't escalate this to the authorities, she could still fuck me over. If she or Patrick spreads their suspicions onto social media, leak the partial audio file onto some gossip forum, or sell it to a salacious news site, it's game over. The general public will speculate and cancel me to oblivion.

I know how Auntie rolls. Her threats are never empty. If I don't acquiesce to her extortion right now, she could come back and demand even more. Considering the shit that I'm guilty of, I'm not in any position to bargain. It's too risky not to take her seriously when everything is on the line.

One point five six million dollars in the grand scheme of things isn't awful if I pretend it's a mortgage, a literal lease on a new life. If I take some extra sponsorships and hustle hard, I might be able to make it back in a few years. Maybe Auntie will let me pay in installments. If I dole it out slowly, the total isn't as scary. Maybe ten installments of $156,000? Or monthly installments of $15,000? When I think about it that way, it's not bad at all!

I keep forgetting that I'm not Julie Chan, cashier at SuperFoods. I am Chloe Van Huusen, influencer. I have the means to generate insane cash flow. A picture of me is worth thousands of dollars—literally.

And when I think about it, keeping my aunt on my payroll could be a silver lining. She's the only person in my past life who could ever threaten my new identity. It's better to have her on an expensive leash than constantly wondering when she might bite.

With this sobering thought, I call my aunt back.

She picks up immediately. "Have you decided?"

"What about one million?"

"How about two?" Auntie immediately replies.

I resist a groan. "Never mind. Let's go with the original amount. Will you accept installments?"

"With interest. Five percent per month compounding."

"Five—" I bite my tongue as fury heats my veins. How can she ask for interest while extorting me? But there's clearly no room for bargaining. They have the upper hand. If my aunt ever opens her dirty little mouth, it's all over. She can't be the reason I get caught. "How do I know you won't ask for more money?"

"You don't. You did a terrible crime and you'll never be forgiven."

I bite my lip, hating that there's a kernel of truth.

"Fine. Send over your banking information."

"What about your sister's body? The morgue has been calling us non-stop."

Flashes of Chloe's corpse revive in my mind. I shiver, try to shake it off.

"I'll deal with it."

25

"Burn her."

"You mean cremate?" asks the woman at the morgue.

"Yeah. That."

She nods. "Would you like a last look at her before we start? A final farewell?"

Christ. I didn't even know that was allowed. I shake my head, pushing the images of Chloe's blue body out of my mind.

I don't know if my twin wanted to be cremated. Maybe she wanted an open-casket funeral. That seems like something rich people do, preserving their legacy by injecting their corpses with formaldehyde and silicone. But I need to get rid of Chloe's body completely, make sure every last trace of her is disposed of, so even if the authorities wanted to, they'd never be able to analyze her DNA against mine. As they say: no body, no crime.

Plus, I read how much a full-service funeral would cost. The casket alone is tens of thousands of dollars. Not to mention the burial site. It's basically permanent New York real estate that you can't sell. I'm rich now, but not that rich. With my aunt's blackmail, I can't squander a single cent.

Chloe will have to be happy with a cremation.

As I make my way out of the hospital morgue, I pass a sign that says Multifaith Prayer Room.

Was Chloe religious? The Van Huusens seem like the type to believe in

Jesus and other religious bullshit. Maybe I should offer a prayer after stealing her life, appease her spirit.

The empty and dim room feels dry yet smells damp. There are four benches and a table holding a cross and some religious texts. I take a seat. The wood squeaks under my weight.

I close my eyes and bow my head. The ceiling lights hum softly as I clasp my hands in front of my chest.

What do I even say?

May you rest well, Chloe?

Please don't haunt me as revenge?

Let this be the end of my suffering?

Let me start a new life? Be reborn?

Please, please, please help me God. Muhammad. Vishnu. Buddha. Zeus. Whoever's listening. I swear I'm not picky. I'm just desperate. I'll do good. Give to charity. Be a kind person. I'll pray to you every day, once an hour. Anything! *Please* give me a sign.

A voice crackles in my ear.

"This is a Code Blue. I repeat, a Code Blue."

I open my eyes and press my lips together. Unclasp my hands.

No God would listen to a sinner like me.

26

I have good news and I have bad news.

The bad news is I have trouble sleeping. Every time I edge toward oblivion, I think of Chloe. Her body. Her eyes. Her hair engulfing me. I catch winks of rest here and there due to pure physical exhaustion, but that's about it. Also, my skin looks like shit. Not even the best skincare can save me from sleep deprivation.

The good news is I've lost a lot of weight. (Mostly because my insomniac body is struggling to function.) I fit into all of Chloe's clothes now, which is fantastic.

In the grand scheme of things, my gaunt appearance helps the narrative. Every story I've posted has followers pooling concerns about me. How I need to rest and heal after my loss. How much they'd love me even if I took a break. They yell in my DMs to value my mental health.

It's nice of them, really.

But I have no time for a break. I have bills (blackmail) to pay and videos to film.

I'm by the Hudson River, dressed in a Burberry trench and matching scarf. Chloe rests in my hand, her body contained in a nice beige urn with a spherical top. Simple. Modern. Deceptively expensive. I think she'd like it.

Fiona points a camera at me. "Okay, I'm rolling."

I open the urn and stare into the gray ashes lovingly. I sigh like I'm about to make an apology video. The wind blows at the perfect dramatic second. I brush away my hair and say, "I'll miss you, Julie." Images of us as children, tiny little twins, pop into my head. Chloe, brave and smiling. The two of us, our chubby fingers intertwined. Sweet mango on my tongue.

Warmth creeps into my chest. Pressure pushes behind my eyes.

Holy shit, I'm actually sad. This is perfect.

I let the somber moment take over. My eyes water. I blink. A tear rolls down my cheek. I sigh again. Biting my lip, I look into the lapping waters of the Hudson River. A plastic bag floats lazily downstream. I tip the urn over and pour the ashes out. Some of Chloe's dust gets blown into my mouth and nose. It's like she's trying to crawl into me, take back her life, infect me cell by cell by spreading down my throat, into my lungs. I cough her out as phlegm and spit her into the water. Her ashes seep into the river in an instant, caught in the current. A human being, gone. Just like that. Longing pervades me as I glance into the empty urn. I didn't think it would happen so fast. Twenty-four years vanished in seconds. Swept into the wind to be breathed in as micro-pollution, sinking to the bottom of the riverbed, food for mollusks.

I clutch the urn to my chest and stare into the camera with an intense look of suffering, my cheeks raw from the cold.

"Grief is not easy to deal with alone. If you or a loved one is suffering from a loss like I am, please seek counseling for support. This video is sponsored by BetterTherapy."

27

Yes, I took a sponsorship on a video of me spreading my sister's ashes. News flash! Extortion isn't cheap. Life isn't cheap. Believe it or not, I need the extra capital.

I barely had time to breathe in this cushy new identity before I was smacked in the face with an influencer's second-worst nightmare, after cancellation: taxes.

I thought finances would be a breeze since Chloe had been raking in a steady six figures per month. But running an operation of her caliber isn't cheap, especially since she tended to outsource. There are several people on her payroll, ranging from salaried staff like Fiona to stylists and artists like Kim and Fernanda, to all the other stragglers and freelancers who help with video and content production. Even the accountant himself costs a pretty penny. And unfortunately for me, Chloe paid them all fair wages—more than fair. Everyone is earning above the market rate. Which is kind of her. But also, kind of fucking me over.

To top it all off, in a few weeks, good old Uncle Sam will come knocking with his grubby little hands, snatching away half my pie to fund foreign wars, since I've meddled my way into a high tax bracket. Seeing the estimate of how much I will have to fork over was a gut punch. It's more than I ever made in a year as Julie.

And look, life in New York is expensive. A good chunk goes to pay off the mortgage on the apartment. Restaurant bills plus tips climb to at least $80 a meal if I get a drink. Not to mention, my Ubers always happen to consistently fall during peak hours. And maybe I've been online shopping during sleepless nights. Also, I got a haircut and a straight perm as a treat-yourself, which totaled $850 after tips. I'm working on fixing my underbite at a boutique orthodontist and the treatment is coming up to five figures . . .

Okay. Fine. I'll admit it! I'm not great with money, okay? Having an AmEx to swipe at leisure is infinitely appealing. I can finally remedy my points of insecurity with cold, hard cash. Let me live like a rich person for a while and I'll get my shit in order before you know it. And in my defense, I can't risk damaging Chloe's clean brand by being caught inhaling a Big Mac.

Anyway, after being hit with the gruesome reality of my financial matters, I realized I needed to get ahead and take more deals. I'm not trying to ruin myself with Auntie's compounding interest, so yes, I did make the executive decision to accept a BetterTherapy sponsorship. But it's not like Chloe wouldn't do this. She literally exploited me for one of her videos. If anything, I'm a mental health advocate. BetterTherapy is paying me fifty grand *and* offering free therapy sessions with a certified counselor.* (*BetterTherapy is not responsible if users are matched to a therapist without a degree or certification.)

I'm watching the final video that my editor sent over to approve. The first half is B-roll of me walking along Riverside Park with the urn, the Hudson in the background. After some voice-over monologues about made-up childhood memories, it cuts to the scene of me dumping the ashes. Fiona expertly zooms in on my misty eyes, then pans up to the gray sky as if my twin is now in heaven. The end of the video is marked by a minute-long stretch of statistics about addiction, hotline directories, and my BetterTherapy discount code.

The total length is thirty minutes, which allows me to stick in three mid-rolls without being excessive about ads.

I click on the thumbnail Fiona sent. It's of me staring wistfully into the distance. You can see my pores since she didn't put blurring filters over my face. It looks authentic. Raw. She pitched a few titles, but I've thought of one that's better.

Logging on to YouTube, I drag in the video, attach the thumbnail, and type: *goodbye* . . . All lowercase with an added ellipsis for emotional emphasis.

I keep the description simple: This is the hardest video I've ever had to make. If you need counseling support, consider BetterTherapy with my code "CHLOE" for a free online trial.

Estimated upload time: fifteen minutes.

While waiting, I click around Chloe's YouTube channel and find some archived videos from years ago. The oldest one was filmed with a mono-chromatic iMovie filter. She's in her room, maybe sixteen years old, a ukulele in hand as she belts her little soul out to Justin Bieber's "One Less Lonely Girl." The cover is horrendous. Thank god she didn't pursue music.

Unable to bear her pitchy voice, I exit and watch the next archived video. This one has no filter, her turquoise wall in the frame. She's attempting comedy: *Sh*t teachers say.* It's not funny, but I chuckle a few times due to the embarrassing earnestness in Chloe's face.

Her archived videos take me back to the old-school internet days when the only people caught on YouTube were weird loners, filming content as a last-ditch attempt at human connection. All we get now are grifters eager for clout.

Near the end of the video her door suddenly swings open. A man stands in the doorway. Chloe jumps to stop recording. The video abruptly cuts.

I frown. Was that Mr. Van Huusen?

I scroll back to when the door opens. His head is out of frame so I can't read his expression, only the brief panic in Chloe's eyes. It's probably nothing. She was likely embarrassed. Yet I can't ignore it. I'm unsettled.

It's been a while since Julie died, and the Van Huusens still haven't reached out.

I bite my lip, curious. Chloe's calendar had a repeating event on March 12 for "Mom's Birthday." The twelfth is only a week away. I can use it. Against all logic, I send a text in the family group chat: Hey. What's the plan for mom's birthday?

As I wait, I scroll through more of Chloe's archived videos. There's a rigidity in her movements, and I can't tell if it's because she's uncomfortable in front of the camera or if there's something else bothering her. "Hi, guys" is her opening. Her voice is soft, almost a tremble. I feel like I'm looking at a mirror version of myself as a teen. I can't take my eyes away. I'm so immersed, time loses meaning.

I startle when an iMessage pings. My heart blares with excitement, thinking it's the Van Huusens. But it's a message from a random number:

> Hey Chloe, I saw your newest video and I am heartbroken for your loss. I know it must be a difficult time, but our previous conversation was incredibly productive, and I don't want to lose the momentum of your story. If you have the energy, could we touch base about next steps? You mentioned wanting to talk about your adoptive parents. Maybe I'm being presumptuous, but it seems like what happened to them was a critical turning point for you and contributed to why you reached out to me. Perhaps unpacking that could help with your current grief too? But of course, no rush. Let me know if I'm overstepping.

My eyes circle the crumb of information about the Van Huusens and the string of numbers floating at the top of the screen. This person was familiar with my twin, but why aren't they saved as a contact? There's no record of a previous conversation either—did Chloe erase them? At first glance, the message seems like something between a therapist and a patient. Could this person be a counselor or psychiatrist?

I plug the phone number into Google with no results. But a search through my laptop produces an email from Jessica Peters that had been sorted into trash a few weeks ago. The name sparks a memory: I had asked Fiona to cancel an appointment with her on my second day as Chloe. The email provides little context. Fiona forwarded a meeting invite and Jessica thanked her, but there's evidence of other exchanges that had been permanently erased by the system. Above her phone number and contact information: Staff Writer at The New Yorker.

I frown. Why was Chloe in contact with a writer at a magazine? About a *story,* no less.

A link in Jessica's email signature redirects to her contributor page, where I find dozens of reports on news and culture—specifically, *digital* culture. These articles aren't simply recaps of the newest social media scandal—quick, biting headlines meant to keep fans clicking mindlessly—but thorough examinations of the online zeitgeist, connecting internet phenomena to broader societal implications. Her most recent essay articulates how a recently viral and seemingly vacuous meme of a duck wearing sunglasses is actually a reflection of the political disengagement of young adults in America, going as far as to interview philosophers and political strategists to evidence her theory. Another article profiles a once popular but now canceled influencer, detailing their quick fall from glory and their grievances with internet fame, drawing an analogy between scrolling on social media and walking through a zoo.

I close the tab, unable to read further, as questions tumble through my mind. Jessica had mentioned Chloe having a story to tell, something that involved her parents. And based on Jessica's previous reporting, it must be related to Chloe's life as a digital creator. Whatever the story was, it must have been important for my twin to reach out. What could she possibly want to say?

Despite my curiosity, I need to consider my self-preservation. I can't have Jessica snooping around me when I'm impersonating my dead sister. Voluntarily engaging with a reporter would be like putting a gun in her hand and giving her permission to shoot. Better to nip this all in the bud before it's too late.

I compose a reply: I've changed my mind. I can't go forward with the story. Please don't reach out to me any further.

After sending the message, I delete the text thread, then block her phone number and email so she can't message me back. I sit staring at my screen with dry eyes, fingers tapping at my keyboard. Doing the right thing didn't chase away my dissatisfaction and curiosity.

Chewing on my lip, I open my chat with Fiona. I'm about to do something stupid, I already know it. But the Van Huusens' silence and Jessica's message have pried open another can of worms. I can't deny myself a peek.

I type: Good work on the video! My brain is failing me these days. What is my parents' address again?

28

Just as I guessed, the Van Huusens live in a brownstone on the Upper West Side. A historic oak with naked branches shades the stoop.

I pad up the icy brick stairs and ring the doorbell. The buzz sends a tremor up my finger. Waiting for an answer, I glance through the window. There's a plant sitting on the sill—or a shriveling sepia skeleton of what used to be a plant.

I ring the doorbell again.

When I'm certain no one is inside, I pull out my jingling key chain and try my luck, finding the match on my third attempt. I twist and it unlocks with such a heavy *clack* that I startle at the noise. Feeling a bit like I'm breaking into someone's house, I glance over my shoulder as if someone will stop me at any moment. An old woman wearing a thick brown trench coat walks her Pomeranian across the street. The dog has little neon-green boots. They don't even look my way.

I take a breath, whisper a quick affirmation—*I am courageous*—and go inside.

Pushing my way into the brownstone, I step over a pile of unopened letters on top of a worn Egyptian rug. Threads of dust dance in the air, caught in the sunlight spilling through the entrance.

My limbs stiffen as I close the door behind me.

"Mom? Dad?"

Nothing.

I'm reminded of the first time I entered Chloe's apartment. Her body. I inhale deep. No smells—none of decay, at least. Maybe a bit of mildew, dust, old wood.

I turn on the light and examine the letters. Judging from the layer of fine dust blanketing the pile, it's been months since someone's gone through these. The first few letters are from the bank, and a few are from the NYU Alumni Association.

While I'm curious about what the Van Huusens' bank statements look like, I have a more pressing task ahead.

This is my first time in a brownstone, and I can't lie, I'm excited. The whole space breathes luxury. Wooden trim and brass features accent furniture that looks handcrafted. Floor-to-ceiling bookshelves slope under the weight of the pages; dust motes rim the edges. Large windows make the narrow space feel lofty and alive. If all the plants were still green, this would have been a vibrant home.

I head upstairs, the steps creaking under my weight. The second-floor hallway is lined with dusty family portraits. In each photo, the family is posed similarly: Mr. and Mrs. Van Huusen in the foreground, dressed in knitted sweaters, their hands on Chloe's shoulders as she stands between them. Her smile is paper-thin in every portrait.

I head into the office, which is equipped with two desks and more bookshelves. Wind wheezes through a cracked window, weathering the crisp plants that sit beside it. When I go to shut the window, I notice the wooden frame is black with mold, rotting and wet. Dead flies and a moth lie with their bellies up on the sill. I brush their carcasses off with my sleeve, trying not to gag. The window struggles to close, the house's foundation groaning in agony as I force it down.

I peek at the Van Huusens' desks. A blue ceramic mug sits on a cork coaster. Inside, a dead fruit fly rests in a bed of sticky brown sediment. The keyboards are dusty. A quick shake of a mouse makes a monitor light up with the sign-in screen. The computers must have been left in sleep mode. I survey the desk drawers, hoping there's a note with log-in information, but find only stationery. After inputting a random string of passwords, I give up.

It almost seems like the house was abandoned in a hurry—not enough time to put away the dishes or power off their computers.

The floor above holds the main bedroom and a small reading nook. Chloe's room, painted turquoise, is on the fourth floor.

I snoop in her nightstand, hoping for a journal or diary. Instead, I find a stack of opened letters that have Chloe's Manhattan address printed on them. Odd. Why would she bring the letters all the way here? It's almost like she was trying to hide them.

I take the one sitting on top, excavate the paper from the envelope, and find an invoice from the Kennedy Nursing Home. For the month of January, they withdrew an obscene total of $35,500 from the "Van Huusen Family Trust" to care for two people. Patient names: VAN HUUSEN, MARGARET and VAN HUUSEN, CHARLES.

My lips part in surprise as I skim the printed text once, twice, three times, trying to make sense of what I'm seeing. I toss the invoice I'm holding and search through the other letters, my heart thundering. They are all invoices. The earliest one is dated August of last year.

That's not long after their last text to Chloe. One day they're making dinner plans, and shortly after, they're in a facility. Is it possible for two people to experience such a steep decline in the span of a few weeks? My mind bounces back to the text Jessica sent. Is this what she meant by Chloe's "critical turning point"? From my snooping online, I know the Van Huusens had retired some time ago. I figured their lack of communication was because they were traveling somewhere remote, but were they actually in a facility? How is there no record of this online or elsewhere? And why didn't Fiona mention this when I asked for the Van Huusens' address? Did she not know the truth? But why would Chloe keep it a secret?

I shake my head to clear my thoughts. No point speculating.

I order an Uber for the Kennedy Nursing Home.

29

On the way to the nursing home, my mind rattles back and forth, attempting to push through the mud of Chloe's secrets. How did the Van Huusens end up in the facility? Were they in an accident? And how did no one find out about it? For someone who credits herself as being open and honest with her audience, Chloe was hiding more than she was letting on. Was anything about her even real?

To cope from the questions throttling my mind, I turn to my phone and review the comments left on my newest video, hoping to find a treasure trove of compassion. The majority of my audience is empathetic; however, a very small but vocal minority disavows me, shaming my sponsored grief. Gritting my teeth, I delete those comments and report the users for bullying and harassment.

YouTube is not providing me with the relief I desire, so I scroll through my Instagram DMs, fielding sympathetic messages from different influencers who wish me health and pray for my loss. Iz, sweet as ever, messaged: Text me your address, and I'll send my famous peach cobbler. It'll make you forget everything for a few moments. I hope you're healing well. xoxo.

I reply: You're my angel.

She reacts to the message with a heart emoji.

Bella Marie uploaded an Instagram story linking to my video with the text: I applaud @Chloe_Van_H for her radical honesty and encourage everyone to watch her incredibly vulnerable video. It is not easy baring your heart to the public like this, especially on issues as stigmatized as addiction and mental health. My mother has struggled with addiction, and I know firsthand how difficult it is to navigate the path forward. I want to gently remind everyone to be kind and compassionate. You never know what someone is going through. x Bella Marie

The next slide reads: If you have the resources and means, please join me in giving. The link leads to the donation page of an addiction research center.

My eyes well up, overwhelmed by appreciation as I click the link. An anonymous party listed only as "B" has made a donation of ten thousand dollars. It must be Bella Marie. Only she could be so generous.

I'm about to send her a thank-you when my phone dings with a new message from the Belladonna group chat. It's from Bella Marie.

Darlings, with spring around the corner, I invite you to check your front door for a surprise. Also, please welcome our newest sister, Isla Harris!! She is such an inspiration and I know she will be the perfect addition to our little family. Yours, Bella 💚 😺

A surprise? I wonder what it could be. Her clothing line? Flowers? A lock of her fine blond hair?

Belladonnas reply in bursts.

Ana: Welcome Isla! Looking forward to the surprise 👀
Lily: It was so nice meeting you Isla, I'm glad you are with us.
Angelique: If you ever have questions about the industry, let us know. I don't know what I would have done without this group. We have your back.
Maya: We are always here for you! We are family!
Emmeline: HI! 😊

Iz replies: Wow, thank you for the warm welcome! I can't wait to see the surprise. I'm itching to get home, but right now I'm at a pole class. She attaches a video of her twirling on the pole.

Kelly: OMG HOT HOT HOT!!! 🔥🔥🔥🔥🔥
Sophia: Please teach me!
Lily: I've always wanted to do pole!
Angelique: Girl? Your body? TO DIE FOR.

I'm about to reply when the Uber driver asks, "Is it okay if I stop across the street?"

I glance out the window. Kennedy Nursing Home is a refurbished mansion estate in Old Westbury that could be mistaken for the set of a historical film. A small brass sign affixed to the tall gates distinguishes the facility from neighboring country clubs and mansions.

"It's fine. Thanks." I stuff my phone into my purse and walk across the street. The gate is locked. There's a camera near the entrance, its black eye staring at me. A metal plate reads: *Dial 1029 for assistance.* I dial the number on the keypad. An automated voice comes on the speaker: "Please look directly into the camera."

Mildly amused, I follow the instructions, positioning myself in front of the lens. A green light scans my face. A beep. The sound of gears turning, and the gate swings open to the brick path.

"Damn," I whisper under my breath, impressed, as I walk toward the nursing home, glancing at the immaculately tended lawn. It's winter, but the grass is somehow still green, so pristine and sumptuous it almost looks fake. I want to roll atop it like a happy Labrador.

When I reach the entrance, the tall black door opens to reveal a pretty brunette employee wearing a cream button-down shirt and gray dress pants. She grins, gesturing for me to enter. "Welcome back, Miss Van Huusen."

Once inside, I begin to understand the value behind the obscene invoices. This isn't your typical government-funded nursing home. There's no smell of medicine or disinfectants. No sterile blue overhead lights and humming radiators. No overworked nurses running around with black under-eye bags and messy hair. I'd almost believe I've entered some sophisticated golf club or hotel lobby—with its limestone floors and runner rugs, fiddle-leaf figs stretching into the lofty ceilings—rather than a facility for the elderly.

The employee hands me a tablet. "If you could take a few seconds to sign in for us."

I take the tablet and work through the rudimentary questions, confirming I haven't been exposed to any illnesses in the past two weeks, and that I consent to be recorded by the surveillance cameras set up for security and quality-monitoring purposes. The last page is labeled: **NONDISCLOSURE AGREEMENT**. The bolded text makes me nervous, but I twist my lips into a smile since the employee is still hovering over me. I skim the hefty chunk of text. The agreement forbids me from releasing anything I may learn on Kennedy Nursing Home grounds, including information about the residents and staff members (among other scary stipulations buried in paragraphs of legalese). This place has some serious security. But it honestly feels a bit overboard. Who are they housing? The president?

After agreeing to everything, I hand the tablet back to the lady, who passes me on to a stout man with inky hair. "This way, Miss Van Huusen." He guides me out of the entrance building and into a large outdoor area at a brisk pace, short legs swishing back and forth, only slowing when we pass a resident, to whom he smiles and nods.

After clearing a line of hedges, we come to a courtyard, where some staff and seniors are gathered. I notice that the workers are mostly Hispanic or Asian, pushing around grouchy white people in shiny wheelchairs with breathing tubes stuffed up their noses, blankets and wool hats protecting them from the cold. It's disheartening to see their transparent, veiny skin and dried, puckered lips. Their eyes have sunk heavily into their sockets like they've been forcefully pushed in. Some are parked near a rotunda to sunbathe, mumbling to themselves. As I pass by, they trace my movement with milky irises.

One man in a wool coat catches my attention. I slow my speed, taking in his sloping features, heavily creased eyes, and silver hair, trying to understand the familiarity unspooling in my memory. And then it clicks. He's an actor—a famous one at that. Former action star in the aughts turned writer-director. He couldn't have been older than seventy, but he looks closer to triple digits. I guess the Hollywood machine really chews through people. But who knew he was here? Last I heard, he was in the middle of writing a new screenplay.

"Is that—" I start.

But the employee I'm following gestures toward the path. "Right this way." I realize he's less a guide, more a security guard whose job is to keep me from wandering.

Zipping my mouth shut, I follow him through the courtyard, glancing over my shoulder one last time at the actor. I can understand the NDA now. The residents here are more high profile than I thought.

"Here we are." He stops in front of a building numbered 4C.

Reading it makes me wince. I guess white people don't believe in four being a bad number. All I can think of is death.

He opens the door for me.

"Thanks."

"My pleasure." He shuts the door behind me.

Building 4C is less swanky than the main entrance, but it still has classy details. Dark wood banisters, warm lamps, tasteful landscape paintings adorning the walls. Soft spa music plays overhead and the air smells vaguely sweet. Two ladies wearing dark green scrubs sit behind the nurses' station, clacking at keyboards. They glance and smile at me before returning to their work with studious expressions.

The third room down the wide hall is labeled VAN HUUSEN. I open the heavy wooden door and step inside. The couple are lying in two separate hospital beds, each hooked up to a million beeping machines. Sterile air, a waft of metal and stale breath.

They look barely alive.

Dread calcifies in my chest as I slink closer to them. Their eyes are at half-mast, barren of soul. They have respirator masks on, mouths open with shallow breaths, red tongues dried to a dot. Their graying skin is dry and flaky like raised fish scales.

"Hello?" No reaction.

The air thins, a veneer of panic coating me. I wave a hand in front of Mr. Van Huusen. He doesn't react. I go to Mrs. Van Huusen. Wave. Nothing.

They can't see or hear me.

They're vegetables.

Their motionless bodies remind me of Chloe's corpse. I stumble away from their beds, hand cupping my mouth, pulse leaping. My teeth chatter as I slide against the wall. Every beep of their heart monitors sends needles of panic into my blood. I'm folding over myself when I remember there might be security cameras. Jolting straight, I smooth my sweaty palms against my coat and try to affect an air of normalcy. I don't want to alert any of the watchful staff with weird behavior. Glancing up at the ceiling, I spot three cameras with blinking red lights, and then I look back at the Van Huusens.

They must have been involved in a severe accident together. It's the only way I can rationalize how two able-bodied individuals have regressed to such a point within months. Being with their withering bodies disconcerts me, but I have a feeling something in this room will give me clues as to what happened to them. I can't leave before knowing, not when I came all this way.

I know I could ask the nurses out front, but I don't want to encourage suspicion with my questions. Searching the desks and cabinets, I attempt to locate a patient file or any source of information. After a few minutes, I find a tablet attached to Mr. Van Huusen's bedside. The only app on the home screen is branded by the nursing home. The app scans my face. An automated voice plays from the speakers over drone footage of the facility grounds, followed by an ensemble of colorful seniors in cardigans waving to the camera. "Welcome to Kennedy Nursing Home, where care is transparent and compassionate. Thank you, Chloe Van Huusen, for trusting us with your loved ones." Slightly unnerved by how the program says my name, I breathe a sigh of relief as the Van Huusens' patient files populate on the portal.

I click on the file labeled CHARLES VAN HUUSEN. There are several tabs, including notes on food and medication, treatment plans, patient room footage, and vital records, which are measured every hour. I navigate to Patient History first, scrolling down to the earliest date.

My lips part with shock as I read the cause of their coma. Patient was involved in a hit-and-run while walking with his wife in Bridgehampton. Despite immediate recovery by emergency services, accident resulted in serious bodily injuries, including complete paralysis below the hip and permanent brain damage. The rest of the file contains notes in complicated medical vernacular and surgery results. Margaret's patient history shows a similar story.

The medical files don't reveal what happened to the offender, so I google it, plugging in the location and date of the accident. The only report I can find is from a local newspaper, which anonymized the victims as "longtime residents" and mentioned "the driver remains unapprehended."

I can barely believe what I'm reading. A car accident, just like our birth parents. What are the chances? And I'm surprised at how little coverage there is considering Chloe's fame.

Nevertheless, I can understand why this incident would change my twin. It might have triggered unresolved traumas from our childhood. Sympathy flows through me, warming my chest. I hold Mr. Van Huusen's dry hand, hoping that even in his comatose state, he'll think his adoptive daughter is here to visit. Remembering that music helps stimulate the brain, I play some Wagner from my phone since the Van Huusens look like the type to enjoy classics. I return to the tablet, reading over the treatment logs. The nurses and physicians are incredibly thorough. Money really does buy the best care. Though perhaps the security cameras keep them on their toes. Since guardians have unrestricted access to footage, you wouldn't want to be caught slipping up.

Out of curiosity, I click into the recordings. The screen refreshes to live CCTV of the room. Seeing myself in an omniscient viewpoint is a bit off-putting, so I swipe to previous days' footage without delay. The app records every time someone enters the room, noting their name and title. I choose clips at random and watch nurses inject things into IV bags and measure vitals. After swiping around a bit, I see a category labeled Guest: CHLOE VAN HUUSEN.

Prior to this month, she dropped by weekly. Reviewing her footage is like watching another one of her vlogs. She often sat by the Van Huusens' bedside, gingerly applying salve to their dry skin. After a few clips, I realize I can unmute the videos. The tablet hums with music. Chloe played classics for her parents, just like I did. This small action lodges a seed of affection within me, and I feel more connected to my twin than I ever had before.

I continue watching her clips, scrolling down through the months, until I reach August, when the Van Huusens were first admitted. Chloe acts more frantic during this period, possibly since the accident was still fresh.

She paces around a lot, her shiny black ponytail swishing behind her small head, or curls up on the sofa, her face tucked into her knees, softly crying. I can barely watch these displays of vulnerability without wincing, suddenly guilty for prying, for sitting on a sofa that she had wept on before.

Soon, I'm on the oldest video, dated the same week the Van Huusens were admitted. She enters the room slowly, hesitant, staring at the Van Huusens' bodies for five minutes, frozen. And then she breaks, crumpling onto the floor with sobs so torrential that I turn down the volume, the razor-sharp wails harassing my ears as she stutters, "My fault, my fault. It's all my fault!"

What the hell?

I power off the tablet and rise from the couch, glancing at the coma-tose couple, my pulse throbbing with unease. Why did she think this was her fault? The first time she called, she'd said something similar. *Mistake, mistake.* Is this what she was talking about? Was she somehow involved in the hit-and-run?

The room spins, the walls closing in as my breaths grow shallow. I can't think about this here, not next to the Van Huusens' waxy bodies, their stale, salty aroma marinating in my nose, clogging my lungs. I need to get out. *Now.*

I rush out the door, avoiding eye contact with the nurses, and I feel thankful for all the NDAs they probably had to sign. I'm out of there quick, sprinting past the employee at the front, who asks me to sign out. I can't stay here another second.

When I'm a block away, I stop to catch my breath. The freezing air chills my throat and burns my cheeks.

Why would Chloe hide this? What happened in the car crash? Why was it her fault? Every little secret and lie is mounting inside me—her prescrip-tions, history of tantrums, and eventual overdose—a physical fortress that cannot be conquered. Is it all connected?

I fall onto the pavement, the cement cold against my jeans.

All I wanted was a new life as an influencer. And now . . . god, what did I get myself into?

30

I clench my teeth during the drive home to keep from crying out, not wanting to alert the driver. He repeatedly glances at me through the rearview mirror. I'm unsure if it's because he recognizes me, or if the small, anxious groans escaping my closed lips are worrying him. I can't help it: the car accident, Chloe's parents' vegetative states, what she said over the phone, *mistake*. Nothing makes sense. I'm on the brink of a panic attack, attempting to piece everything together. A few blocks away from my apartment, we get stuck in traffic.

"I'll get off here." I don't wait for the driver to respond as I tumble out of his car and race for my building so I can panic in peace. My vision is foggy with tears, blurring the pedestrian signals. As I run across an intersection, I almost get clipped by a biker, who swerves out of the way at the last second, skidding onto the road. He shouts obscenities at me, but I ignore him, sprinting for the door, fob gripped hard between sweaty fingers. In the lobby, Ramos is talking to a lady. When he sees me enter, he waves, but I don't acknowledge him, making a beeline for the elevators before spamming my finger on the button. My heart is racing, chest filled with so much pressure, I might explode.

I hear him calling for me. "Chloe!"

I'm shaking my foot, staring at the digital display that shows what levels the elevators are stopped at. The closest elevator is still twelve stories away.

"Chloe!"

I groan and spin toward him. "This isn't the time—"

It's a woman I don't recognize with stringy black hair, rosacea, and wide green eyes. She reaches a mittened hand out to hold my upper arm. "You okay, Chloe? I was calling out to you earlier. I don't think you heard me."

I almost let out a groan of exhaustion. The last thing I need is to expend energy faking in front of one of Chloe's friends. But I set my jaw and twist my lips into a smile. "My mind was somewhere else."

"I'm sorry if I surprised you by visiting your apartment. But I'm just a little concerned after your last text. I tried to reply to you, but . . . I think you blocked me?"

Fuck. It's Jessica Peters. I choke on the alarm crystallizing in my throat and start coughing nervously. She pats my back, but I pivot out from her touch. "Why are you here? I told you I don't want to continue with the story." My words come out fast, anxious. I glance up at the display. The closest elevator is still five stories away.

She tilts her head, lacing her brows. "I know, but I just need to know why you want to stop. You've been trying to get someone to cover your story for months. But now I stick my neck out for you, and you suddenly back out? I'm just worried. I *know* how important this story was for you."

The elevator dings behind me, the doors opening. "I-I just can't. I can't, okay? Please. *Please* just leave me the fuck alone." I back into the elevator, press the button for twenty-seven. When she sticks her arm out to stop the door from closing, I shout, "Ramos! This lady is harassing me! Please help! *Right now!*"

I hear his urgent, clunking steps. Jessica reels back her arms, eyes wide with shock. But then she meets my desperate expression. Sighing, she shakes her head, despondent. "Okay. Fine. I understand. I'm sorry, I'll leave you alone. But Chloe—" The elevator doors shut, muffling her words.

As soon as I'm inside my apartment, I throw off my coat and scream at the top of my lungs, every muscle overwhelmed. Why the hell did Jessica come all the way here? What type of story was Chloe trying to tell? And how did it relate to the Van Huusens? I've spent the entire day trying to grasp at answers, but all I've been able to hold on to is the dreadful feeling that everything is wrong. I'm in over my head, drowning.

Exhausted, I lie on the floor like a fish out of water, gulping in desperate breaths as frustrated tears leak out of my eyes. At a loss for what to do, I take my phone out to scroll and help me cope when I get jump-scared by my own reflection in the black mirror. I'm a mess. Mascara running down my cheeks, eyes red and nasty. But wait . . .

I crawl to the window, where the lighting makes my skin look flawless, and snap a selfie, Facetune my nose smaller, and upload it as a story with the text: Not every day can be a good day #authentic #sad #anxiety #grief #mentalhealthawareness.

In seconds, concerned DMs slide in.

We love you!

Thank you for being so authentic.

You still look so beautiful.

Which mascara is that so I know not to buy it?

We're here for you!

The adoring support of my community never fails to fulfill me. They are the crutches that keep me standing. I'm not alone anymore—never will be again. I stay by the window for an hour, opening every DM, soaking in their sympathy, filling myself up until I'm somewhat whole again. It's such a beautiful escape. Before I know it, the issue of the Van Huusens and Jessica are pushed to the back of my mind. Chloe saying *mistake* was probably nothing, some form of grief manifesting in self-reproach. Survivor's guilt? Possibly, if she were in her last moments. Maybe Chloe had wanted Jessica to pen an article on her experience with grief after the accident. Jessica had mentioned that no one wanted Chloe's story. Maybe what my twin had to say was boring, overdone. Ever since capitalizing on mental health struggles became a profitable thing to do, grief manifestos are a dime a dozen. Sure, the story was important to Chloe, but everyone believes their own story is important. Unfortunately for my twin, she's lost her chance to tell all.

The more I think about it, the more that makes sense. Sometimes, the solution is the simplest answer. I need to think positive. With the Van Huusens out of the picture, my aunt on my payroll, and Jessica blocked from my life, there's no one else to call me out.

Things are fine—great, in fact.

I change into loungewear and throw my dirty linens in the washer. As I'm picking up my jacket, which I flung at the entrance during my burst of panic, I notice a purple envelope scented with lemons and neroli beneath it. Hand-inked cursive coils on the front: *Chloe.*

I drop my jacket and retrieve the letter, excitement spiking. This must be Bella Marie's gift. I had almost forgotten about it with everything else that's happened.

I'm about to rip it open when I think better of it. I can tell the envelope is expensive. Heavyweight, crafted with a blend of linen and mermaid tears. I love how Bella Marie kept it traditional with paper letters. I imagine her making these by large French windows. Sheer white curtains rippling in the breeze, golden rays crisscrossing her pale skin. She's writing on a large wooden desk, an antique of some sort, a candle lit in the corner, a vase of petunias and peonies beside her. Her stationery is in a neat pile next to a vintage typewriter and a butterfly just so happens to flutter into the flower-scented room. Calligraphy pen in hand, she scratches my name onto the card with a smile on her pink lips. As she stuffs the card in the envelope, she spritzes it with the smallest puff of perfume.

I press the invitation to my chest, delighted, inhaling its scent.

Using a butter knife, I gingerly peel open the flap and pull out what's inside. It's nondescript. White card stock with black calligraphy. A dried pink carnation is wax-sealed onto the back. When I flip open the card, chills ripple down my spine.

Chloe, you are cordially invited to the annual island retreat on June 9-16. If you'd like to RSVP, please post a photo within one fortnight featuring this invitation in the background. Remember to keep this event close to your heart. This is a special time shared with only our family
Yours, Bella Marie Melniburg

I bite my lip, my heart pattering with excitement. I don't know how long a fortnight is and I can't be bothered to look it up. My calendar is already cleared for June and every ounce of me wants to go. I don't even have to think.

I'm about to post a selfie when I realize I look like a mess. Deciding otherwise, I rearrange the coffee table toward the windows and assemble different pieces from my apartment to create the perfect still image. A vase of white lilies in full bloom. A Le Labo candle stacked on top of several *Kinfolk* magazines. A glass of white wine. A gold catch-all with some rings and a draping mother-of-pearl necklace. *The Secret History* by Donna Tartt. I didn't know Chloe liked to read and I have no idea what the book is about, but the cover matches the beige aesthetic of the photo. I stick a bookmark in the middle to make a convincing case that I'm actually reading the novel. And lastly, I inconspicuously place the invitation in the top right corner of the frame.

The sun is setting. A golden glow blankets the New York sky. I take a burst of photos and select one that frames everything perfectly. The lighting is so good, shadows so crisp, I don't even have to filter it. I post it on Instagram with the caption How do you cope when life tosses you a challenge? I like to curl up with my favorite book. #selfcare

Bella Marie likes the post after five minutes. My heart skips. She's seen it. I've confirmed my RSVP through a secret language, a game only understood by the inner circle. It makes my heart grow warm, this feeling of belonging.

June can't come soon enough.

———

Throughout the week, RSVPs spill in. Most of them have the invitation in the background during a sponsored post or a vlog. But some were a bit more creative.

Iz posts a picnic spread. Red-and-white gingham blanket, wicker basket, charcuterie board, and a peach cobbler. The little card is tucked beneath a plate, a perfect prop to the whole arrangement. The caption: It's never too cold to enjoy a picnic. Break out that blanket and set yourself up for some fun by having a picnic indoors!

That same day, she hand-delivers a tray of her peach cobbler to me. I'm so delighted at her presence that I invite her inside for some tea.

"What's the trip like?" she asks between sips of orange pekoe. "I asked a few of the other ladies, but they kept dodging my questions. It's kinda weird."

I swallow my tea. It singes my throat. I've noticed how the girls keep avoiding my questions as well. It's frustrating to be in the dark.

"Bella Marie likes to keep things low-key." I hope it sounds legit, though my voice is unsteady. "I can't say too much since it'll spoil the surprise."

"Ugh, I hate surprises. Y'all are too tight-lipped, it's torturing me. Please, I'm begging, give me some hints." She's too desperate for me not to throw her a bone. I don't want her to resent me.

I parrot what forum dwellers have speculated: "Beaches. Ocean. Sun. Rich-people shit. You'll love it."

She blows a slow breath out. "I hope I do. I'm paying a lot of money to have someone watch the kids for a whole week."

The guilt from lying builds in my chest until I make an excuse to get her out of the apartment. She leaves with grace, of course, and my space smells like her for the next hour. Vanilla, peaches, and sugar.

Angelique's RSVP comes last.

The invitation is on the table next to—of all things—an ultrasound to announce her pregnancy. Caption: This little muffin says peekaboo from the oven! Sommer and I are so excited for this new chapter in our lives, and most importantly, to share it all with you. Please join me in my venture into forming life and everything motherhood brings. (Hopefully more desserts!)

She received half a million likes in less than five hours, gained 20K followers, and her comments are flooded with congratulations from verified accounts.

I comment: Congrats!! I am so thrilled for you!!

Delight blooms in my chest when I notice my reply is nestled between comments left by other Belladonnas.

Sophia: Does this mean I'll be an aunt? Congratulations!
Maya: I can't think of a more deserving couple.

Ana: Roses are red, Violets are blue, I love your unborn baby as much as you!!!!!!!!!

Emmeline: The most beautiful family. Congratulations.

Iz: YOU WILL BE THE BEST MOTHER EVER.

Kelly: I am so, so, so happy for you!

Lily: Congrats! I can't wait for our playdates in a few years!

Bella Marie:

31

Belle by Bella Marie launches on the first day of spring. It's an instant hit. I'm not surprised. For the past few weeks, buzz about the brand has reached a crescendo. Keeping the fashion show low-key created mystique and encouraged speculation, which was especially effective since most influencers force their brands in everyone's faces. Her strategy convinced audiences she didn't want to *sell* the products, but that the brand was truly a project of love, of art.

The only press release she did was an interview for *Vogue*—a double spread of her in her brand's figure-hugging lilac dress, which was borderline angelic. In it, she spilled key details about the brand: everything is ethically sourced, female-run, climate-friendly, plastic-free, organic, sustainable, made with net-zero carbon emissions, and is inclusive of every body size: XXXS to XXXXL. Ten percent of all profits will go to endometriosis research.

Once the gates open to the public, everyone clamors, desperate for a peek inside the prestigious club led by the internet's favorite it-girl. Followers are so desperate to buy and support Bella Marie, the website crashes an hour after launch, which only adds to the hype.

Her clothes aren't cheap: $100 for a heavyweight cotton T-shirt made in Italy; $780 for a Belgian wool sweater. Don't even get me started about the dresses made of hand-spun silk.

Before I was Chloe, I could only dream of slipping on these clothes. Now I have the entire collection, since I'm one of the select influencers with early access.

I take pictures for my Instagram feed and make a series of short-form videos unboxing and styling different outfits, tagging the brand and Bella Marie herself.

In a swell of gratitude and admiration, I end up scrolling on Bella Marie's account. Her content is so picturesque, I don't realize I've scrolled all the way back to December. A certain post catches my attention. The photo is of a sunset, strips of pink and orange sky, dark blue sea. The caption: You'll think you're enjoying calm seas, slow waves, open shore, but really, it's the world pulling back, preparing for a tsunami. I've recently been confronted with a tsunami of my own. But it's important to take it in stride, to be grateful and to look forward. Any adversity thrown your way is simply the world's method of guiding you in the right direction. Comments are restricted.

I wonder what happened.

I get a notification that the official Belle by Bella Marie account has reposted my TikTok try-on. Within a few minutes, I gain a few hundred followers. I open the clothing site and find that every single piece is now sold out or on preorder.

I'm so inspired by the success of her launch that I daydream of starting my own brand. The Asian skincare market is hot right now. I've even seen some Western brands cosplaying as Asian through disingenuous marketing, tricking consumers into thinking they're buying products from Korea or Japan. If I play my cards right, I might be able to exploit this growing obsession with Asia.

I message Bella Marie about how she got started with her brand, hoping for some sage advice. She doesn't reply. I guess that's a given. She must be busy with the launch.

After some research and reaching out to Maya, the beauty guru Belladonna who recently launched her makeup line, One Drop, I'm connected with a company that has helped several influencers start successful projects. I send them a query of my ideas, my dreams, going into detail about what I want to make: green tea serums, face masks marketed to look like spring roll paper, cherry blossom lip balms. The ideas flow out of me. Anything is feasible now that I'm Chloe.

They reply after a day, and we set up a meeting a week later, during which I hear nothing but *Yes!* But then they get into the costs, the investments. My eyes widen at the numbers casually thrown my way. I didn't know starting a company was so expensive. I'm hopeful it's still possible.

I consult my accountant.

"Sure, you should have enough funds," he says.

"Seriously? Oh my god, I have so many ideas—"

"You've been diverting twenty grand a month to your savings, so in a few months you should have the necessary capital."

My heart drops. That was the money I'd put aside for my aunt. "I can't use that money. Aside from that, I still have enough . . . right?"

There's a moment of silence. "It will be tough." From his tone, I can tell it's closer to *impossible.* "You could always look into external investors."

"I'll think about it." I hang up.

The reminder of my aunt drains me. Why is she always there to knock me down?

As if on cue, she sends me a text: I'm going to the bank next week. Then she attaches a fifteen-second clip of me admitting to impersonating Chloe.

I scrub the chat history, throw my phone across the room, shattering a vase, and scream. She's a daunting reminder of my past life, the only thing that's holding me back from flourishing, from truly achieving my dreams.

I wish she would leave me alone. I wish I could cut her off somehow.

But I can't. She has me on a leash.

I email the company to cancel our next meeting.

The next morning, I clean up the broken vase, head to the bank, and send my aunt her monthly installment.

32

I'm in my element.

I adapt to Chloe's career like it's always been mine. Making videos is second nature. Taking photos is a breeze. I could write captions without thinking and email brands with my eyes closed.

I didn't know it would all come to me so fast, so easily. Maybe it's because I've spent most of my life absorbing Chloe's content through screens. I've intuitively picked up the nuances of daily vlogs, how to narrate my life in front of a camera, the gimmicks to boost engagement. And if I ever get lost, I can easily outsource. Stuck editing a video? Hire an editor. Running out of ideas? Hire a creative team. Too tired to clean my apartment? Hire a maid. The costs associated with their employment are nothing compared to the money they help me generate.

This is not to say I have it easy. Influencing is like running a 24/7 QVC where I'm the sole spokesperson. I've had to commodify every aspect of my life for profit, tailor my routine for sponsorships and sales. If I'm not posting or filming, I capitalize on seemingly mundane activities by going live. At exactly seven-thirty a.m., I stream myself getting ready for the morning. At nine-thirty p.m., I broadcast myself winding down. Fans will flood my lives and we'll start and end the day together as if we're roommates. Sometimes, I'll even have lunch with them. I've become a safe third place, their ever-present online bestie. A group of lonely followers have even coined themselves the *Chloe Crew* and have become my most valiant supporters. I know some of them by name because of how often they show up or send me donations.

During my rare offline moments, I'm constantly working to improve myself so I can maintain Chloe's happy, healthy brand. I've become an exercise fiend. Every day, I post an Instagram story of my body in a dimly lit exercise room that accentuates my #bodygoals. (I've grown my male audience this way too.) I've gotten my first injection of Botox, which makes me a certified influencer. Barely ten units, just enough to slow down the wrinkling between my brows and forehead, and not enough to make my face look frozen. The type of treatment celebrities get to convince fans they're still natural. The doctor at the clinic almost persuaded me to get lip filler but I declined. Changing too much of my face will tarnish my authenticity.

On the business end, I've rectified Chloe's habit of rejecting sponsorships left and right. Sure, I don't take every sponsor that lands in my lap—that would make me a sellout—I'm just slightly less discerning. In my defense, I have extortion to pay. My aunt's threats are as regular and irritable as my period, and with her egregious interest rate, I'm barely making headway. Every time I receive a sponsor payout that should make my eyes glitter, I have to confront the fact she'll snatch part of it. It's like paying dues to the devil. Worse yet, I have this nagging feeling that even if I do manage to pay her off, she'll continue demanding more, that as long as I live as Chloe, she'll never let me go.

It's the price of my crime.

To make sure I get her payments on time, I've taken a lucrative, ongoing (low-key) sponsorship with this sleep gummy company, SLEEPY BEARS. They're scarily effective. Sometimes, my alarm has trouble waking me up if I chew two before bedtime. Not a single nightmare, either, which is a blessing. As much as positive affirmations helped curb my initial dreams of Chloe, meeting the dying Van Huusens shocked horrors back into my slumber. If it wasn't for SLEEPY BEARS I'd be a straight-up insomniac. I'm not kidding—these tiny lavender-flavored gummies hit like hardcore drugs . . . probably because they are. They're not FDA-approved or government-regulated, which is why I can't outright say I'm sponsoring them. I have to inconspicuously slip the product in mid-vlog or during a wind-down livestream. But hey, money is money.

I also put a moratorium on impulse purchases once I realized PR can fill the hole of online shopping. Every day, I've been receiving at least three boxes of free shit from random brands. Sometimes, the sheer quantity becomes so daunting, I let them pile up in my living room. Once the sight of free stuff becomes too burdensome, I'll film a PR unboxing to capitalize on the effort it takes to organize them. Fiona and I stack the boxes behind me so it looks like I'm in a cardboard fort, me a cute little princess in a brown castle. I pull out packages from behind me like Tetris, an added point of tension for the viewer: *Will my tower of excessive consumption crush me today?* Then I unbox pounds and pounds of sunscreens, face washes, entire foundation lines, body lotions, serums, essences. Hair oils, body oils, tanning oils. Shirts, dresses, jeans, sunglasses, hats. Some companies even send giant boxes the size and weight of my torso only for it to be an elaborate display for one teeny tiny product: a gacha machine fit with working electronics to advertise a brown eyeliner; a box filled with balloons that rise into the air for one bar of soap; a thirty-pound package containing a beach chair, sun hat, and flip-flops for a new coconut-scented body lotion.

The last PR unboxing I filmed went on for eight hours. I'm not kidding. EIGHT hours of cutting open packages, throwing away foam packing peanuts, paper worms, bubble wrap, and excavating the little plastic jars inside. It's hard work. People don't see the effort that goes behind a snappy thirty-minute unboxing vid. By the end of it, my apartment was cluttered with so much trash, it reminded me of those rivers in developing countries that are clogged with plastic bags and green Sprite bottles. Sad. Oh well.

Because I'm so gracious, I donate or host giveaways to get rid of most of the junk. Sometimes, when I get too tired of receiving free things, I'll let Ramos keep the box for his daughter.

On the rare occasion I want something that I'm not on a PR list for, I'll simply send an email with a promise of exposure and the products will be on my doorstep in days. (And unlike many influencers, I'll actually post about the product after receiving it!) I haven't paid for anything for the past month.

I finally understand what people mean when they say the rich keep getting richer.

And I love it.

Let's take a second to be honest here. Cultivate a safe space. Let down our walls and expose the truest, darkest, cruelest parts of our souls. I'm about to bestow a truth that may be hard to swallow: anyone would want to be me. Who wants to pay for shit when you can get it for free? I'm not going to sit here and pretend like I hate the money and attention. Creators who are "down-to-earth" and reject capitalism are nothing more than hypocrites shilling out so-called socialist viewpoints from their mega-mansions or sky-high penthouses. They don't give a fuck. If they did, they'd donate all their money and live in a shitty studio apartment instead of being professional grifters with golden egos. And those who hate this lifestyle are nothing more than envious wannabes. If they had access to my life for one day, they'd cease their righteous comments, standing on their little soapboxes like they're better than me just because they're poor, hateful little internet gremlins. Shit like how I'm being wasteful, ungrateful, privileged, and tone-deaf. Boo-hoo. Who the fuck cares? How about you actually work and get to my level instead of complaining all the time?

And it's not like I'm the worst. Out of the major influencers, I'm at the bottom of the food chain. Imagine what the people in the double or triple millions are doing. At least I'm not running crypto-scams or filming dead bodies in suicide forests or dancing for TikTok in front of Auschwitz. I haven't killed anyone or started any fires or groomed any of my fans. If anything, I save people with my content. My followers literally tell me that every single day: Your livestreams keep me going. They saved me during my darkest times because there's always something to look forward to in the morning.

Hear that? I save lives.

So, in the grand scheme of things, I'm a good person.

A great fucking person.

Everyone in my Chloe Crew tells me so.

33

Something is wrong.

Engagement is sagging. I want to blame it on the algorithm, but I'm not sure if that's true.

A growing portion of my audience says that I don't feel like Chloe anymore. That something about me has changed. That my vibe is different. That I'm less authentic. That they're unsubscribing.

It's fucking bullshit. If only they could see how hard I work behind the scenes to keep up the façade, all the hours I've spent watching Chloe's old videos to replicate her mannerisms. It's not easy emulating a boring lifestyle vlogger with a vanilla personality and a permanent smile. Yet all people do is complain, complain, complain.

At first, I could ignore these comments, shrug them off as trolls.

But then Fiona sends me a link to a video this morning: Have you seen this?

It's a YouTube video made by Samantha, an ex-fan. The Dirty Truth About Chloe Van Huusen. It's an hour and ten minutes long.

Samantha has 1.2K followers. The video has been up for five days and its only garnered a meager 10K views. But the reach isn't what bothers me. It's the content.

The video starts with Samantha telling pleasant stories of how she used to be my biggest fan, buying all my collabs and attending my meet and greets at VidCon. But what follows is a forty-minute psychotic manifesto detailing how I've changed in the past few months. How I've become shallow and obsessed with sponsorship opportunities. How I seem less authentic. How I even *sound* different.

But here's the kicker: during the last twenty minutes, she makes the outrageous claim that I'm actually Julie Chan. Her proof? A deep analysis of *Finding My Long-Lost Twin and Buying Her a House #EMOTIONAL*, where she examines each second of the video, frame-by-frame like a fucking stalker, pointing out all our differences. Like how Chloe had a tiny birthmark on her right arm. How my nose is slightly bigger. How our teeth are different. Chloe had nice gums and a straight smile, while I had an underbite (which I'm fixing). How I pronounce certain vowels weirdly, drawing out the sounds. Or how I say *like* more than Chloe ever did and am less articulate in general—which is elitist as fuck.

Most of the comments seem to agree that the video, while entertaining, is a stretch. Akin to those Avril Lavigne clone conspiracies. That no one is sociopathic enough to switch lives with their twin, and that if it were true, I would have been caught already. But there are enough comments agreeing with Samantha that my mind tumbles into dark places.

How did she find out the truth? Did Auntie or Patrick contact her? I wouldn't put it past them. They always take me down at my lowest point. Maybe this is a threat, a precursor to asking for more blackmail money.

I text Patrick: Do you know Samantha? Is it you?

He replies within a second, always on his phone: Send me $1K and I'll let you know. I'm trying to get a new chara on Genshin. The gacha is fucked.

I text: fuck u. And send him the money.

He replies: I've never heard of Samantha. Should I?

As much as Patrick is scum, there's no reason for him to lie about this. It doesn't benefit him or my aunt if I get caught.

But this means Samantha came up with these conclusions organically. This isn't good.

A few weeks ago, I would have clambered to the bathroom and curled up in a ball to hyperventilate, but my time as Chloe has changed me. The exercise, positive affirmations, social safety nets, and community have given me an intrinsic sense of confidence and control.

I close my eyes, take a breath, and feel the earth beneath my feet, propping me up.

When I open my eyes, I come up with a plan of attack to discredit this idiotic theory before it grows legs. I can't call out Samantha directly. I've been on the internet long enough to know about the Streisand effect. The more I bring attention to it, the more I'm fanning the flames.

I need to be rational and methodical. Drive awareness without naming her specifically.

I decide to address the video on Instagram live, since those who tune in are usually my most loyal fans. Sitting on my kitchen floor, where I look the most distraught and vulnerable, I paint blush around my eyes and rub them hard so they look bloodshot.

Then it begins.

My Chloe Crew trickle in. I pretend to want to converse with them by teasing future video ideas and giving birthday shout-outs.

The whole time, I'm waiting for an inevitable comment about my appearance. And then I get it.

You look sad today. Are you okay?

I jump at the opportunity.

I read the comment aloud like I accidentally saw it. Pause, for dramatic effect. Sniffle and rub my eyes. "Honestly, guys . . . it's been a really tough time for me."

The love showers in.

Omg? Are you okay?

We love you Chloe! Everything will be all right!

"I've seen a really, really hurtful video this week . . . I understand that some of you feel like I've changed," I say, to my eight thousand viewers, "and that's because I have. Grief is something that changes someone from the inside out. You can't compare the Chloe I was before Julie's death to the Chloe I am now. I-I even saw this video . . ." I duck out of the frame and drop saline into my eyes, heave a few breaths. "This video, you guys . . . it was, like, really mean. Like, *vicious*. The person was claiming that Julie took my identity." I shake my head again, distraught. "I don't know what type of sick, sick person would ever say that. How could someone ever accuse my sister of doing something so heinous?"

I sigh, like I'm making a confession, like it's hard to go on. "I guess what I'm trying to say is . . . I'm not just a face behind a screen. I'm a real person. I can read comments and watch videos. And words affect me. *Hurt* me. If you feel like I've changed and you don't like me anymore, that's your prerogative. You can always unfollow me. But there's no need to send hate or make such distasteful videos. Especially not about someone as innocent as my twin."

Omg! Don't cry!
Are you talking about that video from Samantha?
Can someone DM me a link?
Is this about Samantha?
You still look stunning!
I love you Chloe!
You are so pretty even when you're crying. I love how authentic you are!

Hearts cloud up on the corner of the screen from likes.
The Belladonna group chat goes crazy.

Ana: I can't believe someone would make such a terrible video.
Kelly: ugh. Even I think it's gross.
Lily: Call me if you ever need some support.
Iz: my heart breaks for you.
Maya: Some people are so psycho.
Emmeline: I'm so sad for you, Chloe. Remember we are here. We are family!
Angelique: That video is so disgusting. I made a story in support of you. I think we all should do the same.
Sophia: Good idea!

Ten minutes later, eight of the Belladonnas—such angels—have posted a story in support of me, defending my actions and publicly shaming an unnamed content creator who hurt my feelings. (Bella Marie has been silent. She's away in Norway. She's probably too busy.) But the internet isn't stupid. Subtlety doesn't exist in social media. Everyone knows exactly who I was talking about and my Chloe Crew love me enough to blindly bombard Samantha's comments.

By the next morning, Samantha takes down the video and sends me a DM apologizing, saying she feels terrible, that she never meant to hurt me.

I don't feel bad at all. This is what you get for cyberbullying someone.

I leave the message on read for three days until she has to private all her accounts. Then I send her a reply: Thank you for reaching out. I know it's not easy to apologize, even when we do something wrong. If you are ever feeling depressed from this situation, feel free to use my link for one free therapy session at BetterTherapy. Love, Chloe V.

34

'm rotting on my couch nursing a period cramp with a hot water bottle. It's good timing, though. This means I'll have a fresh uterus, bloat-, blood-, and pain-free during the trip.

I'm reviewing the posts I've prescheduled when I hear someone stop in front of my door. A shadow casts through the gap. Lingers. One, two, three . . . ten seconds. I stare at the shadow, waiting for it to go away. Who is that? Why aren't they making a noise? I sit straighter, heart thumping. A parasocial fan? A stalker?

A letter slides under the door.

My nerves are displaced by excitement as I pounce for the message from Bella Marie. For the past few weeks, she's been dropping off letters regularly, but I've never seen the delivery in real time.

Each letter is personalized with her stylish calligraphy, a dried flower attached to the heavy card. Baby's breath. Bluebells. Forget-me-nots. The messages are little hints about the trip. Teasers. I feel like a kid putting together clues in a scavenger hunt.

Chloe, reminder: avoid chemical peels in the month of May.
Hugs, Bella Marie

Chloe, remember to check your passport expiration!
Love, Bella Marie

Chloe, I hope you banked some videos and have scheduled your daily
posts and stories. No posting while we are on vacation! To reconnect,
we must disconnect.
Xoxo, Bella Marie

This time, it's white chrysanthemum. My whole apartment swells with its sharp, musty scent and I become dizzy with nausea. A memory returns: a bushel of white chrysanthemums and lilies—Chinese funeral flowers—next to two caskets, pictures of my parents hanging above, their faces blurry.

I shake the memory out of my head and toss the chrysanthemum in the trash, but the feeling of being watched, exposed, remains.

I pull out the letter.

Chloe, our time together is only a week away. Pack lightly!
Everything you need will be provided. Pickup is at 9PM on June 9.
Yours, Bella Marie

Letter in hand, I stare at the two heavy-duty suitcases sprawled haphazardly on the floor, a hill of clothing climbing out of their compartments. For the past month, I've been excitedly packing items I thought I'd need. I decide to restart after this message. I'll look like a brute with my giant suitcases if everyone brings dainty Rimowas. I look around for Chloe's carry-on but can't find it. I send Fiona a text.

She replies: Apartment storage. Parking level. Compartment 13.

She's a godsend. I make a trip underground. Tires squeak against concrete in the distance. A light flickers on as I enter the storage unit. It smells grimy, like stale water, dust, and metal. Chloe's compartment is at the far end. Her carry-on is stacked on top of a few storage boxes. It's a fancy beige hard shell, very minimalistic, very Chloe. I try my luck with the keys on my key chain and unlock the storage compartment on the first try. The metal cage creaks, scratching against concrete as I swing open the gate. I pull out the luggage and it thuds onto the floor. Objects audibly jostle inside. A combination padlock keeps me from its contents. Four digits. I take a wild guess—our birthday. 0620. It unlocks.

Thank god Chloe was a narcissist.

I pull the zippers to see what's inside.

Dozens of worn-down books—no, *journals*.

Jackpot.

35

I dump the journals on my apartment floor. All Moleskines.

Chloe had written the month and year on each journal's title page, the earliest being from 2010, when she wrote exclusively in pink gel pen and bubbly cursive. We would have been eleven—the start of middle school.

I dive in, excited to unearth the lore of her life. Details on her history will help my impersonation—which is especially important for this upcoming trip, when I'll be surrounded by Chloe's peers. It's the last place I'd want my secret to be uncovered.

The first page of her 2010 journal: *WARNING! This is the private journal of Chloe Van Huusen. If you are not Chloe, stop—*

I flip to the next page.

September 3, 2010
I feel stupid writing this. But Mom and Dad gave this to me so I have to use it or I'll feel bad. What am I even supposed to write here? It'll just be pages and pages of me waking up, going to school, eating dinner.

What follows are pages and pages of her waking up, going to school, eating dinner. Pretty boring. Sometimes she fawns over her crushes, *James, Michael, Callum,* scribbling their names in big bubble letters and swirly hearts, playing M.A.S.H. in the margins. Somehow, she always ends up with a limo and a mansion. Even silly games favor her fortune.

The kernels of drama come from her entries about the Van Huusens. Chloe writes of how she pushes herself to be a perfect child, not to disappoint them, and how she doesn't like going to family functions since her extended family never hides the fact that she's not a *real* Van Huusen. Though the Van Huusens provide a comfortable life, she confesses, *I wish I loved them more. I wish they'd love me more.*

It's a bit sad, really.

July 6, 2011
Mom and Dad are taking me to the Hamptons again. I know I shouldn't be complaining about a vacation, but every time I go, I'm bored out of my mind. None of my cousins seem to like me that much. It's so embarrassing when one of the aunts forces them to play with me. I'd rather they leave me alone.

Lately, I've been thinking more about my birth family. My twin. I wonder if she thinks about me. I wish we were adopted together so I don't have to be here by myself.

This was the only mention of me in the journal. It's not until 2014, a few journals later, that I'm mentioned again.

October 12, 2014
I found out more about my twin, Julie. I had to beg Mom and Dad.

She's living with our aunt. I wonder what her life is like. I want to meet her and talk to her. I want to be her friend.

Chloe wanted to be my friend. A genuine friend. Not just a prop for some YouTube video. When did that change?

October 15, 2014
I keep thinking of my twin. I can't stop. I'm jealous that she gets to live with real family. I wonder if she has photos of our birth parents in our aunt's

*home. I can't even remember what they look like. I wish I could meet Julie,
but Mom and Dad say it's difficult since they don't know where she lives.
That's bullshit. I'm sure they can hire a private investigator. They've done it
before when Aunt Caroline's husband was cheating on her. Why can't they do
it for me?*

I wonder how Chloe would have fared if she was raised by my aunt.
She'd always been the darling child. Maybe Auntie would have loved her.
Or maybe her self-esteem would have been dismantled like mine, maybe she
would have been hounded until she felt useless, stripped of all self-worth.

Soon, I'm enraptured by the journals. I read everything: cringe depression poems, to-do lists, manifestation entries, food tracking (a lot of
black coffee and salad, very little of anything else), privileged-kid rants.
With every new entry, I'm peeling back a layer of Chloe, creeping closer
to who she truly was. By 2015, she was sixteen and had started a YouTube
channel because she was bored and predictably lonely. She documents how
she felt when she got her first hundred subscribers: *I THINK I'M LITERALLY
ABOUT TO DIE FROM EXCITEMENT.*

When she gets to 10K, I'm mentioned.

*April 5, 2017
I can't believe it. 10,000 followers!! What!?!?!?!?!?!?! I'm about to pass out.
And in a few months, I'll be at college. I've already thought of a thousand
video ideas. Tips on how to decorate your dorm, study guides, etc., etc.*

*I wonder if Julie is following me. I'd imagine it'd be weird if she stumbled
onto a video of a girl that looks just like her. Or maybe we don't look alike
anymore. Twins can grow up to look different. Something about epigenetics
and our environment. We might look like complete strangers.*

There are more entries about her YouTube and social media journey.
From her first AdSense check to her first major sponsorship to being
recognized in the street. The Van Huusens make sparse appearances, only
being mentioned after they had a tense family dinner together.

My parents think being an influencer is not a real job and that I should focus on getting into law school. They never say it out loud, but I can tell they're embarrassed by me. They think I'm making a fool of myself for everyone to see. They'll never understand the lucrative potential of this career or how serious I am about my future. Maybe I shouldn't be surprised. They're so old they still use the fax machine. They don't understand the internet like I do.

It's in January when Chloe meets Bella Marie.

January 6, 2018
I've been invited to my first brand event ever!! The event is hosted by Bella Marie!!! OMG. She has over 15mil followers. I can't believe I'll get to meet her. I hope she likes me. I'm freaking out. I don't know what to do!!! I've asked my roommate to style me since she's in fashion school. She put together this super chic outfit with a blazer and turtleneck. I feel so profesh.
    Update from after the event: I spoke to Bella Marie. Actually. That's a lie. I sat beside her awkwardly, scared to talk to her, but then she turned her head and spoke to me. ME! I honestly can't remember what I said. Probably something embarrassing since I was freaking out. She asked me so many questions. I think I told her about Julie and our birth parents??? Why did I do that? What is wrong with me? I can't believe I said that stuff to Bella Marie. I wish I had a time machine.

January 7, 2018
BELLA MARIE FOLLOWED ME BACK ON INSTAGRAM. OH MY GOD!!!!

This is followed by her scribbling *Bella Marie will be my friend* a hundred times as a manifestation exercise.

After that day, they began exchanging DMs. Bella Marie invited her to several dinners and brunches. She got acquainted with the other Belladonnas, who at that time were only Emmeline, Kelly, Lily, and Ana. Then, one spring day:

March 20, 2018
I think Bella Marie just invited me on a trip with her? I had my roommate read
the invitation to make sure I'm not hallucinating. OH MY GOD.

During May, she's preoccupied with preparing for the trip. Getting
waxes, a manicure, planning outfits days ahead. I'm struck by how similar
we are. I did the exact same thing.

But then, June arrives.

June 8, 2018
Someone sent me the grossest email today. It linked to an old article back
in 2003 about Mom and Dad saying racist shit during a conference. The
anonymous sender said they only adopted me because they were trying to cover
their asses. I blocked them immediately. Why the hell would anyone send that
to me? Mom and Dad would never.

The next day:

I think I want to die.
I asked them about the article.
It's true.
Well, they didn't say it outright, but I could just tell. They're so
obvious. They asked: "Where did you hear about this?" instead of just
denying it.
My life has been a farce. A fucking charade. No wonder they never felt
like family. I was only ever a bargaining chip. A Chinese child to attract
Chinese investors.
I feel like such a fool. I want to fucking jump off a building. Push them
off too.
I don't think I can ever forgive them. I wish they'd never adopted me. I
wish they didn't exist.
I'm so glad I have this trip—it's the thing I need. To be away from all of
this. Bella Marie is picking me up tonight. I need to focus on this.

I'm gagged. So that random conspiracy theory I read was true? Only white people would think of adopting a whole-ass kid to pretend they aren't racist. This is so crazy. I almost feel bad for Chloe.

I flip to the next page, eager to know more about the trip, the part I've been wanting to read about the whole time.

It's blank.

"The fuck?"

I leaf back and forth as if I missed a secret section, or a page got glued together. I check the seams—maybe something got ripped out—but no, the rest of the journal is untouched. Brand-new.

That was the last entry.

"You have to be kidding me!" I chuck the journal hard against my windows. The pages flutter onto the ground. I sprint to the elevators, back down to storage, and search through every box. There must be more. There must be more. There must be more!

Nothing.

The journal entries end right before she gets picked up. Nothing about the trip. Nothing about what happened with Chloe and her parents. Nothing about the car crash. Nothing about meeting me.

She stopped journaling completely. A daily habit for seven years. Ceased.

I'm out of breath from my manic search. Filled with rage, I tilt my head to the ground and give the floor a big middle finger.

"Fuck you, Chloe. Rot in hell, bitch!"

She couldn't even give me this one thing.

36

I'm standing at the curb in front of my building, carry-on luggage in hand, the evening sky dark above me. A car honks twice. Someone shouts.

The city is humid and groggy. A group of girls with vivid eyeshadow stumbles my way. Their loud chatter dissolves into whispers as they glance at me, recognition flickering in their eyes. I shield myself with my hand, grinning.

I pull up my phone and refresh my feed, clicking through the Belladonnas' profiles. Not a single post about a trip. A clandestine mission.

Angelique's been posting daily updates of her baby bump. She's in her second trimester, her stomach bulging just slightly over her clothes. And she looks as radiant as ever, smiling confidently with pearly veneers, snaggletooth long gone. I send a heart to her as a heavy black vehicle stops in front of me.

A bald man wearing a black suit climbs out of the driver's side. He lumbers, big and menacing. "Chloe Van Huusen?"

My heart patters in my chest as I nod.

He opens the back door. "I'm here to pick you up."

"Oh! Okay. Thanks."

He takes my luggage to the trunk as I make my way into the vehicle.

The floor is covered with a soft beige rug. The seats are stitched from luxurious leather, equipped with neck and ankle massagers. The car door closes automatically, city din dulling to a hum behind the tinted windows.

Instinctively, I whip my phone out to take a selfie, wanting to share this opulence to all my viewers who live vicariously through me.

The driver's slate-gray eyes latch on to mine in the rearview mirror. "You can use your phone but no photos. Miss Melniburg's orders."

"Sorry!" I squeak, putting my phone down.

The car starts with a low, almost undetectable *vroom*. City lights zoom past the window.

"Where are we heading?"

"Teterboro Airport."

"The one for private jets?"

"That's the one."

I sit back in my seat, biting my lip with excitement.

A private jet. Best trip ever.

———

The driver pulls up right next to the airplane. And I mean *right* next to it.

One step, I'm on tarmac, another, I'm on a red carpet leading up the jet.

They do the briefest security check—no TSA agent verbally accosting me to take out my laptop and liquids—before my carry-on is stowed in the luggage compartment and I'm allowed to board. The whole time, I'm itching to take a photo. This is such a wasted opportunity.

When I step onto the plane, high-pitched shouts of "Chloe!" ripple through the air, battering my eardrums. Eight Belladonnas have arrived before me. They look almost identical in their soft gray sweatpants and tank tops. I'm out of place in my jeans. I must have missed a memo.

Bella Marie stands where a flight attendant should be. Unlike the rest of the Belladonnas, she's dressed in a loose baby-blue dress and welcomes me with open arms. Though she's barefoot, she still towers over me, with her chin hitting my temple. Her hug is perfumed with honey and citrus, her hair smells like salt and the beach. When we part, I'm captivated by her bright smile and crystal-blue eyes. She slides her impossibly soft palms down my arms and clasps my hands as if she cherishes my fingers.

"I'm so glad you could make it, darling." The way she says *darling* is music to my soul. I haven't seen her in person since the event—she's always jet-setting around the world—but the way she locks me in her gaze convinces me we're the closest of friends. "Enjoy your bubbly and have a seat." She takes my Birkin and hands me a glass of fizzy champagne.

"My bag?"

"We're stowing it for the ride. Is there something you need?"

"My phone's in there."

"There's no signal in the air."

"I downloaded *White Lotus* to watch—" Then I remember. No devices! Technology cleanse! Yay! "Never mind."

She smiles and gestures toward the back where I presume my seat is. The jet's interior is sleek and beige, accented by tortoiseshell and glazed wood.

I say hi to all the Belladonnas, who are seated near the front of the plane, gathered in a cluster. The seats aren't arranged in rows, but like a lounge or a conversation pit. Their heads pop up like gophers with perfect beach waves as I walk through the aisle.

"Chloe." The sound of spearmint gum smacking between teeth. Kelly twirls a lock of black hair between her fingers.

I still can't tell if she likes me or not, but I decide to match her energy. "Kelly."

"Chloe, I love your new hair," says Emmeline.

I had lightened it to a warm chestnut shade. "Oh, thank—"

"Yes, yes, just love the new hair," adds Ana.

"Perfect with your skin tone," says Sophia.

"You can't say that, Sophia. Don't you know it's racist?" Lily says.

"Is it?" Sophia asks.

"It's not—" I begin.

"Yes, it is," Lily says. "I'm a mother to a minority. I know this kind of stuff."

"I don't see race, only foundation shades," Maya says. I'm not sure if she's joking, but I am sure that she's had more lip injections since I last saw her. "You look like a 23C Warm. Have you had a chance to try the newest One Drop foundation line? We have over fifty-six shades. Very inclusive for every person. I think I sent it to you last week."

It weighed fifty-eight pounds. I borrowed a cart to haul it into my apartment. "I received it in the mail, but I haven't gotten the chance to use any."

She bats her long fake eyelashes, her blue smoky eyes shimmering. "Oh." She returns to her conversation with Sophia and Lily. They chatter. Something about engagement and click-throughs. Then a ripple of sparkling laughter, a secret joke.

I'm left standing in the aisle, champagne in hand, attention pulled away from me like a slap. I push the feeling aside and make for an empty seat near the back of the plane.

Angelique is sinking into her plush airplane chair, the brown seat belt loose against her bulging stomach. A glazed table is between us. An opened bottle of champagne and a skinny glass, wet with condensation, sit on Angelique's side.

She waves. "Oh my god! Chloe!"

"Hey! How are you?" I ask.

"Just trying to make myself comfortable." She smooths her palm over her stomach. I notice her heavy-handed coral blush and I wonder if she's trying to obfuscate the green peeking through on her cheeks. "I'm sooooooo eager to get this over with."

"Are you sure you should be going on this trip? You don't look well."

Her expression twists, utter shock and confusion spreading through her lips.

"Sorry," I blurt, feeling like I said something wrong, though I'm not sure what.

"Isla!"

The Belladonnas turn like flowers attracted to the sun. Iz appears with a large black tote bag slung over her shoulder. Her curly hair is tied back in a scarf, her brown eyes wide as she scans the jet.

The Belladonnas welcome her with a raucous chitter. With their faces turned away, I can't tell who's speaking.

"Isla, nice to see you!"

"Oh my god! Isla!"

"Isla, congrats on half a mil!"

"Yes, congrats!"

"The algorithm gods are just eating up your content."

"One million in no time!"

Iz seems overwhelmed as she nods and smiles. Bella Marie exchanges her bag for a glass of bubbly. Iz takes the seat beside me.

"Looks like everyone's already gotten a few drinks in." She sips her welcome champagne. "Better catch up."

I nod, downing my champagne as well. It tickles my throat. Angelique tops off our glasses with golden liquid, then fills up her own. Iz and I share a surprised glance.

"Should you—" Iz starts.

"A glass a day is A-OK. My mom drank all the time and look how I turned out!" She giggles. "And this is basically juice anyway. Totes kosher."

Something slams shut, rattling the jet. Conversation ceases. Bella Marie steps into the aisle. I think it's the dim lighting of the plane, or maybe the alcohol swimming in my veins, but her movements are uncannily fluid.

"Darlings, I am so excited to welcome you to our yearly retreat." Her voice is a delicate thrum, at a volume where I strain to hear. "As in the years before, this trip will be an opportunity to reconnect with our true selves, to recharge away from the distractions of technology. I hope this trip brings you all a greater sense of relief and inspiration. Please remember, darlings, everyone on this plane today is a safe space. We do not judge. We listen and we share." She smiles. "We are family."

"We are family," the Belladonnas coo.

Iz glances at me with a dumbfounded smile.

"Without further ado . . ." Bella Marie smiles and turns to knock on the cockpit door.

The engine starts, loud and sharp.

Iz raises her hand. "Can you tell us where we're going now?" Thank god for Iz. She's the only one who can ask questions and get away with it.

Bella Marie smiles. "My home."

"Home," a Belladonna hums.

Iz arches a brow. "Which is . . . France? Moscow?"

"No, no, no, darling. It's in the Caribbean, near Saint Marten. One of our islands is there."

"One of— Like, a whole island? Just for yourself?"

"It's why I asked you to keep this hush-hush. You know how people get when it comes to private islands."

"Owning land is, like, a cancellable offense these days," Ana says.

"We've grown too comfortable criticizing people for being affluent," concurs Emmeline.

Iz glances at me again. I avert my eyes.

"I appreciate everyone's discretion and sensitivity in this matter." Bella Marie looks at Iz. "I can't wait for you to see what my home is like. Before you know it, my home will be your home too!"

"Well," Iz says with a shrug, "I do like the sound of that!"

"With that said," Bella Marie exclaims, "strap in and get ready for takeoff!"

The whole plane cheers as the jet creeps toward the runway. Everyone buckles their seat belts except for Bella Marie, who retrieves a tin from a bar cart. The Belladonnas dip their manicured fingers in, each one plucking a pill and slipping it on her tongue. Bella Marie arrives at our end of the plane. Angelique takes a pill without being asked, a smile curved into her lips as she pops it in her mouth like a mint.

Iz straightens. "Should she be . . ."

Bella Marie smiles wide. "She's an adult. She can do anything she likes. And these pills are totally safe."

"Safe?"

"Totally."

"Very safe!" someone chimes.

"The safest," adds another.

"See?" Bella Marie offers one to me. "Totally safe." Her eyes hold me hostage. Would Chloe take a pill without asking? Everyone's staring, their attention pulling at me like a rope. I have to take the pill, or else they'll be suspicious. I can't get caught, not now.

My fingers wrap around the plain pink pill. I place it on my tongue. Before I can chew on it, it melts into something sweet. Like grape candy.

Bella Marie turns to Iz, the last two pills outstretched.

"I don't take drugs I don't recognize," Iz says.

Bella Marie smiles. "Oh, they're barely anything. Nothing pharmaceutical. You know I'm a strict advocate against the medical-industrial complex."

"No, thanks."

"But everyone else took one. Do you not trust us?" Bella Marie asks.

"It's safe," says Angelique, palming her tummy.

"You can trust us," says one of the girls.

"We are a safe place," adds another.

"We would never harm you."

Their smiles are radiant as they giggle with one another.

"I can take one first if you're unsure." Bella Marie pops the pill on her tongue, closes her mouth, and swallows. She sticks out her tongue again. "See?"

She shoves the tin toward Iz.

Iz shakes her head. "I really don't—"

"We're not leaving unless you take one." Bella Marie's voice pitches lower this time. "This is your week to be free. Let go of all your worries. You can't tell me you haven't had drugs before, Isla Harris. Have *fun*!"

The tension in the plane swelters.

"Do it!" someone says.

"Do it!" adds another.

"Do it!"

"Do it!"

"Do it!"

"Do it!"

"Do it!" I accidentally say.

"Do it! Do it! Do it!" we all chorus.

Iz glances from me to Angelique. She sighs heavily and takes the last pill. Swallows. Sticks her tongue out. "Happy?"

The whole cabin erupts in claps and cheers. I'm clapping too, the energy is infectious.

"You passed!" Bella Marie wraps her in a hug.

Iz frowns. "What?"

"It was a placebo pill. Just sugar."

Iz's jaw drops open. I resist doing the same.

"We all did this during our first trip," Angelique says.

"A silly team bonding exercise," Bella Marie says.

"You were faster than Sophia's first time," Kelly says. "She tried to open the emergency exit before she finally gave in."

Bella Marie's eyes drift to the ceiling, reminiscing. "Ah. The memories." She twirls to the front of the plane. "Now that everyone has passed, let's take flight!" She presses a button and "All Too Well" by Taylor Swift plays through the surround-sound speakers. The Belladonnas belt out lyrics like Jake Gyllenhaal personally affronted them, pale forearms dancing in the air as the jet takes off.

Iz is clearly still in shock, and I am too—though I can't show it.

Instead I grab the champagne bottle and offer it to her. She heaves one last sigh before taking it by the neck and drinking straight from the spout. The foamy alcohol sloshes onto her chin as she pulls the bottle away with a sigh. "Fuck it. Let's party!"

The whole cabin cheers.

37

Someone grabs me hard by the shoulders, fingers digging into muscle. I blink awake with a moan. The light makes my head hurt, a migraine drilling into my temple.

Bella Marie's hair spikes my spit-crusted cheek. "Wake up, darling, we're here." Her breath is a plume of sour and rosé. I am nauseous. When did I fall asleep? Must have been somewhere after ten drinks and our twentieth Taylor Swift song. I was singing too, though I didn't know the words . . . Yet somehow, I did? It was almost like I fell into a Taylor Swift hive mind. I remember wondering how the Belladonnas had so much energy, their bodies wiggling like smoke, limbs impossibly long and twisty, as I faded in and out of consciousness.

"Wow," Iz gasps as she looks out a window. "What a view."

"We're lucky to have such clear weather this week," Bella Marie says. "We've been having bursts of summer storms lately."

I wipe the sleep from my eyes and straighten.

Then I see it.

Blue. A wide stretch of ocean. No land in sight. I've only seen views like this through a screen.

Maya peels a fake eyelash off the wall of the plane. The other girls are frenetic, bodies buzzing as they collect bits of clothes from the floor. Seriously, how do they have so much vigor? It's like they all have balls of lightning inside them, ready to burst out.

The emergency exit opens. Rays of light and salt air suffuse the metal tube. A warm, humid breeze brushes against my skin. The change in temperature gives me goose bumps.

A line of tall white men and women come into the plane. They're all barefoot, dressed in pale linens, crisp smiles painted on their lips, carrying trays of what looks like orange juice.

"Welcome home!" they say.

The Belladonnas clap and yip like hungry dogs as they reach for the drinks on the trays. Bella Marie grabs two glasses. "Fresh orange juice, coconut water, and a bit of caffeine. Great for a hangover." She winks as she shoves the glasses into our hands.

Iz and I down the drink. It is surprisingly refreshing, leaving a sweetness on my tongue that compels me to want more.

After our welcome drinks, we file out of the plane and into the glorious sun.

The island is picturesque. Blue waters, white beaches, tall palms. A cobblestone path leads off the tarmac. In the distance: verdant forest, bushes rife with blooming flowers, buildings with red roofs. Some umbrellas are set out on the beach, shading loungers. A hammock between two swaying coconut palms.

I already feel a tan searing into my skin as Bella Marie hands our bags back to us. I'm relieved as my fingers wrap around my phone—a missing limb reinserted. To my surprise, not a single notification pings through.

No signal.

Iz must have noticed this too. "Is there Wi-Fi on this island?" she asks Bella Marie.

Bella Marie smiles. "We're here to disconnect. There's no signal on premises."

I blanch. No signal? I get that Bella Marie wants to keep this trip low-key, but what am I going to do if I can't refresh my Instagram every three minutes?

"What if my kids need me?" Iz asks.

"Did you give the babysitter the emergency contact information?"

Iz nods.

"If they need help, our staff will relay the message at the utmost expediency. There's an ethernet cable in the main residence if you must plug back in, as well as a landline. But I'd really recommend you resist. Disconnect. That's the whole point of this trip."

Iz is silent as she cups her neck, her lips pressed into a hard line.

It's one thing not to post while we're here, but it's a whole other slap in the face to know we're disconnected from the outside world.

I chew on my cheek, unease creeping into me.

But then I look around. The beaches, warm sun.

I shove my phone into my bag. This is ridiculous. I'm a grown woman. I should be able to live without my phone for a week. I can spend all day lounging on white sands, sipping pretty cocktails, instead of throwing myself down the rabbit hole of social media and living in constant fear of my parasitic aunt messaging me with demands. This will be relaxing. Great! Fun, even!

At least that's what I try to tell myself.

A young man who looks like a cross between a Ralph Lauren model and a Ken doll introduces himself as Viktor. He has a vaguely European or perhaps Scandinavian accent, a fine mop of golden hair, and deep-set narrow blue eyes. His short sleeves reveal his thick biceps, ropy veins crawling up his wrists and hands.

"Viktor will show you around the island and help you get settled in," Bella Marie says. She's beaming under the sun, bright and angelic. "I have to go check on something, but I will see you all during our welcome dinner." She waves goodbye as Viktor leads us into the island.

Behind us, the plane engine roars.

"Is the plane leaving?" Iz asks Viktor.

"Yes."

"What if we have an emergency or need to get home? Is there, like, a boat or something?"

Thank the heavens again for Iz being a new recruit. The other Belladonnas glance at each other and giggle.

"In cases of emergency," Viktor says, "we will make sure to send for help. As of now, there's no way off the island. Unless you're Michael Phelps and plan on swimming the Caribbean Sea. Get it? Because he's an Olympic swimmer?" He laughs, a show of white teeth.

The Belladonnas erupt in giggles.

Iz and I glance at each other. I think we missed the joke. Or is Viktor so hot he gets laughs for saying something utterly dumb?

"But rest assured," he continues, "we have medical professionals who are very helpful in a pinch. In all my years on the island, there has never been a single incident we couldn't handle ourselves."

"It's very safe on the island," Emmeline says.

"Extremely safe," says Ana.

"Literally zero percent crime," adds Kelly.

"America wishes!" chimes Maya.

We follow a path leading into a copse of trees and just before I turn the corner, I glance over my shoulder. Bella Marie is standing there, poised like a doll. Her blue eyes meet mine, yet it doesn't look like she's looking at me. Rather, her gaze is set beyond, staring through me, almost vacant.

38

Most of the Belladonnas decide to jump-start their tans on the sandy beaches. Meanwhile, I accompany Iz on her tour of the grounds—mostly because I need the tour too.

It's a bit awkward, since Viktor keeps bringing up stories of Chloe doing certain things at certain places.

"When we played tennis together, I felt like I was in the Olympics playing against Naomi Osaka!" Or "You girls spent the entire night making friendship bracelets by the beach." Or "Do you remember when we roasted the pig by the bonfire?"

I nod along and ad-lib. If Viktor notices something off, he doesn't comment on it. Perhaps he simply doesn't notice small nuances. His wide, deliberate smile suggests there's nothing going on behind that pristinely handsome forehead of his. Whenever he finishes a statement, he turns toward you with this expression of puppylike longing, as if waiting for some sign of approval. If I punched him in the face, he'd probably smile and say, with dogged affection, "Great aim!"

Nevertheless, the island is impressive.

Like, *really* impressive.

I'm pinching myself every time we venture into a new area, wondering how a family could own this block of the world.

We amble around the glorious sporting areas: a volleyball court, tennis grounds, a squash court that doubles as half a basketball court, and a horse stable. Then there's the main hall, where the kitchen and staff live and work, a three-storied Greek Revival–style building bordered by palm trees. Near the center of the island there's a farm homing free-range chickens, cows, sheep, and other animals. Viktor hands us some carrots and we feed the goats. One of them almost chomps off my pinkie. Next to the farm is a giant greenhouse where they grow their own produce. "Each section of the facility is climate-controlled so we can produce crops from all around the world, year-round," Viktor says, a brightness in his voice, proudly pointing to the zucchini plants, lettuce crops, and citrus trees. "We draw water from the ocean and desalinate it at a plant near the coast. The canals you see running along each crop row not only double as the perfect environment for freshwater fish but the fish also fertilize the plants through their excrement—a technique we learned from Asia." He looks at me as if I was the one who taught them that technique. "Nothing goes to waste on the island."

He introduces us to some staff, who are picking luscious mangoes off verdant trees. They're all tall and lithe and impossibly beautiful. The scene—the workers reaching high, plucking ripe fruit—looks straight out of a magazine. Some dystopian, *Brave New World* shit where laborers are happy to work.

We learn that the island is a big community of sorts. A swanky co-op where the staff live, eat, and work together. A few families, like Viktor's, have worked with the Melniburgs for generations. And we're talking *generations*. Like, hundreds of years. Pre–World War I shit. I'm not joking.

The main house is a rustic but tasteful French-chateau-style mansion with cresting roofs. Viktor shows us giant portraits of the Melniburg ancestors inside a grand entrance fit with symmetrical swirling staircases. The frames crawl up the twenty-foot-high walls, and the paintings' watchful azure eyes seem to follow me. Some family portraits are so old, I'm surprised a British museum hasn't taken them. I'm talking oil paintings straight from the eighteenth century and black-and-white photos of people who could be mistaken for the Romanovs. There are also a few modern photo portraits, including one of the current Melniburg empire. Front and center is Bella Marie. Her dad, a gruff-looking man with red cheeks and blue eyes, is to her right, and her mom, a thin, blond woman with a haunting black stare, is to her left.

"Who's this guy?" Iz points to a small painting near the back corner, her voice echoing around the lofty hall.

The man is sitting on a plain wooden bench. He's wearing a beige frock, has brown hair, and bears a staunch expression, his heavy cheeks weighing down his entire face. A white bandage is wrapped around his left eye, while his other eye stares right into your soul. And I mean *right* into it. It's hard to look away. Every color in the spectrum somehow speckles his painted blue iris—the focal point of an otherwise gloomy and somber painting. The background is a gray brick wall with a square opening that reveals the smallest sliver of a night sky. He's painted in isolation, lit only by an unseen golden candle near the bottom right-hand corner. A long shadow stretches darkly across the canvas. The shadow doesn't belong to him, but to someone just beyond.

"That's Nikolai Melniburg, the patriarch of the Melniburg family." Viktor tilts his head with a smile like he's smitten, almost . . . aroused. I shiver. "According to records, this would have been painted around 1767."

I blow an impressed breath. I knew the Melniburgs were old money, but this is *old* money.

"Nikolai was the start of everything for our family." Bella Marie's dove-like voice pierces the warm air. She slides next to us in a loose white linen dress, a dainty pearl necklace adorning her collar. Her swan neck arches as she looks up at the painting, pale skin ghostly, almost transparent when it catches the sun.

"What did he do? Discover borscht?" Iz jokes.

Bella Marie laughs. "Oh no, nothing that amazing." She drifts closer to the canvas, touching the intricate golden frame with her index finger. "His story is rather funny. Nikolai was a peasant who stumbled upon wealth due to pure luck, wishful thinking, and fealty to the right gods."

Iz places a hand on her hip. "Did a genie in a lamp grant him three wishes or something?"

"Simpler than that. A nobleman of distant relation to the Romanovs had lost a pocket watch." Bella Marie stares at her ancestor, their glittery blue eyes meeting. "It was a watch that belonged to his father and all the fathers before, an important heirloom with priceless sentimentality. The old nobleman had promised to give away his second-born daughter to any man who returned the watch to him."

"Nikolai found the watch?"

Bella Marie nods. "At the time, second daughters didn't inherit anything aside from a title and some noble blood." She shifts her gaze to the painting depicting a family of four. They're dressed in dapper clothes, ruffled dresses. "Their son, Alexander, took advantage of this bloodline and its connections to work his way into high society. And now, hundreds of years later . . ." She spreads her arms. "Here we are."

"But what happened to Nikolai's eye?" Iz asks.

"Luck doesn't come for free." Bella Marie glances at me, as if we're sharing a secret I *should* know. A furtive glance that Chloe would understand. The real Chloe.

My skin prickles under her gaze. I turn my attention to Nikolai, trading a pair of blues for a single one.

"Wait." Iz turns to Bella Marie. "You're saying he gave up his eye for some luck?"

Bella Marie shrugs, smiling. "It's nothing more than an old legend. In truth, he toiled the land owned by said nobleman and happened upon the watch. A serendipitous coincidence, perhaps."

"Lucky guy," Iz comments.

"Very," replies Bella Marie, guiding us out of the hall. As we pass through the tall, swinging doors, it still feels like someone's watching, as if every blue eye in the room behind me has shifted to stare at my back.

39

We each get a bungalow.
Yes. Each.

Ten whole bungalows for ten Belladonnas. I have trouble grasping the magnitude of Bella Marie's wealth. And to think there are families out there even wealthier than hers.

The wooden bungalows run in a row along the shore, like an isolated street, each with its own little garden brimming with tropical plants and a wooden fence for privacy. A crooked mango tree shades my thatched roof, its branches old and gnarly as they reach toward the ground, almost begging in their shape. There's a small window overlooking the front porch. The blinds are pulled shut. Sand scuffs the cobblestone pavement leading up to the entrance, which is accented by a wooden plank that reads: *Chloe.*

There's a padlock on the outside of the door, but no lock on the inside. I guess it's because no one is going around stealing stuff on a private island. The lock on the outside is probably there to barricade against storms or wild animals.

The bungalow's interior is glorious. Tall ceilings, light brown wood flooring, rattan chairs and sofas, intricate, handwoven rugs, and a king-sized bed with plush white sheets and gigantic sleep-inducing pillows. The bedposts have some wear and tear, as if something was tied around them, sanding down the veneer, but otherwise, they look brand new. Slatted french doors lead to a small patio facing the ocean. The bathroom stone tiles are rugged beneath my feet. A long, well-lit mirror sits above a sink that's simply a large rock with its insides scooped out. The freestanding bathtub and shower are outside, surrounded by a bamboo fence and a twisting bush to shield from unsuspecting eyes.

We have two hours until lunch. Bella Marie said we're free to get acquainted with the island—*your home*—during this time: walk around, explore, tan, and socialize with the locals—er, staff.

But there's only one thing I'm yearning for.

I find my luggage stowed in the closet. I dig through my shoes, shirts, SLEEPY BEARS container, and pull out my laptop. Cracking it open, I click on the top bar for Wi-Fi.

No network available.

I stare at it for a while, hoping it might change. It doesn't.

Groaning, I clap my laptop shut and throw myself down onto a rattan chair. How could Bella Marie do this to a group of influencers who depend on their little apps for their careers? Technology is crucial to my existence. I'm not even sure if I have an identity outside of the internet. She's stripping away my livelihood!

Is this what it feels like to be an addict? If so, I think I might be addicted to the refreshing animation on Instagram. The sound of notifications. The sight of views going up. The support of my Chloe Crew. The rush of compliments and praise at my fingertips. I'm itching for it—the fix of social media. Without it, I'm empty, a void. An iPad kid without her iPad.

To distract myself, I spend some time putting away my clothes, arranging my skincare and makeup by the sink, showering off the fumes from the plane, and changing into a billowy linen sundress. After I blow-dry my hair, I reach for my phone, anticipating word from my aunt. She's conditioned me to expect her pernicious messages at random times of day, and the absence of her texts is unsettling. I hadn't told her about this trip because I couldn't give her an opportunity to ruin it. But that also means she doesn't know I'm gone. What if she sent me a message and I hadn't received it? What if she's demanding more money, *right now*? What if she interprets this week of silence as the cold shoulder? That I'm not going to make good on my end of the bargain? What if she leaks the tapes with my confession?

I smack myself in the head, annoyed that I hadn't planned for this before hopping on the plane. I had been too excited, too optimistic. A group trip—what could go wrong? But I'm continually forgetting that I'm not just a regular influencer. I'm a fraud.

Desperation clogs my chest as I sprint outside with my device stretched toward the sky. I go so far out, the warm ocean licks my ankles. "Just one bar. God, please, I'll do anything. Just give me the smallest bit of signal."

Nothing.

I would have screamed if there weren't a line of bungalows housing Belladonnas behind me. Then I hear the sound of someone's feet kicking at sand. I spin around and see Iz. She's reaching her phone toward the clouds too, a lit cigarette in her other hand.

She catches my eyes. We freeze in our ridiculous poses, devices outstretched like we're imitating the Statue of Liberty, and burst into laughter.

"We look insane right now," Iz shouts, heading toward me.

I meet her halfway. "We're on this beautiful island and all we want to do is go on our phones. We're awful."

"It's only been a few hours and I feel myself going crazy. And it's going to be like this for a week. A whole week!" She throws her arms into the air, ash scattering onto the beach. "How did you do it all these years?"

I bite my lip, thinking of Chloe. Was she also this addicted to her phone? "You get used to it after a while." And at least she didn't have a parasitic aunt on her tail.

We fall into a bout of defeated silence, staring at our dark screens.

"Hey," Iz says, her head rising with a grin, "we can't post about our trip, but it doesn't mean we can't take pics to commemorate. We should make the best out of our time here."

Her buoyant smile chases away the dread in my chest. She's right. Even though I can't get in touch with my aunt, I shouldn't spend this entire week moping about it. My foul mood will bleed out and infect everyone. I'll deal with my aunt when I must. For now, I need to stay positive.

"Let's do it."

Iz stubs out her cigarette and we doll ourselves up in her bungalow.

I'm curling my lashes when Iz sighs. "How crazy is it that her family owns this entire island?"

"I can hardly imagine that type of wealth."

"All from a damn pocket watch. What did Nikolai do? Suck God's dick?" I laugh.

"And those family portraits," she continues. "They are just . . . maybe this is mean to say, but the whole time I kept thinking about how her family definitely owned people. Like, *owned* them."

"Oh, one hundred percent. Her dad probably called Asians 'Orientals.' There are at least ten war criminals represented in those portraits. Blood money shit." I apply a thick coat of mascara to my lashes, pausing mid-sentence to focus. When I'm satisfied, I continue, "But honestly, I'd trade my life for Bella Marie's in a heartbeat."

She laughs. "It makes sense how Bella Marie got to her level. She literally has the world at her fingertips. A quintessential nepo kid."

"I guess." But I feel like Iz is discounting Bella Marie. Sure, she has her privileges, but she still worked hard to get where she is.

Iz drops her voice low. "I mean—god, I feel terrible for saying this when she literally invited us onto her island—but frankly, doesn't it just make you a bit sick? Seeing all they have? And not just Bella Marie, the other girls too. Like, they're so unaware of their place in the world, so blasé about their privilege. And some of the things they say . . ." She shakes her head. I wonder if she's thinking about Emmeline's tweets. "I don't know. Maybe I'm just jealous, but it almost makes me *angry*. Sometimes, I feel like I'm holding myself back from checking them every time they say something off-base. And the only reason I stop myself is because I'm sure they get catty when things don't go their way—because things *always* go their way. They can't live in a world where people say no to them. Like on the plane with the pills. That shit was *fucked*."

I see what Iz is saying, but how many other rich people would let women like us into their lives? And it's not like Bella Marie asked to be born that way. Hell, if I was her, I wouldn't be half as compassionate.

"I get that," I say, not trying to argue. "Hopefully things go smoothly for the rest of the trip. If anything, this is your time to LARP as a rich white person. When else will you get the chance?"

Iz doesn't laugh at my attempt at a joke. Maybe it wasn't funny.

I clear my throat. "I'm just saying there's nothing to lose from being on their side. Once you're in with Bella Marie, you'll be at the top of the world. Think of everything her connections will bring. Take it from me: this is your chance to break into the industry, to get sponsorships that will pay for your children's tuition and then some. A weeklong beach vacation is hardly a sacrifice, even if they get on your nerves a little."

"I guess." Iz fingers her curls. "I'm just scared I'm going to accidentally upset one of them." She presses her mouth into a line, observing me in the mirror. "How do you keep your mouth shut? You have so much self-control."

It helps when you're hiding almost every aspect about yourself. "It's all worth it in the end. Trust me. I'm on your side."

This makes Iz smile. She leans in and nestles her head on my shoulder. "I'm so glad you're here."

We head out in our best fits and take photos of us running through the water, posing by the sand, swinging on the hanging daybeds. We change into bikinis and smear our butts with tasteful amounts of sand. I feel like a *Sports Illustrated* photographer as I take gorgeous photos of Iz, her skin shining. I'm in all different poses to get the right angle. Squatting, stomach in the sand, crouching in the bushes, knee deep in water. Iz does the same for me. She keeps shouting compliments as I pose: "Gorgeous! Stunning! Yaaas leg! Look at that booty! Abs for days! Slaaaaaay!" Both of us give our best efforts, even though no one will see the photos—perhaps it's more fun since *I know* no one will see the photos. I don't have to struggle for the perfect pose or angle. Curate my image. Suck in my tummy. I don't even have to strain for a smile since I'm genuinely having fun.

Time flies by, and I'm already feeling the relief of no internet access. Maybe time away from social media is exactly what I need.

40

I hope you've all settled into your homes." Bella Marie stands at the head of a long table, the moon shining above her like a crown. The remains of our outdoor dinner are scattered before her, a charcuterie-style dining experience where deli slices were swapped for steak and every grape had been polished to a jade-stone shine. It's farm-to-table, hands-to-mouth. My fingers are coated with crumbs and meat grease, and my mouth is acidic from wine. The meal's corpse is spread along the table, a river of desecrated crackers like a twisting spine. "Shall we commence our first activity?"

The Belladonnas clap and giggle with excitement.

Iz nudges me with her elbow. "Activity?"

I nod and smile because I have no idea what's about to happen. She holds my gaze for a long while. Have I been dodging too many questions? "It's best when it's a surprise," I amend.

We follow Bella Marie to the other side of the island. Our path is lined with glittering candles. Wisps of smoke trail into the air like specters, leading our way into a forested area. Though it's summer, the night brings a chill. I hug my arms around myself, my skin breaking out in goose bumps. A raging bonfire appears in the center of a cleared field. Viktor is standing near the blaze, his white linens painted orange from the flames. His hands are black from soot; his smiling teeth are white as pearls. When he sees Bella Marie, he almost lifts onto his toes with excitement, bounding to her side. They share a whisper and he nods, disappearing into the darkness. He returns with a wooden box and a bundle of sharp metal sticks. Bella Marie takes the box and opens it, revealing an assortment of graham crackers, chocolate, and marshmallows. "Ta-da! Our first activity: s'mores night!"

The Belladonnas crowd around the box, skewering soft white cylinders through their puffy bodies and sticking them in the fire to roast.

Iz grabs a poker and a marshmallow. "I haven't had s'mores since I was a kid."

I haven't had s'mores *ever.*

Iz grabs a chocolate square. "Are these Hershey's?"

"Never," says Bella Marie disdainfully, as if the brand is below her—which it probably is. "We made these ourselves."

"With your own cocoa beans?"

"We have very talented chefs from the island."

"Wow." Iz's tongue moves inside her cheeks as she tastes the chocolate. "These are *amazing.* Can I get the recipe? I'd love to try my hand at it."

"I'm sorry, darling. I'm afraid the recipe is a family secret."

"I won't tell anyone. Swear on this heart."

Bella Marie presses her lips together. "The ingredients are proprietary. I'm sure you understand."

Iz quirks a brow. "*Family secret.* I get it." She heads toward the fire.

I take a marshmallow and push its soft white body through the metal poker. We stand around the hot fire, roasting. Iz circles around to the opposite side, chatting with Ana and Lily. They're smiling, cracking jokes. I feel slightly at odds with myself, isolated.

Messaging the Belladonnas online provides a pleasant separation between my worlds. I can contemplate my answers for minutes or hours before sending a reply. And last night on the plane, I drank plenty, my inhibitions freed. Without the distance of chat rooms and the blur of alcohol, I notice myself distinctly. I can't help but compare myself to the others. Iz's easy amiable character, the Belladonnas' success and overwhelming beauty. I'm markedly aware of my impersonation, of how I don't really belong. I wish I had more drinks at dinner so I can loosen up, but instead, I'm rigid and uncomfortable, as if my aunt's arms are corseting around my ribs.

My marshmallow suddenly catches on fire. "Shit." I wave it around frantically, encouraging the flames. Angelique appears beside me and extinguishes the fire in one breath.

"Thanks."

"No problem." She regards the charcoal-like object at the end of my poker. Without saying anything, she trades out my blackened marshmallow for hers, which is golden brown all around.

"You don't have to."

"It's all right." She smiles. "Want to see a trick?"

I nod.

She gingerly pulls at the outside of the marshmallow, unsheathing the pillowy white insides from their golden crust. "That's how you know it's perfectly roasted. Say, 'ah.'"

I say "Ah" and she feeds the golden outside to me. It's cavity-inducing and makes me feel like a child in a good way.

She skewers and roasts two more marshmallows to perfection, making both of us s'mores.

"You'll be such a terrific mother," I say, taking a bite, trying to find a topic of conversation. The treat is not as good as I thought it would be—it's too sugary, and the chocolate doesn't melt all the way—but I find myself gobbling it down, since everyone else is already licking their fingers, reaching for another.

"Oh, stop." She laughs.

"No, I'm serious. You have such a motherly vibe."

She's silent, caressing her stomach. I'm not sure what to say, so I change the subject. "How did you and Sommer meet?"

She glances at me. "I thought you knew."

I reach for a new piece of chocolate and start nibbling on it nervously. "I do, but please tell me again. I can listen to meet cutes a million times."

"Bella Marie set us up. Sommer used to be one of her lovers."

I pop the entire chocolate in my mouth and it melts on my tongue, bitter.

That's kind of weird. To set up your friend with your ex. "That's considerate," I say instead.

Angelique nods. "She's saved my life a dozen times by now. If it wasn't for her, I'd still be doing my little YouTube videos in my dinky apartment on my iPhone." I'm reminded of her history, of C-PTSD being listed in her bio. It's clear she's been through some shit. I don't know how she's remained so pleasant when my history has only made me bitter and miserable. "It was Bella Marie who connected me to my amazing talent manager, which led to my book deal. And then she introduced me to Sommer, and he's the best thing that's ever happened to me. In two years, my life has completely changed." She's staring softly across the fire, at Bella Marie, who looks like she's caught in the flames. "I'd do anything to keep this life." She smooths her palm over her stomach.

I think of Iz, who escaped an abusive relationship, and Sophia, who lost her dreams of the Olympics. There's even Chloe and her sham adoption. I wonder what everyone else's story is—Kelly, Ana, Maya, Lily. Maybe even Emmeline. Through the screen, they're all unilaterally perfect. But they must have hurt of their own. It's almost like Bella Marie purposefully finds people who need her, people who are down on their luck, vulnerable, and uplifts them.

There's a swirling warmth in my tummy that almost makes me dizzy. Maybe the wine has settled into my blood, pulling me away from my nerves, or maybe I'm comforted by Angelique's attention, her soft voice as sweet as the marshmallow and chocolate in my mouth. I find myself reaching for Angelique's hand. It's not something I've done before, this tactile outreach, but it feels necessary.

When she cups her hand over our clasp, I feel like I've done the right thing. Our connection is soft and loving, so much so that I have to stop myself from closing my eyes and relishing it.

But then she says something I wish she hadn't.

"I'm really so sorry about Julie."

I stiffen again.

"I keep thinking of losing a family member these days," she whispers, barely audible over the crackling fire. "It must have been so hard. I know you really cared for her." Her eyes are filled with so much sincerity, I have to avert my gaze so she doesn't see my pained expression.

If Chloe had cared, I never felt it. Not for a second.

"I wish I was better to her," I say, staring at my fingers woven between Angelique's, feeling her warmth travel through my palm, into my arm. "I wish I was better to Julie." My voice comes out in a wobble. It's hard to say it out loud; it hurts in a way I didn't expect. As much as I wish it were really Chloe saying this, that my twin was the one wishing she had been kinder to me, I also wish I had been kinder to myself, softer to myself.

I've always believed I was of little worth—perhaps because my aunt would tell me so. But what if I hadn't? If she had cultivated my strengths, could I have been successful without stealing someone's life? I've been thrust into Chloe's identity and have adapted to it with ease, like my sister's life was never out of reach, like I was always capable.

Angelique is silent for a moment. I hear the sound of drums, music. But when I look around, I don't see anything. Maybe it's my heartbeat, all in my mind.

"I think you saw how influencers exploit their families," she says finally, "how ugly it can get. Maybe you didn't want Julie to endure that. You were good to her in your own way."

A part of me has trouble believing her, not only because she's on her way to becoming a family vlogger—making her seem hypocritical—but also because I feel like she's saying empty words to be nice. If Chloe had cared, why exploit me in the first place? But the other part of me, the part softening near the bonfire's heat, wants to believe Angelique. This desire feeds on my hunger for a connection to my twin.

Chloe's dead. Can never make her intentions clear. But this could be my chance to believe that she cared for me in her own way—to believe in a prettier truth. I want to gift myself a better, forgiving future, and sometimes that means writing over the past.

I squeeze Angelique's hand tightly. "Thank you. I think you're right."

The box of chocolate claps shut beside me, and I flinch.

Bella Marie smiles. "Darlings, I hope you've all enjoyed your treats tonight. Shall we adjourn this dessert party and embark on part two?"

41

As I step toward the flames, a piece of paper clutched between my fingers, my eyes water from smoke and wind, making everything wobbly, like I'm drunk or tired. The swaying shadows beneath the trees are animated, their creaking branches reaching out. Again I hear, somewhere in the distance, the beat of drums, the din of strings. Iz is to my left, Angelique to my right, and the blazing fire burns in front of us. I resist staring into the flames, their hypnotic dance; it makes me dizzy, makes me want to fall.

"Is everyone ready?" Bella Marie had instructed us to write down one thing we wished to leave behind for good after the trip and then to throw the paper into the fire to burn. *A cleansing ritual to help manifest good energy.* It feels like self-help bullshit, but everyone else is enthusiastic about it. I guess it doesn't hurt.

I glance down at the paper in my hand. It only has one word: *Aunt.*

Yes, a human.

Tucked away in my dark corner of the forest, my aunt was the only thing I thought of. Her barking voice, her vile tongue, the cut of my earnings that she demands every month. Even on this faraway island, she's the one thing that pulls me away from joy, the one thing holding me back from flourishing. If she were gone, if she left me alone, I know I'd be able to reach my potential. Without my aunt I'd *truly* be able to start anew.

And in my defense, Bella Marie hadn't set the parameters properly. I know she meant to write down something like *self-doubt,* but at no point did she say we *couldn't* write a human.

"Now," Bella Marie says, "close your eyes and focus. Breathe in your intentions, and exhale to exorcise all the negative energy into the paper." With my eyes shut, her voice is intimate, like she's close enough to lick my ear. I do as instructed, the hairs on my neck rising. "Open your eyes and let the paper find the fire. Allow your negativity to be burned with it, gone forever."

Everyone lets go of their paper. They drift into the flames like flower petals. But there's a sudden kick of wind and mine flails out of its path.

"Shit," I whisper under my breath, bending to pick up the paper. The word *aunt* has been smudged with dirt. I go to toss it again—

"STOP!"

I recoil from the fire, eyes snapping to Bella Marie. She comes running, and rips the paper out of my hand. The music stops suddenly as I glance around. Everyone's staring at me. Their dire faces cut with long shadows.

"W-what?"

"You've been chosen."

"Chosen?" My heart thumps hard into my ear.

"Yes, chosen," Bella Marie says, the fire's reflection dancing in her icy blue eyes.

"Chosen!" exclaims Sophia.

"Chosen," says Maya.

"Cho—"

"What does that mean?" Iz asks, interrupting Emmeline.

"Her paper shall not be burned," says Bella Marie. "Not like this. Not right now."

"Um. I kind of prefer it to be burned." I reach for the paper. Kelly snatches it and hands it to Bella Marie again.

"It's not about what you prefer," Kelly says. "It's about what the world is asking of you."

Bella Marie keeps my paper in one hand, not looking at it, as she holds my shoulder with the other. Her breath is chocolate and smoke. "Be honest, darling, you have something ailing your heart, don't you? Something dark and heavy. Something that you must confess. I can feel it, the unease. You've changed these past months, become a whole new person with your pain."

Her words strike a chord of panic and I suddenly notice that I'm sweating—perhaps I have been sweating for the past while. My clothes are wet and cling to my skin. But wasn't I cold earlier? Why am I feeling so feverish now?

"Your paper," Emmeline asks. "What did you write?"

"Um . . ." I search for a savior. At Angelique—she looks away—at Iz.

"Wasn't it supposed to be personal?" Iz says. "Just let her burn the paper. It's not a big deal."

"No!" someone says, I don't know who, can't sense who. I'm beyond stressed; the trees surrounding us are starting to spin. Shadows breathing, pulsing. I feel like I'm floating, just slightly, losing control of my limbs.

"I want you to tell us," Bella Marie says. "What did you write? You can trust us, darling. We're your safe place, remember? We've been your family for years now. Return to us. *Confess.*" Her blue eyes are the daytime, safe and serene, compelling the truth out of me.

"M-my aunt."

After looking at me for a long while, as if searching for something that isn't there, Bella Marie releases me. "Your aunt."

"Your aunt?" Lily asks.

"Why your aunt?" Emmeline adds.

I can't tell the truth. I can't reveal how she's blackmailing me. It would expose me entirely, let everyone know that I'm not Chloe.

Why did I confess? Why didn't I just rip the paper out of Bella Marie's hands and toss it into the fire? The words had slipped out before I could control it. How can I cover my tracks? "I mean my biological aunt—Julie's aunt. I didn't really know her, but ever since Julie died in my apartment, she's been threatening me."

Bella Marie tips her head. "Threatening you?"

"Yes, like demanding money. She's"—I swallow—"been threatening to leak Julie's secrets. I think my twin was involved in some nasty stuff. And I-I don't want my sister's name to be tarnished. I want to protect her."

"I see." Bella Marie crumples the paper in her hand and holds her arms wide, welcoming. I go to her, letting her hold me. "I feel your pain, Chloe. I feel Julie's pain too. Thank you so much for confessing." I lean into Bella Marie's body, her warmth, her bones. She smells impossibly sweet, like candy, and I almost want to lick her skin, her sweat. She pulls away. "I know just the thing to help you."

"Oh, you really don't have to—"

"Nonsense!"

I'm glad Bella Marie says this, because I want their help, their saving. I want their support. She leans forward, kisses me on the forehead, sealing her words in. I am disarmed, at the mercy of her touch as she holds my hand and guides me through the forest like a child. Bella Marie starts picking up twigs from the ground and the Belladonnas follow suit. By the time I am aware of the bundle of tiny sticks clutched in my fingers, I'm already heading back to the bonfire. Viktor appears with twine and a piece of muslin. We gather in a circle, the fire cracking and cackling. We sit cross-legged.

Iz's knee bumps into mine, and she reaches out to touch me. Her fingers are clammy and smell like dirt. "Do you feel a bit weird?"

I'm about to answer, but my attention is pulled away by Bella Marie, her soft skin, the smell of chocolate. She uses her thumb to anchor onto my chin, pulling my lips apart, and slips the crumpled piece of paper with my aunt's name into my mouth. I salivate at the uninvited object, the paper gritty with dirt yet somehow saccharine. Then, slipping two fingers between my lips, making me quiver, she pulls out the moist clump, my saliva curving into the night. The bundle of sticks we'd gathered has been tied together into a nest. Bella Marie places the wet paper in the middle and wraps it with the muslin cloth. There's tinny music rising somewhere in the air, an orchestra beyond the trees, singing to us.

"Together, as a group, we will save Chloe." Bella Marie hums, and I'm lifted, my head a balloon on my neck. "Come." We huddle together, all ten of us, hands held. Everyone's energy surges into me, their support palpable. "I hear you, Chloe," Bella Marie says, louder now, hoarse. Her voice is a blistering crackle, burrowing straight into the mushy parts of my brain. "I feel your hurt. Your agony. Your rage. Your pain for yourself and your twin."

Then, everyone else says it back to me. *I hear you. I feel your hurt. Your agony. Your rage. Your pain for yourself and your twin.* Even Iz says it, though her voice is softer than the others, a slight slowness, perhaps confusion, resistance. I feel like I'm truly heard. Like they're listening. They understand my pain, my rage, they're sharing my burden without complaint, and they're pushing everything to the surface, my repressed frustration burgeoning to a point.

"What do you want, Chloe?" Bella Marie asks. "What do you want to happen to your aunt?"

"I . . ." The world blurs. I'm out of breath, though I've barely moved. It's like I'm shoplifting; I'm hyperaware of some watchful presence that may catch me at any minute, but my heart also beats with an unmistakable rush. "I want her to suffer like I have. I want her to be fearful of me. To never bother me ever again." Warmth creeps down my cheeks and I realize I'm crying uncontrollably. Hiccuping.

Bella Marie holds me as I sob ugly, salty tears, her breath warm on my skin. Her tenderness is beautifully suffocating, yet I crave it.

"Then that is what you shall have."

It takes over us, a mass hysteria, a frantic energy that compels our limbs forward. We come together in an act so ungentle, so ungraceful, so ugly, as we kick and smash the bundle of sticks under our feet, cracking and breaking each twig, screaming and huffing, until it becomes a brown pile of wood chips and paper waste.

Bella Marie scoops the remnants of the nest, soil between her fingers, staining her nails, and hands its corpse to me. The fire before me is raging, an inferno, heat pulsing through my body, calling me forward. I scream, a guttural sound, releasing and cleansing, and toss the bundle of broken sticks into the flames. The Belladonnas whoop and howl, their dancing shadows crisp against the oscillating orange tendrils. My body is alive, like the gesticulating trees around me. I gaze into the clear twilight, and it's like something releases itself from my chest in a hot burst. I look back in the fire, the burning bundle, and see my aunt's face in the dancing wisps of orange and yellow and red—see her burn to a crisp, to a char, to nothing. And I feel—I believe—that she won't bother me anymore. I know it. I just know it.

I am free.

42

I jolt awake. My mouth is dry, and I have a small headache. The back of my throat is sweet but sooty.

I try to go back to sleep, but vignettes of last night flash in my mind, vibrant bursts of memory. The dinner, the bonfire, the s'mores . . . the burning of my aunt? Or at least the burning of some effigy. It's ridiculous, almost surreal. Maybe I had too much to drink. I downed a few glasses of wine and I've always been a lightweight. Was I drunk the whole time? Seeing things?

I roll over to my side and check my phone, as if it will give me some clarity. But I left it on my nightstand last night, so there are no videos or pictures to jog my memory, no follow-up texts, no social posts.

How can I tell what's real without a record?

When we have breakfast, no one comments on what happened. Everyone is fresh-faced while sipping on their juice, forking fruit into their mouths. Bella Marie taps at her soft-boiled egg, which is nestled in a porcelain eggcup, with a golden spoon, creating a jagged crack along its hemisphere. As she peels back the beige shell, she glances at me with a smile. "Would you like one? It's delicious when you dip a slice of toast in it." She points to the well of bright yolk, yellow and goopy.

I look away without answering, suddenly sick. Everyone is so normal, I almost convince myself that it was all in my head, some odd dream or hallucination.

Only Iz is out of sorts. She's off to the side, sucking on a cigarette without rest, flicking her golden lighter, *schwing, clack, schwing, clack*, making the flame appear and disappear. When our eyes meet, she raises her brows in an expression of disbelief. Neither of us say anything, as if we don't want to be guilty of disrupting their pleasant and peaceful breakfast.

But as I scrape butter on my toast, I can't help but summon memories of the absurd night. When I try to recall what I was thinking, I stumble onto a dead end. It's like I *wasn't* thinking—like I was acting without rationale. And there's the issue of my aunt. I can't deny it: I feel lighter. Like something heavy has drained out of my chest. When I looked at my phone earlier, I didn't even think about her texts. I wasn't anxious about her, couldn't hear her biting voice in the back of my head. Even now, it's all . . . gone.

Is my current state because of what happened last night? Did it release something inside me? Detach her spirit from my chest? But how does that make any sense? I wish my aunt could send me some signal, confirm that nothing has changed, that everything I feel right now is a farce.

After breakfast, Bella Marie tells us we have some time to ourselves before our morning group activity. The mention of *group activity* gives me the chills. If it's anything like the last one, I'll have to tap out.

I'm heading back to my bungalow when I hear someone behind me. I turn around, hoping it's Iz. I want to talk to her about what happened. If anyone could understand the confusion in my head, it would be her. But to my surprise, it's Kelly. Her inky hair is clipped back. Without makeup, she resembles her teenage self in her viral hair-curling video. Regardless, her presence makes me wary. I pivot, not wanting to deal with her passive-aggressive remarks, but she grabs my arm. "Let's talk."

"Oh, I don't—" But she pulls me toward the beach. In my periphery, I see Lily dragging Iz toward the greenhouse. Bella Marie is farther down the path, eyes trained on them, and I wonder if she sent Kelly and Lily to talk to us. She must have sensed something awry at breakfast. Embarrassment heats my cheeks. What if I spoiled the group mood? I bet Chloe never acted this way.

Kelly sits me down on a wood bench shaded by a palm tree. I can barely look at her, casting my gaze along the horizon. The sky is so blue, it's like it's one with the ocean.

"Where's your head at?" Her voice is gruff and impatient.

"I'm not sure what you mean." I dig my thumbs into my thighs, wondering why it's Kelly here and not Angelique or Sophia. Hell, I'd even take Ana. She could recite some bad poetry about feelings, bat her pretty doe eyes at me, and then we'd be on our merry way.

"We used to be pretty close," Kelly says. "Before your break, you could share anything with me."

I arch my brow. Given how mean she's been, I have trouble believing it. Nevertheless, this conversation is drifting toward being too personal, so I attempt an early evacuation. "My stomach is really disagreeing with me—"

My butt is an inch off the bench when Kelly says, "Sit down."

Her tone is so commanding, I obey without thought, swallowing a knot of tension.

"Things have obviously changed between you and me, but I guess this is our opportunity to set things straight. So, let's not beat around the bush. You're obviously concerned about what happened last night. Tell me what's going on in your mind right now in one word."

"One word?"

"Congratulations on demonstrating active listening! Do you want a ribbon?"

I bristle at her sarcasm and turn over responses in my head. Better to go along with whatever she has planned than to fight against it. "Overwhelmed?"

"Given everything that happened, it's natural you'd be overwhelmed. I know you've been having memory lapses recently—"

"It's because my twin—"

"She died and you found her body. Super traumatic or whatever, rest in peace, yada, yada. Will you let me continue now?"

I nod meekly, picking at my nails, scraping out soil from last night that had escaped my notice.

"When all of this happened to me the first time," she continues, "I was overwhelmed and confused too."

"You burned an effigy of your aunt?"

"Not exactly, but something like that. And can you stop interrupting me? Seriously, it's so annoying. The Chloe I knew didn't do that."

I bite my tongue. "Sorry."

She sighs. "Years ago, I had a string of viral videos and was growing faster than I ever thought possible. My parents even let me drop out of high school and move from Oklahoma to New York to pursue influencing full-time because they recognized my potential. These days, I know that audience loyalty is a fallacy, but back then, I was naive and *so* hopeful. I didn't know how easily everything could be pulled out from under me." She shakes her head. "To be honest, I still don't know why my audience lost interest, but a few years into my career, my videos barely surfaced four digits and my subscriber count had plateaued. Brands stopped working with me because of limited engagement, and I didn't have enough views to make good AdSense. I tried to chase trends, change my personality—anything to recover what I'd lost. But people didn't seem to care."

I had known about this vaguely. Kelly, like countless other content creators, had fizzled out of the mainstream, often through no fault of their own. As soon as you lose your grip on the attention ecosphere, you slip and fall into a void of obscurity, reduced to another bullet point in a long list of dated internet references. By the time you realize what went wrong, followers have already turned the other way, and the small window to capturing their attention has closed again.

"I was a twenty-year-old has-been without a high school diploma. Getting in front of the camera became shameful and embarrassing, like I was a monkey asked to perform in front of an empty audience. After a year of no progress, my mind was in a dark place. I couldn't see hope. I was anxious and depressed. In my desperation, I made a last-ditch attempt at regaining my following by reaching out to trending creators for a collab. I was a pitiful case, and most people didn't even have the decency to reply. But then one person said yes."

"Bella Marie," I say, the answer obvious.

A rare and genuine smile curves on Kelly's lips. "She was my second wind, guiding me through my trouble, giving me solutions to things I thought impossible. Like chewing a strong gum to combat my anxiety by grounding me through my taste buds, simple things like that. And when I was invited on the trip, my career began to soar. I'd had the resurgence I'd been searching for and I finally found hope again."

"What did she do?"

This time, Kelly doesn't chide me for interrupting. Her eyes glimmer as she turns to face me. "Close your eyes and feel your body. Compared to who you were before, how do you feel now?"

I do as she asks. Behind the darkness of my eyelids, I consider my present state intensely. "I feel . . . buoyant."

"That lightness is your chest is a sign of alignment. Because of our group effort last night, the universe has heard what you've been manifesting and has given you a taste of what's ahead. But this marvelous feeling isn't permanent. If you want to make your wishes everlasting, you have to truly believe and accept the positive energy we are gifting you. Otherwise, this is only temporary. Can you do that?"

I lace my brows. It's true. I feel buoyant, lighter, detached from any concern, as if at any moment, I could rise to the sky. But it isn't an aimless weightlessness, I'm not a mote of dust being pushed by the wind, a molecule at risk of being vaporized by sun. I am solid, in control, ready to make the world mine. If I could remain like this forever, without concern, without burden, protected from the leaden mass my aunt had buried within me, I would do anything they asked.

But a thin thread of hesitancy anchors me to the ground. Is Kelly telling me the truth? Are these sensations a result of a group manifestation? Last night wasn't a pleasant memory. I hate my aunt and wish she'd stay away from me—but burning her? That has never been my intention.

I open my eyes to see Kelly staring at me intensely. The raven pools of her pupils shoot goose bumps down my spine. I shiver, though the breeze is warm.

"After I became one with this group," she continues, "accepted what everyone was providing me, protected by our mutual understanding and effort, I was able to be born anew. My dreams became reality again. Don't you want that too?"

I gulp. "I do."

"We can do that for you. But to do so, we must maintain a positive group synergy. This means we must trust each other. Believe in each other. That's the only way we can help uplift and protect each other. We cannot grow tall and command our dreams unless we are supported. Remember, not everyone gets a second chance. We only have your best interests in mind. Do you understand?"

Her words buzz in my chest, making my pulse jump. The string of hesitancy that grounds me frays after everything Kelly has said. I don't want to be tied down when I could soar to impossible heights.

"Yes. I do. I understand." And once the words are out in the air, I am weightless once again.

43

Morning sun drapes my skin. The breeze is cool. Every inhale is a refreshing gulp of salty sea air.

"Now open your eyes and feel the changes in your body," Sophia says, capping off our five-minute breathing meditation. She's the leader of our morning group activity: vinyasa yoga by the gardens. Sophia is a certified yoga instructor, and a damn good one at that. I don't think I've ever down-dogged as well as I have today. My body is limber and reenergized, like I've somehow wrung the worries out of me.

Sophia is dressed in white linen—we all are, breezy and free. She insisted we change since looser clothing is more *authentic* to how they practice yoga in India. Sure, whatever. Admittedly, this garb is way more comfortable than skintight leggings and a pinching sports bra. The best part is, I don't have to worry about my stomach skin rolling over when I bend to touch my toes. It's kind of empowering.

"Before we conclude, I want us all to say one positive thing about ourselves, and for the group to repeat it back as *you* statements. I can start and we'll go around in a circle."

After what Kelly told me, I'm assuming these affirmations are yet another instrument in their group manifestations. I've been slowly understanding the power of affirmations, but it still feels narcissistic to praise yourself so openly.

"I am successful," Sophia starts.

"You are successful," we say. I push through my internal cringe, reminding myself to protect our group synergy.

"I am beautiful," Ana says.

"You are beautiful," everyone says with smiles, easily.

Huh. Why am I the only one having so much trouble? Oh my god. Have I internalized misogyny? You know what? She is beautiful. And so am I!

"I am a hard worker," says Kelly.

"You are a hard worker."

"I am a good person," Angelique says.

"You are a good person."

"I am loyal." Lily.

"You are loyal."

"I am a good mother," Iz says.

I glance at her as we repeat, "You are a good mother." Whatever Lily said to her this morning must have struck a chord. Her Zen vibrates at everyone else's frequency.

"I am smart." Emmeline.

"You are smart."

"I am brave." Maya.

"You are brave."

There's a brief lull and I realize it's my turn.

I clear my throat, embarrassment licking me.

"I-I am worthy," I say.

"You are worthy."

They repeat it without a hitch. Without an ounce of doubt. Like it's true. Obvious. A brightness erupts inside my chest, pulsing hot through my veins. My lips curl into a smile and I sit taller.

I feel worthy. Genuinely. The group has gifted me with glowing worth and there's no one to tell me otherwise, no hounding voices or clawing threats.

I am worthy.

Last is Bella Marie. We all turn to her, and she smiles a perfect little smile.

"I am a leader."

"You are a leader," we say to her.

24

Lunch is a picnic by the ocean. Fizzy pink drinks in sweating champagne glasses, sandwiches cut into diagonal quarters, tropical fruit platters, kale salads topped with pomegranate, and miniature strawberry shortcakes sit on top of a gingham blanket. An umbrella shades us from the sun.

After our yoga session, golden energy ripples through me. I am worthy with every step I take. I am great and beautiful and brave and kind. I haven't felt this good—this free—in a long time. We are a group of women, young and alive with the generous desire to uplift and listen. We've sweated off our makeup, stripped our defenses, changed into similar linen clothes. We are barefaced and vulnerable, imperfections and all.

If this is how the rest of the week goes, I'd never want to leave.

"I can't thank you enough," I say. "This was such a much-needed break."

"Of course, darling," Bella Marie replies, handing Emmeline a napkin after she spills orange juice onto her white pants. "We don't listen to our bodies enough. It's an honor to host you all."

"It's good to have a moment to ourselves," Ana adds.

"Especially for us moms," says Lily, glancing at Iz. "Otherwise, we'd lose ourselves entirely. Not to scare you or anything," she says to Angelique.

"Oh, no worries." Angelique strokes her belly. She glances at the distant waves, a solemn expression threading her Botoxed brows. "I'm not worried about that at all."

Iz forks some salad into her mouth. "Lily took me on a walk earlier this morning and it really hit me. I can't believe you have an entire island." She chews, then swallows. "This is . . . a *crazy* life. And you do this *every* year?"

"It's all thanks to Bella Marie," Kelly says. "She gives up so much for us."

"So generous," says Emmeline.

"And so perfect." Lily.

"Beautiful too." Maya.

The Belladonnas glow at Bella Marie, who smiles sheepishly. Her golden hair is almost white in the sunlight. "Oh, stop it," she says, covering her mouth.

"We all work so hard," Kelly continues. "This is the one week a year we get to take a break."

Everyone nods in agreement.

But there's a laugh. The slightest chuckle from Iz. Attention whips to her. She looks around, lips pressing into a line.

Kelly tips her head, agitation pinching her eyes. I smell spearmint, even though she isn't chewing gum. "What are you laughing at?" She's smiling, but her tone is clipped.

"Isla," Lily says, gripping her glass of juice tight. "Remember what we spoke about earlier?"

"Yeah, but, I mean, it's just that . . . You know." Iz tries to laugh it off. But no one laughs with her.

"*You know* . . . what?" Kelly asks.

Iz glances around as if hoping someone will finish her sentence. Everyone falls quiet.

"We're *influencers*."

"What's that supposed to mean?" Kelly asks.

I still, and my core tightens. Water crashes on the rocks a few paces away, splashing spikes of water onto my thigh.

Iz picks up her fork, like she's hoping we'll move on. When no one speaks up, she puts down her fork and speaks softly. "I'm just saying, being an influencer isn't, like, the hardest thing in the world." She glances at Kelly. "You literally make reaction content."

Kelly arches her brow. "And?"

"Are you seriously going to make me say it?" Iz sighs. "Like, that doesn't require a lot of work."

I clutch the bottom of my blouse, my breath shortening. *What is she doing?*

Kelly's mouth falls open in a surprised, angry laugh. "Do you know how long I've had to work to get to where I am? And for the record, I have a very, *very* high production value. I have a team of five. I feed families."

"Right. But at the end of the day, don't you just press play and record a reaction?"

"I abhor that characterization of my work."

Iz whistles. "*Abhor.* Wow."

I bite my lip, eyes flipping from Kelly to Iz. I want them to stop fighting. I want us to return to what we were moments ago. Family. Supportive. What happened to Kelly's whole sermon on group synergy? Do the rules not apply to her if she's the one affronted?

"We should all calm down—" Emmeline begins.

"If you think it's so easy," Kelly says, "why don't you do it?"

Iz leans back, her hands in the air, making a gesture like, *Isn't it obvious?* "I'll never be applauded for mediocrity because I'm not a stereotypically beautiful white girl."

I wince at how Iz has spoken the truth aloud and glance at Bella Marie, waiting for her to relieve the tension. But her jaw is set. Her eyes don't follow who's speaking, as if she's deep in thought.

Kelly clenches her fists. *"Mediocrity?"*

"Race has nothing to do with Kelly's content," Ana says.

"Of course, *you* say that." Iz rolls her eyes.

"I think we should all take a breath," Sophia chirps, "practice some positive meditation—"

"Excuse me?" Ana spits. "I worked hard for my followers! Do you know how much I sacrificed to get to where I am?"

"Your entire career is defined by your appearance," Iz continues. "I mean, no offense, but you have to acknowledge it's true. That's literally your niche. You don't sing. You don't do makeup. You aren't into fitness. You're just pretty. You take selfies and do body checks."

"That's not true. I write poetry!"

"Putting paragraph breaks between a fragmented sentence is not poetry!" Iz's back is straight as an arrow, a horrid line between her brow. "I mean it's— Why are we even debating this?"

Angelique downs her orange juice and pours herself a glass of wine as Lily palms her forehead.

"Just because we're white doesn't mean we work any less hard for our following," Maya says.

"Social media creates an equal playing field for everyone," Emmeline adds.

"Equal?" Iz jolts. "Is that a joke? You do realize the basis of social media starts offline, right? Social media is inherently unequal. I mean, even if we disregard race entirely, there are so many barriers to accessibility. Who can afford a phone? Who has access to stable internet? Who has time to scroll and learn about trends instead of clocking in to a double shift to feed their families? Even what country you're born in affects it. There's nothing equal about social media. Sure, once in a blue moon it uplifts creators from under-served backgrounds, but that's like finding a unicorn amid a stable of horses."

"God," exhales Emmeline. "You don't have to sit there and make a speech like Obama—"

I flinch.

"*Obama?*" Iz repeats.

"—it's patronizing and belittling."

"I'm disappointed in you," Lily says. "I thought you understood."

Iz rolls her eyes. "I'm not going to silence myself for something as dumb as *group synergy.*"

The girls gasp in horror and a tense silence chokes the air.

"You're being awfully rude and antagonistic today, Isla," says Maya.

"Very rude," says Ana.

"Terribly antagonistic," echoes Kelly.

"Christ. I'm just saying we should take some accountability. *Especially* you, Emmeline."

Emmeline jerks straight. "Me? Why are you singling me out?"

"You know exactly what I'm talking about."

Fuck.

Emmeline is visibly shaking, as if there's a timer within her, *tick, tick, tick,* about to explode. Her pale cheeks bloom red as her eyes grow misty. "Those tweets were from *years* ago."

"It wasn't cool to be racist in 2010!"

Emmeline starts tearing up.

"Look what you did!" Kelly holds Emmeline's hand, patting her back. "Apologize."

"What?" Iz pushes her plate of food away. "No! Are you fucking kidding? I feel like I'm going crazy right now."

"That's obvious," Ana says. "Your jealousy is showing and it's not pretty."

"Very ugly," says Maya.

I scan the table and notice that Ana, Maya, Lily, Kelly, and Emmeline have somehow joined hands, their shoulders pressed together like a solid wall. They all bare their teeth. Their expressions are so similar that for a second, I can't tell them apart.

"Okay? So now we're just attacking *my* appearance?" Iz blows out a breath, exasperated. "Fine. Let's talk about appearance and race since you are all so desperate to pretend it's not a factor. Well, news flash. It is! It's inherent in the business of photo and video content." She turns to Emmeline, who has two rivers streaming down her cheeks. "Like your videos. I love the aesthetics—which I don't doubt is thanks to your editor and entire creative team—but you never fail to complain about how hard your life is. About how you're depressed and lonely all the time. Meanwhile, you're jet-setting to Paris, attending fashion shows, eating hotel brunch, and lounging in your little New York penthouse with your dog. You have the *luxury* of boredom and people eat it up. Why? Because you're a stereotypical beauty. Desirable by Western norms. People are sympathetic to your struggles because your appearance makes your whining palatable. And I'm not saying your feelings of depression aren't genuine. They're valid. I'm only saying if a Black or Hispanic, or hell, even Asian"—she turns to me and I recoil—"person said the same things you do, they'd be labeled as ungrateful. If we rotted in bed like you, our oily hair would be seen as dirty and lazy instead of relatable. We have to confine ourselves into these perfect yet nonthreatening boxes, while you have the privilege of complaining because you fit the aesthetic of the sad white girl that society thirsts for."

"That's not true," Emmeline says, dabbing her tears with a gingham napkin. "You don't know how hard I worked to get to where I am. What I've given up. You're making me upset."

"You can't cry your way out of everything, Emmeline." Iz sighs, while the rest of the table gapes. "Obviously, we all worked hard to get to where we are. But acknowledging our privilege is still important. We all put in our hours. We are all on the grind. We've all sacrificed. But some people sacrifice less and get more. And other people work themselves to the bone and get scraps. That's the nature of life and social media is not an exception."

There's a deafening silence as a cool wind blows around us. Emmeline hiccups. The sun retreats behind the clouds. My skin tickles with the feeling of winter.

"Isla," Kelly snarls, "just because you're less successful than us doesn't mean you get to be a bitter, envious bitch and gaslight us about our hard work."

"A *bi*—" Iz gapes. "Are you fucking serious?" She's met with nothing but angry stares. Simmering resentment.

But then she turns to me.

Her eyes are desperate. The air seems to thin as my throat constricts. I shake my head slowly. *Please don't bring me into this.* But it's too late.

My heart whirls in my chest as everyone shifts to me. All nine faces and eighteen eyes staring, waiting for me to say something. To take a side. This whole time, I avoided being swept in, letting them fire at each other. But now the Belladonnas are wide-eyed, eyebrows rising.

You agree with us, right? Don't you want to become one of us? Don't you want to be accepted and happy and buoyant?

Iz is breathless. "C'mon, Chloe. You see what I'm trying to say, right?"

"Uh, um. I—"

Two sharp claps ring through the air. We all twist to look at Bella Marie. She stands, a mother about to lecture her children. "I think we've all hurt each other in this heated conversation." She turns to Kelly, specifically. "You must be understanding of Isla. She's new to this. She doesn't know what we've given. What we've sacrificed. Hasn't experienced what we have. It's only day two. We've barely gotten started. Give her time to understand our world. Remember, darlings, we are family."

No one affirms this.

There's the slightest twitch in Bella Marie's eyes, the smallest crack in her perfection, a fracture before an earthquake. "Kelly, I would really appreciate if you apologized to Isla for calling her a b-word."

Kelly blows out an annoyed sigh. "I'm sorry if what I said offended you."

Bella Marie turns to Iz. "And? What about you, Isla?"

"You aren't serious, right?" Iz asks. But everyone waits for her to apologize. She shakes her head, glancing at me, disappointed, and then looks away.

Guilt burns inside my throat. Hot, acidic, and paralyzing.

She gets up from the table and no one stops her.

I'm the only one who hears her whisper, "That's not even a real fucking apology."

45

can't bear being around the Belladonnas. The vibes are off. But most of all, I'm disappointed in myself. At how I didn't speak up for Iz. Sure, she could have been nicer, but she wasn't entirely off base. I knew where she was coming from.

I wander around the island and wind up in front of Iz's bungalow. I'm tempted to knock. To say sorry and offer an ear. But something pulls me back. The whole island has this heaviness, an overwhelming sensation of someone observing, breathing down my neck. I'm reminded of Bella Marie the day we arrived, how she stood on the tarmac with an empty gaze, and shiver.

I wish things could return to how they were this morning. I've lost the heady energy and I yearn to have it back.

Instead of going to Iz, I wander around pointlessly. I pass by some staff, dressed in their spotless white linen as they trim grass, manicure trees. They smile at me with their straight teeth, eyes sparkling, looking like models out of *GQ* or *Vogue*. What the hell is in the water here that gives their skin that uncanny glow? I wonder if they have a community dentist or if they pop out of the womb with perfect pearly whites, artificially selected for their teeth and luscious skin. "Good morning, Miss Van Huusen," they chirp, tipping their heads. "How are you doing? Need any help? Where are you going?" As much as I love the attention, it's getting annoying. Everyone is too keen on my actions, like a doctor observing a recovering mental patient.

To avoid eager eyes, I walk to the edge of the island, around the shore. My bare feet make imprints in the soft sand, each granule warm against my skin. The slosh of waves gathering and retreating, tasting my toes. I lose track of time. Somehow, I end up near the back of the island, where the sand merges into rocks and green. Putting on my sandals, I hike uphill and navigate through spindly trees that aren't as manicured as the ones in the front. I come to a clearing that leads to a rocky bluff. Blue sea and endless skies stretch before me. The wind cools my damp skin and I spot a rock that would be a perfect place to take a break. Maybe some positive meditation to calm my thoughts. Sophia would be proud.

I'm situating myself on the rock when I hear branches snapping. A figure bursts through the trees. An old woman. She's thin, dressed in brown-and-white linen, moccasins on her feet.

I knit my brows. Something is familiar about her.

She's in a daze, doesn't notice me. Her skin is wan under the harsh summer sun, blue veins running up her jaw. Eyes red and bleary. She creeps closer and closer and closer to the edge of the cliff, rocks crackling under her shoes. I glance from her to the edge and back to her, as the gap between them draws uncomfortably thin. Three more steps and she'd go plunging to her death.

Why isn't she stopping?

Should I say something?

"Um. Excuse me? There's a cliff there, so be careful." My voice comes out weak, childish.

She stops, dust kicking under her shoes. Her head creaks toward me, her neck twisting like ropes. She stares not at me, but beyond. Behind me.

Goose bumps prickle my arms as I gulp, following her gaze. Nothing is there. Only trees, rock, and blue sky. I return my gaze to her, unsettled.

"Um . . . Hello?" I say, managing a smile.

She registers my words this time. Sharpness enters her eyes, and she darts toward me in fast, short steps. I jump off my rock, alarmed by her approach.

"You're not from here," she says, her voice hoarse and raspy like a smoker's.

"N-no, I'm not. I'm a guest of—"

"You should leave before it's too late." She grabs hold of me, her dry, skeletal fingers prodding into my warm skin. "Leave before they get you too!"

"Um. What—"

Then, the sound of approaching steps. People running. Shouts. "Mrs. Melniburg!"

Mrs. Melniburg?

Now that I look at her carefully, I see the resemblance. Their long, swan-like necks, pointed chins, delicate frames.

"What are you standing around for?" she asks, breathless. "Go! Run!" She pushes me away.

I don't know what it is. Maybe it's the desperation in her irises or the sound of people approaching in search, but my legs move before my mind catches up. I stumble in retreat while my eyes are still on her.

Four workers dressed in gray appear beyond the trees and they lunge for her, grabbing her arms. I'm far enough away that they don't notice me.

"Let go!" She struggles against them violently.

"It's dangerous here, Mrs. Melniburg. Let's get you back inside."

A branch snaps under me. Four heads whip my way.

Fuck.

The biggest one, tall and menacing, separates from the rest. He glimpses me through the trees. My limbs are frozen, heart pattering up my narrowed throat. I only manage a squeak as I urge my legs to move. Move.

Move!

Fight or flight finally takes over. I spin around, legs breaking into a sprint as I dash in the opposite direction. He charges toward me. I risk a look over my shoulder as he closes in, burly hands reaching, grasping. I slam into something hard and fall onto my ass, knocking the wind out of my lungs. The world spins. A pale face looms, casting me into cold shadow.

I scream and shield myself. But there are no fists or kicks or grabbing arms. Only the sound of waves.

"Sorry. I didn't mean to scare you."

That voice. It's familiar. I peel my eyes open and glance through my fingers.

Viktor. He shakes his head at the other man, gesturing at him to back off. "She's a valued guest of Miss Bella Marie."

The other man grumbles something under his breath and jogs back to the group, who have a screaming Mrs. Melniburg wrapped tight in their arms.

"Are you all right?" Viktor offers his hand.

I'm apprehensive as I take hold. His fingers are rough, calloused. He pulls me up in a quick swoop, air rushing into my face.

"Y-yeah," I stammer. Dried grass pricks my thigh through my linen pants like needles. I dust them off. "What the hell was that?"

"Sorry about my friend there. He's under strict orders to watch Mrs. Melniburg. He can get quite protective."

"Protective enough to run after me like he's ready for murder? A bit of an overreaction, don't you think?"

"Not to us. Don't you get jumpy when you think your family is in danger?"

I don't have any family of value, so maybe I don't understand. Swallowing hard, I wipe my forehead, which is slicked with sweat. "That woman said some weird things to me."

Viktor nods, unsurprised. "The doctors say she's sustained many traumas to the brain. Her falls as a gymnast, and now her addiction and her recent stroke. We're also suspecting dementia. Sometimes, she says things that don't make sense. It's a shame what old age brings."

She did seem in a daze. Like her head isn't in the right place.

I think back to the Van Huusens. The two of them, vegetables in their hospital beds. It's fucking depressing.

"Shouldn't she be in a home or something?"

"She receives the best care here on the island. And she's surrounded by family. There's no better place to be."

I guess he has a point. There's clean air and fresh food here. Plus, knowing the Melniburgs, they probably have fancy doctors up their assholes. I wonder how much Viktor gets paid.

"You look frightened." He puts his hand on my shoulder with a grin. "I have something that might cheer you up."

46

Viktor hands me an axe. The sharp edge glints in the sun.

I gawk at him. "Are you serious?"

"What's wrong, Chloe? You used to beg to chop wood with me."

I bite my tongue. Damn Chloe and her weird hobbies. Who the hell chops wood for fun?

Reluctantly, I take the axe. When he lets go, I almost fall forward, unprepared for the weight.

Viktor sets a fresh log in front of me and crosses his arms. Waiting.

Sweat trickles down my armpits. I take a deep breath and steel myself. Squeeze my abs and tuck in my pelvis like I'm in Pilates. I'm a SoulCycle queen. I can do anything. I am a warrior beast!

I aim the axe at the middle of the log, then lift my arms over my head. With all my might, I swing forward with a grunt. The axe cleaves right through, ripping the wood in half with a satisfying crack. The pieces fall off to the side. Fresh cedar wafts into the air, its wooden flesh exposed.

I jump, surprised at my strength. Holy shit! I'm stronger than I thought.

Viktor laughs and angles the pieces again so I can chop them into quarters. Maybe Chloe was onto something. This is pretty stress-relieving—more fun than I thought it would be. No wonder lumberjacks seem like such chill dudes. It's impossible to feel anger if you are constantly whacking away, breaking shit in half.

Eventually, Viktor tells me I've chopped enough wood for tonight.

"What's tonight?" I ask.

He smiles. "Dinner by a campfire."

"Oh, sounds fun." I hope this meal will be more relaxed than the last. Maybe Iz has simmered down and the girls will be able to forgive her. I just want everyone to be together again.

I help him stack the wood onto a wheelbarrow. After putting in the last piece, I take a satisfied breath and pick the wood chips off my clothes.

Warmth spreads onto my back. Viktor wraps his arms around my torso, his face deep in my hair, long nose poking my cheek.

I freeze. "Uh. Wha—"

He gropes me, kissing my neck, one hand swimming to my breast, the other traveling down my legs, squeezing. He moans, breathless.

I scream. Push him off me and scramble away. Somehow, my hands find purchase on the axe. I hold it out in front of me. "Get away!" I shriek.

His eyes widen, hands flying up in the air. He paces backward.

"What the fuck is wrong with you?" I scream.

His brows furrow with confusion. "Y-you normally like it when I do that!"

"What?"

"After you chop wood, you like to do it by the barn. To burn off all the extra energy. That's our thing."

Our thing?

My mouth is so wide, a moth could make a home in it.

It makes so much sense now, why Viktor had all these memories of Chloe. They must have spent a lot of days *and* nights together.

I put down the axe and try to laugh it off. "Sorry, I'm not in the mood. The image of Bella Marie's mom is just, like, *seared* onto my brain. Not exactly, uh, the best aphrodisiac."

He nods like he totally understands. "I hear you. But whenever you need me, I'll be at your service."

"Yeah." I clear my throat. "I'll, uh, give you a shout when I need you, I guess. For . . . sex." Okay. Fully cringing now. We're silent for a bit, a rippling awkwardness between us.

I palm my forehead, still recovering from when he groped me. I'm desperate to change the topic. "So, you mentioned the campfire tonight, right? I can help set up."

He's surprised by this offer. "Really? Okay!"

We bring the logs to the beach and stack them next to a long dining table. After which I help him set up some tiki torches that are boxed up in storage.

"I'll grab some lighter fluid," he says, disappearing into the small wooden building.

As I wait, I hear squeaking. The pitter-patter of tiny feet. They might have a rat infestation. I get chills just thinking about it. Even though I've lived in New York for a few months, I'm not used to walking the streets at night when the rats are out.

Viktor returns with a bottle of lighter fluid. We coat the torches so they catch and stay burning for longer. By the time we finish, night has tinted the sky and the staff are setting up for dinner. They roll a long burgundy runner along the center of the dining table and place twisty candles and vases of flowers on top. I ask if they'd like help and they're all surprised. "Oh, no. Please sit down, Miss Van Huusen," they say, moisture gathering along their temples.

It's a bit awkward, sitting there alone as the staff bumble around me. Viktor tries to rope me in for conversation, something about how he wishes wood chopping was part of the Olympics, but the memory of his rough hands flares in my mind as soon as he opens his mouth.

Even though there are only ten minutes till dinner, I decide to leave for my bungalow, making the excuse that I want to change into another outfit. When I'm back outside in a luxurious Belle by Bella Marie silk emerald dress with a high leg slit, the table has been set. Bella Marie and seven Belladonnas, sans Iz, are waiting for me. Some staff members play live music—violin, cello, and harp—a few paces away. The music's lush tones resonate in the air, backed by the sound of the ocean. I don't recognize the tune—an original, perhaps.

I hang back for a moment and watch the Belladonnas. Their voices are as soothing as birdsong as they chirp in high tones, their wind-chime giggles perforating the air. French braids crisscross their heads, the strands as tight and binding as their friendship. Small flowers are slotted between each knot:

peonies, daisies, petunias, camellias. I missed out, apparently. I finger my loose, inky strands. My bones ache for it, the desire to be included. I wonder if Chloe braided her hair like them. I wonder if the others sense that I'm different from the woman they used to know.

Bella Marie finds me. "Chloe!" she says, beckoning with her hand.

The other seven turn to me. "Chloe!" A high and sweet chorus, welcoming me. Their gravity is irresistible.

I go to them.

47

We pass around the food. Bread, freshly baked, soft and slathered with butter. Salad. More salad. Butternut squash soup. Roasted asparagus. Sun-ripe heirloom tomatoes. Potatoes with sage. The main is roasted chicken with a ginger sauce, served on top of couscous. Everything I eat is delectable. Even the alcohol is delicious. It's the type of wine I like, not too dry or acidic but jammy and sweet, sliding easily down my throat. By the time I finish my potatoes, I've had four refills and my insides are warm, buzzing.

"We missed you today," Bella Marie says. She saved me the seat next to hers, like at her launch party. She's at the head of the table, and I'm across from Emmeline. Angelique is beside me. They smell of lemons and freesia.

"Yes, we missed you," Emmeline echoes.

"Very much," says Ana.

"You missed our hair-braiding session," Lily says.

"We picked flowers for you and everything," Angelique adds. "Now they're all wilted." She sticks out her bottom lip in a pout.

They missed me. Had picked flowers for me. "I'm sorry. I was walking around, getting some fresh air."

"See anything fun?" Sophia asks.

My mind floods with images of Bella Marie's mother. Her warning. I shake my head, clear my thoughts.

"Nothing much. Found a nice rock to meditate on."

Sophia nods, glowing. "I love that. I hope you did some positive affirmations. You are worthy."

"You are worthy," they all echo.

I sit taller at their words.

"I heard you spent some time with Viktor earlier today"—Ana bites her lip with a sly grin—"*chopping wood.*"

The whole table breaks out in high-pitched giggles, their bodies swaying.

Oh my god. Is chopping wood a euphemism here? Do they all know about Chloe and Viktor's relationship? I glance at Bella Marie nervously. She has a pleasant, mild smile. No indication of anything awry as she sips red wine.

"I hope Viktor was a gentleman," Maya says. "Oh! Unless you like it rough. Manly like a bull."

More giggles. More laughs.

I put down my fork, unease slithering into me.

"I do love it when Viktor chops my wood," Ana says. "Especially near the beach."

"The beach?" Emmeline asks. "Where on the beach?"

"By the banyan tree, where the swing is. Or, I should say, *on* the swing." Ana winks.

"The swing!" Emmeline exclaims.

"The swing is a good place," Sophia purrs.

"A great place," Lily says. "I love swings."

The campfire beside us pops, logs collapsing. Holy shit. Viktor is their shared sex-toy-man-thing. What in the actual ya-ya-sisterhood living fuck is this?

I glance around the table. Has everyone—did everyone? Even Bella Marie? I'm sick. The wine in my stomach is a pool of acid, sloshing back and forth as the Belladonnas' giggles grow louder and louder.

Bella Marie catches my gaze, tips her head softly. "Something wrong, darling?" Her hand finds my thigh under the table. A finger slides beneath the slit of my emerald dress. Her skin is soft and warm on mine, tingling, enticing. I remember how she said I look *splendid* in emerald during her launch and I gulp, shrinking away from her, desperate to change the conversation.

"Where's Iz?"

The laughter stops. So does the music, just briefly, to switch to another song. The ocean tide pulls back. Everyone looks at me. Sharp razor blades to my bones.

"If you're talking about Isla," Bella Marie says, "she's elected to take dinner alone by the telephone to talk to her daughters. It seems she misses them dearly. Though I do wish she was disconnecting like the rest of us."

"Oh. I see."

Kelly's knife grates hard against her plate. "You're nothing like Isla," she says to me, poking her fork hard into her chicken. Metal against porcelain. "So much more well behaved."

"Not teeming with jealousy just because the algorithm doesn't favor her," says Emmeline. "Not lecturing us like we're a group of idiots."

"Women like Isla aren't truly feminists," Ana adds, "always pitting women against each other when we should uplift."

"Exactly," Maya says. "Men dominate social media in every industry and niche. Even in beauty, an empire built on exploiting womanly vulnerabilities, the top creators are men. Women like Isla only bring down our efforts by making us seem antagonistic."

"You are so much better than Isla," Kelly says. "And you don't speak with food in your mouth."

"And you don't smoke," says Sophia, "inhaling those toxic carcinogens, poisoning your lovely body. She's not even trying to quit!"

"Less angry," says Ana. "Less bitter. More beautiful. Stunning."

"Very beautiful," Lily joins in. "Gorgeous, really."

"Not just gorgeous. Sublime," Maya says.

Sublime? I resist a smile. I am warm and heady from their compliments, even though part of me wants to defend Iz.

"I want to take a bite of you and savor you under my tongue because you are so sublime."

"I love you so much, Chloe," Emmeline coos.

I stop resisting. A smile breaks across my face. "That's so sweet. Thank you. *Thank you.*" I say it twice. I can't help myself. I am so thankful.

"I love you too, Chloe," Angelique echoes.

"I love you, Chloe," says Lily.

"I love you, Chloe," says Sophia.

"I love you, Chloe," says Kelly.

"I love you, Chloe," says Maya.

"I love you, Chloe," says Ana.

"I love you, Julie."

My heart stops. I whip my head to Bella Marie, pulse thrumming. "W-what? What did you say?"

She blinks. Smiles. Tips her head. "I said 'I love you, Chloe.'"

I take a breath. I must have heard wrong. Had too many drinks. The world is dipping in and out. Her beautiful figure is wobbly from wine, yet she is still godly. I'm reminded of my teenage self, scrolling endlessly on Tumblr, reblogging her every time she came on my screen. My idol.

Bella Marie returns her hand to my thigh, slipping her fingers up the sensitive parts of my upper leg, as if she belongs there. The thin fabric allows me to learn each groove of her finger, study the swirl on her pinkie. I sit straighter and move without thought, cupping her pliable hands, buttery on my skin. She intertwines our fingers. Then she leans over to Emmeline, holds her hand too. In a blink, we're all linked. The nine of us. My palms are sandwiched by Bella Marie and Angelique, their energy channeling into me like lightning. Hot and dangerous yet loving, shooting through my limbs, melting into my muscles. I am warm and light. Floating, but tethered and supported.

"I love you all," I say. It comes out naturally. Glides out like air, true. Overwhelmingly. "I *love* you."

"We love you too," they say.

A drunken giggle bubbles up my throat, pure euphoria slipping out, unrestrained. It catches, harmonious. We all laugh until we're out of breath. Happy. Even as our laughs dull, our hearts are full. Our hands are still interlocked as the staff clears our plates, trades them out for slices of key lime pie and matching green fizzy drinks. Carbonation crawls up the chilled, sweating glass.

"Enjoy dessert, my darlings." Bella Marie lets me go, and I wish she hadn't. I'd rather eat like a dog, a beast—face in the plate, licking, slurping—than let go.

But I pick up my fork like a human and dig in. The pie is perfect. Citrusy and sweet with the slightest tang. Cool as it melts on my tongue, the crust crumbly with butter. I swirl the contents in my mouth, salivating as the violin notes swell, pushing the custard-like filling between the gaps of my teeth. When I swallow, I'm left with an empty mouth that begs for hydration. I tip the green drink to my lips. It is effervescent, sweet, tangy, and the slightest bit bitter. Gritty and fresh with herbs, cleansing my palate, a perfect pairing with dessert. I sip and I eat and I sip and I eat and I sip and I eat and I sip and I eat until there is no more.

The world is hugging me, the night air warm as my insides fizz with delight. The musicians switch pieces and I think I recognize the tune. It's familiar, slightly haunting, but I can't pick it out, not when I'm surrounded by laughter and beautiful women. I cannot pay attention. I will not pay attention.

An energy within me begs for release. I stop resisting.

"Let's dance!" I jump out of my seat, my feet somehow landing on the table. I make it my runway, spinning around the candles, the vases, the baskets of bread. The girls laugh and clap and they love me oh so much. Their faces stretch and twist with pure adoration. They join me, some in their chairs, dresses sashaying around their spindly hips, showing off their long, tanned thighs; others dance in the sand, their arms snaking through the air, the flowers in their hair blooming. We come together and pirouette past the campfire, twirling near the edge of the foamy water, carried by the triumphant cello, its strums forcing my legs to buckle. The water is icy, chilling, but I do not care. I kick and I kick and I kick, soaking my dress until I'm all wet. The other girls do too. Beautiful creatures illuminated by the moon.

48

I wake up.

It is dark. Cold. I blink at the wooden beams above me. I am in my room.

My skin is dry, the remnants of salt on my lips. Sweetness and tanginess in my throat. Key lime pie. My feet are sandy, aching, tired. Tired from what? I try to make sense of it.

The dancing. Oh, how we laughed and danced.

I close my eyes and melt into the memory.

I must have had so much fun I passed out. Yes, yes. I remember. The girls, my lovers, they carried me from the water after my eyes tired of staying open, their dresses and hair soaked like seaweed, dripping. They held me as their baby, a thing to be loved from first breath and sight. They were laughing, giggling, delighted. "Oh, you are so beautiful," one of them said. I can't remember who. My vision was blurry, their figures dark and similar in the night. Only the barest outline, blond hair. But that's half of them.

"You are so charming," said another as they tucked me into bed sweetly. "I love you."

"You are worthy."

"You are kind."

"You are warm."

"You are a lie."

My eyes pop open, heart thudding into my throat.

I turn to the voice. My blood runs cold.

Chloe.

She is alive. Sitting on the sofa, with her back turned to me. I can pick out her dusty black hair from anywhere, the shape of her head, which mirrors mine. She smells rotten, acrid.

Why is she here?

"A fraud," she says. "A miserable human being. Selfish and narcissistic. Nothing more than a leech. A parasite. A *killer.*"

"N-no." I'm choking. Gurgling. My voice is weak. "I didn't kill you. You died from a drug overdose. It wasn't my fault. It was your own fault!"

She stands. I flinch and look around for someone to help me. But there's no one to witness the ghost. My girls have left. I am abandoned—*again.* Am I destined to be alone?

I press my back hard into my pillows, wanting to sink into the plush fibers, become one with the thread and goose feathers, erased from this world.

"Then why?" Without turning, she floats toward me. Her feet never leave the floor. "Why did you take my place, Ju-Ju? Take my identity? Steal everything I have?"

"I-I didn't steal anything. It was—y-you died! It would have gone to waste otherwise."

"No." She slowly turns around. And then I see her, finally. My mouth dries, eyes widening with horror.

She has been devoured. Nothing more than bone and hair. A few maggots nibble on some tendons around her jaw, but their grip is weak. As she looms, her foul breath a cloud around me, they shed onto my sheets, weightless bugs squirming for meat and decay.

"You've stolen everything I worked for." Her jawbone clicks as she speaks. "You are a cheat and a fraud. I wish you were not my family. That you were not my sister. Not my twin. I hate you."

"N-no. I loved you. I wanted you in my life but you abandoned me. You left me alone again and again."

"You stole my life without an ounce of guilt."

"I'm sorry. I swear, I feel bad, every day."

"Liar."

I flinch, knowing she's right. I am a liar. The lines of our lives have blurred so much that Chloe's life truly feels like mine. There's nothing to be guilty for.

She climbs onto the bed, reaches for me with her bony hand, scraping my cheek, yet I don't move. A part of me yearns for her touch. My sister. My twin.

"For so long," I croak between sobs, "all I wanted was for you to come back into my life. I wanted a family. Mom and Dad. Our home that smelled like rice and broth. The sticky counters and dusty corners. The small, dark cabinets where we could hide together. All of it. I just wanted my family back, but it's too late. You're all dead, so I took what I could. The last remnants of what was left over. It just happened to be the outline of the life you left behind." I finally dared to say it out loud, the words that were always locked inside me.

"Family," she whispers harshly into my ear. Rattling. "Is that truly what you wanted? Not my life?"

"It's true," I say, desperate.

"Then it's not too late."

I sob harder, my palms wet, salty, and wrinkling. "It is."

"It is not."

She puts her hand on me again. I jolt. But then I notice it's different. Soft, light. Fleshy and real.

The sweet smell of flowers. Of love. I take a risk. Open my eyes. Chloe is gone, replaced by eight beautiful women in bed with me. Their stares are loving, even in the dark. They all lay their hands on me, soft and delicate. I am a wilting flower they are trying to revive. A baby bird that has fallen from a tree.

"We are your family now," Bella Marie says. She's right next to me. Her warm breath sweet on my cheek. A caress. "Close your eyes and focus on my voice, Julie."

My breath catches in my throat. *Julie.* They know.

"H-how?"

"We could feel your energy, the difference. Chloe was always a cool blue, but your soul is golden and warm. Better, in some ways. The truth of you has never been hidden from us."

My chin trembles, I shake my head. "I'm sorry. I-I—"

She shushes me. "It's okay. We accept you, Julie."

"We accept you, Julie," the rest say.

Breath enters my lungs again. They accept me. As Julie. They knew I was a fraud but they still welcomed me into their arms, held my hands, danced with me. As family.

"Why?"

"Because, Julie," Bella Marie breathes, "we can hear you. Understand you."

"We hear you," hum the others, their hands all over me, rubbing, soothing. "We understand you."

"We can see your hurt," Bella Marie continues, "your vulnerabilities, all that you've had to overcome with your aunt and your childhood. Being taken from your family, a victim of this horrible world. You've lived with that weight, a mountain of pain, yet you've dug yourself out with your grit and resilience. Like last night, how you exorcised your rage through fire. It was powerful."

"So powerful," says Emmeline.

"Beautifully powerful," says Ana.

"Perfect," says Maya.

I hear bones rattle and see Chloe in the corner of the room. She has retreated, unable to break through the barrier of love that is my girls, my echo chamber of protection. She stares at me, envious. My teeth chatter with fear. I cannot take my eyes away from Chloe no matter how hard I try.

"But what about Chloe?" *She's here. Can't you see?*

"Hush." Bella Marie presses a finger to my lips, smooths her other hand through my sweat-soaked hair. I focus on her. Only her. "It was supposed to be *you* all along. The wrong twin found us at first. *You* were the one missing."

"Me?"

"When your sister died, you saw the opportunity and you held on to it. You acted on the unthinkable; you took a risk and maneuvered yourself to the top. *Others* might deem you shameful, immoral, psychopathic, but not us. Not *us*. You did what any of us would do. We will never judge or admonish you for your courage and determination. You are just like all of us. We understand you. Don't you see it? We can become your family. True family. We are the *only* people who will be able to see you and accept you."

I'm breathless, dizzy from her words. I wonder briefly if I'm in a dream. Such kindness only seemed possible in my head. But their energy is visceral, their sugary breaths cannot be make-believe.

"You are our pride."

Her words are a rush of validation. I want to drown in it. "Pride?"

"Our most beautiful pride," they all say.

I drink their words in. I am their pride. They understand me and all my faults. They understand why I did what I did, taking Chloe's life. They don't deem me a monster or a criminal. They won't exploit me for their own gain. They respect me, admire me.

I can be their family—I *am* their family.

Trust makes my eyelids grow heavy. I shut them and focus on her voice, at her soft mercy.

"Julie, you are safe," she says.

"Julie, you are warm," says another.

"Julie, you are loving."

"Julie, you are selfless."

"Julie, you are caring."

"Julie, you are innocent."

"Julie, you are worthy."

"Julie, you are one of us."

"We are your family now."

"We will protect you."

Their words are laced with magic, leeching the fear from my bones. I can breathe again, full gulps of air scented like lavender and lime. I am relaxed and soothed. I take a few breaths as they hum affirmations at me.

Loving. Selfless. Caring. Innocent. Worthy.

When I open my eyes again, Chloe is gone. Exorcised. Never to return. I know this is true from the sparkling buoyancy in my chest, just like how my girls released me from my aunt. My new family—they saved me. My girls who accept me for who I am. They coo over me, massaging my arms sweetly, wiping my tears, giving my aching feet a rub, kissing my forehead, braiding my hair, stuffing it with flowers. I am loved. They love me. I am their family. Even as Julie. I erupt into sobs again, but this time not out of fear. Out of love. Of triumph. My heart is so full I must burst into tears to release the pressure or else I'd explode into a goo of pink and gold.

Then, a clamor outside. I think I hear someone scream for help. It sounds like Iz. But I'm not sure.

Wait.

Where's Iz? I haven't seen her since lunch. Since she stormed off.

I turn my head to the french doors, slits of light slashing through the hazy darkness. But Bella Marie grabs my wet cheeks. "Focus on us," she says. "Focus on me, Julie. I love you, Julie."

Even at night, her blue eyes are striking. I want to kiss them, suck them like a lollipop. She leans in and gives me a kiss on the lips. I melt. Disappear into her taste and smell, sweet and bitter like key lime pie and fizzy green drinks. I am in love. I am love. I am surrounded by it. Can feel it in the touch of those around me. The belonging. The acceptance. My family. New, beautiful, and perfect.

49

I wake up but I am not afraid.

I am warm, golden, surrounded by love.

The girls pile around me, white bodies in linen like blankets born to hug and warm. They stayed with me throughout the night. Protected me and guarded me like their own.

I shift and accidentally wake Bella Marie, who has fallen asleep beside me. The light streaming through the slatted french doors illuminates her golden hair.

"Morning," she says.

"Morning," someone else says, rising near my feet. Emmeline.

"Morning."

"Morning."

"Morning."

"Morning."

"Morning."

"Morning." Angelique is on my other side. She cradles her stomach and I reach for it. She lets me palm her bump, feel the baby's kick. A girl. I know it. It must be. Another one of us, growing, becoming. Another family member for us to love. A warm pressure pushes against the back of my eyes, and I want to cry again. Angelique, this creator of life, is so beautiful, and her baby will be even more perfect. I already want to hold the babe in my arms, coddle and kiss her soft cheeks. Sniff the back of her sweet newborn neck. I am so happy.

———

Sophia runs another morning yoga session for us.

We swoop and bend into different positions. Our bodies are pliable. Full of energy.

When we complete savasana with a ten-minute meditation, it is with ease. My thoughts are nothing more than clouds floating in a blue sky. Everything passes. We are at peace.

We do our group affirmations.

"I am loved."

You are loved.

———

In the afternoon, we knit by the farm. A piano player soundtracks our activity, the musician's fingers light on the black and white keys. Each of us is tasked with completing a square that we'll sew into a knitted blanket. I choose a design that has a small daisy in the center, even though I've never knitted before.

"It's a hard choice, but I'm sure you can do it," Ana says.

"We'll help you if you don't know how," Kelly adds.

"Even if the piece is imperfect, it'll be perfect because you made it," Lily concludes.

Bella Marie teaches me how to cast on and stitch, her hands working with mine, soft and patient like kisses, like flowers brushing your palm. Our needles *click, click, click* as I loop and push and wrap and pull. I fall into a rhythm. Loop and push and wrap and pull. Loop and push and wrap and pull. Occasionally, I stop to drink the pink juice they've given me. Something with guava and grapefruit. Maybe mint.

"You are such a fast learner, Julie," Bella Marie says.

"So fast," Emmeline echoes.

"The fastest of all of us," Angelique says.

I am glowing, pride bursting out of me.

We somehow knit for hours. I finish my square. My daisy turns out ugly. Misshapen. Uneven. But the girls love it.

"It's beautiful."

"Perfect."

"Has so much character, I'm obsessed."

"Obsessed!"

We stitch the nine pieces together. They make a perfect square. Even and gorgeous and whole, just like all of us together.

Bella Marie grabs my hand and kisses me on the cheek. I love her so much, it hurts. I want to devour her whole from the inside out, leaving only her skin so I can wear it and become her, that's how much I love her.

"You can decide what to do with the blanket," she tells me. "Do you want to keep it?"

I shake my head. I know what I want to do. Something better.

Bella Marie hands me the blanket, the yarn heavy with love.

I pass it to Angelique. "For your baby. Our newest family. So it can be wrapped with our affection."

The girls *awww* at my gift.

"That is so sweet, Julie."

"So sweet."

"The sweetest."

Angelique hesitates. My arms are outstretched with the blanket, which grows heavy at the looming denial. There's something in her eyes. A bleariness. Glassy. As if close to tears.

I've upset her.

Oh no! I've upset her!

"What's wrong?" I say, dropping the blanket to hold her hands so she can feel my warm, loving energy course through her.

"She's sad," Ana says.

"Why are you sad?" Lily asks.

"Don't be sad, we love you," Sophia adds.

"We are family," says Emmeline.

Angelique shakes her head, ripping her hands out of mine. She wipes her tears and picks up the blanket. "I am not sad. I am happy. I am so happy that I cried."

"She's so happy she cried!" Emmeline exclaims.

"We are so happy you are happy," says Kelly.

Angelique bursts into a smile and throws the blanket around her shoulders. "I am so happy," she says as she skips, the blanket a cape. We dance again, carried by our bountiful joy.

But something isn't right; I glance at Angelique. She says she is happy, yet I don't believe her. I was holding her when she said it. Her skin was on mine, our energy, shared. My aura was warm, golden, euphoric, but hers was cold and blue.

She is a liar.

She is not happy.

She is pretending and only I know the truth.

Time passes so fast.

Somehow, it is dinner.

We fill our bellies inside the Melniburg mansion tonight. The French chateau's floors are marble, the walls are white, the ceilings soar so high, they could disappear into the sky. Our voices echo against the building like ghosts repeating back our laughter.

The table we eat at is a grand thing. At least five yards in length. Carved from a sequoia, a single tree, no cuts, no planks, an earthly relic. It must have lived hundreds of years, perhaps more, before it was cut down, sanded, polished. Our feast doubles as a masquerade party. We've donned intricate lace masks of purple and gold, blue and black, white and crimson, that hide our pretty faces, showing only our painted lips. I love my girls so much I can identify each of them by their teeth, their Cupid's bow, and how many cc's of lip filler accentuate their perfect pouts.

The Asian dinner is to honor me, they say. The kitchen staff have prepared steam buns and dumplings and Peking duck. Edamame salad, sashimi boats, and miso soup. Gimbap, japchae, and kimchi for sides. Bottles and bottles of rice wine. I drink until I'm flushed bright red. The music is vaguely reminiscent of something they'd play in an Asian historical drama, wood and string instruments filling the glorious space with full and round sounds.

Bella Marie watches me with a smile. Her mask is green and her blue dress shifts shades, seeming to change color with every movement. Iridescent like a hummingbird. I want to go into her arms, have her hold me in her vibrant wings.

"To Julie!" she says, raising her glass.

"To Julie!" Everyone holds their drinks aloft, alcohol sloshing in their glasses.

We swallow the liquid and grow warm, mutual fires lit within. We fill our mouths with delectable food. I dip a piece of sashimi in soy sauce and wasabi, place it on my tongue. The hearty flavor of tuna bursts onto my palate.

"I must say," says Emmeline to Ana, "you are so correct."

"Correct?" Ana asks. "About what?"

"About Viktor and the swing!"

"Ah! The swing!"

"The swing!" Lily coos.

The group breaks out in giggles and I glance at Viktor, who stands near the door. He stares into the distance. I wonder if he can hear us over the flute and strings and bouts of laughter. I wonder how he feels. I wonder if he is as happy as us.

"He works with the oscillations." Ana swings her spoon back and forth like a pendulum. "It is wonderful."

"The best," says Sophia.

"So good," says Emmeline.

"I just remembered," Maya chirps. "Julie hasn't experienced Viktor yet since she isn't Chloe."

"Oh, that's right!" exclaims Emmeline.

"You should try soon," says Maya.

"Yes, soon," says Kelly. "Should we call him over for a bit of dessert?"

"Oh, I don't know." I glance at Bella Marie, who holds me in her blue eyes, Mother Earth reflected back to me.

She smiles. Perfect natural lips. "Maybe Julie doesn't like to *chop wood*," she says simply.

"Oooooh," coo the others, understanding me entirely as if we were one.

50

We are outside by the beach.

A campfire blazes between us. The hot flames roar, kissing the night sky, tinting our skin with an orange glow. Violin and drums in the distance. Bouncing, sharp tones that strike crisp in my ears.

We are laughing about something when Viktor comes around with a box.

"Oooh!" say the girls as he goes around the campfire. Everyone grabs whatever is inside, hiding it in their palms, making kissy noises to the secret within their fingers.

I am last. Viktor lowers the box in front of me. I gasp.

A tiny mouse, fleshy and pink. I pick it up. It is warm in my hand, the size of my finger and terribly sweet. It's still a newborn, its eyes not fully developed, black beads hidden behind a layer of translucent flesh. In this miniature form, it has little resemblance to its final shape. For now, it causes no disgust, not like its uglier rodent brothers, those fat and pesky rats that scamper desperately in dirty city sewers.

"Oh, you sweet little thing," I coo. It wiggles on my palm, stretches its limbs wide. I must have woken it up. It flips onto its stomach and crawls feebly. Tiny, fleshy feet stamping, stamping, stamping, tickling my palm in its weakness as it corrals the strength required for a meager squeak. It strikes me that I was once this small, this innocent, this lovable, a clump of cells in a belly.

"Julie," Bella Marie says, "we're almost halfway through our trip and I am so sad."

"So sad," repeat the girls.

"So sad," I say.

"I want to celebrate you, our newest family member. Share our bond, our secret. Tonight, we will let you into our world, a small step, to make us an even truer family. I remember when Chloe was in your position. It was such a beautiful moment."

Though she had abandoned me, I am happy for Chloe, pleased that she was able to experience the true meaning of family, especially after uncovering the truth of her adoption. Everyone deserves this joy. These girls rescued her at the right time.

"Are you Christian?" asks Bella Marie.

"No," I say.

"Buddhist?" asks Kelly.

"No."

"Shinto?" asks Emmeline.

"No."

"Muslim?" asks Ana.

"No."

"Atheist?" asks Angelique.

"Mmm. Agnostic?" I suggest.

"Agnostic!" laugh the girls.

The mouse twitches in my hand. Alive and well. The air smells like ash. Burning.

Bella Marie strokes her mouse with her pinkie. "Do you remember Nikolai's story?"

I nod. The pocket watch he traded for a wife.

"Well, I wasn't being entirely honest. It wasn't pure luck. He had sworn fealty to a holy being and prayed hard for a changing tide. A break from toiling peasantry."

I understand why they asked about my religion now. If I am to be family, of course we need to respect the same gods. To worship the same spiritual being. I am okay with that. I will do anything to be family. I want to be one of them, body and soul.

"Which god?" I ask.

Bella Marie is delighted, eyes glinting with excitement. I have said the right thing.

"This is the beauty of Eto," she says. "There is not one singular god. No singular entity. Eto shifts and flows with time, molding itself to best serve us."

Eto. I've never heard of it, yet it feels familiar, as if it's been whispered to me in the gauzy space of a dream, right before I woke.

"What does Eto take the form of now?" I ask.

The girls giggle.

"Eto takes the form of whatever empowers us," Bella Marie says. "Have you ever wondered how we've reached the hearts of millions in the span of a few years? How we've solidified ourselves in positions of influence in the ever-changing zeitgeist? It is all because Eto has blessed us. And once the world tires of influencers—and such a thing is inevitable—Eto will empower us in different ways, ways we cannot even fathom with our simple minds now."

"But how?" I ask, trying to piece it all together. Trying to make sense of this idea that seems so foreign, so silly, so impossible. Is this what Kelly meant by group synergy and manifesting? Were they simply praying to some god? "How can Eto do that?" I glance at all my girls, considering their legions of followers, how Kelly was able to have a comeback despite dipping into obscurity. Do they truly believe it was down to Eto?

Bella Marie shakes her head. "Eto is not for us to understand. Eto works in unknowable ways. You will see it soon. Once you've opened your heart and served Eto, Eto will repay you in kind."

The girls all nod except for Angelique, who is staring at the mouse in her hand, holding it up to her belly so her baby can hear the squeaks through her swollen abdomen.

"Like Chloe," Bella Marie continues. "She gained millions across each platform soon after swearing her fealty. It is all because of Eto."

I find myself frowning, though I don't want to. Is Eto really the reason for Chloe's growth? Did Chloe once believe this too? I can't imagine it.

Chloe, my twin, who had felt so steady and solid since she was a toddler, believing in something as nebulous as this.

"Julie?" Bella Marie smiles at me, her eyes so warm and lovely I could drink from them and taste the humid summer sky. "Where have you gone? Return to us."

Return to us.

My girls, who are all so beautiful and talented. Of course they'd be loved. Of course their followings are organic and true. Of course they are successful. I hadn't ever considered anything else at play.

But I can read the frequency of their humming bodies, their curving smiles, the steady beat of their hearts. They truly believe some god is the reason for their success. That it is some amorphous celestial body that controls the numbers on their screens.

Us.

They believe in Eto. I can sense it now: their belief is a necessary ingredient to their synchronicity, their togetherness, their group synergy.

I must conform to become one of them. I must believe in Eto for *me* to become *us.*

It doesn't matter what I truly think, what logic or reason is ticking in my brain, holding me back. I must sacrifice it all into the fire, let it burn away. I can't lose the chance to be accepted, to become inextricably linked, not when I've finally found kin who understand my faults, who hold me with affection, who love me as *Julie* and no one else. They are the blood running through my veins, the bones holding my body together, the heart beating in my chest.

I will force myself to believe if that is what they need. Even if it means putting faith in a god I'm not sure exists. I would do anything to be *us.*

I am ready.

"How do I swear fealty?"

The girls love my declaration. Their bodies vibrate with excitement, compulsive and electrifying. It strikes my chest like I took a bite of the sun, and I know this is the beginning of it all, a heady sign that I am being welcomed into *us.*

Bella Marie grows tall with a beaming smile. "Eto lives within us through our love. Our dedication. As long as we show Eto our heart and our devotion, Eto will love us back." She sits down next to me and shows me the small mouse in her hand. The little pink babe. It yawns, opening its tiny mouth wide.

She takes one of my hands in hers, the other cupping her mouse. "Repeat after me." She stares at the little creature. "You will grow to be strong."

I do the same. We all do. Stare at our mouse, shower it with our intent, our affection.

You will grow to be strong.

Then, Bella Marie passes her mouse to me, and Ana takes mine. We each trade mice in a circle. A new pink creature twisting in each of our palms.

Emmeline is next. "You will grow to be beautiful."

You will grow to be beautiful.

We trade mice again. We do this several times. A new mouse each time, a new wish for each trade. The little animals are showered with our devotion, our dreams, the lucky things, as they squirm in our hands.

You will grow to be rich.

You will grow to be loved.

You will grow to be safe.

You will grow to be brave.

You will grow to be adored.

You will grow to be successful.

Then it is my turn. My original mouse is back in my hand. I bestow it with my intent.

"You will grow to be worthy."

You will grow to be worthy.

"And now," Bella Marie says, "we must accept the love we gave Eto as ours. Absorb Eto into us."

"Absorb?"

"Yes," she says gently. "Watch."

The violin screams. Its notes are sharp and cutting as Bella Marie parts her lips and places the mouse on her tongue. A tiny thing, barely a tenth of her glorious, beautiful mouth. I am enraptured as I stare into the mouse's beady eyes, black behind a layer of skin, blind, as Bella Marie seals it behind her lips, as she chews, slow, methodic, as the bones *crunch, crunch, crunch.* I think I hear a squeak, but it might just be the fiddle. She swallows. Opens her mouth. The mouse is gone. Only tongue, gums, white teeth, and a pink uvula.

I stare at her open mouth. For a moment, I think it's some magic trick, or a game like the pills on the plane. That the mouse is simply behind her back, not deep in her throat. But then her lips meet in a grin and I realize it was no ruse. She swallowed it. My breath hitches and I blink rapidly, as if a mosquito is stuck inside my eyelid.

"Now, your turn."

My mouse twitches. It moves its head lethargically, as if craning, as if it can see, as if it's not actually blind, but aware. Aware of the mouth that may eat him. My breathing is shallow, sweat shedding across my skin.

I don't feel happy or good or beautiful. I don't want to eat it. I don't want to absorb it. I am scared.

"Don't be scared."

I glance across the campfire at Maya. How did she know what I was thinking?

"There's nothing to be scared of," says Lily.

"You have us now," says Sophia.

"We are here," says Angelique.

"We will protect you," says Ana.

"We are family," says Kelly.

"Family," says Emmeline.

Then, they all pop their mice into their mouths. Chew, chew, chew, *crunch, crunch, crunch.* Swallow. They look refreshed, happy, aglow. I want to be like them. Happy and aglow. Not afraid.

Bella Marie kneels, her dress dusted with sand. She cups my hand, sidling close so her bony hips are pressed hard into my legs. Her breath, scented blood and flesh, wafts toward me.

"You will be one with us," she says. "And I love you. Now eat."

"Now eat," they say.

Their eyes pierce me, poke holes in my skin, draining all the warmth in my chest until there's nothing left but a vacuum of darkness. I need to do this, or they'll hate me. If I don't eat this mouse, they won't consider me family. If I stop here, I will never be *us*. I will be cast out, ignored, abandoned again.

What's a little mouse to eight beautiful girls, the family I always wanted?

There's a hush in the air, a sudden lull. I stare at the mouse, my senses dissolving, dulling. I am not scared or happy. I feel nothing. The mouse is nothing. I need it inside me to revive. To become whole again. I need to eat the mouse to receive their love.

I lift it to my mouth, drop it on my tongue. It moves, tiny feet clambering to get out of my wet, sticky cage. I gag as I close its escape route. I feel its panic. The beat of its limbs on my tongue. The press of its head against the inside of my lips. I flinch and chomp hard, end its misery, iron coating my tongue, soft skull in my molars. I do not chew even though I might choke, and swallow it whole, though I've never done that before, not even with a pill. The mouse jostles my uvula. Slides down my throat. Tiny nails cut my trachea, as if it were still alive, desperate to escape, crawling up my esophagus. It passes through the tight channel of my throat. I can't feel it anymore, disappeared somewhere inside my chest.

I open my mouth. Show my girls I've done it. I'm one of them. Family.

They explode toward me with precious screams and crowd their protective warmth around my body, patching up the holes they'd pierced just earlier. Bella Marie wraps her arms around my torso, pressing her face into my thighs. They are my chamber of affection, cooing, doting, filling me back up again with glowing love.

In their ardor, I forget about what we ate.

51

I am alone in my room.

I can't sleep, though my eyes have been closed for hours. Something within me is not right. Like a living being is trying to crawl out of my throat, come alive, seek vengeance. I sit up since I fear that if I stay down, I might puke and choke to death like Chloe, foam in my throat. I take deep breaths, fighting nausea and telling my body I am in control.

But I have this odd feeling. Like I'm forgetting something. A figure is curling into my mind, her name right at the tip of my tongue.

But then, a scream.

Piercing, guttural, hoarse. The sound is from a few bungalows over, yet it is so loud it might as well be in my ear.

Angelique.

Worry tramples my acrid nausea and I run to her bungalow and push open the front door. The room smells like iron—like blood.

Angelique is on the floor, moaning, mumbling something that sounds like, *I'm sorry, I'm sorry, I'm sorry.* Her skin is pale, wet with perspiration, scarlet staining her white dress, down her thighs.

I rush to her and gather her in my arms. Her muscles spasm at my touch. "What happened?"

She grabs on to me, her bloody hands slippery on my skin. I can't make out her whispered, incoherent words.

Kelly runs in, then Maya, who says she'll get Bella Marie, running back out again.

"What happened?" I ask again.

"My baby," Angelique says, voice hoarse. "It's done."

"Done? What's done?"

She blinks slowly, her voice a whisper only I can hear. "Am I . . . a good person?"

"What?"

Her head falls to the side before she can answer, and she passes out in my arms.

I shake her, panicked. "Angelique? Angelique! Can you hear me?" I'm crying, throat closing with worry. I look at Kelly as she stares at the blood. She's quiet, her hands to her heart as if in prayer.

"What do we do?" I ask. "She needs help. A hospital. A doctor!"

A thunder of footsteps. All the other Belladonnas rush in. Emmeline, Lily, Ana, Sophia, Maya. Bella Marie is last, accompanied by Viktor and another burly white man holding a stretcher. They grab Angelique's body and lift her on the stretcher. A heave and they carry her out of the room. The rest of us follow behind them as they bring her to the service building a few minutes away. There's a small medical bay. The light is harsh and sterile, illuminating Angelique's severe blood loss, the warm, sticky vermillion pond between her legs.

I'm about to go in with them, to make sure she'll be okay, when Bella Marie stops me.

"She'll be fine. We have a doctor." But she's chewing on her fingernails.

"You have to call emergency services," I say. "What if she needs a blood transfusion? She lost so much a-and—" My breath hitches as I think of the baby. That warm spirit that breathed into my palm, beautiful and whole. I had felt the babe only this morning and now . . . It's barely been twelve hours. How did this happen so quickly? "She should be with her husband, Sommer. With her family."

"We are family," Bella Marie says.

"Bella Marie!" I shout.

She jolts. Stumbles backward, her veneer of perfection cracking.

Everyone stares at me, all fourteen eyes. They are in shock that I yelled. I am in shock that I yelled too.

Why aren't you happy? Why did you yell at your family? This is not nice of you.

I don't like this feeling growing inside me. It is not peaceful, not nice. It is red agitation, bristly and spiky. Yet I can't push it away, not when Angelique, her baby, are dying. I can't let it happen again, cannot allow another family member to pass away. I take a breath, close my eyes, and gather my thoughts. Then I step forward, grab Bella Marie's hand, and speak to her softly. "My love, my beautiful dove, I'm worried about Angelique."

"I'm worried too," she replies.

"So worried."

"Very worried."

"I just . . . I think she might need transfusions or . . . something else. I know you have good medical facilities here, but I worry. She's Angelique! Our family. What if . . ." I shake my head and let her fill in the blank with her worst nightmare.

Bella Marie opens her mouth wide with realization. "You're right." She jumps toward me, wraps me in her arms. "You are so right, Julie. I love you so much. Angelique needs to be safe. You're right."

"You're so right, Julie," says Emmeline.

"So right," says Ana.

"Very right," echoes Lily.

"I will call emergency services right away. Wait here." And then Bella Marie takes off running. I think it's the first time I've seen her run. She looks weird. Gangly. A collection of coltish limbs that don't quite go the right way.

The door to the medical room swings open and Viktor steps out, covered in blood. "I'll pack Angelique's bags. You girls wait here." Then he runs off, long strides, into the darkness.

"Angelique will be all right," Maya says.

"All right," Emmeline echoes.

Ana pulls me into her arms. "She will be fine."

We all gather in a hug. Their arms twine around me as they affirm themselves of Angelique's safety.

I hug them back and force myself to believe, to conform, my mind whirring with nausea. "Everything is fine," I say, arms still bloody from Angelique.

52

Half an hour later, the rescue helicopter arrives.

It is a big alien spaceship, its gray body blending into the night, whirling propellers booming across the quiet island, swaying treetops.

It lands in a field, flattening the grass below it like a crop circle. I watch from a distance as the orange paramedics haul Angelique onto the rescue vessel. Bella Marie is there too, her stick body ghostly under the searing lights of the helicopter, her shadow stretching sharply across the grass.

The helicopter takes off into the sky, Angelique safely tucked inside. Just before it disappears into the cloak of night, I catch sight of "CG-484" painted on the tail. Must be an identifier; the helicopter's PLU code.

Bella Marie returns to us, an unusual line pressed between her fine, blond brows. The night paints her skin purple, a tongue after choking on a handful of grape Nerds. Her beige dress is stained with browned blood and some of it has gotten on her cheek, smeared on like a bruise.

"Oh, Julie!" She holds my hands, her eyes wide and wet. "You were so right. The paramedics said if I had called them a minute later, Angelique's life would have been at risk. I am so thankful to you. A lifesaver!"

"Lifesaver!"

"Lifesaver!"

"Lifesaver!"

"Lifesaver!"

"Lifesaver!"

"Lifesaver!"

I cram a wide smile on my cheeks even though my gut is bubbling with corrosive liquid. "Thank you. Thank you." I really want to be thankful. I really want to be a lifesaver, to drown in their pretty love, gobble it up like a fresh summer peach. Yet I keep having this feeling that something is wrong. A force that's pulling me back from being swept in even though I want to, dearly.

"My loves," says Emmeline, her doe eyes drowning in tears. She looks like a giant baby. "I'm scared. I don't like seeing blood. It triggers me. Be with me tonight?"

"Oh no!" Maya exclaims. "Don't be scared, we are here."

"Think of happy things," adds Sophia.

"We will be with you tonight, keep you safe," says Maya.

They coo at Emmeline, dancing around her in a circle and whisking me into the tornado of their love as we pirouette into Emmeline's bungalow and fall in her bed. A nest of beautiful girls scented like fresh grass and blood.

"Good night," says Emmeline.

"Good night," replies Maya.

"Good night," adds Sophia.

"Good night," murmurs Ana.

"Good night," whispers Kelly.

"Good night," says Bella Marie.

They all wait for me.

"Good night," I say.

The girls bury their faces in the white blankets. The room is dark and sickeningly warm. I'm sweating up a storm, sandwiched between Ana's thighs and Sophia's armpit. Someone's leg is sprawled across my stomach, caging me in, pressing against my ribs.

Their breaths have grown deep, restful. Somehow, they've all fallen asleep. I try to join them, to escape into black night and smooth slumber, but my stomach is a riptide and I can't shake off Angelique, her blood on my hands, a pool of red between her legs, her baby. *It's done*, she'd said.

What was done?

Why does it all feel so wrong?

My stomach gurgles. Something is coming back out.

I scramble out of the sheets, the tangle of pale, bloody limbs, and kneel over the toilet, spraying the porcelain bowl with pink foam and chewed tuna. Then, something hard and slick regurgitates from my esophagus. It hits my tongue first as it slithers, slimy, before plopping into the toilet.

I blink.

The mouse. Half digested. Its eyes are black, almost alive.

Dizzy with nausea, I puke up everything else: the sashimi, the alcohol, the pink and green drinks, the key lime pie. The whole time I have this perverse feeling roiling through me.

What the fuck did I do?

When there is nothing left in my stomach and I'm gagging on putrid air, I flush everything down the toilet. I can't even look at the mouse, the poor pink thing, as it swirls into oblivion. I hobble to the sink and rinse my mouth, glance in the mirror.

My reflection makes me jump. I palm my face, my cheeks, stretch the skin around my eyes. I'm ghastly, uncanny. Almost like . . . Chloe the night I discovered her.

"Fuck." I shake my head to get rid of the images. How did I end up like this? I replay the past two days. A hummingbird and a mouse and a lumberjack. Lots of dancing and laughs. It was fun, I remember; I was elated, joyous. I was loved. It was good. Beautiful. Until . . . the blood. Until Angelique. My stomach gurgles though it's empty, a reminder that I'm missing something important.

Someone important.

The taste of peaches and sugar. The smell of vanilla.

My ears buzz. I cup my mouth.

How could I forget?

Iz.

I straighten with a gasp, my breath sour. What happened to her? Why hasn't she been with us?

I'm about to turn for the door, find Iz, when Bella Marie intercepts the exit. She's muddy with clumps of blood. Her arms stretch outward as she wraps me in a foul hug, suffocating my nose in the crook of her shoulder. I can't breathe. I try to tell her that, *I can't breathe*, but my sounds are muffled against her clothing and skin.

"Oh, darling," she coos, "do you need an IV drip? It's a must when I purge."

I push her away. "What? No, I—"

"It's okay, Julie, it's nothing to be ashamed of."

"No, it's not that, I'm worried about—" I can't bring myself to say Iz. Her name is caught in my throat. "About Angelique."

Bella Marie exhales, rubbing my back. "You are so kind, so considerate. But don't worry. Angelique is fine, I can feel it in my heart. Go to sleep, my sweet, and tomorrow you will wake up better."

She pets my head like a child, soft and loving. For a moment, I almost let myself walk into the mist of golden happiness, elusive and tender. But then I remember Iz. I need to keep her at the front of my brain. We haven't heard from her all day, and no one has brought her up. There's no way she wouldn't talk to me if she was planning to leave early. Something is very, very wrong.

But for now, I say, "Okay," and let Bella Marie hold my hand and guide me to bed, allow myself to be buried in the pile of ribs and legs again.

53

I can't sleep. The Belladonnas' limbs are a suffocating, sweaty net. My head spins in circles as I try to piece everything together. Angelique, Iz, the mice, Mrs. Melniburg's warning, this whole island. Something is off. I can't ignore how everything we've done is perversely fucked up. My throat itches with an intense need to scream. Maybe it's the ghost of the mouse residing within me, the remnants of its soul scratching at my esophagus.

I can't believe I ate a fucking mouse as a show of devotion.

I can't believe all these girls stuffed mice down their throats too.

I tremble, recalling how I was swept into their coos of affection, falling headfirst into the persuasions of the ever-elusive *us*. It was intoxicating, that golden, rippling energy. But now that the heat has worn off, my chest and stomach cold and empty, I'm forced to confront my actions.

These girls.

What is wrong with them? I can't believe I witnessed them swallow a whole mammal and still wanted to be one with them.

Which begs the question: What the hell was wrong with *me*? Where had my head gone? It's like logic had slipped out between my fingers, disintegrated like sand. Was I so desperate to be their companion that I swore fealty to some ridiculous, amorphous, godly being just so they'd accept me into their group? I know I can be a lonely, miserable wreck at times, but I wouldn't be so susceptible to this shit if my mind was clear. Is it possible that they're drugging me with all those drinks? With the food? It would explain why I always feel groggy after dinners, why my memory appears in fragments.

And now I wonder: What more was I *going* to do if I hadn't snapped out of it? What if I hadn't puked out the carcass of what I ate? Would I have held their soft hands and blindly twirled into the depths of insanity?

Time crawls at a snail's pace as I mentally comb through every horrific thing I've done. When sunrise arrives, I stir, waking the Belladonnas, who blink lethargically to consciousness, eyes crusted over with sleep. They look ugly and smell pungent. Acrid morning breath, blood, and sweat stewed between Egyptian cotton sheets.

"Morning," begins one.

"Morning," replies another.

"Mor—"

"I'm going to take a shower." They all stare at me, eyes wide and confused. Quickly, I add, "Morning, my loves. Excuse me." Though I am sick from what we did, I can't bring myself to upset them. I can't tell if it's fear or if a small, lonely part of me still hopes to have their love within reach.

I untangle myself from their sticky web. As I pad out of the room, their songbird choruses hypnotize each other. *Morning. Morning. Morning.* It takes everything in me not to be pulled in.

I don't put on my shoes. Stones jab at my feet as I navigate the gravelly path that leads through the avenue of bungalows. My pulse thrums as I get closer to Iz's house, which is near the end of the row. This is my chance to investigate. I push on her door, but it doesn't budge.

The padlock. I pull. It's locked tight.

What the fuck?

I'm about to pound on the door when I hear footsteps. I run back out onto the path, heart hammering.

A staff member crosses my path and I almost bump into her. She's brunette, dressed in a white linen frock with an intense smile on her lips. "Need help with something, Miss Chan?"

Chan.

Does this entire island know I'm Julie? That I'm basically a felon who stole her twin's identity? And they're still smiling at me?

I know I'm fucked up, but these people are a whole new level of fucked.

I grin nervously at the worker, eyes flicking to Iz's door, the padlock. What if she's been locked in? No, the Belladonnas wouldn't do that—Bella Marie wouldn't.

Yet it gnaws at me, the *what if.*

I had thought they were all perfectly beautiful creatures. But after the mice, I can't look at them the same way. I don't know what they're capable of.

"Fine, thank you. Just, uh, trying to shower off this blood. Haha." I hope she'll leave me alone so I can check on Iz.

"Of course! Let me know if you need extra towels." She stands there. Staring.

I walk past her, past Iz's bungalow, glancing over my shoulder as the worker smiles. I can't investigate now, not with this attendant gawking at me.

It's okay. There are chances in the future. I have three more days here.

As I head back to my bungalow, my mind drowns in thoughts of Chloe. For five whole years, she was a member of the Belladonnas, a believer in Eto, one of the family. Then, she dies, and the girls barely blink an eye, accepting a replacement at the snap of their fingers. I knew my twin for four hazy years of childhood, yet I continued to think of her for most of my life. And when I couldn't connect to her, when she abandoned me, I filled her image with hatred and envy because I couldn't fathom a life where she didn't take up space in my mind. That's how much she mattered to me. That's what being a family should be like.

When I confront the truth this way, the Belladonnas' cruelty toward Chloe is apparent. Would I be any different? Is their pretty affection nothing more than fantasy? A mirage that vanishes once I open my eyes? At one point, I desired their connection, their friendship, their empathy, and group synergy. But I have this sinking feeling that everything I receive here is false and shallow, as authentic as a sponsored post.

I hate what's unfurling within me. The knowledge that the Belladonnas are not the people I hoped they were. I wish I could shut my eyes to all the creeping unease, not just about who the Belladonnas are, but what they've done to Iz. Everything would be so much simpler if I could shut myself off from the truth and live happily in their toxic bubble of positivity.

But I can't.

I can't shake it off. I need to see the truth for myself.

As I'm showering, washing off the remnants of Angelique's blood and sweat, the dirt between my toes, the smell of the Belladonnas from my hair, a few sprigs of flowers caught between strands, I think of a plan: I move at night, when everyone is asleep, no staff lurking around. I need to break into Iz's bungalow. Just to confirm that Iz is okay, that my worst suspicions aren't true. I don't have a key, so I'll have to use brute force. The axe by the farm we use to cut wood. That's perfect.

Okay, so I'm going to break into Iz's bungalow.

What then?

In all likelihood, Iz will be safe, right? And if she is, then everything is okay. I can shove these worries into a dusty corner of my brain, label them as unfounded worries, and pretend that everything is totally fine.

But what if my worst fears *are* true? What if Iz is locked up and it's the Belladonnas' fault? I won't be able to deny reality any longer. I'll have to confront the fact that these girls, who I want to believe are pretty and innocent, are anything but.

If Iz has been captured and harmed by the Belladonnas, there's no way we can stay on the island. I need to devise a way to leave.

There's a landline and ethernet access in the main house that we can use to call for help. We have to be close to some country—Saint Marten?—that could send a helicopter over.

But I can't just ask to use the phone. That would be suspicious as hell. I'm supposed to *disconnect*.

Should I play along until the end of the week and jet out of here safely? But what if weirder shit happens? One night we're munching on mice, the next night might be worse. Horses? Turtles? Maybe they'll hack off a chunk of Viktor's juicy thigh and sear it medium-rare for me to devour.

God, what did I get myself into?

Biting my lip, I get out of the shower and towel myself off. I can't think about this too much. First, I'll focus on Iz, check to see if she's okay, and when the time comes, I'll make the decisions that are necessary.

Three knocks on my door. "Julie, darling, will you be joining us for yoga?"

I take a breath and stare at myself in the mirror. My dark hair, thinning brows, deep, inky eyes, tan skin, and thin lips.

Remember who you are. Don't fall for their deception. Don't get swept in.

For now: blend in.

54

You are humble," the girls affirm after yoga. The zap of heady confidence I usually feel is absent. I mask my antipathy with a broad grin. No one questions me.

In the afternoon, we have açai bowls for lunch. As soon as I have time for myself, I purge my stomach since I'm now certain they're drugging me.

I wonder if Chloe's vices were rooted in these island trips. If she developed an addiction to euphoria and happiness that crumbled into a dependency on pills and alcohol. I can understand it. That golden energy inside me is something I was desperate to have.

But that's exactly why I can't take risks with anything they feed me. One wrong step and I'll be swallowed into their addictive stream of *I love yous*, lungs clogged with so much liquid ardor, it'll be impossible to breathe.

It's movie night in the chateau. I've tucked myself into the corner of the room.

The girls are debating between *Beauty and the Beast*, *Miss Americana*, and *Midnight in Paris*.

"Didn't Woody Allen groom his daughter?" Maya asks.

"It's important to separate the art from the artist," Kelly replies.

Everyone claps and nods like what she said was oh so poignant.

There's a knock on the door.

"Who is it?" Bella Marie calls.

"Viktor."

The room breaks out in giggles as the girls tuck strands of hair behind ears.

"Come in," says Bella Marie.

The double doors swing wide. He smiles at us. "Hello, ladies."

"Hello, Viktor," they purr.

I wonder what Viktor's life must've been like. Born on a small island, molded into a little plaything. I had thought him brainless at first, but now I pity him. Could he still break out of it? Or is he permanently tainted?

He hands Bella Marie a flash drive and whispers in her ear.

Her eyes grow wide with delight.

As Viktor leaves the room, he catches my gaze. He must know I'm Julie now. I wonder what he's thinking. He shuts the door behind him.

"I have an update on Angelique," Bella Marie says, hopping over to the projector.

Pressure releases from my chest. The fact that she's smiling must mean Angelique is okay.

"I miss her so much," says Lily, though this is the first time she's mentioned Angelique since last night.

Bella Marie plugs in the flash drive and clicks a few buttons on the projector.

It's a screen recording of a YouTube video. The title is only: "."

Yes. A period.

It has three million views.

Angelique's eyes are bleary, tearstained. Sommer has one arm wrapped around her shoulders. He's staring into his lap.

Bella Marie dims the lights and presses play.

The video starts with a *beep . . . beep . . . beep*. Sounds that remind me of the Van Huusens' hospice. The couple is silent, holding hands. Angelique's hair is unusually messy, lips pale. She's wearing an ugly white gown—a *hospital* gown. My chest tightens when I realize they are in a hospital room. The beeping is her vital monitors. Five seconds into silence, she sighs and makes eye contact through the camera.

"I really didn't want to make this video." Her voice cracks, at the cusp of a cry. "But I promised to be transparent and vulnerable at every step of our pregnancy."

My mouth dries, heart pattering. I know what will follow.

"Last night," Angelique continues, tears welling in her eyes, "I miscarried our baby."

And there it is.

I bite my lip, cover my crumpling chest with my hands. My heart breaks as I listen to Angelique express the dreams she had for her child; the names, *Celine* if girl, *Thomas* if boy.

But then.

"This is so sad," Lily says.

"So, so sad," Emmeline echoes.

"The saddest. I might cry," adds Ana.

"So sad," says Maya, "but she still looks so beautiful."

"Yes, gorgeous," says Kelly.

I glance at the Belladonnas. They're staring at the screen—smiling, white canines bared, catching the light of the projector, like they're filming a sponsored video for a tooth-whitening kit.

"She's glowing," says Sophia.

"Like an angel," adds Lily.

"And Sommer is so handsome," says Kelly.

"Not just handsome," says Maya. *"Hot."*

"So hot," Emmeline coos.

"The hottest," Ana concludes.

They turn to each other and giggle, their dainty little fingers covering their mouths as if this video is oh so sweet, beaming as they watch their friend bawl for her lost child. I repress the urge to slap each of them in the face, to roundhouse kick in their fake lips so the silicone explodes, break their veneers so their collective giggles sound like whistles.

The only silent one is Bella Marie. She's stoic, emotionless. And perhaps that's even worse. It's as if the sight of her weeping, grieving friend doesn't bring her sadness. Just . . . nothing.

I curl my knees into my chest, hug myself tight.

The video is short but heartbreaking. Five minutes. No ads.

The next slide is comments. I can barely read them because my eyes are clouded with tears and confusion, but I get the sense that they are overwhelmingly positive, from how the Belladonnas coo and smile and giggle and clap.

The next slide: YouTube analytics. In the span of five hours, she's gained over 30K subs. Millions of views. Thousands of comments. The next slide: Instagram analytics. Similar growth and numbers. Finally, her TikTok. Angelique has cut the video into two parts. Each with about five million views. She only gained 2K followers, which is par for the course on TikTok, where views rarely translate to follows. But then Bella Marie shows us another screen recording. A TikTok live where the only thing in frame is Angelique's ultrasound and a pair of yellow newborn shoes with cupcakes on them. The corner graphic indicates there are 10K live viewers. Next to the ultrasound is a piece of paper that says: all gifts to the live will go toward my baby's memorial fund.

Donations are turned on.

The thirty-second screen recording begins. There's background music. "See You Again" by Charlie Puth from the Fast and Furious franchise. I'm horrified not just by the song choice, but by the donations that roll in. Twenty roses. A hundred more roses. Someone sends a cowboy hat. The animation clips onto the ultrasound, like the dead fetus is wearing the hat, the uterus growing a little mustache. A different viewer donates a disco ball. It spins near the top of the screen, holographic lights pointing to the black-and-white picture. A corgi now, its tongue lolling out in delight as it shakes its little butt at the gray fetus.

"Angelique wanted me to show you this," Bella Marie says as she flips to the next slide. A screenshot of her earnings from the five-hour live. $32,982. TikTok will take a 50 percent commission, which means she netted just over $15K.

My jaw drops as the Belladonnas clap and squeal, elated, their slapping palms ringing into my ear.

The projector shuts off and we're cast in momentary darkness. Bella Marie flicks on the light. It beams over her head like a halo, her hair the color of piss.

She floats to the center of the room, her hands clasped in front of her heart. "I am just *so* delighted for Angelique. Thanks to Eto, her growth has been explosive. And with how special and holy her sacrifice was, in due time the whole world will see how kind and beautiful and lovely she is."

My blood runs cold.

Sacrifice.

The baby.

Her firstborn child.

Of course. How did I not realize?

She sacrificed her *firstborn child* to Eto for *followers.*

Well, I guess it's official. There's no more denying it.

They're all batshit insane.

"Angelique is so kind," says Emmeline.

"So kind." Kelly.

"And so beautiful." Maya.

"Gorgeous." Sophia.

"Incredibly lovely." Lily.

"Just so lovely!" Ana.

They all turn to me, waiting for me to join along. There's a rock stuck in my throat, it doesn't budge even as I try to swallow it down, the primal urge to scream: *WHAT THE HELL IS WRONG WITH YOU ALL?* But not now. Not when I'm stuck in this room with them. Their long, pointy acrylics could rip into my flesh at any moment. Their white teeth could chomp my fingers like carrots.

"So lovely, so beautiful, so kind," I say, urging the tears that threaten to leak out of my eyes to suck themselves back in. "And I miss her so much."

Bella Marie smiles. Her features are so symmetrical, it's almost uncanny, inhuman. "I knew you'd understand, Julie. You're just too beautiful to not understand." She shakes her head, a single finger tapping her lips. "Darlings, I have a really wild idea."

"Wild?" Ana asks.

"What type of wild?" Maya asks. "Fun wild?"

"No, no, no." Bella Marie looks at me. "I think we should make it official."

My pulse jumps into my throat. "M-make what official?"

"Make you one of us." Bella Marie's eyes are wide, stretched, revealing the bloodshot webs in her white sclera. "Part of the family."

"I thought I already was. I ate—last night by the campfire."

Giggles ripple across the room.

"Oh, silly goose," says Bella Marie. "That was just the first step. An initiation."

Sweat breaks across my back. Eating a fucking mouse was an *initiation*?

"It was a gesture to Eto to show what you are willing to do," Bella Marie explains. "To swallow down your fears, to put away morality for a brief second. A show of dedication."

"Right." I gulp. "Dedication. So, um, what's the real thing like?"

She smiles wide, so wide I can see her uvula. I think of the mouse again. How easily she swallowed it, like a snake. She grabs my arms and rushes me out of the movie room, into the grand entrance hall with all the paintings of the Melniburgs—*Eto* worshippers, cult leaders—crawling up the wall.

"Viktor!" Bella Marie screeches. "Ohhhhh, Viktor! Where are you? Come right this instant!"

"Yes?"

I jump, his voice to my right. He's appeared out of nowhere.

"Ready the main hall. We're about to let Julie into our family!"

Someone steps behind me, too fast for me to turn around. A whoosh. *Bang!* I topple onto the ground, ears ringing. My temple throbs with pressure as my vision goes in and out. Pretty little ankles dance around me, the sound of their cooing voices.

Darkness.

55

The smell of something sharp, cutting, ammonic.

I jar awake and cough out the putrid scent that is caught in my nose hairs, singed into my brain.

My eyelids are dry, tacky, sticking to my corneas.

Bella Marie kneels in front of me in a sheer white dress, almost bridelike. Her hair is twisted into two braids, black bows tied at the ends. She sets down the pot of foul powder—it's that scent that must've shocked me awake.

I glance around. High ceilings, marble floors. We're in the dining room. They've taken away the tables and chairs and drawn all the blinds, casting us into darkness except for a few flickering candles here and there.

My head throbs like my skull has been split. "Did you hit me over the head?"

"We had to," she says, a crease forming between her brows like she's truly pained. "But trust me, we didn't want to. It hurt us a lot to do that."

"I was the one who bonked your head," says Sophia. She's with the rest of the girls at the far end of the room. They're all wearing matching white dresses, their hair tied up in milkmaid buns. "It might have hurt extra since I've been taking kickboxing classes. I hope it's not too bad."

"It hurts a lot, actually." I lift my hands to rub my head. Resistance. I glance down. My arms are shackled to the wooden chair with metal chains.

Panic beats into my throat in choking pulses. What the fuck? They've tied me down?

"Oh no! I'm sorry!" Sophia weeps.

"Ouchie," says Lily.

"Poor, poor, Julie," coos Emmeline.

"Don't worry, it only hurts for, like, three days," says Maya.

"Four for me," says Ana. "But I have a low pain tolerance. You are so strong, Julie. I'm sure it's not going to be a problem."

It takes everything within me to play nice. Not to scream: *Fuck you!*

Is Iz also tied up somewhere right now? She must be so scared and alone. I have to get out of here and help her. I just need to get this last step over with, and then I'll escape. I'd rather throw myself into the fucking ocean, get torn to shreds by sharks or squished by a colossal squid, than be stuck here.

"How do I become a part of the family?" I ask. "I'm desperate. Want it quick because I love you all so, so much."

"Oh!" Bella Marie exclaims, jumping in the air. "I love your enthusiasm and I love you, Julie. Let's get started then." She floats to the end of the room where an old gramophone lies and adjusts the needle. Mozart's *Confutatis* scratches into existence.

"Viktor!" she calls. "Bring in Nikolai."

Viktor comes in with Nikolai's portrait. He sets the painting on a marble pillar and places a candle in front of the frame.

Nikolai stares at me with his single blue eye, the flickering candle making his outline twitch.

Viktor stands behind the painting.

Bella Marie caresses the frame gently. "Nikolai was the first to swear fealty to Eto. One night, in a dream, Eto gave him a message. Asked for something dear: an eye. And when Nikolai woke up, he knew in his heart he had to follow Eto's instructions. So, he took a spoon and—" She gestures gouging out one of her eyes. "A week later, as he was hoeing the fields, he found the pocket watch and his life—all of our lives—were changed forever."

Christ. Who did Nikolai think he was? An off-brand Joan of Arc? He probably had psychosis from being a peasant with malnutrition and chronic stress. One bad dream and some dumb luck later, he makes his entire lineage follow some delusional religion.

And now, here I am. Just perfect.

Bella Marie flattens her palm over the back of my hand. "For you to truly join the family, for Eto to listen to you, you must do the same."

I wince, pulse spiking with alarm. "Gouge my eye out?"

She laughs, a quick *ha*. Delighted.

The other girls giggle too. Titter, really.

"No, no, no, darling. Promise something dear to you. Something close to your heart. The more significant the promise, the more significant the reward." Her eyes are intense. She really believes this.

"What about you? What did you promise?"

Her gaze softens. She looks down at her belly, strokes her stomach. "My father had me perform the ritual when I was thirteen. It coincided with the first time I bled. I hated PMS so much that I offered my womb to relieve the agony of my cramps. At fifteen, I was diagnosed with endometriosis and a year later I was declared infertile because of primary ovarian insufficiency." She takes a long breath and closes her eyes in grief. I wonder if this was why she was so stone-faced about Angelique's supposed sacrifice. "My father was beside himself when he realized what I'd done. I was rash and immature: one wish and I put an end to our lineage, severed our history by the head. But I was only a child in pain, desperate to alleviate it. I didn't know what my sacrifice truly meant." Her voice is hoarse and tired. Reluctantly, my heart strains. Her hurt is so ardent that I'm disarmed, shrinking in front of Nikolai's portrait, the shadow looming behind him.

"But I promised to rectify my mistakes. That's why I have you, my darlings. A family of my own to carry on my history." Opening her eyes, she rests her hands on my shoulders. She stares at me lovingly, like a mother giving her daughter advice. "Think carefully. Don't make the mistake I did by promising too much. Whatever you offer, Eto will collect as payment. Even though the timing is out of our control, it is inevitable. But the offering must be grand. Eto will not accept something too small nor easy."

My nails dig deep into my palms, every part of me tense. I want this to be over. This is too much to take in. "And how do I do this offering?"

"This is the miracle of Eto. As soon as you declare it in your heart, set your intentions, Eto will hear you. The reply will be felt in your soul, clear and crisp. You will know. For me, it was like a hummingbird had entered my heart, a trembling, buzzing energy. But we each feel something different."

"Soft for me," Lily says. "Like clouds. Sweet like cotton candy."

"I was struck by creativity and inspiration," says Ana. "Anything felt possible. I could pen a hundred soliloquies!"

"Mine was hurt," says Sophia. "It tore me apart. I thought I would die."

"I was sad," Maya adds. "I cried for hours when Eto finally heard me."

"Mine as well," Emmeline echoes. "I was inconsolable."

"An orgasm," says Kelly, eyes wide. "I felt Eto come inside me. Multiple times. It was triumphant. My limbs were spasming the entire night."

Okay. Thanks, Kelly. Absolutely did not need to know that.

"Then why is Nikolai here?" I ask. "If all I have to do is speak it in my mind?"

"For encouragement, obviously," Bella Marie says. "It can be so lonely and terrifying swearing fealty, giving up something dear. His painting is here to remind you of all the greatness that resulted from his sacrifice. A show that it's all worth it."

"Won't you be here?"

"The offer is a sacred process. It should be endured only between yourself and Eto. A family member cannot bear witness as it may bring undue pressure. However, a witness must be present to know the ritual is complete." She gestures at Viktor. "Once your sacrifice has been accepted, you pass the knowledge to the witness and the secret is kept forever."

"Wait, so Viktor knows all of your promises?"

Bella Marie nods. "It was the duty performed by his father and all the fathers before. A family legacy he is bound to uphold."

"And what if he tells?"

"He explodes in a ball of holy fire."

I burst out laughing but Bella Marie jolts, harsh surprise pressed in her frown.

"Oh." I clear my throat. "You're serious."

"Darling, I've been serious this whole time. I'm unveiling the truth of the world to you. It's not a laughing matter."

"Right." I bite my tongue. "Sorry."

She smooths her white dress. "It's fine," she says, though she's clearly displeased. "We will leave you to it now. The three of you, behave." She smiles at me, Viktor, and Nikolai, before beckoning the other girls to follow her out of the room. They march behind her like little ducklings, waving goodbye.

"Good luck," says Bella Marie.

"I'm praying for you," says Kelly.

"Soon, you will be family," says Maya. "Officially. One of us!"

"Family," adds Emmeline.

"I hope your head doesn't hurt for too long or I'll feel really bad," Sophia says. "You still look pretty, though."

"So pretty," echoes Ana.

"Stunning," says Lily. "Really."

The door slams shut behind them, echoing through the empty hall.

I glance at Nikolai. One-eyed like a pirate. At Viktor, who stares blankly at a distant wall.

I lift my arms, testing the restraints. The chains clink, pressing hard against my wrists.

I sigh.

How did I even get here? All I wanted was to be an influencer.

I stare at the looming shadow behind Nikolai.

Time to make an offering to the devil, I guess.

56

W hat do people usually offer?"

Viktor's eyes slide to me. "I'm not permitted to say."

I roll my eyes. "Right. The whole bursting-into-holy-fire thing. Do you actually believe that?"

He frowns, clearly upset I'd even ask.

Fair enough. He's probably been brainwashed. A whole line of Viktor Seniors indoctrinated as sex-toy-witness-things. Pretty barbaric.

This may be my one chance to get some answers out of him, since the Belladonnas cannot pry. "Do you get paid for all you do?" I ask.

"Serving the Melniburgs is all the payment I need. It is the world's greatest honor."

Okay. Uh. Wow. So, he's literally a slave.

"Have you been off this island?"

He grits his teeth, resistant to answer. With enough silence, he shakes his head, gaze downcast to the floor.

"You'd be a hit outside," I say. "You have that European white man appeal. A bit like Alexander Skarsgård."

"Alexander Skarsgård?"

"*Tarzan? Big Little Lies?*"

He tips his head, confused.

I gape. "Don't you watch TV here? Movies?"

"Only what Miss Melniburg permits. The Olympics, sometimes. We love the Olympics." No wonder he keeps going on about the Olympics.

"What about *Succession*? You must have watched *Succession*."

"What's *Succession*?"

Holy crap. "Only the greatest show —" I sigh. No point in explaining this to him. There are more important things at hand. "What about Chloe? Can you tell me what she offered?"

He glances at me. "I must keep it all a secret—"

"I know, I know. Ball of holy fire or whatever. But she's dead, so technically, she can't tell me even if she wanted to. And I'm her sister—twin! I think she'd want me to know."

His mouth presses into a thin line.

I tilt my head cutely. "Please? I really don't think this will bend the rules. I'm basically Chloe, anyway. I'll give you permission." I tap his shin with my foot.

He squirms and I almost feel bad making a grown man fidget and sweat. But whatever. It's not like this Eto thing is real. He's not going to burst into holy fire. And I really want to know Chloe's sacrifice—need to know. I have this feeling that once I get the answer, everything will click into place.

How can I pry information out of him when his mind is barbed with holy rules?

He's a bit simpleminded, his deprivation and lack of knowledge by design, but he's human. He must have desires. The less you have, the more you want; I know this well. Could I use this to my benefit? I might as well try. There's nothing to lose.

"What if I make *you* an offer?" I ask.

His eyes widen. "M-me?"

"How about this: in exchange for telling me what Chloe sacrificed, I'll give you anything you want."

"Anything?"

"Yeah, like goals, aspirations, an object. Anything." I'm setting a high bar for myself, but it's not like I plan on fulfilling this promise. Once I get this over with, I doubt I'll be seeing him again. A lie or two won't change much for me.

He ponders this hard, biting his nails. It's almost sweet, really, his excitement. "An Olympic medal?"

God. He's so easy. I might even be able to fulfill his wish. There are probably a few replicas floating around eBay. I doubt he'd be able to tell.

"I'll do you one better," I say. "I can get you a *gold* medal."

He jumps closer to me. "What? Really?"

"Yes! I promise I'll get you a gold medal if you tell me what Chloe sacrificed, and if I don't, Eto can strike me down with holy fire. Swear on this heart."

He considers this seriously, making a lap around my chair and staring at Nikolai, as if asking for permission, moaning and groaning all the while.

"Her adoptive parents," he answers finally, squinting, clearly afraid he'll explode. And when he doesn't, he opens his eyes fully, shoulders relaxing. He glances around and blows a steady breath out his mouth, surprised. "The Van Huusens are who she offered."

Oh.

So that's why she thought the Van Huusens' hit-and-run was her fault.

Although . . . what are the chances?

No. I need to get a grip. Our parents died in a car accident, and no one jinxed them. Millions die the same way every year. And the Van Huusens would have kicked the bucket eventually, given their age.

It's all a coincidence. Surely.

Viktor brushes himself off, looking grateful that he's not a ball of fire.

"See?" I say. "You can trust me. I knew you wouldn't be harmed. I'm on your side. But while we're on this topic . . . Did the Bell—did the others have anything to do with Chloe's death?"

"Miss Melniburg would never hurt family. Never." He's offended that I'd even ask. "But sometimes, after Eto takes, the offerer can experience extreme guilt and remorse." He leans closer, tentative. "Like Mrs. Melniburg," he whispers. "She tried to . . ." He mimes a noose.

So, it wasn't just a stroke and dementia.

"Are you saying Chloe might have . . . unalived herself?"

"Unalive?"

Right. Internet lingo to a caveman Skarsgård who only watches the Olympics. Why am I self-censoring anyway? "Suicide," I amend.

He shrugs. "It's a possibility."

The more I uncover how awful this island is, the more suicide makes sense. Maybe the Van Huusens' accident was the moment of reckoning that forced Chloe to confront how fucked up her so-called Belladonna "family" was. If I were somehow swindled into this shallow friend group for five years, I think I'd end up doing something drastic to escape too.

But that still doesn't explain why she called me.

At the very last second of her life, the words she said to me were: *I'm sorry.*

It was an apology. Not even a call for help.

Why?

I've heard people's lives flash before their eyes when they're close to death. Maybe she had thought of me—her family—before her last moments.

But what was she apologizing for?

Our childhood? No. Those years needed no apology.

The video? Yes. That makes sense.

She had filmed that video exploiting me after being indoctrinated by Bella Marie, after being swept into this whole fucked-up, mice-eating group, her mind addled by drugs and hysteria. What if, after she snapped out of it all, she realized how awfully she'd treated me? Maybe she wanted to apologize before it was too late.

Chloe hadn't always been a self-interested influencer. She had once been kind and loving. But the promise of connection and power is corrupting, can push us to do terrible things when we're lonely and desperate. When we finally free ourselves from those protective yet toxic echo chambers, open our eyes to the wounds we caused, it's only human to feel regret and guilt, to want to make things right, even if it means confronting an ugly reality.

Maybe that's what my twin was trying to do with her call and apology. Make things right with me.

Chloe's story ended a long time ago. I can never know the truth of her intentions. All I can know is what I tell myself. What I believe.

And this is a reality I wish to believe.

Still, accepting this possible truth slashes a gaping hole of remorse through my chest. Her last words were an apology, and yet . . . I took everything from her.

I really am terrible. I deserve everything that's happened to me.

After all of this, I need to leave Chloe's life behind. Build something new for myself. Let her rest in peace.

I close my eyes, take a breath.

But first, I have to get this over with. To be frank, I'm just glad that I don't have to munch on a bat or a bunny.

My task seems simple.

I need to make an offering to some fake god. But it needs to be good enough to trick Viktor. He's witnessed at least seven Belladonnas complete their offerings. He'd know if I'm lying. I need to think of something convincing.

What do I have to offer?

My firstborn? That one is pretty good, but Angelique just did that, and I don't want to seem unoriginal with my offering to the devil.

Family seems like a good bet.

But who? My cousin? My aunt? It's odd: even now, as I think of them, they don't bother me anymore. Chloe is dead, so the closest thing I have are the Belladonnas—

A flash of light rips through the curtains. Thunder booms overhead and vibrates through the chateau right as *Confutatis* crescendos into hammering drums, a belting choir roaring above the storm. My heart is elastic, beating like crazy. A vision of fire explodes onto my retinas. Orange flames lick the sky, columns of smoke, high-pitched screams. Euphoria bursts into my chest, rippling hot, torching my bloodstream with adrenaline.

Then, without warning, it dissipates, leaving me panting, yearning for more.

I blink back to awareness. Viktor's eyes are alight with excitement. "The offer. Eto has accepted it."

Warily, I glance at the portrait of Nikolai. Of the shadow.

"Holy shit," I whisper to myself.

Are you fucking real?

57

The way to end this.

It struck me with abrupt and specific clarity, like Eto had commanded me to carry out the terrifying plan. Like I'm a puppet at its whim.

But it can't be. Eto is not real. Eto is a creation of delusion and psychosis.

The thunder was a coincidence. Didn't Bella Marie mention they've been having summer storms? And those visions of fire . . . it must have been a scheme of my own nightmarish creation. Perhaps my burning anger toward the Belladonnas mutated to a more literal form. And they've been drugging me—hallucinogens could have remained in my blood, making me have horrific visions. The fires in my head are merely bursts of violent fantasy, not something to be actualized. Everything can be explained rationally and logically.

Eto doesn't exist. Surely.

I step into the grand entrance hall where the Belladonnas are huddled, giggling. When they hear me, they cease their chittering and smile wide.

"Julie!" they coo, rushing to me with quick little ballet steps. "Have you done it?"

I nod.

They scream and giggle, clapping.

"What did it feel like?"

"Sadness?"

"Elation?"

"An orgasm?"

"Yes, yes, tell us!"

I swallow and glance at Viktor, wondering if he'll warn them. He's returned to his empty, thousand-mile Skarsgård stare. He cannot go against Eto, what Eto has accepted—if Eto is real. And, maybe, he trusts me.

The Belladonnas grasp at my dress, fingering my locks as if yearning to tie little knots in my hair, bind us together forever.

I whimper. They salivate.

"Girls," I say sweetly. "It was really scary. Really, *really* scary. So scary, I almost cried."

"Oh no!"

"You should think happy thoughts."

"Yes, yes, happy thoughts."

I glance over their buzzing heads to Bella Marie. She's poised, ever elegant. Her thin, wiry fingers smooth down her blond hair. I stretch my arms out. She arrives without resistance, folding into me.

"Because I am so scared, I need you all. I need my family." I peel myself from her cold, bony body. "Stay with me tonight? Protect me?"

She parts her lips and inhales deeply, as if smelling me, wanting to savor the scent of Eto that has just touched me. "Of course, my darling Julie. Anything for you. Anything for family. We will protect you. I love you."

The Belladonnas coalesce, forming a net around my ribs with their arms, lifting me into the air, spinning me around. "*Of course! We love you. We will stay with you all night, all the time,*" they coo until we are back at my bungalow. We collapse on the bed. A mass of bodies piled like fresh, flopping fish. They nest into me, brooding chickens watching over their fragile egg, smoothing my hair, massaging my arms with their damp fingers.

"Let's go to sleep now," they say.

"Wait." I snake myself out of their grasp, their eyes burrowing into me with curiosity. I disappear around the corner. There's temporary relief from this minor separation. But I can hear their collective breaths. It's like they're doing group meditation, coordinated inhales and exhales. My pulse hums as I roll my thumb over my padlock. I unlock my carry-on and find the SLEEPY BEARS. The plastic safety seal shines in the evening dim. Little purple bears stare at me with their dull smiles.

I step out with the bottle behind my back. "I feel so scared. You girls couldn't imagine the sense of doom I feel."

"Doom?" Maya asks.

I nod. "Like I'm getting canceled."

There's a clap of thunder. They all gasp, horrific lines cutting into their faces, mouths gaping wide. Even Bella Marie looks terrified.

I nod, desperately, thankful they are reacting the way I wanted. "I am so terrorized by these thoughts that I know I won't be able to go to sleep tonight." I show them the bottle of SLEEPY BEARS. "I know taking these will help me fall asleep. But . . ." I swallow. "It would feel so lonely to take them all by myself." I break the safety seal and pour a few gummies into my hand. I look at the Belladonnas with wide, adoring eyes.

They glance at one another, exchanging uncertainties.

Are you fucking kidding? They were gobbling baby mice like Sour Patch Kids, but they can't accept some non-government-regulated, non-FDA-approved, drugged-out sleep gummies?

Get real.

My hands tremble, outstretched.

"They're safe," I say to Bella Marie. She's the only one who can convince everyone else. I step close to her, take a gummy myself as a show of intent. "They taste like lemonade and lavender."

Her eyes glaze with concern.

"Please," I say. "I am just so lonely, and so sad, and so, *so* scared. And I don't want to be the only one to take it. I thought we were family."

Bella Marie considers me deeply. Finally, she nods and pops a gummy in her mouth. Seeing this, the other Belladonnas join in. But for security, I say, "One is never enough. It takes two for them to be effective." I pop a second bear on my tongue. Maybe it's because they're chewing a gummy already, but they don't question it and accept second bears.

Truth is, one dose is enough to make anyone drop like a dead fly. Two is overkill, especially for a new user. But I've been using SLEEPY BEARS every day for the past few months. I've built up a tolerance. Normally it takes six to lull me into a night of sleep. Two is nothing. But to the uninitiated . . .

Already, Sophia opens her mouth in a yawn. It catches like a disease. Everyone stretches their jaws wide, blinking lethargically.

I yawn with them and crawl into bed.

They huddle close to me, limbs stretching over my body like lace.

"Good night," I say.

"Good night," says Bella Marie.

"Good night."

"Good night."

"Good night."

"Good night."

"Good night."

"Good neugh . . ."

Their breaths fall into slow sleep.

I am awake. And alive.

And holy fuck, this is actually happening.

But first: Iz.

58

Even though SLEEPY BEARS pack a serious (and possibly illegal) punch, I can't be too careful. If one of them wakes up, it's over. And I'm still not sure if I'm doing the right thing. If my thoughts and actions are even mine—or if they're Eto's. (But Eto can't be real. Right? *Right?*)

Heart pounding hard against my ribs, I gingerly untangle myself from their lithe limbs, moving arms and thighs like they're sleeping cobras. The bed shifts under my weight as I navigate through their bodies. Kelly moans and I freeze, pulse electric. She smacks her mouth as if tasting something delicious, and giggles. Goose bumps prickle on my arms as the giggles spread among the girls, contagious.

I slide off the bed and land on my tiptoes, barely making a sound. The bungalow groans. Wind whips at the thatched roof, whistling through the slatted windows. The door creaks as I open it into the night. Before I shut it behind me, I listen to see if anyone stirs.

Muffled snores and deep, sleepy breaths. My thundering heart.

I let out all the air from my lungs as I gradually close the door behind me. I keep my eye out for any prowling staff members. No white-teethed workers in sight.

Fog and rain scent the cool evening air. I keep to the line of trees until I reach the farm, then creep into the wooden shed. The rusty door shrieks as I pry it wide. I glance over my shoulder to see if anyone heard. Nothing but night.

The shed is pitch black. I feel around the walls for a light switch, but I can't find one.

I wish I brought my phone as a flashlight. All I can see are vague shapes: shelves, boxes, tarps. Shadows shift with the rapid current of clouds covering the moon. Something skitters across the floor. I shiver at the memory of the mice. From the corner of my eye, I spot a long cylinder that looks like the handle of an axe. I fly toward it, eager to get it in my hands. But it's only a garden hoe.

There's a creak behind me.

The hairs on my neck stand, itchy, like someone's watching.

Bang! The shed door slams shut, the walls shuddering. Dust coughs from the shelves, landing in my face. Heart thundering, I spin to the door.

A shadowed figure holding an axe, the sharp end pointed toward me.

I try to scream but nothing comes out. My heart is jammed into my throat, sheer panic crashing through my body.

The figure reaches up and I shrink away, scrambling to hide behind a series of boxes, but the light clicks on before I make it. A moth throws itself against the humming bulb. *Splat, splat, splat.*

"You look like you've seen a ghost."

I blink, my eyes adapting to the brightness.

It's only Viktor.

I'm frozen with fear, staring at the axe. It doesn't look like he'll harm me. I think I'm safe—for now.

"W-well, I mean . . ." I gesture at the axe.

"Oh! I was putting it away after I sharpened it." He swings it toward me and I jump back.

"What the hell!"

"Sorry! I just wanted to see if you cared to examine my work."

"Um . . . Okay?" I step a bit closer and glance at the raw edge. It's pristinely polished, shining like a mirror, reflecting his eager expression. "It's . . . very sharp."

He nods excitedly. "It takes a lot of skill to sharpen an axe, you know. I spent the past two hours honing it down with a file. It should chop through a log like butter now." He stares at me, waiting for more compliments.

"Really impressive." This Skarsgård boy toy just made my life that much easier. Luck is finally on my side. "Could I borrow it for a second?"

"Want to chop some wood?"

"Something like that."

He grins, handing me the axe, but just as I wrap my fingers around it, he pulls away and steps back. His head cocks to the side, lips curving into a frown. "You weren't thinking of doing anything *bad* with it, were you?"

Fuck.

"Bad?" I let out a nervous laugh. "No. Nothing bad at all." Which is the truth. Breaking Iz out isn't bad. Hell, I'd be a hero by most standards.

He narrows his eyes. "You're lying." His grip tightens around the wood handle.

Why has he chosen this moment to be perceptive? "I'm just trying to help Isla."

He backs away, shaking his head. "Bella Marie wouldn't like that." He's already halfway out the door.

"Stop!" But he doesn't. What should I do? I can't physically overpower him, and he has a literal axe in his hand. Right as he's about to run out, I shout, "Chloe's sacrifice!"

He freezes.

"You broke decades' worth of ritual by telling me. Bella Marie wouldn't like that very much."

He's stiff as he turns toward me, eyes sharp. The muscles in his jaw worm up to his temples.

"If she hears about it," I say, voice cracking with nerves, "she'll be mad. She might even get rid of you."

A grim expression creases his forehead. "That's not a very nice thing to say. I don't like you very much right now." He points the axe at me, but I step toward him. My gut tells me I have the upper hand. He's a brainwashed minion with a nice smile. He's a victim too. There's a way to take control.

"If you try to stop me," I say, "it will be the end of you."

He furrows his brow. "How?"

"I scheduled a message to Bella Marie detailing everything you told me. It's set to send tomorrow morning." There's no such message, obviously, but this caveman Skarsgård doesn't know any better. "So even if you deal with me tonight, you could still get in trouble."

A sheen of sweat drenches his fine upper lip.

"*But* . . . Bella Marie doesn't have to know. If you let me go and give me the axe like the good boy you are, I'll delete the message." I lay a trembling hand on the weapon.

"How can I trust you'll delete the message?" His voice is tight.

"Why would I lie? And also . . ." I push the blade away from me. It goes down without resistance. Whatever I'm doing, it's working. "You must remember what Eto has accepted as my offer. Soon, Bella Marie and all the other girls will be gone." I step closer to him and place my hands on his arms, hoping he doesn't notice how nervous I am. "With Bella Marie gone, who will take care of you?"

Fear widens his eyes. He shakes his head in agony and drops the axe. I resist swearing when it clangs to the ground an inch away from my foot.

"But you can trust *me*," I say. "Outside of this island, I have millions of fans. Hell, some videos I make get even more views than the Olympics."

He chews his nails with the energy of a frightened mouse. "Really?"

I nod. "Really. And I told you before, didn't I? You have the white European man appeal. With the two of us together, I know we'll make something great out of you after this all blows over."

He bites his lip and pivots. Wiping the dust off a flat side of a shovel leaned against the wall, he glances at his reflection. "You really think so? Can I be like a Skarsgård?"

"Yeah! Totally. Well, Skarsgård-adjacent, maybe. We could work on the branding together." I inch toward the axe and grab it now that he's distracted by his own appearance. With the weapon in hand, I am much more secure. But just in case, I seal in the deal with some validation. "I know you're scared, but I know something else too: you're smarter than you think. You need to believe in yourself. I will let you make the decision about whether you let me go tonight. A show of my trust. I'm putting my life in your hands." I'm mostly gentle-parenting out of my ass, hoping he'll believe me. But just in case I need to do something tragic, I grip the axe so hard I fear it will slip right out of my hands like a bar of soap.

He glances at me through the reflection on the shovel. "You promise not to tell Bella Marie?" His gaze is sincere.

"My lips are sealed. I promise. You can trust me."

He considers me intensely. I hold my chin high, serious. He sighs and cups his palms over his eyes. "Oh! It's so dark in here, I can't see anyone or anything. If someone were to walk past me right now, I'd never know!"

59

I lift the axe above my head and heave it straight for the padlock. It breaks without resistance, clattering heavily onto the ground.

Inside her bungalow, I'm greeted by the pungent smell of sweat and piss. "Iz?"

A moan.

"Iz!"

Her wrists are tied to the bed frame, mouth taped over. "Holy shit." What the fuck did they do to her? I rip the tape off. "Are you okay?"

She screams when she sees the axe, closing her eyes tight as if I'm about to kill her. I set the axe on the ground. "It's me. I'm here to help you."

She slowly blinks her eyes open, squints. "C-Chloe?"

Being called my twin's name confuses me for a moment. I forgot she doesn't know my secret.

"Y-yeah." I untie her wrists, which are knotted with, of all things, Hermès silk scarves. What is wrong with these people?

"W-water," she rasps. I run to the bathroom and fill her a glass. She chugs it.

I wipe off her sweat with a scarf. "What happened to you?"

She shakes her head, palming her chest like she's about to cry. I urgently want an answer, but I give her space to collect her breath. I turn on the bedside lamp, illuminating the haggardness of her face. Her eyes are red and wet, lips cracking, bleeding. She's sweaty, drenched in her own oil and crusted spit. Her usual bouncy curls have matted into a firm ball at the side of her head.

"It all happened so fast," she finally begins, voice hoarse. "After that lunch, I couldn't bear being around you all, so I used the landline to connect with my daughters for dinner. By the time I finished my call, I'd cooled down, so I thought about joining you guys. There was even a stupid part of me that convinced myself I'd overreacted. B-but then I saw you all and . . ." She shakes her head. "It . . . didn't feel right. You guys were dancing and singing but the closer I got, the more it felt . . . off. The energy was just . . . it was like you were coked-up zombies or something. And the giggles! God, you were all giggling like you were stoned out of your minds, while the servants were standing there, staring at you like you were zoo animals. It was so fucking creepy."

I smooth a palm over my forehead. Is that how it seemed from the outside?

"The whole vibe was off, so I ditched and went to hide out in my room." She turns to me. "But then I heard you screaming a few hours after."

"Me?"

She nods. "When I went to check on you, your door was locked, so I went around the back and peered through the slats in the french doors. That's when I saw all the girls surrounding you on the bed. You were screaming and crying and they were chanting something like—" She glances up at me.

My mouth dries. "Like what?"

She shakes her head. "It doesn't matter. Anyway, out of nowhere, two dudes tackle me to the ground. I scream for help, but someone puts their hands over my mouth."

So the person screaming that night *was* Iz.

My chest burns with regret. While Iz was crying out for help, I let myself be cooed into complacency. I sat back and watched the girls debase her at lunch. I gloated as they compared us at dinner. What the hell is wrong with me?

"The next thing I know, they hauled me back here, tied me down, and taped my mouth shut." Her voice is rich with vitriol. And it's justified.

I think of the markings by my bedpost. How long has this been going on? How many others were treated this way? And the Belladonnas, they're all complicit in these horrible machinations. I can't believe I wanted to be them—that for a moment, I *was* one of them. I can't believe we were prancing and singing about how we're all *oh so happy* when they literally imprisoned Iz. None of them felt guilt. Not even a smidge of remorse or empathy.

What the hell is wrong with them?

And how much longer will they get away with this shit if someone doesn't put an end to it?

Earlier tonight, I wasn't sure if I was going to finish what flashed in my mind. The idea of sacrificing seven human beings is twisted, an act that should never be realized. But it's dawning on me: if I don't do it, there's no clean escape. Even if I somehow get off this island, as long as the Belladonnas are alive, they will continue to enact whatever psycho cult bullshit they deem necessary. Worse yet, once it becomes obvious that I've defected, that I no longer want to be *us*, be family, they will come after me. If Iz was imprisoned in response to screaming for help, what awful nightmares would they wreak upon someone who betrayed them?

I can't sit around and twiddle my thumbs, hoping for things to be okay. If I don't finish this, it will drag into the outside world and the Belladonnas will never meet justice. I'm sure of it. With how much power the Melniburgs have, I wouldn't be surprised if someone on the Supreme Court also danced with their devil—hell, even a president or two. I can't wait for the system to serve justice because justice doesn't pertain to people like the Melniburgs. I need to do it myself while I have the upper hand. While no one is expecting it. While Eto—whether it exists or not—is on my side.

It needs to end right here. Right now.

"I'm so sorry, Iz. I'm sorry I didn't come and help you. I think they drugged me or tried to mind-control me or something. I wasn't acting right—wasn't thinking right. It wasn't until they made me eat a mouse—"

She grimaces. "A what now?"

"It's a long story. But I eventually snapped out of it." I tell her about what happened to Angelique, what I learned about Eto.

"You didn't offer anything, did you?" she asks.

I ignore her question. "Look, we don't have time to waste. I drugged the girls, so they won't wake up for a while. We have to act fast. Do you have your lighter on you?"

She staggers to her suitcase and unzips the lighter from the front compartment. The gold catches the moonlight.

I take it from her. "I know you're probably starving and sick to your stomach, but I need your help. Those girls—" I swallow. What if she thinks I'm taking it too far?

Abruptly, she stands. "Tell me what to do."

Thank god.

60

Under the cloak of night, we sneak into the wooden shed used for storage and haul every bottle of lighter fluid we can find back to my bungalow. Iz and I quietly stack all the patio furniture against the french doors so no one can force their way out through the rear.

"Okay," Iz says, dusting off her hands. "Now what?"

I haven't told her the full plan. It doesn't feel right to drag Iz into this, but beyond that, I have a feeling I need to do this alone. In my brief vision, she wasn't present. Not as a member of the Belladonnas, or as a perpetrator of fire.

I know there are no hard-set rules about sacrificing human beings; it's not like there's a handbook detailing do's and do-not's on how to trade human souls for power. (Hell, I'm still not sure if I believe in this Eto thing.) But if I'm going to murder, I might as well murder right. I don't have the time nor privilege to dip my toes and test the waters. I need to dive straight into the deep end and believe I'll come up on top.

I can't take any risks. Having an extra variable might fuck this all up.

And anyway, getting Iz out of this situation is a net positive for her. She gets saved *and* she doesn't have to commit a crime.

"You shouldn't do this," I say.

She frowns. "What do you mean? Aren't we just making a fire signal so we can get help?"

"Um . . ." I cast my eyes to the lighter fluid, then to the bungalow. "About that . . ."

She follows my gaze. Her eyes widen and she palms her forehead like reality is suddenly hitting her, the initial rage-fueled adrenaline wearing off. "Shit," she whispers. "Shit, shit, shit. Holy fuck. You aren't thinking of seriously harming them, right?"

"Don't freak out."

"How can I not freak out?" Her voice is pitched high. "You're thinking of burning—"

"Shh! You're going to wake them. We—*I* have to stop this. Look, I know you have a family, kids to take care of. You don't have to be involved in what happens after. I can take all the blame."

"But—"

"It's the least I can do after I left you hanging like that." She tries to protest but I shake my head. "I'll be fine. Run toward the main house and hide out somewhere nearby until you see the flames. The staff are bound to notice and run out to extinguish the fire. At that time, go inside. You still remember where the landline is?"

She nods.

"Call for emergency services. Tell them the island they sent the helicopter CG-484 to yesterday needs further assistance since there's a fire. And once you confirm they're sending help, hide until they come."

"Oh my god." She paces around, then drops to a crouch, panting deeply. "I can't believe this is happening. This is all so fucked! We can't do this."

"No! Fuck that." I bend down and grip her shoulders. "I know it's scary, but this is the only way it ends. Do you really think they'll let you out of here after everything they've done? Even if by some miracle we get off this island, do you think these girls will let us waltz back into society unscathed? Think of how much power they hold. It'll be the word of eight beloved white women against *us*."

Desperation clouds her eyes. "There must be another solution. Some other way we can all get out of this safely."

I can understand Iz's concerns, but I know it in my gut. This is the only way forward. "I can't explain the details to you, but I'm sure this is the right thing to do. You have to trust me." I say it full of intent, wide-eyed and true.

She closes her eyes and groans, fisting her hair. "This is seriously *so* fucked up!"

"I know. But there's no other choice. Now go before someone notices you're gone."

She stands and collects her breath. "God! This is the worst vacation ever." She trudges forward. A few paces away, she stops and glances over her shoulder. "Good luck."

"You too." I watch as she runs toward the main house.

I turn toward the bungalow entrance with two bottles of lighter fluid and take a deep breath, trembling.

I am strong.

I am brave.

I am a warrior.

I am going to be okay.

I push inside.

61

I rest the axe near the door and creep into the room. The women are fast asleep, mumbling sweet nothings under bitter breaths. Slipping past them, I push my weight against the french doors to check that the patio furniture is securely barricading the rear exit. The hinges don't shift an inch with all my strength. I upright myself and take a nervous breath.

No going back now.

I work quickly, dousing the room with lighter fluid. My hands are so sweaty from nerves that I almost drop the bottles twice. I soak everything thoroughly. The walls, the couches, the fancy rug. The blinds, the closet, between dresser drawers. I can't believe I'm doing this. I'm literally about to murder seven people. What the fuck? Yet I don't stop. Instead, I try to think of what happens next, what I'll do when everything catches aflame, how I'll return to the outside world and somehow justify my crimes.

By the time I'm finished, the room is pungent with the dizzying smell of butane. My clothes are damp with perspiration and lighter fluid. I'm a walking combustion engine with a lighter in my pocket. The only place I don't soak is the bed, wary that if I get too close, one of the sleeping devils will wake and accost me.

With the last bottle emptied, I creep toward the closet. When I open it, the automatic light inside flickers on, illuminating a small pocket of the otherwise dark room. I take the padlock off my carry-on so I can use it to barricade the Belladonnas inside.

The sound of rustling sheets. A groan. One of the girls is stirring.

My heart patters against my chest. I stay still. Madly still. A cornered mouse waiting for the big bad wolf.

"Ugh." Bella Marie. "What is that smell?"

I glance at the door. Should I start the fire now? Light the flames and run out?

But Bella Marie's awake. What if she manages to rouse everyone before the fire takes? The seven of them slamming against the door would overpower a shitty luggage lock. I need most of them asleep when the fire starts, so by the time they are awake, their lungs are filled with smoke, carbon monoxide clogging their tracheas, a floor of ripping flames beneath them, no method of escape. .

I hear her climb off the bed. "Julie?"

Shit. She's noticed I'm not there.

But her voice is that of a worried mother hen. She doesn't know what's going on yet.

Against my better judgment, I step back into the room. "Hey," I whisper, hoping the darkness hides my panic, the sweat glistening across my temple.

"Darling, do you smell that?" She wipes the sleep from her eyes.

I take a big whiff that slaps me in the back of my head. Stars spin in my eyes from the sharp butane. "Nope! No smell. We should get back to bed."

She doesn't move, staring. The blue of her eyes glows at me. "Why are you creeping around, Julie?"

I swallow. "No reason. Just needed to stretch my legs because . . . I had a nightmare."

"A nightmare?"

"Yes. Very bad nightmare. Cancellations and everything. Why are you awake?" The SLEEPY BEARS should have put her in a coma.

Her white teeth shine in the dark. "Darling, I only pretended to take the bears for your mental support. I spat them out when you weren't looking. You know I'm strictly against the medical-industrial complex. Sorry to disappoint." She steps toward me. Jolts. Peers down. Her feet have landed in a puddle of lighter fluid.

Fuck.

The shadows of her face contort as her brows arch, lips curling into a frown. She lifts her foot, swipes a dainty finger across her arch, and sniffs. Her body snaps straight and she stares at me with wild eyes, stalking closer. The closet light illuminates her sharp profile. "Julie, what were you doing with the lighter fluid?"

"Nothing." I back away, remembering the axe by the door. I yearn to lunge for it but I fear that if I move too quickly, she'll tackle me with her spindly limbs before I get to the weapon.

I gulp and move slowly. My muscles creak and my bones pop as I inch through the entranceway. The whole time, I can't tear my eyes away from Bella Marie's blues.

"Don't lie." Her eyes are inhumanly wide. Like a Cheshire cat. She comes so close my stomach roils with fear. I can somehow smell her honeyed skin through the butane. "We're family, remember? Family doesn't lie to each other."

"But we keep each other tied to beds?"

She freezes. Tips her head to the side with a mild smile. "You found Isla?" Her voice is disturbingly light, almost playful. The tone you'd use to congratulate a toddler for performing a simple math equation. "You must understand, what we do is for the good of the family. Out of love. After a few days, Isla will come to her senses. Everyone does."

"It's inhumane."

"Inhumane? Me? Inhumane? You're the one who stole your sister's life." I flinch. Didn't she proclaim it to be a brave act? "Don't you see what I've done for you girls? I'm uplifting you. Welcoming you into the family. I'm generous. I'm kind. I'm beautiful and loving. Things usually work better than this. We normally introduce one new member at a time so as not to overwhelm. But it's all because of my dear cousin's tweets and *you* that we've had to improvise." She opens her arms for a hug. "But it's not too late. We all make mistakes. If you repent, we can take you back."

Only a day ago, her open arms filled my heart with warmth. But now my blood runs cold as I take another step back. "F-fuck you," I spit.

She's in front of the light now, her skin sallow. She drops her arms and sighs. "I should have known that Chloe's twin would cause problems." She steeples her temple. "After all I did to take care of her."

My teeth chatter. "Take care?"

She tips her head, makes a small *aw* sound. "Darling, are you slow? Chloe would never die from something as blasé as a *drug overdose*."

"Y-you—" The words catch in my throat. "You killed her."

"Don't be so crass. *Killed* is a very dramatic word. I simply eased her into eternal sleep by lacing her water with some drugs that interacted poorly with her anti-depressants."

I'm breathless at how easily she says this. Like she's gotten away with this before. "Do the girls know what you did?"

"Everyone but Angelique. She's still a fledgling, has only just fulfilled her promise, so she's not privy to it all."

I'm grateful that Angelique doesn't know. Maybe her words from s'mores night were genuine. But I can't believe the rest were pretending the whole time. I guess I wasn't the only one wearing a mask.

"And anyway," Bella Marie continues, "I think your twin must have felt guilty for what Eto took. The Van Huusens' car crash was the start of her mutiny. It was a shame, really. But I think you'll be pleased to hear that until the last second, your sister was an affable person—well, except for the brief period where she threatened us. Silly girl thought she could expose us by going to a journalist."

"Jessica Peters," I whisper to myself. *This* was the story Chloe had wanted to tell.

"*The New Yorker* has been a compatriot of ours for a while. It was a simple catch-and-kill." She grimaces. "I really don't like how that sounds. Catch-and-*kill. Kill. Kill. Kill.* It's so ugly. We should think about re-branding that."

"You killed Chloe!"

"I told you not to use that word! After going against me—against the family like that, putting a gun to my head—she knew how it would end for her. You must snuff out the sound before anyone can let out a scream. It's a doctrine of our family, which you would have learned tomorrow morning if you'd been more obedient." She sighs. "Though, I will admit, it was my fault for not staying through her demise. I felt her pulse slow, so I thought it was finished. I never liked the face of death. It's very violent, not pretty at all, I don't recommend it. I also had a *Vogue* photo shoot to prep for later that evening. And when Anna Wintour tells you to come at six, you come at six. Not a minute late."

I'm reeling. How can she be so casual about all of this? As if mixing murder and *Vogue* in the same breath is as natural as syrup on pancakes.

"Of course, I also hadn't accounted for you," she continues. "But I figured you were a gift from Eto, given your past. The loneliness, the guilt, the need for community and validation. It made sense."

I'm so close to the axe, its gravity pulls on my fingertips. The presence of the weapon empowers me to speak. "What? So I'm more susceptible to your fucked-up cult? To your fake god?"

Bella Marie gasps, palm slapping her mouth. The bungalow groans under the wind, wooden slats creaking. *"Fake?"* She shakes her head slowly. "How can you be that dense? Don't you see the miracles happening around us? Look at us, our influence. The bonfire and your aunt. You feel the change, don't you?"

I hate that I do. But there must be another explanation for everything that's been happening. "These girls are all beautiful and talented—is it so unbelievable that they'd attract fans? That maybe being in your orbit, having access to your connections and wealth, would boost their influence? There are *thousands* of rational and grounded explanations. It's not like every influencer swears fealty to some god."

"Angelique," she says, stepping a hair too close. "You saw her. You saw how Eto took her baby." Her breath is sour, acidic.

"She was drinking the entire trip, taking weird-ass drugs you gave her—which, by the way, is not very anti-medical-industrial complex of you—"

"It's holistic!"

"She ate a fucking *mouse*! And even if it's not for any of those fucked-up reasons, miscarriages happen all the time. It could all be some horrific coincidence. And of course she gained followers after posting such a heart-wrenching video. People thirst for sob stories!"

"Then what about me?" She's shouting now, desperate and ugly. "What about me?"

"People have fertility problems without sacrificing their womb to the devil!" My fingertips make contact with the wooden handle.

Bella Marie shakes. "Eto is *not* the devil!"

"Fine! People have fertility problems without sacrificing their fucking womb to Eto!"

She bares her canines, expression crumpled with fury. "Not. To. People. Like. ME!" She lunges. Before I know it, my hands are around the axe handle and I swing blindly for her right as she wraps her fingers around my neck, squeezing. I feel resistance against the weapon as it hacks into something firm. Warm fluid splashes onto my cheek, into my eye, stinging. Bella Marie's grip weakens, drops from my neck. I pull the axe out with a grunt, my sight impaired.

The air is iron, metallic.

I wipe the gloop out of my eye, pulse racing. Blood, I realize, as I take in my scarlet fingers. Red gushes down Bella Marie's shoulders, her bony clavicles, drizzling onto the floor, from a giant, horizontal gash in her neck. In my panic, I didn't hit her hard enough, and the axe didn't go all the way through.

There's a beat as the world slows. My mind is empty. Our breaths are heavy, out of sync. My legs tremble, weak from the sight of the gore. Her figure sways slightly, and she stumbles from shock as she palms her neck, violent crimson pulsing between her fingers. Her eyes meet mine, pupils dilated like a wild animal's. She opens her mouth to scream. But before any sound leaves her lips, I brace my core and swing the axe toward her neck again—toward the woman who killed my twin. Soft skin, tense muscles, vertebrae. The bloodied axe clears through to the other side, splashing the wall with gore. Her body thuds hard on the floor, shaking the entire bungalow. Breath struggles into my lungs as something brushes the tip of my toes. I glance down. Blond hair. Blue eyes. Pale skin. Her head. Bella Marie's mouth is suspended mid-scream, face frozen with horror as her empty blue eyes, barren of soul, stare at the ceiling.

My pulse is on fire, my heart beating so fast I can't move, can't think. My eyes are fastened to Bella Marie. The axe slips from my fingers. The sharp clatter of the blade hitting tile flips a switch in my head. My mind churns.

Bella Marie.

I did that. I killed her. I am a *killer.*

Every part of me is wet with sweat, my brain high and dizzy from the butane that swims through my nose. My limbs are jelly, and I want to puke, but I need to get a grip. There's no going back now. Not after I've bloodied my hands, murdered Bella Marie. I need to finish this. *Now.*

Fueled by pure adrenaline, I stumble past the body, feet slapping through warm, sticky blood, and check the bed.

The rest of the Belladonnas are still asleep. But their bodies twitch, fighting for awareness.

With all my remaining willpower, I fumble the lighter from my pocket with one hand, the padlock with my other, and stagger to the door, avoiding Bella Marie's decapitated head. I flick open Iz's golden lighter, the metal cool to the touch, grounding. I roll my thumb against the jagged spark wheel. A thin blue-and-orange flame appears. I toss it to the line of lighter fluid I had drizzled earlier. It catches, a monstrous display erupting in a blink, engulfing Bella Marie. I back away, slam the door, shut and lock it. Smoke billows out from the gaps near the hinges.

By the time I let go of the padlock, my body is so weak I fall to the ground. I crawl on all fours away from the burning bungalow, my dress stained with Bella Marie, leaving a crimson trail behind me. The thatched roof catches like kindling. Wisps of black smoke curl into the dark sky, highlighted by yellow flames. The window becomes a night-light, an orange portal into the bright, burning insides. I think I hear a scream, something guttural. *Bang. Bang. Bang.* It might be a human. It might be the foundation collapsing. It might all be in my head. The thatched roof caves in, clearing way for a large cloud of smoke. The fire crackles, a dancing figure, a bonfire for the gods. The suffocating miasma of a sacrifice. Heat sears the tips of my toes, but I don't move. I watch as the entire bungalow is engulfed in golden orange, roaring as the staff rushes over. They helplessly throw buckets of water on the blaze, but soon, they simply stand and watch, soot staining their pale faces.

My vision clouds with smoke. A cry cracks up my throat, or maybe it's a laugh. A scream? I can't quite tell.

As I take in the beautiful bellowing creature of my creation, an evil monster that has swallowed up seven lives with ease, I pray.

I pray that Eto is real. I need to believe this wasn't all for nothing.

Then, darkness.

62

I wake up chained to a hospital bed. A police officer is sitting beside me, half asleep. When he hears me pulling on the clinking metal cuffs, he startles awake. His eyes widen and he presses a button beside him.

"What happened?" I mumble, mouth dry.

But the man refuses to talk to me. I'm disoriented, a screaming headache gnawing at my brain like it's been cleaved in half. My lungs are harsh, tight. Every breath is a rattle and a cough. A blurry rush of doctors, nurses, police officers. Their murmurs are deafening and disturbing. It reminds me of cooing girls.

I close my eyes and escape into sleep again.

63

Look straight into the camera."

A pop. Light bursts into my eye and I squint. When I breathe in, my lungs rattle. The doctors told me I was lucky to be alive after how much smoke I inhaled. Though their definition of *lucky* is a bit different from mine. After two weeks of critical care in a Saint Marten infirmary, I was forced into a garish orange jumpsuit that pairs awfully with my tanned skin and hauled onto a plane to be booked for my alleged crimes. As it was explained to me, since the Melniburg island is located in international waters, I am subject to the laws of my and my victims' home country: America. And if anyone knows anything about the great United States of America, it's that we love guns, bald eagles, freedom, and have *fantastic* state-of-the-art penitentiary facilities. Nothing inhumane and unwelcoming about them, *at all*!

So, no. I don't feel particularly lucky.

"Turn to your left."

The metal handcuffs between my wrists clank as I pivot left to face the gray brick wall. I find myself sucking in my cheeks and mewing even though I'm taking a mug shot, not a selfie. But if there's a chance that this ever gets leaked, I might as well look hot in it.

Another pop of light.

"Now turn to your right."

Pop. Light.

"All right, Julie, you can head into the next room."

I jolt at the name *Julie*.

That's right. The world knows I stole my twin's identity and that I'm really Julie Chan. And you would never guess who exposed me.

Iz.

Yep. That Iz.

Isla motherfucking Harris.

After I saved her ass from those psychopaths and prevented her from being a murderer—from *being* murdered—she ratted on me while I was passed out. She claimed she overheard the girls calling me Julie in some cult ritual, and it didn't take long for the authorities to piece two and two together.

A part of me wants to be angry at her betrayal. But after all I've gone through, the blood on my hands, I'm too resigned to feel any emotion as pointed as anger.

Still, sometimes I think about what might have happened if I had just left Iz in that bungalow.

I'm ushered into a room near the back of the station, where my court-appointed lawyer waits for me. He's wearing a drab checkered blazer two sizes too big, his hairline resembles McDonald's Golden Arches, and he keeps clearing his throat into his fist. A pile of yellow manila folders is stacked in front of him. The room smells like stale coffee.

He stands and extends his hand for me to shake. "I'm David, your publicly appointed defense attorney?" His voice is mousy, and all his statements sound like questions.

I take a seat across the table, folding my arms.

He awkwardly drops his hand and sits down. "Okay, so uh, let's just quickly go over everything you've been charged with?" He moves the pile of manila folders in front of him and flips one open. "I'm seeing here . . . identity fraud, obstruction of justice, theft, arson, eight counts of first-degree murder—"

"Wait." I uncross my arms, lean forward. Bella Marie, Kelly, Sophia, Lily, Ana, Maya, Emmeline. Seven girls. Seven deaths. "Eight? That can't be right."

He glances at his paper. Points to a line. "It says right here, eight counts."

"It can't be. I only ki—only seven people died in that fire."

"Well, I think, um . . ." He fusses over his stack of papers, pulling out another manila folder. But when he flips it open, he accidentally knocks over his cup of coffee. The black plastic lid pops off and the murky brown contents spill onto the floor. "Oh gosh, oh no." He bends to clean up his spill before realizing he has nothing to wipe it with. "Uh. Let me get someone to clean this up?" He leaves the room.

I close my eyes and huff a tired sigh, praying that I won't have to deal with him too long before Fiona finds me a replacement.

Reaching out to an employee with my single phone call was pathetic and embarrassing. The pain of having no one hit me hard that day. I was worried that Fiona would be apprehensive about still working for me, considering that the story about the island massacre had already been blasted across the news. But to my surprise, Fiona picked up the phone with interest. As fate would have it, she's a true-crime enthusiast. She agreed to continue working for me, as long as she got to tell people she's employed by *the* Julie Chan. Assistants to influencers and A-list celebs are a dime a dozen, but an assistant to an alleged mass murderer? Just one! Social clout goes a long way these days.

I stare into the security camera in the corner of the barren room. Its black eye stares back.

I'm left alone for a dreadful length of time and since there's no clock, I can't tell exactly how long it's been. Could be five minutes. Could be thirty. Restless and antsy, I pull the papers out of the manila folder and read all the notes David has scrawled onto them.

Details of my crimes, the events before the fire, and then a list of the seven victims found in ashes. But then, at the very bottom of the page: *Defendant is charged with the first-degree murder of her twin, Chloe Van Huusen.*

I read the line over and over and over, the words not making sense. *First-degree murder of her twin, Chloe Van Huusen. First-degree murder of her twin, Chloe Van Huusen. First-degree murder of her twin, Chloe Van Huusen.*

What the *fuck*?

My blood boils at the accusation. I'm shaking, the metal handcuffs jingling like Christmas bells. While in the hospital, I'd been planning on pleading guilty. There was no way I'd get away with killing the Belladonnas. I was literally covered in Bella Marie's blood. But killing *Chloe*? No. Fuck that.

I did not kill my twin.

It was all a coincidence—a horrific coincidence.

I need to set this straight. I *did not* kill Chloe Van Huusen.

When the door finally swings open, I twist toward the entrance, desperate to shout the truth at David.

But the person who strides through the door is no sad sack of a public defender. She's a tall woman, dressed in a well-fitted navy pantsuit. Her ginger hair is slicked back in a tight, pristine bun. She steps over the puddle of coffee, heels clicking, before clunking her heavy leather briefcase on the metal table.

Before she even introduces herself, she pulls the chair out, sits across from me, and looks me dead in the eyes. "This is how I'm going to get you out of here."

64

Shannon is a no-bullshit lawyer who isn't afraid to get dirty to win. And win she does. Fiona heard about her through the assistant grapevine: three years ago, Shannon had worked on a case where a financier had allegedly (definitely) killed his wife. Every piece of evidence pointed toward the husband after he'd caught his wife having an affair, but Shannon was able to work magic during cross-examination, making witnesses contradict the evidence presented in court. She got the first-degree murder charge knocked down to involuntary manslaughter and her client walked away with three years of community service, when he was originally up for fifteen-to-life.

Shannon has a hefty price tag, but she's already proved her worth. After I signed the documents for representation, she somehow secured my conditional release from jail with a surprisingly low bond. It's a miracle I'm allowed to sit inside my—er, Chloe's—apartment without an orange jumpsuit on, considering my alleged crimes include the murder of eight beloved women. Now, I'm enduring house arrest as lawyers and paralegals bumble around me, a scratchy black GPS monitor wrapped around my ankle.

My eyes crawl to the nightstand, where I've hidden my phone. It's been a month since I've touched it. Yes. One month. Four weeks. Thirty—going on thirty-one—days. My abstinence is out of fear. I'm sure people online will eviscerate me. I don't need the additional blows to my already fragile mental state.

Time away from social media has been somewhat cleansing. My mind has slowed down, I've learned to listen to my body more, and I get less distracted. It's like my neural receptors are literally repairing themselves. And yet . . . the slim metal of the phone continues to entice me. I crave its heft in my palm, the connection at my fingertips. The love. The community.

Just one swipe. How bad can that be?

"Julie?"

I turn to Shannon. "Sorry, my mind wandered."

She's sitting across from me with a clipboard. "It's important that you focus. We can't have your mind wandering like that in court. The jurors will read that as unreliability."

"Right. Sorry."

Shannon is training me on my story in preparation for trial. It hasn't been too difficult. My claims of cultlike activity and brainwashing were corroborated once the authorities ransacked the island and found pounds of toxic psychoactive plants and a legion of indoctrinated pearly-white slaves.

Two people even agreed to testify in my defense: Bella Marie's mom, who claims she's been held captive on the island for five years, and Iz, who agrees that the cult was real, that she was held hostage for two days, and that our lives were in genuine danger. (They questioned Angelique. She's pleaded the fifth on everything thus far.) With all this evidence in my favor, Shannon says it's realistic to mitigate my Belladonna murders with self-defense. *I was only trying to escape a threatening situation. I had to kill to survive.*

The "truth" muddies when it comes to Eto. Confessing that I promised the Belladonnas to Eto would show intent for my murders, thus destroying any argument for self-defense. As far as Eto is concerned, in the court of law, I've been instructed to shrug and say, *I don't know.* Thankfully, no one alive can attest to the fact that the burning was nefariously motivated, not self-defense.

Well, except for Viktor. But last I heard, after being flown straight to America to be interrogated, he seemed to have kept his Abercrombie & Fitch lips sealed.

The sticky part is the issue of my twin.

Although Bella Marie confessed to Chloe's murder, since she's dead, it's all hearsay. Not to mention, it's not great that I just so happened to show up at Chloe's apartment, stumble upon her body, immediately lied to the cops about being Chloe, then proceeded to switch identities without guilt for a few months after her death. My actions don't paint a pretty picture. To an outside observer, there's reasonable grounds to argue I planned Chloe's death to steal her identity.

"Okay," says Shannon. "Let's go through everything that happened, step-by-step, again."

"I was walking home from my shift at SuperFoods when Chloe called me."

"What was said during the call?"

Although there is evidence of the call, there is no recording. All the court can go on is my word. "She seemed to be struggling for breath. And she kept apologizing to me for something. Saying something was a mistake. And then in her last breath . . ." I breathe in, try to be convincing. "She said something about it being Bella Marie's fault." This lie is my golden ticket out of jail. Sure, it might be struck from the record for hearsay, but once the jury hears this, they'll struggle to erase it from their minds.

"Is it true that you had two days off work the week Chloe was found dead?"

"Yes."

"The paramedic on the scene noted that Miss Van Huusen had been dead a few days, but since no autopsy was completed, the exact timeline of death is unclear. The security camera footage of the building also remains unclear, as you and your twin cannot be told apart. Is it possible that you went to New York during your days off and killed your sister?"

"What?" I shout. "No!"

"Calm down. Don't raise your voice. This is just what the prosecution might argue."

My lungs rattle and I fight the urge to cough. The issue of the security cameras triggers me. I'm unable to deny being in New York, since anytime Chloe was spotted on CCTV, she could be mistaken for me. Go figure. My face, which unlocked the world for me, might also be my downfall.

Bella Marie was never captured on camera near the building, since it just so happened that the cameras near the back-door fire escape had "mal-functioned" during the time of the incident. I would bet my life that Bella Marie tampered with them.

"No," I say, resigned.

"Is it true that you requested Chloe's body be cremated?"

"Yes."

"Did you do that knowing the timeline of death would remain uncon-firmed?"

"If I knew, I would never have done it."

At length, Shannon needles me about the timeline, if it was possible that I coerced someone else to call me on Chloe's phone, why didn't I request an autopsy, etc. It's painstaking and frustrating.

"After you discovered your sister's body," she continues, "why did you decide to take her identity?"

This is part two of the plan. "When I found her dead, I only assumed her identity because I needed to unravel the truth of how she died. I could sense something amiss after she mentioned Bella Marie in her last call to me. I knew that Bella Marie was somehow involved. When the police arrived, I lied about my identity because I needed to personally avenge my twin. A white woman like Bella Marie would never be brought to justice through regular means. It was a cruel means to a good end. I am not a killer. I am a truth-seeker. I strive for justice in my own way."

"Um . . . Okay, so we're going to have to work on that and unembellish it a little. It sounds like you're telling a story rather than the truth, but it's a good start."

"It is the truth." I haven't told Shannon anything else except this story. I need her on my side.

"I'm not saying it isn't. I'm just saying we'll work on it, okay?"

Her doubtful tone stings. I tap my feet as the need for validation grows in my chest, accompanied by a shadow of regret. What if I hadn't killed the Belladonnas? What if I'd just closed my eyes and let myself be absorbed into their current?

"You say you swapped identities for the sake of finding the truth. But there's evidence you've been living quite freely and happily as 'Chloe.' If you were trying to seek justice, why did you continue to do brand deals and sponsored content?"

Ah, the one time in my life where my aunt has come to save me. "My aunt has been extorting me, saying she'll expose my real identity. I needed to pay her off, so I took sponsorships in order to continue seeking justice for my sister."

Despite the weird fire ritual, my aunt is (unfortunately) alive. Though she might wish she were dead, considering her present circumstances. After my true identity was revealed, I told the police she possessed an important recording with evidence I didn't kill Chloe. Since the recording also included evidence of her crime of extortion, my aunt refused to relinquish it, which resulted in a warrant being issued to search her home. On top of the recording, the authorities uncovered a history of other petty crimes, and now she's suffering under investigation for extortion, aiding and abetting a crime, and a slew of other infractions. She hasn't gotten in touch with me, saying that she is *afraid* of me. Of *me*! Can you believe it?

But thanks to her, I'm able to justify my actions during my influencer era.

"We have email evidence here stating that—"

Two knocks. A paralegal opens the apartment door and Fiona walks in with a man beside her. He's holding a single hammer. His gaze is angled toward the floor, the rim of a black baseball cap obscuring most of his face except for his sharp jaw.

"Who's this?" Shannon spins out of her seat to shoo the man away. "We aren't allowed to have unregistered guests."

"Just here to fix the internet." He glances up at Fiona, revealing a tight and eager smile.

My heart drops. I can recognize that tight grin anywhere, an expression that's wholly desperate for validation.

Viktor.

65

e needs to go," Shannon says, pacing around the living room. We've cleared out the rest of the team.

I glance at Viktor. He's sitting on my bed, his knees pressed together. Somehow, he had gotten hold of Fiona and told her I'd promised to help him once we got off the island. Fiona didn't question it, likely because she was too busy fawning over his cheekbones. I should be concerned at her poor security discretion, but whatever; Viktor being here might be a good thing.

"You can't speak with witnesses unless you're under court supervision," Shannon continues. "This could get you in a lot of fucking trouble."

"I'll only need a few minutes. Tops. I have a feeling he can help us."

After some further convincing, Shannon begrudgingly allows me a moment with Viktor. I sit on the bed beside him and put a hand on his shoulder. "How are you holding up?"

He shakes his head for a few seconds, chewing his lip, before breaking into a torrent of tears. Between sobs, he muffles a few words I struggle to decipher. "Not . . . good . . . everyone's dead! You . . . you were gone too."

I don't think I've ever seen a grown man cry, and I certainly didn't expect Viktor to wail so loudly. All I can do is pat his back awkwardly. "I know. I'm sorry. I was quite literally locked up."

He wipes his runny snot with the back of his wrist like a toddler and I resist cringing, leaning over to hand him a tissue box. He pulls one out but doesn't use it, bawling openly for a few more seconds before recovering his hiccuping breath. "I don't know what to do. People keep asking me questions, asking if I'm okay, if Bella Marie had ever done bad things to me . . . I don't know how to answer. I never thought it was bad. I was just doing my part, what I was told. But maybe it is? They make it seem that way. I don't know. I'm so confused. What should I do?"

"You're asking me?"

"Who else can I ask? You're all I have now. You promised you'd help me."

I sigh, thinking of how I'll let him down easy. How am I supposed to help this man? But I can barely bring myself to disappoint him. I recognize the desperate confusion. He's lonely, hopeless, lost all he's ever known. He's a trained dog without its owner. And now, all he has is me . . .

Me.

I recognize the blight of cruelty infecting me, but I'm not dissuaded. "I can help you."

His eyes widen with hope. "Really?"

"Yes. I'll help you through all the questions authorities are throwing at you, and I'll help you through everything after too. Like getting you an Olympic medal and building you up to be a Skarsgård-adjacent icon, just like I had promised you on the island. But it's only possible if you do everything I say. And I mean *everything*."

He nods ecstatically, holding my hand. I try to ignore the film of snot touching my skin as he says, "Thank you. Thank you!"

I give him a pat on the head and turn on the TV. The first channel plays *SpongeBob SquarePants.* It seems to capture his attention.

In the living room, I whisper to Shannon, "We can use him. He's on my side."

"We can't be sure of that."

"We *can*. He's been brainwashed and . . ." I lean closer. "On the island I manipulated him just a little. He's convinced that I'm the only one who can help him. He trusts me. And isn't it advantageous to have one of the cult members on my side?"

Shannon shakes her head. "He could be a loose cannon. There's no guarantee—"

In the bedroom, Viktor laughs, voice clear and loud, at the cartoon, a flash of gleaming, handsome white teeth. Shannon's eyes go wide.

"Huh." She taps her index finger to her chin. "Maybe you're right."

It's a week later. Fiona and I are sitting in front of the TV while Shannon stands by the couch, her arms crossed, nervous breaths entering and exiting her mouth.

The program we've been eagerly waiting for starts. A man with white hair sits in front of a brick background. "Hello, this is Keith Morrison, I'm live with *Dateline NBC*. Today, our guest, known only as Viktor, has been at the center of the biggest news storm of this century." The camera cuts to Viktor. He's wearing a dowdy brown sweater that is clearly supposed to make him seem relatable, but his powdered face makes him look like a model. Peeking from under his collar is a line of blue, the 2010 Vancouver Olympics replica gold medal that I bought him on eBay.

Before Viktor, we'd been declining a barrage of media requests. Shannon advised me to stay out of the spotlight, since my words could be used against me. But we decided to send out Viktor, since nothing instills public faith more than an attractive white man.

Still, it's a risk. Shannon said it's never advisable for a witness to speak to the media, and that Viktor may even be reprimanded by the court. But we're gambling that there will be no severe repercussions since the judge is handling this case sensitively, and penalizing an innocent cult victim who's only trying to speak out could translate into bad optics. At most, Viktor would lose the chance to testify for me, but given all the other Melniburg servants who could vouch for cultlike activity, we decided Viktor was worth the gamble.

As much as the law is about legal matters, it's also about PR. Whipping up a positive media storm and shaping the court of public opinion early could be our key to victory. "It's impossible to perfectly sequester a jury these days," Shannon had told me. "With how quickly information spreads online, they're bound to accidentally skim an article or hear something in passing. Those subliminal messages can impact their subconscious and shape the outcome of the case, if we play our cards right."

I'm tense as I watch the interview. It's live, so a slipup could spell game over. The program starts as we predicted. Keith goes on a spiel about the island, giving the audience a summary of the latest news and the court case. Then, he directs questions to Viktor. *What was life like on the island? Were there schools? Did you ever doubt what you were being taught?* Viktor answers the questions, working in the talking points we trained him on, which include details on his brainwashing, crazy cult stories, forced imprisonment, grooming for sexual pleasure, and other criminal Melniburg activities. In general, he lets the truth speak for itself. Based on his honest account, it's objectively difficult to deny any wrongdoing from the Melniburg family. So far, I'm pleased with his performance. He's followed our instructions to a T and is surprisingly genial to the host, who seems charmed by his good looks and eager smile. I guess Viktor is used to being told what to do.

About halfway into the hour-long program, Keith focuses his questions on me. "What was your first impression of Julie Chan?" I clench my fists. I'm on the edge of my seat.

"I had no idea she'd switched places with her sister, as Bella Marie never informed us about what she did to Chloe."

"Did she seem off to you? Were you ever suspicious of her?"

"Not that I noticed. Though every time we have guests on the island, I tend to get excited, since we rarely see different faces." This makes Keith shake his head sympathetically. "So, I might have been distracted."

"You mentioned that forced sex was part of your role on the island. Excuse me for asking, but I'm sure audiences want to know: Were you ever forced to engage with Julie?"

"I had offered my services as stress relief once, but she rejected me."

"Really?" Keith looks surprised.

"Yes." Viktor's gaze falls down to his lap. "For the first time in my life, I was treated like a human rather than a toy." He takes a breath, speaking slow. "In that moment, I realized that things could be different. That there were people out there, like Julie, who wouldn't use me for their own gain."

These aren't words we fed into his mouth. These are his genuine feelings. I'm riddled with guilt as I listen.

But then Fiona shouts, "We're trending across every platform!"

"Positive comments too," Shannon says, disbelief lacing her voice.

My heart races with excitement. "Can I see?" Fiona hands me her phone and I scroll through some live tweets. It's a whirlwind of sympathy. Viktor has become the hottest victim the internet could thirst for.

If what he's saying is true, Julie did nothing wrong. There are so many iterations of this I lose count. (That being said, there's a good portion of: Viktor is so hot! Julie must be a saint for keeping her hands off him!! He can fuck me on a swing any day! In all three holes!)

I swipe and swipe and swipe, absorbing the waves of positivity. Vindication bursts into my chest, melting into my core.

When I finally peel my eyes away from the phone to look back at Viktor, he's staring at the camera, the beginning of a rehearsed line poised on his lips.

"I feel lost now that I know the truth of the island, a place I once thought of as home. But I know one thing for sure. Julie is my liberator. She is the one who freed us all."

66

After the success of the *Dateline* interview, I simply can't restrain myself. Once everyone leaves for the day, I dig my phone out from my nightstand, plug it into the charger, and power it on. As soon as my wallpaper glows to life, a burst of notifications unfurls onto the lock screen.

I check socials first.

On Instagram, Chloe's profile has gained a staggering two million new followers. The comments are filled with snake emojis, but also a surprising outcry of support. Some of the Chloe Crew even rebranded themselves as Julie's Jewels. A loyal member said, I only started watching after Julie took over. She's the one that I've always been a fan of. If what Viktor said is true, I don't think she did anything wrong. My YouTube views have exploded. People are replaying my content constantly, time-stamping certain parts of videos they find suspect. (Unfortunately, YouTube removed me from the partner program due to my alleged crimes, so I haven't earned a single cent from the boost in views.) Overall, engagement has gone up over 5,000 percent on all platforms.

There are even stan-accounts of me.

And I mean *me*.

Accounts that support Julie Chan. Edits of me to TikTok sounds, Reddit threads that attempt to justify my actions, and thirst-traps litter Instagram. As one internet dweller said, I support women's rights *and* women's wrongs.

The people love me. (I've also become the Second Coming of Christ to certain shadowy corners of the internet after validating their evil-cabal-of-elite conspiracies. Tinfoil hats aren't part of my brand, but they've become my loudest supporters regardless.)

I'm enamored and surprised by the overwhelming support, a lot of which came before the *Dateline* interview even aired.

Shannon has been drip-feeding me information on what's happening in the media. Like how some of the extended Melniburg family members are running a public smear campaign against me, spearheading the Julie-killed-Chloe conspiracy to discredit my claims. I worry the Melniburgs will have sway over public opinion, since the powerful always get to rewrite history.

But while it's true that many major news outlets are in support of or lukewarm about the Melniburgs (likely because they operate on the Melniburg dime), nobody can control the actions of a few curious content creators.

For instance, someone made a four-part docuseries on YouTube (thirty million views and counting!) about the Belladonnas and their toxicity. The creator deep-dived into Bella Marie's history and unveiled a world of hurt through intensive internet sleuthing. Cults were just a footnote in Melniburg history when you account for their long list of alleged offenses, including but not limited to: supporting dictators, aiding in eliminating democratically elected leaders of developing countries, contributing to several economic collapses, high-level tax fraud, suspicious deaths—political assassinations?—the list could go on. (You have a lot of time to do evil shit when you're in power for several centuries.) This one docuseries spurred a hundred other videos digging into the Belladonnas, bringing their most infamous moments into the light. Some internet sleuths went even deeper, examining old photos of Melniburg ancestors and who they hung out with, and looking through flight records of who's been to the island. It's been unearthed that several politicians, celebrities, and *of course* Supreme Court justices have been friendly with the Melniburgs over the years.

Shannon tells me the courts are scrambling to compile a list of judges who have not been touched by the Melniburgs—which is about as difficult as compiling a list of Catholic priests who haven't touched young boys—but I didn't know it was all thanks to some internet truth-seekers with too much time on their hands.

Because of them, Bella Marie and the Belladonnas have become the biggest villains of the internet and I've somehow become the poor little victim. I just so happened to be a perfect sob story: orphan, abusive childhood, dead family.

On top of that, the *Dateline* episode, which aired with record-breaking views, is already helping in more ways than I imagined. Only three hours after the live broadcast, a barrage of clips have been uploaded onto every video platform, each with thousands of views and thousands more comments. With one interview, Viktor has shaped my public image from *victim* to *liberator*.

Someone even started a Change.org petition that claims I'm too pretty to go to jail. It has half a million signatures.

When I click into my email, hundreds of requests from screenwriters and production studios populate my inbox. They are hoping to buy my IP to write a movie or series based off my experience. Offers worth millions. Biographers and publishing houses are wondering if I want to pen the next bestseller. (Apparently, Iz has already signed a book deal of her own.)

I reply to each email in earnest and message Fiona to get in contact with an agent to see if we can start a bidding war on *The True Story of Julie Chan*.

Then it hits me.

I've transcended what it means to become an influencer. No longer will I have to paddle the treacherous open waters of the internet, chasing seconds of attention and kernels of power. I have become the lighthouse people swim to.

People are making video essays and podcasts of my story. Mainstream executives are wanting to produce shows in my name. But I've been around long enough to know: the only one you can trust is yourself.

Right now, the world wants to watch, to listen, to follow my light. This is my chance to guide them through truths that wouldn't be illuminated otherwise, to mold their understanding of Julie Chan.

I have that power. It's right at my fingertips.

67

Shannon advises me to stay off socials. Viewing is okay, but posting? Bad, bad, *bad* idea.

"People are sitting on the lines," she said. "They know you took your twin's identity, but the chaos of the case and the NBC interview is taking that weight off you. If you speak out, the attention will shift and the fallout will be unpredictable. I beg of you, for your sanity and mine, stay off social media." *Blah, blah, blah.*

Shannon is an amazing lawyer. Fantastic. But what does she know about social media? She was too busy sticking her nose in law school textbooks instead of doom-scrolling like the rest of us.

Everything is different now.

For a brief moment, I was caught in a limbo where I didn't have access to the outside world. I rejected my phone, my only source of influence, for fear of humiliation and hatred. But I can see it with my own eyes. The cascading outpour of support for me.

Me.

Someone accused of burning and killing seven people—seven gloriously beautiful, powerful, loved white women. Ana, Kelly, Sophia, Emmeline, Lily, Maya, and Bella Marie. Seven deaths at my hands. Eight, if you include Chloe. And yet, the world doesn't revile me or condemn me. Instead, I am an object of *obsession*. They salivate for more, *hungry.*

The love is uncanny. Almost, dare I say, *impossible*.

The longer I sit with it, the more obvious it becomes.

Tell me, what other explanation is there?

This is my prize in exchange for seven lives. The promise of freedom, euphoria, it's been delivered. Yet I can tell that this is only the start.

Eto would never be so stingy. Seven human souls for a few million followers and a boost in views? Yeah right. Nikolai received a whole dynasty in exchange for one measly blue eye.

I know there's more coming. I *need* more. I deserve it. But I can't just sit on the sidelines and wait for it to come, not when my time is growing increasingly precious, my court date looming. Now is my time to reach toward the skies and grab hold.

I decide to quadruple-stream on Instagram, Twitch, YouTube, and TikTok live. (Gifts enabled, of course.) Within five minutes, I have over 100,000 viewers across all platforms. I'm trending worldwide. Everyone is waiting for *my* tell-all. In ten minutes, 200,000 viewers. Then, 600,000. The numbers don't stop growing. Gifts are piling in. Comments are going so fast, I can't read them. I'm blitzed with the same light I had the night of the fire. A wonderous, holy, and powerful excitement, dopamine and adrenaline straight to my bloodstream.

This is it. Today, I will step into the light. Not as Chloe Van Huusen, but as Julie Chan.

It is time to make my mark. I am finally in control.

I stare into the camera on my phone.

"One thing needs to be made clear," I say. "I did not kill my twin sister."

Acknowledgments

Thank you to my agent, Samantha Haywood, for picking up this novel and championing it into something real. And to the others at Transatlantic Literary Agency as a whole, especially to Eva Oakes and Megan Philipp. Also to Laura Cameron and Dana Spector, for finding this book a home in the TV/film world.

To my editors, Loan Le, Alison Hennessey, and Brittany Lavery, thank you for working patiently with me through all the drafts and shaping this weird little book into something incredible. I can't even imagine where it would be without your sharp suggestions and developments. To all the editorial staff, publishers, marketers, publicists, cover designers, and everyone else behind the scenes at Atria, Simon & Schuster Canada, and Raven Books, thank you for sprinkling your magical dust onto this novel. I appreciate you!!

To my first readers and critique partners, I have learned so much from you all: Jane Benoit, Juliet Wilde, Jered, Emily Klein, Dorit D'Scarlett, Heather Hooper, Lia Lao, Tayo Oriade, Ry Surujpaul, Jenny Pang, Flora Pan. This book wouldn't have existed without your early encouragement and guidance.

Thank you to Claire Lam, for taking my author photos and for lending me cute tops that hid my awful tan lines.

To all my friends who had to listen to me waffle about a "secret project" since I was too embarrassed to say I was writing a book: Thank you. Truly.

Thank you, from the bottom of my heart. Thanks for not getting annoyed and blocking my number, because I was very much that: *annoying*. You are all too patient and kind and supportive—dare I say beautiful and saintly? I am obsessed with each and every one of you. There are too many people who have supported me to name individually, but especially to Emily Wang and Heather Yuan, who were always there and the first people I told about writing. Thank you! I am so grateful.

To my parents, who ensured I had no student debt and remained financially secure so I could spend my spare hours in university writing silly books instead of worrying about corporate internships, jobs, or bills, like most students. Especially to my mom. Just in general. For literally everything. To my sister, Kassie, who is nothing like Chloe or Julie. I will not steal your life! I promise!! (Mostly because we look nothing alike and I'd never get away with it if I tried.)

To all the YouTubers and influencers I watched growing up that literally formed my personality and sense of humor. I will withhold naming any of them just in case they get canceled in the future.

To me. Because I wrote this book. Also, it's always nice to practice self-affirmations. So: Thank you to me, myself, and I!!! You did it, girl!!

And to you, the reader. Are you still here? Wow. Congratulations! You are perfect, beautiful, so smart, and hot—sublime, really.

About the Author

Liann Zhang is a second-generation Chinese Canadian who splits her time between Vancouver, British Columbia, and Toronto, Ontario. After a short stint as a skincare content creator, she graduated from the University of Toronto with a degree in psychology and criminology. *Julie Chan Is Dead* is her first novel.